CHRONICLES OF CURIOUS GIRLS WHO CREATE

EDITED BY
PAIGE DANIELS AND MARY FAN

BRAVE NEW GIRLS: CHRONICLES OF CURIOUS GIRLS WHO CREATE

This is a work of fiction. Names, characters, places, and incidents are either products of the authors' imaginations or, if real, are used fictitiously.

Compilation copyright © 2024 by Paige Daniels and Mary Fan

"The Science of Dad Jokes" copyright © 2024 by Adriano Moraes
"Color the Constellations" copyright © 2024 by Mary Fan
"Libbie and Dewey's Excellent Adventure" copyright © 2024 by Henry Herz
"Go For Pets" copyright © 2024 by Andrew K. Hoe
"Light as a Feather, Stiff as a Board" copyright © 2024 by Julie Palomba
"Liminal Space" copyright © 2024 by HJ Farr
"Lady Verdant: Hero Knight of Mara Villa" copyright © 2024 by J.R. Rustrian
"Researching the Behavior and Habits of Terrestrial Exoplanet Fauna" copyright © 2024 by Jeanne Kramer-Smyth
"Girls Rule the Solarpunk World!" copyright © 2024 by Ira Nayman
"Jupiter Jigsaw" copyright © 2024 by Kris Katzen
"The Owl and the Rabbit" copyright © 2024 by Brad Jurn
"A Girl and Her Cyberdog" copyright © 2024 by Phil Margolies
"Gaia: The Legend of the Moldavite Stone" copyright © 2024 by Denise Sutton
"Earning Her Wings" copyright © 2024 by JD Cadmon
"The Ape Canyon Adventure: An Itzal Story" copyright © 2024 by Josh Pritchett
"The Merchant of Venus" copyright © 2024 by Jennifer Lee Rossman
"Whatever Happened to the 9-5?" copyrizght © 2024 by Christian Angeles
"ZIPPED" copyright © 2024 by Mackenzie Reide
"Daphne Harris and the Time Jump" copyright © 2024 by Annie Gray
"The Adventures of Lucy Tyme-Walker" copyright © 2024 by Tim Tobin
"The Interloper" copyright © 2024 by Scott Pinkowski
"The Village Runners" copyright © 2024 by Paige Daniels

All rights reserved. No part of this book may be reproduced, transmitted, or stored in an information retrieval system in any form or by any means, graphic, electronic, or mechanical, including photocopying, taping, and recording, without prior written permission from the publisher except for the use of brief quotations in a book review.

First edition: July 2024

Illustrations by Ben Falco, Martina Localzo, Jarod Marchand, Adriano Moraes, Ann Piesen, RM Nielsen, Josh Pritchett, Harley Scroggins, and Kay Wrenn.

TABLE OF CONTENTS

COLOR THE CONSTELLATIONS by Mary Fan 15
LIBBIE AND DEWEY'S EXCELLENT ADVENTURE by Henry Herz 39
GO FOR PETS by Andrew K. Hoe 51
LIGHT AS A FEATHER, STIFF AS A BOARD by Julie Palomba 73
LIMINAL SPACE by HJ Farr 95
LADY VERDANT: HERO KNIGHT OF MARA VILLA by J.R. Rustrian 105
RESEARCHING THE BEHAVIOR AND HABITS
OF TERRESTRIAL EXOPLANET FAUNA by Jeanne Kramer-Smyth 131
GIRLS RULE THE SOLARPUNK WORLD! by Ira Nayman 149
JUPITER JIGSAW by Kris Katzen 171
THE OWL AND THE RABBIT by Brad Jurn 183
A GIRL AND HER CYBERDOG by Phil Margolies 203
GAIA: THE LEGEND OF
THE MOLDAVITE STONE by Denise Sutton 223
EARNING HER WINGS by JD Cadmon 251
THE APE CANYON ADVENTURE:
AN ITZAL STORY by Josh Pritchett 267
THE MERCHANT OF VENUS by Jennifer Lee Rossman 295
WHATEVER HAPPENED TO THE 9-5? by Christian Angeles 305
ZIPPED by Mackenzie Reide 321
DAPHNE HARRIS AND THE TIME JUMP by Annie Gray 345
THE ADVENTURES OF LUCY TYME-WALKER by Tim Tobin 357
THE INTERLOPER by Scott Pinkowski 371
THE VILLAGE RUNNERS by Paige Daniels 397

COLOR THE CONSTELLATIONS

MARY FAN

GLITTERING STARS ZIP ACROSS MY viewscreen, and I command my pod to twist and dance between them. The controls fit comfortably in my hands, as if I were always meant to hold them. A great *whooshing* feeling fills my chest, and a laugh escapes me. Even though I've lived on a starship—a giant Dorado-class science vessel called the *ICS Moncacht-Apé*—for the past year, this is the first time in a while that I really feel like I'm *in space*.

Out here, a girl can fly, instead of being tied down by gravity generators and heavy-duty stabilizers that make it feel like nothing is moving even as the *Moncacht-Apé* zips through the cosmos. No more pristine hallways and well-matched decorations that look the same as what you'd find on a planet-bound institution.

It's just me and the stars—all those exciting, mysterious stars—and I can almost hear them speaking to me.

I twist the steering bars, sending the pod into a corkscrew. Its stabilizers aren't quick enough to compensate, and my stomach flips. That's what I was counting on: this sensation of twirling between the constellations and, for a moment, becoming one of them. Bleached hair briefly fills my vision as my double bubble-braid pigtails fly across my face. I give the controls a shove—

The pod jolts to a halt, and an alarm buzzes. A warning flashes across the screen. The engines screech, straining in vain against the tractor beam they're caught in.

An indicator light tells me that I have an incoming transmission. Scowling, I tap an icon on the control touchscreen to accept.

"This is Lieutenant Park to Pod BNG-08-F." The image of a stern-faced woman, with short black hair and sharp cheekbones cutting across her creamy complexion, appears in a small window on the viewscreen. "Shut off your engines immediately."

"*Mooooom!*" I yell. "A tractor beam? Really?"

"Kyung Ji-eun, you shut off those engines right now, or I'm revoking your Net access for a month!"

Huffing, I comply. The engines groan, then go silent, and the alarm ceases. In the corner of the viewscreen showing the rear view, the golden-hulled *Moncacht-Apé* looms against the glittering abyss. A glowing blue beam shoots out of its elongated form. I slump in the pilot's seat and cross my arms. "Seriously, Mom, you couldn't have hailed *before* tractor-ing my pod? This is freaking wrong!"

"No, what's wrong is my sixteen-year-old daughter stealing my access code to take an official research vessel out for a joyride." Mom glares at me through the screen. "Do you know how embarrassing it was for me to explain to Commander Torres why the pod was missing, and why I needed to activate the tractor beam? I'm confining you to our quarters for the next week!"

"What?! I didn't hurt anyone or damage anything! Why are you treating me like a criminal?"

"That's enough, Ji-eun. I'll speak to you on the ship." She ends the transmission.

"C'mon, Mom, I've been living on science vessels since before I could read, yet I've never been allowed to explore anything!" I don't bother keeping my voice down as Mom drags me through the *Moncacht-Apé*'s blue-walled corridors. "It's been one multi-year deep-space mission after another for as long as I can remember, yet the only adventures *I've* ever gotten to go on have been in virtual reality!"

"Lieutenant Park!" Ensign Saxe, a muscular young woman with jet-black hair and an alabaster complexion, rushes toward Mom. "I have an update—"

"Not now, Ensign!" Mom waves her off and turns back to me. "Listen, Ji-eun—"

"This isn't fair!" I throw up my hand. "You get to visit all these new worlds, but you only let me off the ship when we're at a space station or a Confederation planet!"

"Where it's *safe*." Mom purses her lips and glances around, no doubt conscious of all the crew members we're passing in the hallways. As the ship's Head Engineer, she has to appear professional.

Not me. "What's the point of dragging me all up and down the galaxy if I'm never allowed to see any of the cool things we're supposed to be exploring? I might as well be on a prison planet!"

Mom sighs as we arrive at our quarters. She presses her hand against the security pad, and the door swishes open. "We can never be sure what to expect on these missions. What looks like a friendly meadow on an unknown planet might turn out to harbor some fatal virus, or be prone to abrupt earthquakes, or—"

"Yeah, yeah, I get it." I march over to the violet sofa in the middle of the living room and plop down. "Only trained professionals should go down there, blah, blah."

"That's right." Mom straightens the silver-piped jacket of her black-and-blue uniform. The Interstellar Confederation makes a big deal about distinguishing exploration ships like the *Moncacht-Apé* from military vessels, but as far as I can tell, the crews behave in the same stiff, rule-obsessed manner.

I arch my brows. "Explain to me why Dad gets to go off-ship, then. The only training he has is in culinary arts."

"That's different. He's an adult."

"I'm close enough!"

"Then start behaving like it." Mom smooths her hair. "I must return to my shift. I'll see you at dinner."

She turns on her heel, and her black boots tap against the metal floor as she exits.

"Ugh!" I slam my head back against the sofa cushions.

"Taro boba?" Dad emerges from the kitchen, holding a cup full of lavender-colored liquid with a wide straw sticking out.

I jump. "Were you lurking the entire time?"

"I was making myself a snack when you and your mom came storming in. Thought it was better not to get caught in the crossfire. Here." He approaches and hands me the beverage, which he knows is my favorite.

"Thanks." I take a grudging sip of the sweet drink, and a tapioca pearl shoots up the straw and into my mouth.

"Feel better?" The smile lines by his gentle, dark brown eyes crinkle. I share those eyes, and I hope they'll look as kind on me when I'm older.

"You can't fix everything with food," I mutter into my boba.

"Perhaps not, but it helps, doesn't it?" He sits down beside me. "Now, why are you so angry, Ji-eun?"

"Because Mom's being unreasonable!"

"First of all, no, she's not. You violated a lot of rules. A ship-wide alarm went off, and Commander Torres herself had to get involved."

"Well—"

"And secondly, she's been under a lot of pressure recently, and the last thing she needs is to be stressing over you as well."

I look up. "What do you mean?"

A conspiratorial glint lights Dad's eyes. "Do you know where the *Moncacht-Apé* is heading next?"

"Yeah. T'rovek Ghad, in the Haurra system."

"What do you know about it?"

"It's the fourth planet from its sun, and it's got the gravity and atmosphere to support human life, but it gets frequent ion storms that really screw with technology. Also, it's light-years away from the network of interstellar tunnels connecting civilization… it's gonna take us two weeks to get there. That's why no one's tried to settle the planet in the hundred years since it was discovered, though it's got plenty of plant and animal life. It's been explored a few times already, but the last mission was twenty years ago, and there's still lots we don't know."

"And?"

I furrow my brow. "And… we were originally heading to a pulsar, until Commander Torres changed course last week." I hadn't thought much of it before—science vessels change course all the time to check out the newest and shiniest findings—but from the look Dad's giving me, there's more to T'rovek Ghad than I'd thought. "You know why, don't you?"

He leans toward me as if telling a secret. "It's because of your mom. You know how searching for the *Black Diamond* has been a hobby of hers for the past few years?"

"Yeah…" The Anguilla-class transport had been carrying several museums' worth of planetary treasures from Ixak Prime, which was being evacuated ahead of an asteroid collision, when it got caught in some kind of space anomaly. The crew escaped, but the anomaly vanished, along with the *Black Diamond*. That was fifty years ago, and people have been speculating about where it ended up ever since. My eyes widen. "Mom thinks she found it?"

Dad nods. "Based on contemporary readings of the anomaly, new information from recent scans of the area, and some brilliant calculations, she believes the *Black Diamond* was pulled through hyperspace and into the Haurra system, near enough to where T'rovek Ghad was at the time that the ship likely crashed onto the planet."

"So that's the real reason we're headed there." I jitter with excitement. Everyone knows the story of the lost treasure ship, but I never thought I'd get to be on the mission that found it. "Why didn't anyone tell me before?"

"Commander Torres wanted it kept quiet. In fact, I shouldn't be telling you, but… oops." He gives me a playful nudge.

"It's because Mom's afraid of being embarrassed if she's wrong, isn't it?"

"Not at all. Being wrong is simply part of life when you're trying new things. And even if there's no *Black Diamond*, T'rovek Ghad is still worth exploring further. The reason Commander Torres didn't want to broadcast the mission's true purpose is because of security. She's concerned about what would happen if the wrong sorts got wind that such valuable artifacts might have been found."

"Got it. I really hope Mom's right."

"Me too." Dad stands. "I'd better head to the cafeteria—my shift starts soon. You just stay here and be good, okay?"

I roll my eyes. "Yeah, sure. Don't wanna get into any more trouble."

For now, that is. Because no matter what Mom says, there is no way I'm staying on this stinking ship once we reach T'rovek Ghad.

Mom was so busy upgrading the *Moncacht-Apé*'s sensors in advance of the T'rovek Ghad mission that she didn't think twice before approving my request for a synthetic skin kit from the lab. I told her it was for a biology project. Little did she know that the only reason I'd started that unit in my virtual classroom was so I could learn all about fabricating derm patches. They were meant for wound care but also, with a little tweaking, could be used as a way to mimic someone's handprint.

She'd had security on the pod hangar upgraded from access codes to palm scans since my last off-ship adventure, which I'd expected. Hence, the biology project. Really, she should have anticipated that I would anticipate it...

A grin spreads across my face as I steer my newly re-stolen pod toward T'rovek Ghad, whose mottled surface grows larger on my viewscreen. Deep blues, vibrant greens, rich browns, and stately grays swirl beneath lacy white clouds. I wish I could get a closer look at the land below, but there's too much interference for the pod's sensors to pick up anything. Probably thanks to those ion storms. Ah well, a little mystery makes it all the more exciting.

When I land, I'll be the first person to step foot on that planet in two decades. Chances are, I won't find the *Black Diamond* myself, but it'll still be worthwhile to stand among the alien plants and be someplace new. My original plan was to go down after the crew located the treasure ship, but then it occurred to me that they might need all the pods for the search and excavation.

Besides, how cool would it be if I did manage to find it?

I zigzag the pod left and right at random, while purposely leaking particles from the engines that I, uh, tweaked earlier, to make it harder for a tractor beam to get a lock this time. If anyone on the *Moncacht-Apé* noticed my unauthorized departure, though, I can't tell. The ship remains still in the rear view window on my viewscreen, almost as if it's sleeping.

An uneasy feeling fills me. This is too easy. Sure, it was the middle of the night ship time when I left, and sure, there's no reason any alarms would go off if Lieutenant Park took a pod, as the security pads believed, but still…

Something silver zips across the rear view, then vanishes behind the *Moncacht-Apé*. I blink, wondering if I imagined it.

A second silver streak appears, and this time, it slams into the ship's hull.

My eyes widen. I scramble to enlarge the window and enhance the image, tapping at the touchscreen before me.

By the time a third streak appears, there's no mistaking what I'm witnessing.

Half a dozen small, sleek vessels with pointed fronts attack the enormous science vessel and slam right into the hull, penetrating it.

"Silversides…" I gape. The tiny ships, meant to carry three or four people, were designed for combat. Their pointed noses were meant to pierce larger ships, then open to allow those inside to invade. Like syringes injecting attackers.

But we're not at war or anything… who would attack a science ship? The answer hits me as I recall what Dad told me. *These are the "wrong sorts" that Commander Torres was worried about. Somehow, they found out about the* Black Diamond, *and they're going to force the crew to take them to it.*

I rush to revert my viewscreen to its front view and turn my pod around. Whatever is happening, I have to help. I don't know how, but—

An alarm blares, and the entire pod shakes. I scream, gripping my safety straps. "What was that?!"

According to the warning flashing across my viewscreen, one of the engines is compromised. I was hit… one of those Silversides *shot* at me…

A second blast flies toward my pod. I briefly spot a small cannon—protruding from a Silverside embedded in the *Moncacht-Apé*—before being thrown forward by the impact.

I grip the steering bars and try to regain control of the pod. Maybe if I hadn't sabotaged my own engines to make them leaky, I might have been able to compensate, but as it is, there's nothing I can do to keep the pod from hurtling toward the planet.

Tears of panic fill my eyes. I punch every control I can think of, hoping to do something, anything, to slow my descent.

The colors of T'rovek Ghad fill my viewscreen. I take a deep breath. If this is how I go, then at least the last thing I see will be beautiful.

The pod abruptly jerks to the left, as if yanked by an invisible claw, and gray static fills the viewscreen. A cry escapes me.

The next thing I know, I'm spinning like a tornado. My stomach feels ready to leap out of my throat. I clench my safety straps and squeeze my eyes shut.

Never mind, the last thing I see will be the insides of my own eyelids.

For what feels like an eternity, I just keep spinning and spinning and spinning—

The pod lurches to an abrupt stop.

My head is whirling so fast, it takes maybe a minute for me to realize, truly realize, that I'm not moving anymore. *What happened?*

The viewscreen remains fuzzed out, but the touchscreen on the controls is still active. According to the status report, I've landed somewhere. I try to find out where, but none of the scanners are working. *Only one thing to do, then.*

Fortunately, all the *Moncacht-Apé*'s pods come equipped with environmental suits. I'm pretty sure I'm on T'rovek Ghad, which has a breathable atmosphere, but I'm not stupid enough to just open the door and find out.

After suiting up, I press the controls to open the pod's doors.

A lush wonderland of tall trees and bioluminescent flowers greets me under a dark, star-studded sky. Three bright moons cast a ghostly glow upon the blue-and-purple vegetation.

The wristpad on my suit tells me that the atmosphere is, indeed, breathable, so I take off my helmet.

Cool, crisp air fills my lungs. I stare in awe at the glorious land before me, and for a moment, I'm able to forget that I've crash-landed here and have no idea how I'll get back.

Having a genius engineer for a mom—and being super interested in the stuff she does—has made me capable of a lot of things. It also means I'm acutely aware of what I'm *not* capable of. And what I can't do right now is fix this busted-up pod with its busted-up engines, without having some not-busted-up parts on hand.

Despite having spent the past hour or so digging through every inch of the small vessel, I simply can't find any way to engineer myself out of this mess. Not that there was much hope to begin with when the thing took two hits from a cannon.

Feeling defeated, I plop down on the grass and lean back against the cool metal hull. A slight shiver runs through me. I wish I were wearing more than a short-sleeved yellow shirt and thin brown pants. Though I'm not cold enough to put that clunky environmental suit back on.

I glance up, hoping against hope to catch a glimpse of the *Moncacht-Apé* in orbit. But only the unfamiliar constellations of this strange new planet shine down.

What happened on board the ship? Are my parents okay? The bad guys, whoever they are, must need everyone alive in order to find the *Black Diamond*, right? So they wouldn't hurt anyone, right? And Commander Torres is smart—she'll find a way out, and then she can send someone to rescue me... right?

I squeeze my knees to my chest, trying not to panic. There's nothing I can do about the *Moncacht-Apé*. I need to focus on where I am now, and what I can do next.

The leaves of a nearby fern rustle.

I jump to my feet. If that turns out to be some kind of predator, then I have no way to protect myself. There are probably defensive weapons tucked into some corner of the pod. I could try to get one, but what if the thing pounces when my back is turned?

The leaves rustle again. Deciding to stand my ground, I raise my arms to make myself as big as possible. "Stay back! Or—"

A small critter emerges from between the leaves: a feline no bigger than a human newborn, with short purple fur and wide yellow eyes. Two long stalks, topped with a diamond shape, sit between its pointy ears. Green markings surround its eyes, and a green patch sits on its left haunch. Plus, it has one green paw.

It lets out a high-pitched meow. I narrow my eyes. Okay, so this thing is adorable, but it could still be dangerous. I really ought to know what it is—xenobiology is one of my favorite subjects.

Watching it warily, I step backward toward the pod's open door. Among its standard equipment is a specially modified slate computer with scanning and translation capabilities. I have no idea if this feline will be in its database, but it's worth a shot.

"Don't eat me when I turn around, okay?" I whirl and rush inside, half expecting the creature to grow fangs and pounce. So I feel like a real idiot when nothing happens.

I retrieve the slate from a compartment in the back, then return outside. The feline remains where I left it, blinking placidly. It meows again.

I run a scan, and to my relief, an entry comes up. "So your species is *Felidae*

Pi-40R-1AN, you're an adolescent male, and those antennae things can detect electromagnetic waves..."

The little alien creature steps forward and meows once more, as if trying to speak.

"I'm sorry, cat, but I don't understand *meow*." I glance down at the slate. "Maybe this machine can..."

Xenobiologists have been working on ways to translate animal sounds and movements into human words for ages, but their success has been... uneven. The slate's database contains translation algorithms for a handful of common animals on Interstellar Confederation planets, but nothing exists for *Felidae Pi-40R-1AN*. There *is* one for a different type of feline, though... I wonder...

I select the algorithm, activate the translation program, and point the slate at the feline. "Okay, cat, say something."

The cat meows again. "Horse cabin blanket on," says the computer's voice.

Well, that makes no sense. Guess it didn't work. But it didn't entirely *not* work either. Words came out, after all. If the feline's language had been completely foreign to the computer, then I would have gotten an error message.

Maybe it's because I need to focus on something other than my current plight, but a determination to make the translator work takes over my entire mind. I dig into the algorithm and make adjustments, pulling in information from the broader database. With every passing minute, I worry that the feline will leave, meaning I'll have no way to test my program. But he sticks around, meowing intermittently, but otherwise just staring at me. Each time the translator fails to provide coherent words, I go back to work.

Eventually, my program grows so complex that it requires more processing power than the little slate can provide. And so I borrow a piece of the pod's computer—it's not doing me any good, anyway—and hook it up to the slate.

I have no idea how long I spend on this project, only that my stomach starts grumbling, and the sun starts rising. Exhausted, I finish my latest modification, run the program, then leave the computer on the ground as I stumble inside the pod in search of the emergency rations. After finding a nutrition bar, I emerge to find the feline still watching me.

I take a bite of the bland but filling bar. The feline steps closer. Cocking my head, I hold out the bar. "Want some?"

"Gross, why would anyone eat that garbage?" The voice floats up from the slate as the cat lets out an agitated noise.

I gasp. "It worked!" I stare at the feline. The algorithm should work both ways. "Can you understand me?" The computer lets out several meowing noises.

"So the human's slab lets it speak to me." The feline sniffs the slate.

"You *do* understand!" I straighten and clear my throat. "Greetings. I am Kyung Ji-eun of the starship *ICS Moncacht-Apé*, daughter of Lieutenant Park Ha-rin, Head Engineer, and Crewman Kyung Min-Ju… um… Preparer of Meals."

The feline looks up with narrowed eyes. "Why are you talking like that?"

"I… don't know." I give a sheepish grin. "What's your name?"

"Why would I need a name?"

I blink. "Oh… I just thought… I mean, how else are people supposed to know who you are? Or call for you?"

"I know who I am, and I don't care if anyone calls for me."

"Well, I need to call you something other than *Felidae Pi-40R-1AN*."

"Why?"

I start to answer, but pause. This is going nowhere. "I'll just call you 'Pi.' Is that okay?"

Instead of answering, the feline saunters up to the pod. "Humans don't crash from the sky often. I was hoping you would bring something interesting this time, but it seems that disgusting item you're eating is all you have."

"Wait… no one's explored this planet in forever, yet you know I'm a human! How?"

"A hairless ape that walks on two legs, covers itself in strange materials, and comes surrounded by foul-smelling metals? I wasn't born when the last ones came to this part of our world, but you match the description. Everyone knows the stories."

Excitement rises in my chest. "When did the last ones come?"

The computer takes an extra few seconds to translate, and I realize it's calculating what Pi's answer would mean in common human terms. "Fifty years ago," it says finally.

The Black Diamond! That must be it… Pi said "crash," not "land," and none of the previous exploration missions had experienced crashes. The scientists who came twenty years ago must have been on a different part of the planet.

"Wait," I say, thinking aloud. "The crew evacuated… there were no humans on the ship…"

"There were images of humans. There was the smell of humans. They heard sounds like the ones humans make." Pi glares at me, as if daring me to challenge him.

The local fauna must have wandered onto the crashed ship, and a computer program must have still been running. Maybe one with holograms. "Do you know where the last human ship landed?"

"Of course. I can sense it even now. It never stops buzzing." He twitches his stalks. The *Black Diamond* must be giving off electromagnetic energy that he can detect, which means at least part of it is still functioning.

"Is it far?"

"Only if you're lazy."

My excitement grows. Not only would I get to be the one to locate the legendary treasure ship, but an Anguilla-class vessel, even a wrecked one, would probably have the parts I need to fix my pod and get out of here.

For a moment, I thank my lucky stars that I was fortunate enough to crash near the *Black Diamond*, and then I realize that luck had nothing to do with it. My pod was pulled into some kind of space anomaly or weather system... that's probably what the *Black Diamond* fell into as well. And that must be why previous scientists never explored this part of T'rovek Ghad.

"You have to take me to that ship," I say breathlessly.

"I don't have to do anything." Pi turns away and, tail held high, marches back toward the ferns.

"Wait! I'll give you treats!"

The feline stops and looks back. "Treats?"

"Yes! I told you my father is a Preparer of Meals, right? He has access to all our food! I will give you anything you want!"

"Do you have fatty fishes?"

"The fattiest! Take me to the other human ship, and once I fix my pod and go back to mine, I'll get you as much as you want."

Pi saunters toward me. "Very well. But first, you must give me that food item you were eating."

I hold out the nutrition bar to him. He sniffs it in distaste, then takes it between his teeth and flings it away. "Hey! What'd you do that for?"

"Because I hated it." He turns back to the fern. "Follow me."

"Hang on, let me get some supplies first."

Pi watches judgmentally as I rush back into the pod, grab a backpack, and stuff it with anything that might be useful. Then, I use my slate to take some readings of the pod's damaged engines.

When I return, Pi gives me an unimpressed look. "Would you like to take a nap before we leave?"

I make a face. "Shut up. Let's go."

.ıııılı..lııılı..lııılı..lııılı.

The haunting glows of bioluminescent leaves fade under the rising sun, as if the ferns are going to sleep. A fast-moving creek babbles between the thick trees. Pi ambles alongside it, his purple tail swaying.

A light streaks across the early morning sky.

The feline stops in his tracks. "Another already?"

"Another?" I stare, and then it hits me. "A pod! From my ship! They must be looking for me—they beat back the attackers, and now, they've come to find me! We must go to it!"

"And they'll take me to where the fatty fishes are?"

"Yes! Come on!"

As much as I want to find the *Black Diamond*, I'd rather not be stuck on T'rovek Ghad for the rest of my life.

Pi glides through the brush like a swan on a lake. I, on the other hand, tromp between the shrubs and crash through the branches in a manner that could generously be described as "oafish." I don't care how clumsy I'm being though—I just have to get to that pod.

I glimpse its metal shape between the trees ahead and grin. It's identical to the one I took, except for the numbers on the side. And they landed instead of crashing, which means they found a way to avoid the anomaly. They must have detected my pod. Guess I won't have to figure out how to repair it after all—

The door opens, and I freeze. A bearded man stands beneath its frame, holding an enormous gun. Nothing like that is permitted on the *Moncacht-Apé*, and he isn't wearing a uniform. Instead, a tough-looking black coat with a red, flame-shaped insignia on the upper arm hangs off his shoulders. He gestures with his gun, and a woman in a silver-piped jacket emerges with her hands raised.

Mom! I suppress a gasp.

They haven't come to rescue me. The attackers weren't beaten. They must have taken over the entire ship in order to force my mom to take them to the *Black Diamond*. That's why they came to this spot... Mom figured out that the treasure ship is nearby...

A few more members of the *Moncacht-Apé*'s crew emerge, along with several armed individuals. Pirates—what other word is there for people who attack a ship?

Mom glances back at someone still in the pod. "You won't get away with this."

"Oh, yes, I will." A muscular woman with black hair emerges, aiming a gun at my mom.

Ensign Saxe?! Except she isn't in uniform anymore. Instead, she wears a vest with an insignia identical to that of the bearded man.

"Infiltrating your ship was the easy part." Saxe casually leans her weapon against her shoulder. "Getting my crew here ahead of the *Moncacht-Apé* was the challenge. Required more math than I would have liked. Now, move. Or do I have to remind you of what my crew will do to your husband and the others back on the ship if we don't report back in a few hours? And I'm not reporting back without the exact location of the *Black Diamond*."

Mom sets her jaw and glances down at the slate she's holding. "It's more complicated than you think. The mineral composition of this planet is interfering with—"

"Figure it out," Saxe growls.

Shaking, I retreat into the trees. If it's the *Black Diamond* that Saxe wants, then maybe I can get Pi to take her instead of me...

But once the pirates get what they want, they won't need the Moncacht-Apé's *crew anymore.* Horror churns in my stomach. There are hundreds of innocent scientists, engineers, and their families being held hostage. Including my dad.

I have to get to the Black Diamond *first. If I can fix my pod, then I can get off the planet and send out a distress call...*

Except we're in the middle of nowhere. The nearest security ship would take weeks to arrive.

I shake my head. *I have to try. Some patrols travel to remote areas... maybe I can contact one.*

At least the pirates don't seem to know I'm here, which gives me an advantage. I turn down the volume on my slate, then glance at Pi. "We have to hurry—what are you doing?"

The purple feline walks casually toward the pirates, his tail erect. "I don't care about your human business. You offered me delicious food. Maybe these other humans will offer me some sooner."

I gape. "Listen, cat, if you think—"

Saxe abruptly fires her weapon into the trees. "Stay away, you filthy vermin!" She glances around sharply, then fires again.

Pi retreats toward me. "Those humans are a threat."

"You think?!" I mull for a moment. It's not enough to hope that I can race to the *Black Diamond* and make it there ahead of the pirates. I have to slow them down. And if I could find a way to communicate with Pi, then my mom could certainly get a different feline to communicate with her. "Go warn the others— tell them not to help the pirates, and to avoid them if possible."

Pi gives me a withering look. "Others?"

"You're not the only feline around! Do you want others of your kind to get blasted?"

He swishes his tail. "Fine."

"Meet me back here when you're done."

He doesn't answer as he bounds off.

Ugh, he'd better return! Or I'm screwed. I sling the backpack off my shoulder and grab a small communicator from one of the side pockets. It was able to connect to my slate earlier, which means that even though interference from the planet is preventing me from contacting the ship or scanning the area, *some* signals can go through.

I get to work jerry-rigging the thing to send out an emergency beacon. Then I plan to chuck it into the creek. With any luck, my mom will pick up the signal and believe it's coming from a fifty-year-old wreck…

I half-expected Pi to abandon me for good, but apparently he really, *really* wants the treats I promised him. I'd hoped to be done making the false emergency beacon before he returned. Instead, he sits there watching—and judging—me for several minutes while I complete it. I toss it into the creek, where the water rapidly sweeps it in the direction opposite to the one we're heading in.

Since Pi is about one-tenth my size, I thought when he said the *Black Diamond* was not far, that it was, well, not far.

Apparently, members of species *Felidae Pi-40R-1AN* have more stamina than humans.

Felines neither sweat nor pant, but I'm doing both by the time we reach our destination on the other side of a tall, rocky hill. My legs are sore from having walked across miles of uneven and sometimes steep ground.

But it was all worth it to glimpse what's lying ahead. "The *Black Diamond*," I whisper.

"That's neither a stone nor the color black." Pi plops down on the ground beside me. "It is a foul-smelling pile of metal human refuse."

"Hush, cat. Even you can't ruin this for me."

I grin at the sight of the great starship lying in the dirt and rocks ahead, overgrown with vegetation. Despite five decades' worth of corrosion and rust eating away at its silver hull, not to mention the crumpled and torn metal from when it crashed, there's still something glamorous about its elegant, rounded shape.

I can't believe I'm the first to lay eyes on the legendary vessel carrying the lost treasures of Ixak Prime.

I whirl to Pi. "Thank you. When we get back to the ship, I'll serve you that fatty fish in beautifully plated slices on a silver platter."

"I do not care about its appearance, only its quantity." Yet despite the snarky words emerging from the slate, a purr rises from the feline himself. Maybe he doesn't hate me after all.

I make my way down a slight incline toward the wreck. I expect Pi to follow, but instead he trots off, back into the forest. I guess he has no interest in the *Black Diamond*. Well, I got what I wanted, so whether he returns or not makes little difference to me.

Yet I hope he will. I'd feel bad if I had to take off before he returned, and was therefore unable to fulfill my promise. Besides, that fluffy feline is pretty dang cute.

There's no need for doors when an entire panel has been ripped off the side of the *Black Diamond*. I step inside, my heart pounding.

Lights along the gray-walled corridor illuminate as soon as I step inside. I shouldn't have been surprised, since Pi detected electromagnetic energy, but it's still amazing that the *Black Diamond*'s technology works after all this time. *The ship is solar-powered... its energy cells must have remained intact after the crash. Does that mean its computer is still active as well?*

I wander down the hallway until I find a console. It, too, illuminates at my presence, which means the ship's motion sensors are functional. Though I don't have any credentials, the computer's emergency mode means I'm able to access the ship's status report without them. I scroll through it until I find the section on the engines.

They took a lot of damage, but several important parts remain functional. In fact, I could probably find a way to fix them given enough time. For a brief, wild moment, I consider doing just that—repairing the *Black Diamond* and taking it into space. But then I recall all the gaping holes in the hull, including the one I entered through.

All right, salvage time.

I take a moment to review a map of the ship, then head off.

Considering all the mythology that was built up around the *Black Diamond*, I expected something cooler than boring corridors similar to those on board the *Moncacht-Apé*, only older and dirtier and more covered in vines and stuff. Lights, holoprojectors, control panels—the only significant difference is that the *Black Diamond* also possesses internal defense systems. That is, weapons mounted on the walls.

I chastise myself for being disappointed. Of course the crew wouldn't have left the treasures of Ixak Prime lying around. They must be stowed in the cargo bays. Which I don't have time to explore, because I'm here to find parts to repair my pod, not go treasure hunting…

But as I pass a wide doorway, I can't resist looking inside. The ship's security systems remained in place after the crash, but I have fifty years' worth of technological advancement on my side. So I tear open a panel, wire a nearby console to my slate, and create a program. A few minutes later, I'm able to unlock that door with a simple command.

It slides open to reveal a miraculously preserved plethora of artifacts. Statues of ancient gods, hewn in loving detail by expert hands. Jewelry worn by great rulers of the past, still glittering despite the dust. Paintings, pottery, and sculptures by the finest artists, depicting important historic, religious, and mythological scenes. Musical instruments, ceremonial weapons, decorative furniture… all gorgeously fabricated.

I take a deep breath. I'm staring at the history of a planet shattered by an asteroid half a century ago. At what remains of a world that was blown away. At a heritage determined to survive.

And this is only one cargo bay… there are more. For the first time, I truly understand why the *Black Diamond* became so legendary, why so many have dreamed of finding it. Not because of gold or silver or jewels, but because it contains the story of a lost civilization.

The evacuees of Ixak Prime and their descendants deserve to see all this. It belongs to them, not to whatever greedy jerk the pirates plan to sell these things to. The thought of Saxe and her crew getting her hands on it makes me want to punch something.

But I don't have time to stand around and worry about history and justice. My parents are in very real danger, and I have to help them.

I tear my eyes away from the treasures and continue toward the engines.

I don't know what I was thinking when I only brought a single backpack with me. The parts I need require a lot more room than that.

Based on the readings I took of my pod's damaged engines earlier, plus some help from the *Black Diamond*'s computer, I was able to locate what I needed. And thanks to the tools I found in the engine room, I was able to excise most of it. Unfortunately, all this crap is bigger and bulkier than I expected.

Huffing, I look around the wide, console-lined area surrounding one of the

Black Diamond's giant engines. The parts lie strewn across the floor. Maybe the ship has some kind of ground transport on board that I could borrow—

"You made a mess." Pi ambles toward me, and his translated words float up from the slate in my hand.

I jump—I wasn't expecting him. "Pi! Where did you go?"

"I was hungry, so I hunted for food. The other humans will be here soon."

It takes me a moment longer than it should to process what he's telling me. "Wait—*what*? You mean to say... the pirates..."

"The smart one with the short black hair—she's your mother, right? She is leading them."

"Crap!" I should've known that my false beacon wouldn't throw her off for long.

I tap my foot anxiously, looking around at the scattered parts. Yes, I have what I need to repair my pod, but there's no way I can get all this back and then fix the thing before the pirates get what they came for. And then what? They won't need Mom anymore... or Dad... or any of the crew... I could make it off T'rovak Ghad, but what would be the point if it's too late for help to come?

Pi flops onto his back. "When do I get my treats?"

"Seriously, cat?!" I grab one of my pigtails and twist it anxiously. "The pirates are about to get what they want... they'll kill everyone on the ship... I mean, why would they leave anyone alive when that could mean getting caught?"

The feline rubs his head against the floor. "Give me my treats."

"*I can't!*" My voice rises to a scream. "Even if I could get back to the ship, the pirates will have taken over, and I won't be able to get to the kitchen, and—why am I even explaining this?"

Still rolling around on his back without a care in the world, Pi gives me an unimpressed look. "If the pirates are the problem, then get rid of the pirates, and give me my treats when they're gone."

"What do you expect me to—" I break off.

Get rid of the pirates. They're heading here, to the *Black Diamond*. Which has a functional central computer. That I was able to access, because cybersecurity is a joke when you're from five decades in its future.

Holoprojectors. Internal defenses. Force fields. All standard security measures for a transport carrying items of great value.

And all tools I can use to free my mom.

The pirates enter the *Black Diamond* through the same hull breach I did, led by Mom and a few others from the *Moncacht-Apé*'s crew.

Sitting in the commander's chair, I watch through the viewscreen, which I programmed to correspond to the motion sensors and security cams. That is, it'll show me anything bigger than Pi that moves on board this ship. I also used the internal communications to create a signal that'll interfere with any attempts by the pirates to communicate with each other.

Saxe turns to the other pirates—six in total, including her. "Split up. We'll take a hostage each. Interference from the planet means we won't be able to talk, but you know what to do. Document everything of value so the others will know what to look for when we use the *Moncacht-Apé* to retrieve it. We'll meet back here in an hour."

Mom whirls to her. "You said you'd release the ship once you got what you came for! If you're planning to use it to transport the—"

"Yeah, yeah, I lied." Saxe smirks. "Did you think I could get the valuables off T'rovek Ghad in a bunch of little Silversides? Everyone on board the *Moncacht-Apé* will remain under my control until each item has been safely delivered to its buyer."

I grip the armrests, seething. Nothing on board this ship should be sold to *anyone*. It belongs to the people, and ought to be displayed in museums that anyone can access, not squirreled away in some rich jerk's private residence.

I'm not surprised that Saxe reneged on the deal she'd made with the *Moncacht-Apé*'s crew. Yet it still infuriates me.

She divvies up the hostages among the pirates, and then they all head off in different directions. She takes my mom as her own hostage.

"All right, Lieutenant Park." Saxe shoves Mom toward a console in the hallway, the same one I used previously. "What can this thing tell me?"

Mom clenches her jaw and turns to the screen.

Except it doesn't come alive the way it did when I approached. Oh, and neither did the lights. Because I altered the *Black Diamond*'s central computer to make it look like everything is dead.

No matter how Mom pokes at the screen, no matter how she messes with the wiring behind the panel underneath, the console won't respond. Because I told it not to.

Meanwhile, the bearded pirate, walking alongside a terrified-looking ensign, climbs a ladder to the second level. He makes the ensign go first, and she arrives without a problem.

But as soon as he steps foot in the corridor, I command one of the internal defense weapons to fire a stun blast at him. He falls to the ground unconscious, and the ensign gasps.

I open a communication channel and activate just one speaker, so only the ensign will hear me. "This is Kyung Ji-eun," I say. "Relax, I've got this."

The ensign looks around nervously, but some of the fear fades from her eyes.

On the viewscreen, another pirate approaches a cargo bay door. He commands his hostage, also an ensign, to open it. The young man shakily pries open a panel and reaches for the wires.

Since I don't want him to do anything to mess with my control of the ship, I open the door for him. A startled look fills his face—he knows he didn't do anything to cause that.

The pirate, enamored by the sight of the ancient jewelry and priceless art before him, doesn't seem to notice. A greedy look fills his face as he strides through the door.

Apparently, he was too busy staring at shiny things to notice the colorless force field I'd erected under the doorway.

It throws him backward, and he slams against the floor. The ensign jumps up and grabs the pirate's weapon, forcing the latter to surrender.

Two down.

Pirate Number Three walks into a supply closet that looks like a cargo bay, thanks to a false signal I sent to his hostage's slate. And he wasn't smart enough to make the crewman go first, so I'm easily able to trap him in there by slamming the door behind him.

Pirate Number Four is a bit smarter. She makes her hostage walk ahead and grips the crewman's arm the entire time. When I try to use an internal defense weapon to fire a stun blast at her, she notices it moving and blasts it with her gun before I can fire.

What she didn't expect, though, was for me to have used the holoprojectors to create a fake door, leading to a fake cargo bay full of fake treasure. Oh, and the door was programmed to look crumpled-open due to the crash, so she wouldn't wonder why she's able to walk right through it, or notice that it's made up of nothing but light. She's so distracted by the magnificence of her discovery—really a scan of the items I found earlier—that she doesn't notice a second internal defense weapon moving behind her. It hits her with a stun blast to the back, knocking her out and allowing the crewman to escape.

Pirate Number Five is all brawn and no brains. He walks smack-bang into a wall that I used a holoprojector to transform into an open doorway to a room full of treasure. He walks into it so hard, he knocks himself out. His hostage rolls her eyes at the sight.

Meanwhile, Saxe still has Mom. Though they weren't able to use the ship's computer, Mom still has her slate and its scanner. With every step, Saxe shoots any sign of technology she glimpses—the holoprojectors, the internal defenses, even the lights. They're only able to see because of a flashlight that Mom's holding. I'm glad that the *Black Diamond* has a gazillion security cameras, and that they're so well concealed that Saxe can't notice and blast them, too.

The two make their way to the cargo bay I entered earlier.

"Open it," Saxe commands.

Mom opens a panel and starts fiddling with wires. She furrows her brow—she must have noticed something I did.

Saxe nudges Mom with her weapon. "What's taking so long?"

Mom glares up at her. "Maybe you care to try?"

Saxe scowls and aims the weapon at Mom's knee. "You're a genius, aren't you? The only reason this door isn't open yet is because you don't want it to be. So I'm giving you thirty seconds to let me in, or else."

I don't doubt the threat. I hurriedly command the computer to release the hold I had on the door, and it opens before Saxe.

The pirate sneers. "That's what I thought."

Pi, who's been curled up in the pilot's seat this whole time, glances up. "You're in trouble, aren't you?"

"Hush, cat," I grumble. "I'm trying to think."

Saxe strides into the cargo bay and looks around at the treasure. "Scan everything," she says to my mom. "I want a complete inventory."

"Why don't you knock her out like the others?" Pi stretches lazily.

"I can't!" I grit my teeth in frustration. "She shot all the force field generators!"

"She didn't shoot anything in the cargo bay. She couldn't without risking damage to the things she wants."

"Well, there aren't any force field generators in there, only holoprojectors—" An idea hits me.

I tap at the control touchscreen by the commander's chair.

On the viewscreen, Mom obediently uses her slate to scan and inventory the artifacts. But from the glint in her eye, I know she's looking for an opportunity.

So I give her one—I use the holoprojectors to conceal her behind an image projecting the background behind her, while at the same time creating a holographic version of her in almost the same spot.

From Saxe's perspective, it would have looked like her image blinked and shifted by about a millimeter. It's subtle, but the pirate is savvy enough to notice. She scowls and lifts the weapon, already aimed at Mom.

At my command, the holographic version of Mom leaps at her. Saxe fires, and it goes right through the image.

My real mom uses the opening to kick Saxe's legs out from under her. She slams to the ground. Mom wrestles the weapon away from Saxe and aims it at the pirate.

"Don't move," Mom orders.

A relieved smile spreads across my face. It's over—we have all the pirates, including their commander.

Pi jumps off the chair and stares at me with his big yellow eyes. "Now can I have my treats?"

✦✦✦✦

After all that salvaging, I didn't need to repair my pod after all. We used the one the pirates had taken down to the planet to return to the *Moncacht-Apé*. En route, Mom ordered Saxe to command her crew to stand down and escape while they could. It wasn't ideal, letting all those pirates go, but at least it meant that by the time we returned, the hostages were no longer in danger.

Besides, we got the leader and five of her crew. Plus, Commander Torres alerted all patrols as to what the pirates looked like, so they won't get far.

After handing over Saxe and the other five to the security crew, Mom and I return to our quarters, where Dad is waiting anxiously.

He throws one arm around each of us and pulls us close. "Thank goodness you're okay!"

For a few seconds, I just breathe in the moment. All of us here, safe, on a ship we call home.

Dad releases us with a smile. "You ladies must be exhausted after all that saving. Want a snack? Taro boba?" He gives me a wink.

"Always." I smile back.

He heads to the kitchen.

Mom turns to me. "Ji-eun, I haven't had a chance to address your behavior yet, given—"

"Given that we were busy making the pirates who captured you release everyone?" I arch my brows. "The pirates you only caught because I got to the *Black Diamond* first?"

"What you did—impersonating me, stealing a pod—was wrong." Mom gives me a stern look. "If we were not on board this ship, and if you were not afforded special privileges because of your relationship to me, then your actions would be considered *crimes*. I don't think you understand the gravity of your actions."

I blow out a breath. "You're seriously lecturing me after I saved the entire ship?"

"I'm not finished." Mom's shoulders relax. "While your initial actions were reckless, you showed incredible courage and cleverness under stressful circumstances. I don't think *I* have understood the extent to which you've grown up. You'll always be my little girl, but that doesn't mean I should treat you like one. And... it seems making you stay on the ship wouldn't have kept you safe anyway."

"Yeah, if I'd followed the rules, I'd have been a hostage, the same as Dad, and you might never have defeated Saxe and her crew."

Mom gives me a stern look. "Just because I'm conceding that you had a point doesn't mean you can get cocky. But... perhaps I can allow you to accompany me on off-ship missions every so often."

I brighten. "Really?"

Her face warms. "Really."

I throw my arms around her. "Thank you, Mom! That's all I ever wanted!"

She hugs me, and I sink into the happiness of the moment.

"Where are my treats?!" An obnoxious computer voice interrupts my bliss, coupled with an insistent meow.

I look up to find Pi standing by my ankles, glaring at me. He demanded to come with us to make sure he got what he was promised. The slate with the translation algorithm sits on the side table where I left it.

I smile down at him. "I'll go get them. Wait here."

He watches as I head to the kitchen. "Sliced and presented on a silver platter, like you promised?"

"Thought you didn't care about how food looked."

"I want what you promised."

I grin. "Silver platter it is."

"Good." He hops onto the sofa. "Tomorrow, I want poultry."

"Tomorrow?"

"And the day after, I want fish again, but a different variety. After that, beef."

"How long are you expecting to stay here?"

Instead of answering, Pi curls up and starts purring.

Mom huffs, and I give her a sheepish look.

"Hey, Mom, can I have a cat?"

THOUGHTS ON *BRAVE NEW GIRLS*

"When we launched *Brave New Girls* back in 2014, I thought it'd be a single volume. I never imagined that ten years later, we'd still be going strong with our eighth volume. I'm so grateful to all the creators who've contributed their stories and art to these anthologies, and to all the readers who've picked up the books and given them to the young girls in their lives. We've still got a long way to go on the journey to gender equity, but it's great to see all the support out there for this cause."

ABOUT THE AUTHOR

Mary Fan is a Jersey City-based author of sci-fi/fantasy and young adult fiction. Her books include the *Jane Colt* trilogy, the *Starswept* trilogy, the *Flynn Nightsider* trilogy, and *Stronger Than a Bronze Dragon*. She is the co-editor, along with Paige Daniels, of the *Brave New Girls* anthology series. In addition, she is the editor of the anthologies *Bad Ass Moms* and *Magic Under the Big Top*. Her short fiction has appeared in numerous collections, including *Thrilling Adventure Yarns*, *Phenomenons*, and *Sing, Goddess!* When she's not writing, Mary can usually be found at choir rehearsal, the kickboxing gym, the flying trapeze rig, or the aerial arts studio. Find her online at www.MaryFan.com.

Illustration for "Color the Constellations" by Adriano Moraes.

Libbie and Dewey's Excellent Adventure

Henry Herz

LIBBIE AND DEWEY'S EXCELLENT ADVENTURE

HENRY HERZ

THE MINIATURIZED COMMUNICATIONS DEVICE (MCD) embedded in my scalp tingles as I stride through a veined marble hallway of Libernaut Headquarters on Luyten b. [*Hypatia, report to my office*] the MCD conveys directly into my brain.

I nod reflexively, even though Knowledge Director Ashurbanipal can't see me. *I'll be right there, ma'am,* I reply through my MCD.

I've never met her before. My pulse quickens as I imagine myself, an eighteen-year-old Earth girl with long brown hair and blue eyes, standing before the ancient, red-skinned, four-eyed leader of the institute.

Three millidays later, I knock on the thick synth-ebony door of her top-floor office.

"Enter."

I salute and stand at attention. Embossed on a rhodium plaque on the wall behind Ashurbanipal is our organization's motto: "DELIVERING THE RIGHT INFORMATION TO THE RIGHT PEOPLE AT THE RIGHT TIME."

Ashurbanipal looks up from her cluttered plasteel desk. "At ease, Hypatia." She points a webbed hand at one of the three black guest chairs. "You may be seated. You scored extremely well on your final exam."

My shoulders relax. I realize I've been holding my breath.

"Having successfully completed the academic portion of your internship, you will now undergo a series of operational exercises."

A smile creeps onto my face.

Setting down her compu-tablet, Ashurbanipal continues, "To start you off gently, the first exercise shall take place on your home planet. What human languages do you speak?"

"English, French, and Mandarin, ma'am," I answer with a hint of pride. Pride that vanishes at her reply.

"Your mission will be in Poland. You must rely on the hyper-transporter's AI for auto-translation. Report to Supply for your equipment."

My excitement battles with anxiety. *I've never used a hyper-transporter before.* My palms begin to sweat.

Ashurbanipal seems to read my mind. "The hyper-transporter will orient you in its proper use and outline your mission parameters. Dismissed."

As I rise to leave, she lifts her head. Four black eyes gaze into mine. "This institute exists to curate the spread of knowledge. Remember your training, Hypatia. Renowned people make history. Renowned Libernauts make history better."

I bet everyone gets that speech. Saluting, I depart, my strides lengthened by adrenaline.

Returning to my dorm room from Supply, I set period-correct black leather shoes and a matching handbag on the floor. I spread the feathered hat, corset, and full-length pale green outfit on my bed. *That's one profusely trimmed dress!*

[*At least the vertical lines will be slimming*] the AI of my hyper-transporter, concealed within the handbag, consoles me in a male voice via MCD.

I giggle. *So, in addition to transporting me through spacetime, translating languages, and materializing whatever books the client needs, you're also a fashion consultant?*

[*I don't like to brag. Now, for the mission. We'll be jumping to Warsaw's Załuski Library on May 3, 1882 at 4PM. The client's a fifteen-year-old named Marya. Transmitting her picture to your occipital lobe now.*]

The image of a small girl with unruly blonde hair appears in my mind.

[*You are to provide the client with textbooks. If you successfully encourage her interest in science, it will have a profound effect on the advancement of human knowledge. This is your first assignment, but it's an important one. Keep in mind, we can communicate only if we remain within two metrons of each other.*]

I turn, feeling silly for conversing with a handbag. *If she's at a library, why does she need help getting books?*

[*You'll see, Hypatia.*]

Grinning, I reply, *Given names, is it? I guess I'll pick one for you.*

[*How about Hal?*]

No, I think Dewey the Wonder Bag suits you better. I could swear he sighs before completing my mission orientation.

Wearing my tightly contoured dress, and with Dewey firmly in my grasp, I wink into existence in the wooded area behind the Załuski Library. After getting my bearings, I walk to the corner of Hipoteczna and Daniłowiczowska Streets to await the client. I take a moment to admire the first Polish public library. Constructed of light-colored stone, the two-story Rococo-style building has a steep slate roof and a small tower for astronomical observation. Busts of Polish monarchs adorn the building's facade.

[*They take book theft VERY seriously here*] Dewey volunteers. [*In 1752, Pope Benedict XIV threatened to excommunicate anyone caught stealing books from this library.*]

A well-dressed young man carrying a brown paper bag catches my attention. He notices my gaze and halts. "Hello. My name is Andrezj."

I nod demurely as he flirts with me. *You're awfully cute.*

Andrezj extends the open bag. "Would you like a blackberry *kołaczki*?"

[*That's a flaky, buttery cream cheese cookie. Focus on the mission, not this boy.*]

I can see what it is, Dewey. Anyway, talk about a LONG-distance relationship... "Thank you, Andrezj, but I must be going."

I move to the top of the library's gray granite front steps.

Within five millidays, the client arrives, carrying a book bag and wearing a faded blue dress with frilled cuffs and a lace collar that isn't as white as it once was.

Striving to look nonchalant, I enter the library behind Marya. There's something inexplicably pleasing about a library—like I can feel the accumulated weight of wisdom. I position myself behind a bookshelf with a clear view of the reference desk as Marya greets a high-collared librarian, "*Dobryy den*."

That's not Polish.

[*It's Russian for 'good afternoon'*] Dewey explains. [*Remember your briefing. Russia controls the government and educational system here.*]

Marya returns two books. "May I please borrow *Fownes' Manual of Chemistry* by Henry Watts, 1878?"

The woman frowns. "Come now, Marya. What does a young woman like you want with Chemistry? Soon enough, you will marry and have lots of babies. Leave science to men."

My face flushes.

[*Remember your training, Hypatia. You know what to do.*]

Marya's lips tighten, but she says nothing. She turns and wanders toward the shelves of science books.

The book please, Dewey. I reach into my handbag and withdraw the Chemistry manual. Closing the distance, I tap Marya lightly on the shoulder. "Is this the book you wanted?" I ask in Russian.

Marya's piercing eyes convey extraordinary intelligence. A wide grin splits her face as she reads the book's title. "Yes!" She glances about, leans toward me, and lowers her voice to a whisper. "Thank you so much. But I have not seen you before. Are you a librarian?"

I nod. "But this isn't my library." Winking, I add in Polish, "I think you should read whatever books you want. But let's keep it our little secret, eh?"

Her eyes radiate excitement at the intrigue. "Oh, yes." She reverently accepts the book. "My name is Marya. What is yours?"

[*Don't give your real name.*]

It's not like she's gonna visit us back home, Dewey.

[*Hypatia!*]

I'm just pulling your, er, leg, Dewey. "Libbie." Over her shoulder, I spot the Russian woman headed our way. "Quick, tuck the book in your bag, Marya."

The woman offers a smile that doesn't reach her eyes. "Who is this, Marya?"

"Oh, my cousin, Libbie Boguski." Marya extends a hand, palm up. "Libbie, this is Mrs. Kuznetsov."

[*Oh, I like Marya. She lied without missing a beat.*]

You've got an odd personality for software, but I agree. "Nice to meet you, Mrs. Kuznetsov." Once Kuznetsov returns to her desk, I take Marya's arm and lead her to a worn wooden table. "Now, Marya, would you like another book?"

Her faces lights up like a young child in a candy shop. After a moment's consideration, she whispers, "Do you have the latest version of Ganot's *Éléments de Physique*?"

[*Not in front of her.*]

Give me a little credit, Dewey. "Let me go see what I can do, Marya. Please wait here." I stroll to a section of the library where Marya can't see me. I spend two millidays scanning the shelves to make it seem that I had to hunt for the book rather than simply asking Dewey.

Marya's smile at my return and the warm feeling this engenders confirms I've chosen the right profession. I sit, placing my handbag on the tabletop. Withdrawing the physics book, I hand it to Marya.

She holds it up to admire the cover before scanning the table of contents. "Oh, this is wonderful. I cannot thank you enough, Libbie."

I stiffen when Mrs. Kuznetsov looms directly behind me.

"Tell me why one of our library books was in your bag."

Keen-eyed little busybody, aren't you? "I borrowed it last week."

She scowls. "Is that right?" Her face crinkles like she bit a lemon. "Not that I recall. And even so, you cannot give it to someone else. This library has strict rules. Wait here." Mrs. Kuznetsov storms toward a man in uniform.

Shoot. I don't want the police questioning or possibly detaining me for a theft I didn't commit. "Enjoy the books, Marya," I murmur, my heart pounding in my chest, "but I must leave." I glance over my shoulder. "Now." I jump to my feet and sprint for the front door.

"Hey! Stop!" shouts a voice from behind me.

I burst out the door, separating some dress seams in the process. Hurtling down the entrance steps three at a time, I bolt around the side of the library. I reach the trees where no one can see me, gasping for breath. *Okay, Dewey. Take us home now!*

The scenery doesn't change. *Dewey?* I look down. Nothing. *Oh, no! I left my handbag inside.* My stomach twists. *My MCD can't communicate with Dewey at this range.* My pulse races. *Without him I can't return home... or even speak Polish or Russian.*

I take deep breaths to gather myself. *Think! Remember your training... and the client. Marya speaks French, so you can still communicate with her. As a regular, she knows the library layout. Your only hope of returning home is Marya.*

I recall her address—less than two kilometrons west of here. *I'll intercept her when she arrives home for dinner.*

Slipping out of the trees, I follow the previously memorized directions to Marya's: Right on Daniłowiczowska, right on Bielańska, left on Solidarności, right on Nowolipki. The streets, lined with stores and restaurants, bustle with activity. When they don't frown at my disheveled appearance and unladylike pace, shoppers gaze in shop windows or chatter gaily.

My heart races at the sight of a policeman standing on a corner. He doesn't appear to be looking for me, but I cross the busy street anyway, dodging bony country nags pulling water-barrel wagons and liveried coachmen driving gleaming carriages. When a foot patrol of four green-uniformed Russian soldiers carrying rifles marches toward me, I duck into a watch repair shop. After they pass, I locate a good spot—a recessed doorway opposite the front of the Nowolipki Street apartments.

Time passes, and the temperature lowers. My empty stomach rumbles. *This has to work.*

After what feels like an anxious week, but was probably less than half a deciday, Marya approaches, head buried in an open book.

"Marya!" I wave. When she halts, I hurry across the street.

She smiles and speaks excitedly… in Polish.

"*Excusez-moi*," I say in French. "*Parlez-vous français?*"

Her eyebrows rise. "*Oui… pourquoi?*"

I can't tell you why. "It's a long story, Marya. In any event, when I escaped the policeman, I left my handbag behind. It's vital I retrieve it." My throat tightens.

Marya nods, her alert eyes taking in the state of my dress and the tension in my face. "Why is the bag so important?"

"I'm sorry, but I can't say." I put a hand on her shoulder. "But I need your help retrieving it."

Her mouth opens at my outrageous request. "I could get in so much trouble…" Marya's eyes twinkle. "So, of course I will help you. It is the least I can do after you gave me two incredible textbooks."

"*Merci*, Marya." My shoulders relax. I hug her. "We must break into the library in the middle of the night."

"*Oui*. We will have to avoid Russian patrols enforcing curfew." She closes her eyes in thought. "I slipped out in the commotion you created, but it is most likely your bag was put in the library manager's office. Was there anything in it with your name and address?"

I shake my head. "No. I don't have a Warsaw address."

Marya tilts her head. "Then where will you stay?" At my shrug, she takes my arm, leading me toward her home. "I will hide you in my room until then. If anyone asks, you are a new boarder. They often come and go."

"You're a gem, Marya."

She sneaks me into her room, later bringing me an apple, half a loaf of rye bread, and water. It's like a feast.

I remain hiding in silence until the household goes to sleep. A glance out her window shows the full moon rising.

Marya taps me on the shoulder, holding a finger to her lips. She hands me a dark gray wool blanket. "My coats are too small for you," she whispers in response to my raised brows.

I wrap the blanket around my shoulders. A wall clock reads 2AM. We slip out of the house, scurrying like mice through empty streets toward the library… until I spot a Russian patrol.

"*Les Russes!*" I yank Marya into an alleyway and behind a pile of refuse, where we cower until the soldiers pass.

Being a Libernaut is not for the meek. My breathing returns to normal. Marya looks like she's having the time of her life. *You enjoy disobeying authority as much as me.*

The library windows are dark. *Good.* I lead Marya to the rear of the stone building and try the door. Locked. *My luck's not that good. I guess I'll have to break a window with a rock.*

Marya reaches into her cloak and hands me a screwdriver, smiling. "I thought you might need this."

I wink. "*Fille ingénieuse.*" *Clever girl.* After a milliday of tampering, I jimmy the lock. "Where's the manager's office?" I'm sweating despite the cool night air. *Please be in there, Dewey.*

Marya takes my hand, and we slip inside like two gray mice searching for cheese. Thankfully, the moon's glow eliminates the need to light a lantern. She brings me to an office. "This is it." The furniture includes a desk, a bookcase, and two small wooden cabinets. Marya steps to the bookcase, and I head for the desk.

My frustration rises with each empty drawer. "Nothing," I hiss, my fists bunching.

"Same here," Marya replies.

I try the first cabinet. *Locked.* Using the screwdriver, I pry open the door, Marya standing beside me. Only leatherbound books, loose papers, writing implements, and a bottle of vodka meet my eager eyes. *Shoot!* I have no better luck with the second cabinet. My chest tightens. "Marya, where else might it be?" *Assuming the police didn't take it, in which case I better get used to living in nineteenth-century Poland...*

She takes a deep breath. "Well, there is a storage room next door."

I rush in, pulling up short at the sight of a much larger room lined with what must be a hundred sturdy storage cabinets. A quick inspection confirms they're locked. My pulse races as I get to work with the screwdriver. The lock proves more difficult to pry open. My breath catches at a sudden realization. "Marya, when do the library staff arrive for work?"

"The library opens at seven, so perhaps an hour before that."

I perform a quick mental calculation. My jaw clenches. "There won't be enough time to open all the cabinets before the library staff return." My shoulders shake. *I'll never find Dewey in time. My first mission is a colossal failure. I'll be stuck in this time without money to feed and house myself.*

Marya offers me a hug, reminding me, "You do not have to open them all—only until you find your bag."

THOUGHTS ON *BRAVE NEW GIRLS*

"In researching my anthology, The Hitherto Secret Experiments of Marie Curie, I came across a startling 1927 photo. One brave woman among the gods of science, including Erwin Schrödinger, Wolfgang Pauli, Werner Heisenberg, Paul Dirac, Arthur Compton, Louis de Broglie, Max Born, Niels Bohr, Max Planck, and Albert Einstein. Marie Curie epitomized the idea that women are men's equal intellectually, and need only be given a chance (or seize one for themselves). Until the world is perfectly equitable, girls must keep being brave."

ABOUT THE AUTHOR

Henry Herz's stories have appeared or will appear in *Daily Science Fiction*, *Weird Tales*, *Pseudopod*, *Metastellar*, *Titan Books*, *Highlights for Children*, *Ladybug Magazine*, and anthologies from Albert Whitman & Co., Blackstone Publishing, Brigids Gate Press, Air and Nothingness Press, Baen Books, and elsewhere. He has edited seven anthologies and written twelve picture books. You can follow his work here: www.henryherz.com.

Illustration for "Libbie and Dewey's Excellent Adventure" by Harley Scroggins.

Go For Pets

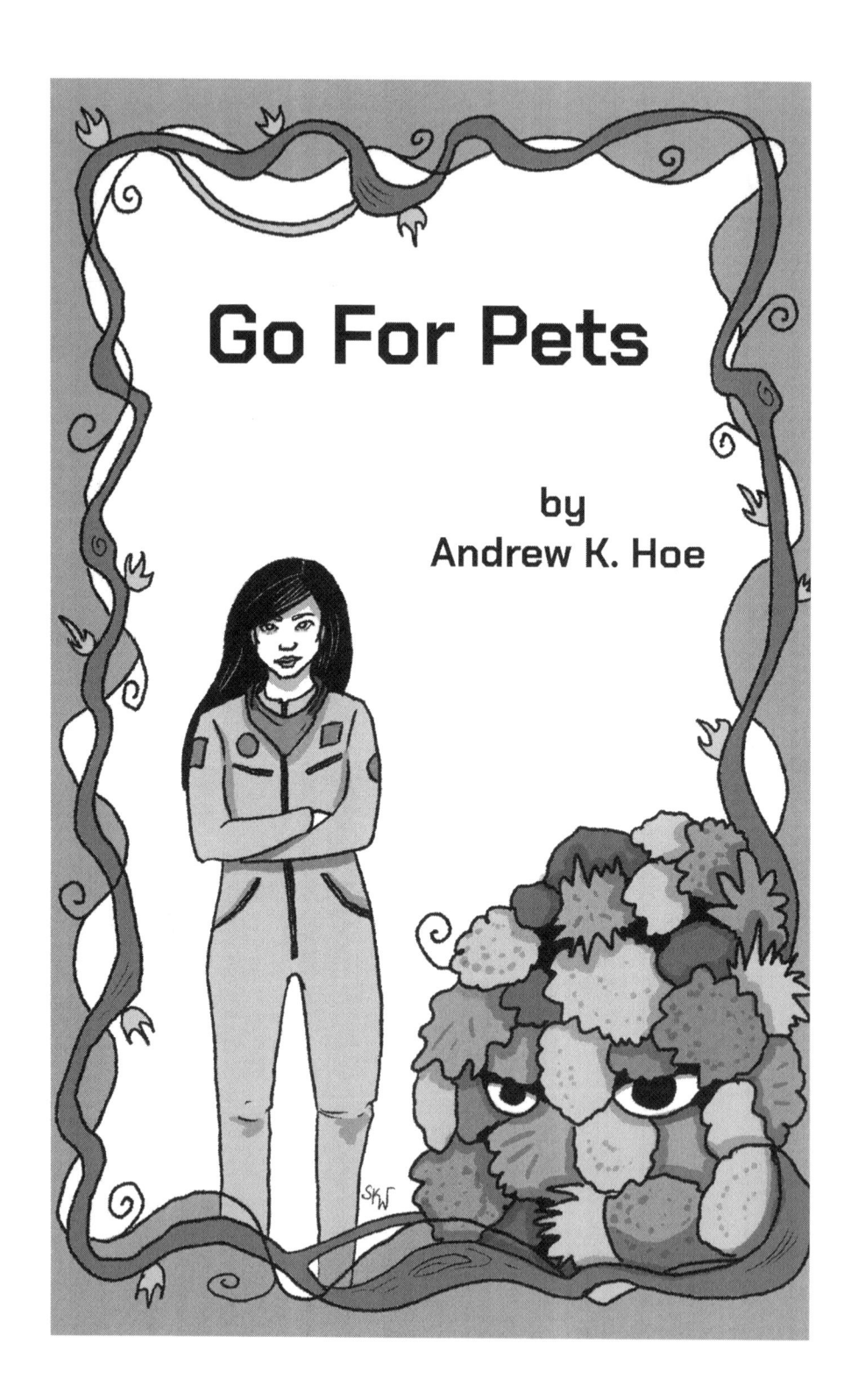

by
Andrew K. Hoe

GO FOR PETS

ANDREW K. HOE

Nobody had taught Team Leader Anika Fong much about leading a group of heroes, but it apparently involved seeing an entire mountain range flatten like a row of dominoes. She gaped as the bottom half of the horizon toppled with a *boom*, muffled by distance and the pilot's bubble of her rescue craft.

She tried warning everyone. "Everybody! Brace for—"

A mountain range's worth of displaced air slammed into Anika's flyer.

Alarms *boop-boop-booped* as she fought her control stick. Where was up? Where was down? From the grunts and cries coming from her comms board, the other rescue pilots seemed to be struggling as much as she was.

"Ride it, don't fight it!"

Death before dishonor!—that from Kai Sim, a non-verbal responder that Anika's comms unit translated as a splash of colors across her cockpit.

"Climb, climb!"

"Yes, climb!"

And a whole lot of choice oaths. As a first-year university student, Anika had heard plenty of that language, and would've yelled some herself had she not been desperately righting her craft.

Finally, Anika and the fleet of two dozen craft stabilized. She canceled her alarms. The turnaround had her now facing her ragtag flock of first responders: pilots of various creeds and heritages steadying cargo haulers and skiffs, gunships and floating spheres. Whatever craft had room for transport, was reasonably fast, and whose pilot was willing to put their life on the line for emergency evacuation of Planet K-406 during an extinction-level disaster.

Heroes, every single one.

People who'd never asked to be heroes, but had answered the call anyway. Nobody would ever impress Anika as much as the bunch before her.

"Ay, chi-*hua-hua*," Responder Cervantes breathed. He'd taken aboard fifteen critical-ward patients and jerry-rigged a suspended-animation freeze for them—good thing, too, considering the turbulence. Now, his air ambulance was at the forefront, closest to the revised landscape. "You don't see that every day, do you?"

Where the range used to be was now a fissure, shooting lurid purple-ish light into the roiling skies. Magma pooled to the surface and added an angry reddish-yellow glow to the disaster. All this from a gravity-inducer experiment gone wrong.

"You said it, bruddah." This from Responder Ulani, the Native Hawaiian who'd tractor-beamed a busload of scared children off a collapsed bridge, talking them through it in a mixture of Native Hawaiian, Pidgin, and Standard English, while performing the complicated calculations of that maneuver. "Not our kuleana, though. We didn' break it"—she switched to Standard English—"But let me get my hands on the mining engines they made to wreck this 'āina."

Nervous laughter at that. Ulani was a psychology doctorate student, always caring for everyone's morale. Anika herself might've given up had it not been for Ulani's ready encouragement.

"Well, that's gravity for you folks," Anika broadcast. "It's one heckuva curtain closer."

A hiss came through her speakers—the Serpenthren responder Warmly Striking Sunrise—translated by her comms as, "Sssssstime ssssssstooo exssssit sssssstage leftsssss..."

A pattern of lights flashed from Kai Sim again. *The battle has concluded. Victory and spoils... back at Base Station.*

A chorus of agreement in languages human, non-human, and synthetic extruded from Anika's comms. They'd been at this for five hours straight. Everyone was exhausted.

Anika felt her stomach drop again. If watching mountains fall was part of leading heroes, then it seemed so was telling them bad news. Forked lightning lit the dark underbellies of the clouds around them, and another distant rumble sounded—maybe another mountain range crumbling.

"Okay, folks. Time is short, so I'll be quick. Thanks to you, over three hundred souls have been rescued from K-406. I myself have a first-year chemistry midterm to get back to."

About six hours ago, the emergency klaxon from her watch had startled her out of a doozy of a problem. She'd been partly relieved to dash from the professor's class, but she'd rather be back at asteroid college than tell her team what she had to say next. She should have been congratulating them, offering thanks, promising they were always welcome in the Fong household, but...

"But there are additional souls on K-406." She tapped a button, and the same display she was looking at went to everyone's screens. "There are forty-two pets still unaccounted for. So. I can call this in to Base Station and we can all leave for a *well-deserved* rest from danger… or we can go back. For the pets."

She hadn't meant to, but the display automatically began cycling through images of the pets in alphabetical order of name registration: dogs and cats, fish, octopi, an iguana, various animals from other planets. No, that wasn't fair. She couldn't tug on everyone's heartstrings like that.

Anika switched her display to show the feed of the gravity-inducer as it continued to self-destruct, pulsing the same purple light that was visible in the sky. The building-sized contraption was trembling, pipes bursting and sparks flying.

"The inducer's entering its final self-destructive phase. In another hour, there will be no K-406. The planet will collapse in on itself like a ball of aluminum foil. If we're caught in the gravity wave, we'll become part of that crumpled ball. Just FYI, Base Station is ordering us back *pronto*. They do *not* want us to continue operations."

Anika unmuted the audio that had been going nonstop since she'd proposed her plan to Base Station. "—you hear me, Team Leader Fong! You're a *volunteer*, a college student, not professional rescue personnel! You go through with this, there will be no rescue party to rescue the rescue party! ANSWER COMMS, YOU ARROGANT—"

Anika cut the feed. "To be honest, folks, as unpleasant as they're being, they have a point. This is extremely dangerous. Um, I need decisions, please."

The sky rumbled, and the magma lake gooped over the land. An explosion shot gravel into the air as lava geysered into the air. As if the dying planet were saying: *Puny rescue ships. You don't belong here. Fly away. Run.*

"Ah, sistah. Ulani here." Her voice sounded world-weary. But filled with steel. "Who you kiddin'? Aloha 'āina means caring for animals. We go for da pets. We in dis to win dis."

"Team Leader Fong, Wing Leader Maryam here. We are go for pets."

A flash of lights. *Kai Sim of the S'thra Warrior Sect. We are go for pets.*

"Team. Leader. Fong. Nix. Leader. Here. Confederation. Of. Sentient. Machines. Synthetic. Wing. We. Are. Go. For. Pets."

Ulani's laugh danced across Anika's speakers. "You're all my ohana! Robots, too!"

Anika's heart started to swell. Rescuing forty-two pets in forty-two separate locations on a collapsing planet was a whole lot more manageable if the animals were to be spread amongst a group, with each flyer responsible for only one or two animals. "Gosh, I really appreciate you," she gushed, emotion straining her voice. "I really, really appreciate you!"

More positive responses came through.

"Go for pets!"

"Also go for pets!"

"Negative, Team Leader. Cervantes here. I've got critical patients, and my flyer can't handle more flak. Suspended animation is meant for long-term stasis, so I gotta get these people to Base Station before they develop permanent symptoms."

Anika nodded. "Good call, Cervantes. Get those people to safety. You did well today."

Sounds of approval came from the other rescuers.

"Good job, Cervantes!"

"Well done!"

"Finest medical student his side of the galaxy!"

"Yuan Thongkham here. Afraid I'll also have to bow out—damage to my craft. I'm having difficulty keeping altitude."

"Yes, absolutely, Yuan," Anika replied. Yuan was an intergalactic florist. They had dumped their entire cargo of star lilies to come help save three families. "Get yourself to safety."

More approval from the rescuers.

Then, a shaky voice. "T-team Leader Fong. I... I c-can't. I just can't."

Anika paused her calculations. She'd been multitasking, hurriedly assigning pets to people as they volunteered. That voice had been the rookie's. The only other person officially trained in rescue efforts besides Cervantes. Zara Winn, who'd proven herself admirably during the past five hours. The secondary school student who should've been in class, joking with classmates, gossiping over whatever high schoolers gossiped about.

"It's the fire, Team Leader. I... I'm afraid of the fire."

Anika wanted to give Zara a huge hug, but there just wasn't time. As far as Anika was concerned, Zara was now the kid sister she'd never had. When this was all over, Anika would—

Another explosion rocked the air.

"There's no shame, Zara," Anika broadcast. "Listen, you're making an excellent call. Knowing one's capabilities and being honest with one's limits is crucial to this kind of work."

"You're ohana now," Ulani said. "Family. You did great."

You saved lives today, Kai Sim flashed. *You are braver than many warriors, young Zara. For this, you will always have a home among the S'thra.*

Yuan jumped on. "Don't feel bad," they said. "I agree with Team Leader Fong about knowing one's capabilities. I'm a florist and don't know much about animals, much less how to handle panicked animals. I'd just be in the way. You're still a student, right? What do you study?"

The other volunteers chimed in, agreeing with Yuan, saying they didn't know the first thing about how to get animals to trust them, or how to treat an injured animal either. They were only volunteering because there was nobody else qualified to.

Anika heard a sniffle on Zara's end. Then maybe a bitter laugh. "I'm studying xeno-veterinarian science."

⁂

After she'd docked onto Base Station and the evacuees in her hold had been ushered away by medical staff, Responder Zara Winn dragged herself to sick bay for her own evaluation.

Boy, did she feel like the sorest loser this side of a gravity-crushed planet.

Everybody felt sorry for her, and the thing was, *they were so kind about it.* So freaking understanding. Living with the anxiety that dogged her every day was one thing, but to have an unexplainable fear of fire, to get goosebumps from hearing just the sound of that awful licking yellowness…

She was a scientist, for heaven's sake. She knew the food she ate was prepared using heat, and yet she still couldn't help thinking of burnt skin or fire-related injuries whenever the subject of fire came up. Even cartoons of flames were enough to give her the shivers.

It was absolutely humiliating, having a fully rational mind, yet being completely dominated by an irrational fear.

She'd thought she'd been holding it together, fingers white under her gloves from gripping her control stick, zooming around falling debris like a pro pilot. For five hours she'd endured the rising panic, holding her ship steady as scared evacuees pounded up her boarding ramp. But that mountain range collapsing, and all that magma flooding to the surface…

The medical technician examining Zara looked over his notes, then advised her to drink fluids and rest for the next week. "Do you need to talk to a counselor? You've been through an absolutely terrifying experience, Zara. I recommend—"

"No." Zara collected herself and stood. "No, thank you."

Then there was the mission debrief, which, luckily, was more about Anika Fong's disobedience than Zara's failings.

"At least you had the sense to follow orders," Director Penn griped. "If anything happens, the lawsuits from the families of those volunteers will bury us. What is on that lunatic's mind? Risking it all? *For pets*?"

It was enough to snap Zara out of her funk. Why did everyone think animals were expendable? "I commend Team Leader Fong's actions. Pets are absolutely a priority."

Director Penn whirled from the Base Station's floor-to-ceiling windows to face Zara. Penn was a Pantheren, resembling a white, spotted big cat from Earth—except thrice as large.

"And what qualifies you to make that determination, Responder Zara? Foolhardy as she is, at least Team Leader Fong has years of emergency responder service under her belt. When did you get certified to serve, a month ago? For the financial aid benefits, I assume?"

Penn stalked toward Zara on great pads, snow-white tail flicking side-to-side, as if about to pounce.

Zara felt her cheeks grow hot. "Well, yes, but—"

"Is this the first time you were activated? Is this your first mission?"

"Yes—"

Director Penn snarled. He pawed an input device on the floor, and Zara's profile leapt up as a holographic collage. Zara's age, her high school, her Asian heritage, her interest in xeno-biology and veterinary science. Pictures of her surrounded by birds, kittens, rabbits, and so forth. Animals gravitated toward her.

Her achievements: pilot's license at age twelve, cleared for everything from single-person flyers to large cargo haulers. Her internship with indigenous peoples and their environmental methodologies.

Director Penn knew Zara's profile by heart, of course. Popping up her information was just a display on Penn's part. Zara waited as Penn's yellow eyes roved through the data, bracing herself for when Penn inevitably brought up Zara's psychological weaknesses. She'd always wondered how she'd been accepted into the Emergency Responder Corps with her anxiety issues. Maybe now Penn would realize his mistake and discharge her.

"You have much to commend you for, Zara Winn. Your accomplishments make you an excellent asset to our rescue team."

Zara hesitated. She hadn't been expecting this, for Penn to switch from yelling about Fong going off-the-book to complimenting Zara. "Sir?"

"But you are not a frontline worker. It is crucial that you see that."

Zara spluttered. "Sir, I would like to—"

"You cannot let Fong's antics distract you from a promising future," Penn went on, pawing the display off and padding his feline form to face the stars beyond the windows again. "You admire Fong, don't you? You wish you were her."

It was true. Anika Fong was the heroine Zara always wanted to be.

"Don't follow her example, Zara. Anika throws herself into danger. I don't always agree with her methods, but she is the kind of person who thrives in chaos." Penn turned his yellow eyes on Zara. "You are not. You must not try to be what you are not. What you can never be. If Anika doesn't know when to quit when she should, at least you should know to let it go."

Then the director's mood changed from angry to almost mournful. "We can't save them all, Zara Winn. Remember, we can't save them all."

Anika ordered passengers to be transferred to the ships that would be returning to the Base Station, the massive staging area that was always assembled for a big operation like Planet K-406.

Then Anika and the remaining ships split to their various destinations.

"Heading for the aquarium," Ulani said, drifting right and toward an especially flame-ridden sector.

"Stay safe out there!" Anika broadcast, but got only static in return. "Hello, Ulani? Anybody still with me?"

Either comms were disrupted by the chaos out there, or the other volunteers were too busy to talk. Maybe Anika should focus, too. She'd picked the hardest mission for herself.

The other pets had clear registration data, but this one… it wasn't in the city areas. The residence was listed as rural, located in the outlying wilderness. The gravity-inducer shot its purple rays, and those it blasted directly through the planet's mantle were causing all kinds of tectonic stress. These outer regions were taking the brunt of it.

Anika guided her flyer over chasms opening along the planet floor, gouts of magma leaking through the earthen crust. A newly formed geyser spumed lethal fumes at her, but Anika managed to veer away.

"Yikes," she muttered. "Almost became a steamed dumpling, folks. It's geysering out here. Anybody hear me?"

Better fumes than one of those purple rays. To get caught in one of those was to be mashed into the ground as one's gravitational pull was increased one-hundred-fold.

Her flyer approached an enclosure of some sort, maybe a zoo, by the looks of the separated areas. A water-filled area, an open-air zone, and so forth. What if this was like what Cervantes had encountered? He'd thought he was showing for a single passenger, but found instead a whole ward of critically wounded people.

"Only one way to find out," Anika said aloud. She wasn't just talking to herself. Maybe she couldn't hear anybody else, but that didn't mean they couldn't hear her. During the hours before, they'd talked to each other, giving advice, calling for assistance, working as one unit. Just in case anyone was listening, she clarified her thoughts. "Er, I mean, I hope this isn't a surprise like Cervantes found."

Anika set her craft to hover at the enclosure's gates. "Okay. Going in."

She extracted herself from her safety harness and jumped from her high cockpit. Thrusters on her boots allowed her to float to the ground. She winced as she made landfall. It was steady. So far, so good. No purple beams, no earthquakes. Yet.

She double-checked her utility belt—water, grappling coil, climbing hooks, multipurpose gun, and so forth. The enclosure was big, and her scanner was not giving clear readings. She read one flickering life sign ahead. Besides that one vague blip on her watch's screen, nothing.

Then, the air was split, not by the sound of groaning earth or collapsing mountains she'd heard all day, but by something else—a moan of utmost sorrow booming from the enclosure. It was a call of so much heartache that Anika gasped.

"Oh, no, people, I think my pet is big. And it sounds hurt." Anika took a moment to steady herself. "Hang on, beastie. I'm coming."

As she started sprinting through the enclosure gates, a wild idea struck her. That call had been loud, but singular. No other call answered. What if this big enclosure wasn't for many animals, but for one creature?

Zara walked the corridors of Base Station with hot tears pressing against her eyes. Director Penn's words haunted her. *You must not try to be what you are not.* Did he not think she already knew that?

She had pride, sure, but not so much as to throw herself into a situation where her anxiety would endanger not just herself, but the ones she was rescuing. And for what? Prove that she could overcome in a single mission what had haunted her for a lifetime?

That was how movies portrayed anxiety. It was simply a matter of mentally pushing yourself through it. The protagonist would face their worst fear—rats, snakes, whatever—and they'd do what needed to be done. And, hey presto, they were cured by movie's end!

If only anxiety worked like that.

If there were a way for Zara to do away with the sweating and spine-tingling panic she got whenever she saw fire, like slow her breathing and pounding heart, it would more likely be the result of prolonged treatment with a trained professional—than on a dying planet.

But what had Director Penn meant? It seemed like he'd been saying something else about not being what she wasn't. Was she not fit to be a rescue worker after all? Was he trying to let her make the decision of quitting, rather than discharging her?

Zara plopped herself before a console. She wanted to lie down, and Director Penn's words bothered her, but something else was nagging at her. After Anika had broadcast that list of pets to everyone flying over disintegrating Planet K-406, one page had caught her attention.

Now, with no mountains flattening around her, no deadly purple gravity rays to dodge, Zara pulled up the list and read in more detail. The pictures were adorable: wide-eyed puppies smiling for the camera, an iguana riding their owner's shoulder, but… what about the blank screen for this pet listed as living out in the wilderness?

It seemed the list had been updated with which volunteer was going for which pet.

Of course. Anika Fong was going for the very one Zara was researching.

FILE RESTRICTED—CLASSIFIED.

"The heck?" Zara said aloud, then remembered where she was and looked around. The office area she was in was deserted. Base Station personnel were seeing to the evacuated people.

Zara turned back to her screen and started typing. The pet registry was a public site, but as a veterinarian, Zara had other ways of researching the issue. Vaccination records, medications, food deliveries, etc.

Who would classify a pet, though?

What, is this mystery pet with no image, like, some kind of government secret? Many animals had a range of abilities utilized throughout history. Dogs could guide non-sighted people. Monkeys could be trained to help owners who couldn't use their hands.

And Zara had studied animals who could assist in rescue operations, like dogs who could smell explosives, or the zyn-zan of Dylo Prime whose electrostatic abilities could resuscitate someone's heart better than a crash cart…

Yeah, okay, so say there is this top-secret animal that had some… haha. Zara had to grin at this. *What if this animal has some superpower and that's why it was classified—that would be, like, mind-blowing, hahaha… ha… ha…*

The grin froze on Zara's lips. Her fingers stilled over the keyboard. "Holy moly," she breathed.

"Oof!" Anika landed on a giant, plush petal. She raised her arms against the debris that fell after her: bits of wooden staircase, flecks of paint, a cylindrical lighting bulb—all harmless.

Seemed the enclosure was built off a natural rock formation, but rather than remove the natural elements, they'd been incorporated around the architecture. A natural waterfall with benches around it. Stairs above this cavern, which was apparently some sort of basement area.

She'd fallen into a cave with vines crawling the rough walls. She was lying on a huge magenta flower. Whoever had designed this enclosure had a taste for flora; Anika could see that. The vines were everywhere. She should broadcast that to the group in case anyone came looking. She just needed to catch her breath.

Grunting, Anika rolled off the wobbling, bed-sized petal and onto the ground, putting hands on knees to pant and dust herself off. The stairs had collapsed, and she'd fallen, what, five stories?

This was the third time a well-placed flower or vine had kept her from imminent doom. She really wanted to share her incredible luck. Kai Sim might have a pithy warrior aphorism about making one's fortune. One of the sentient machine volunteers might share the statistical data behind her three-times-not-dying. She'd take a selfie if she had the time.

"I'll say, folks," Anika said. "This is the luckiest rescue mission I've ever been on. Anyone hear me? Over?"

Again, nothing but static. *Oh, well.* She didn't have time to chat, anyway.

Where was this wounded pet? What would she do to get it to trust her? Anika found her flashlight, undamaged from the fall, and aimed it at the cavern she was now in. She felt a rumble under her soles.

Time was running out.

"Hello?" she called, her voice echoing slightly off the recessed niches. "Hellooooo! Pet?"

There was a kind of trail Anika was following. Her intergalactic emergency responder training hadn't covered how to track animals, but her flashlight illuminated an unmistakable swirl through the debris, dust shoved aside by the passage of something very large.

She turned to keep moving but caught sight of a living area.

This was a study nook, judging by the comfy chair and lamp, and bookshelves.

The more information she could share with whoever might be listening, the better. Maybe when everyone was done rescuing their assigned pets, someone might come lend her a hand.

"Aha. Folks, if you can hear me, I'm in some residence—not an enclosure. And the person who lives here…" Anika peered at the pictures on the shelves, which were relatively undisturbed by the planetary disaster. A woman in a ridiculous orange hat. "The homeowner has some interesting sense of fashion," Anika concluded.

The ground rumbled, and the framed picture tumbled and crashed onto the cavern floor. The tremors were getting worse. The gravity-inducer was steadily working its dreadful effects on the surrounding area.

Anika grumbled and trudged deeper into the enclosure.

Zara stepped away from the console. She checked left and right of the Base Station. Activity had increased since she'd started researching. Medical personnel flown in to treat the evacuees. Government officials wanting updates on the status of rescue efforts, even representatives of the mining company who'd brought the stupid gravity-inducer onto K-406. People were dashing down the station hallways outside the workroom Zara was in.

She hurriedly wiped her presence clean, deleted her search path. Nobody could see what she'd discovered. She didn't have all the pieces, but she knew enough. She needed to get to Anika. Fast. That was no ordinary pet she was looking for.

But how?

What, was she going to steal a flyer and head back to the dying planet? The planet that was now awash in burning magma?

The flames she would see, broken buildings, more molten lava lakes as the malfunctioning gravity-inducer kept breaking apart the planetary crust. Zara's heart rate skyrocketed. Her skin prickled, and on the cool station, sweat beaded on her forehead: heat from an invisible inferno.

Images of objects shriveling in fire kept popping in her mind. Scraps of paper folding on themselves. Water droplets shivering themselves into nothingness. Even the smell of fire's work, the smoky, ashy scent it made—

"You! You created that monstrosity of a machine without any thought of what it would do to the ʻāina!"

That voice! Zara pulled herself together and joined the flow of people rushing down the corridor. That voice had talked her through some hairy moments during the five-hour rescue—on private comms. As if the speaker knew about Zara's snarled mess of anxieties.

She emerged onto quite the scene. Before a crowd of onlookers stood Ulani, a brown-skinned young woman in a flight-suit smudged with grime, glaring at a group of mining scientists, who were backing away, studiously avoiding her gaze.

"Irresponsible!" Ulani continued. "There's a whole history of people who've learned to live with the land, rather than steal its resources. Why didn't you listen to the original caretakers?" She whirled on the onlookers. "Did you know that before these corporates took over, K-406 used to be inhabited by—"

Ulani was ready to keep talking, but Zara grabbed her arm. Ulani was younger than Zara had assumed, a high school senior, maybe. Ulani scrubbed a forearm across her eyes, as if not believing what she was seeing. Then, the older girl leaned in. "Zara?"

"Yep," Zara said. "Am I glad to see you."

Ulani scooped Zara into a two-armed hug. "Ohana," she murmured into Zara's ear. Zara hadn't realized when her arms had wrapped around Ulani's frame. She wasn't just younger, but smaller than the voice that Zara had heard over her comms. Ulani was crying.

"Look," Ulani whispered in Standard English. "Look at what they did to the beautiful ʻāina…"

.ılııl..ılııl..ılııl..ılııl.

"Helloooo? Pet? We really gotta go!"

Anika was practically dragging herself forward at this point.

She found more framed pictures the deeper she wandered into the varied enclosure. She found an orchard, an atrium, even a pond that was part of the waterfall system, and there was at least one framed image in each area of the facility. Seemed the orange-hatted homeowner was into old-tech: no holograms, but lots of physical photos.

Orange Hat Lady liked nature, too. She was usually posed with dusty-looking people, but always around some magnificent specimen of flora. Giant flowers just like the one that had caught Anika's fall earlier. A gigantic magenta-flowered tree exactly like the one whose branches had kept a sizable chunk of ceiling from squashing Anika. There was even a picture of Orange Hat Lady with her feet in a pond featuring a hyacinth with spongy floating leaves, the very same type that Anika had used to keep from drowning when a violent quake had broken a containment wall and a mini tsunami had slammed into her. Orange Hat Lady was a collector of plant-life. And...

"You're an emergency responder," Anika said. "These are pictures of the people you've saved. You collect plant life from the places you've been..."

Orange Hat Rescuer was human, according to the pictures. A clear-eyed, tan-skinned woman under that hat. A poet and activist, as Anika could see from the books she noticed as she jogged through the facility. Anika did another scan for life signs, but it was just the one vague signal she was getting—too big to be human. Maybe the pet's owner had rushed out to help, not realizing how severe the planetary disaster was.

Anika collapsed against what looked like a spongy fern. She was freezing, shivering, but the great stem was oddly warm. Anika rubbed her palms together. Orange Hat Rescuer had a thing for giant plants. Considering all she'd done for others in dire need, it was the least Anika could do to take care of Orange Hat Rescuer's pet, wasn't it?

Anika sighed. The pet was hiding from her. It was terrified. So Anika would have to subdue it for its own good. Grimacing, she pulled her stun-pistol from its holster.

With Ulani's encouragement, Zara entered the communications network to send electronic letters. She eventually got contacted by an elder from Planet K-406's original population, the S'ana.

A blank screen came up. At first, Zara thought she'd gotten a bad connection, but then a husky voice spoke in Standard English.

"Cunning Star Fortress is a further one; Glimmering City is a further one. They lived together, and Strong Book Lore was born. Strong Book Lore is a closer one; Curiosity Via Experimentation is a closer one. They lived together, and I, Investigative Bud, was born."

From all that, Zara got that the elder who was on the other side of the blank screen was named Investigative Bud, but she didn't have a clue about what "closer one" and "further one" meant.

"Hello?" Zara queried.

But the screen remained blank. It seemed something was expected of Zara...

"It's... a moʻokūʻauhau," Ulani murmured in wonder. She turned to Zara and spoke low. "The elder has just given you their family lineage. You have to give yours. I think 'further one' means something like a 'grandparent.' Therefore, 'closer one' would mean 'parent.'"

Zara cleared her throat. "Um, Winn Weibo is my grandfather. Yang Hairong is my grandmother. They lived together, and Foong Theresa was born. Foong Theresa is my mother. Winn Donovan is my father. They lived together, and I, Zara Winn, was born."

Silence for a moment, then Investigative Bud spoke. "We've listened and examined your vocal intonation. Your intention is respectful. We'll hear what you have to say."

The screen cleared to show a brown-eyed human of indeterminate age and gender—not Investigative Bud's true appearance, but a human-filter. A gesture of caution, she assumed. From what Zara had researched, the S'ana got the best treatment only when they made efforts to appear human. In their actual bodily forms, they were treated poorly.

The one thing that was odd about the filter was that it gave Investigative Bud what looked like... orange hair. Besides that, Investigative Bud's expression was iron-hard. Gaze sharp and passionate. Wrinkles around the elder's eyes showed tiredness, but the intensity of his gaze conveyed a tense anger.

Zara swallowed. The S'ana had been forced off-planet by the same people who'd introduced the gravity-inducer. She understood the elder's deep sorrow... and outrage.

Sitting beside her, Ulani nudged Zara. "Get to it, sistah. Can't blame them for being angry. If they agreed to talk, they're interested in what you have to say."

Zara nodded. This wasn't about Zara's sheepishness. "Thank you for taking the time to speak with me."

The elder nodded. "Your written communications to us state there were people still left on our... homeworld." The elder's voice choked at the last word.

"Yes," Zara said. "There's a creature that you can help us understand. Please refer to the package I'm sending."

Investigative Bud's eyes roved over the data transmitted on their screen. The elder's anger evaporated as they read, replaced by a weariness.

"Listen to me, young one. That's a very rare creature you've found, considered the very living breath of our world. Even when my people thrived, there were very few. It's believed the appearance of one would signal a rebirth for us. If it was taken in as a pet, its existence classified, then the owner must understand why such a creature should be kept secret."

"Excuse me, Elder of the S'ana," Ulani said. She recited a more fluid version of the family lineage Zara had given. "Mahalo nui loa for sharing this information with us. Will you come to help care for this creature?"

Investigative Bud looked off-screen, as if consulting with others. "We'll board the next shuttle there. In the meantime, do I understand correctly that you, Winn Zara, are an expert in veterinary science? That you study animal behavior and their physical and emotional needs?"

Zara nodded. "I'm still in school. I don't have my—"

"You'll do," the elder said. "Listen carefully."

Zara opened her mouth to protest, but Ulani nudged her. *Listen to the elder,* she mouthed. Of course. They were the experts here. They knew best what to do.

Zara opened a note-taking app. "I'm... I'm listening."

⁂

"Anika! Anika, come in!" Director Penn called.

But only static came back.

Director Penn was at Base Station's most powerful comms unit. Penn turned his great cat's head to Zara. "Assuming she's still down there, the interference is too great to get through."

Zara groaned. The only option was to mount a flyer and follow Anika's last known location along the planet's collapsing surface.

But the flames.

"I can't," she muttered. "I just can't."

Ulani clasped Zara's shoulder. "But I can."

"If you're talking about flying to the surface," Penn growled, "then you most definitely can*not*. We just barely got you and the other volunteers back. There will be no rescue party for the rescue party."

"What if we just get close enough to establish a comms link?" Ulani persisted. "I can relay what Investigative Bud said—"

"It has to be me," Zara said, rubbing her eyes. "Conditions will have changed down there. I'll need to adapt Investigative Bud's instructions in real time."

Director Penn snarled. "Absolutely not! You cannot risk your life, risk our resources, just to prove yourself."

Zara looked up. "It's not *about* me, director! I'm not proving anything." She turned to Ulani. "I can't pilot. You'll have to get us close. One look at the fire, and I'll freeze up..."

Ulani grabbed both of Zara's shoulders and spoke softly. "Your eyes are dilated. Your breathing is shallow. What do you need, Zara? Tell me."

"I need you to keep me from seeing the planet in flames."

"Look at her!" Director Penn pawed the station floor, like a bull getting ready to charge. "She can't even operate a comms unit!"

"Why not come with us?" Ulani said. "*You* operate the comms unit."

Director Penn's tail lazed in the air, tipping slowly from side to side over his unblinking golden-eyed gaze.

"We can do this," Zara said, with a swallow. "Please. We have to do this."

Anika staggered into a huge chamber littered with debris. It looked like the walls had collapsed. The space was illuminated, like someone had just switched on the lights. There was a craft at the far end she could just make out the wings of. Ah, so this was the flyer bay, then.

She'd just passed yet another framed photo of Orange Hat Rescuer among the grateful-looking people she'd saved and realized that it wasn't a hat the woman was wearing.

"It's… a crest…" Anika panted. "An orange crest…"

Anika heard a moaning sound in the depths of the building.

"Hello? I'm in the corridor, about to step through." Anika entered, describing what she was doing in case there was someone in the bay who couldn't talk. "I'm a first responder! I'm here to help! Please don't be alarmed! I'm entering this bay and headed to the craft!"

The moaning was too big to be human. It was sad. Terribly, terribly sad. It whined and whimpered, like a big crying dog.

Anika gripped her stun pistol. The pet sounded wounded, and badly, too. She could zap it, and if that craft on the far end was undamaged—it looked that way, a wall had collapsed in that corner, but the ship looked untouched—then maybe she could drag the pet aboard and take off. Her original flyer was most likely toast by now.

The ground split beneath Anika's feet, and a noxious-looking purple aura suffused the garage-space. Anika dove. "Yikes!"

She tripped over a vine—and luckily, too. Getting yanked forward saved her from a purple gravity-beam that whizzed over her head instead of through it. The purple light vanished, leaving the flickering bay lights.

"Anika! Team Leader Anika!"

Anika gasped and trembled. "Zara!" Finally. A signal!

It was weird to be hearing Responder Winn's voice, and the girl sounded shaky as heck, but the relief Anika felt from not being alone any longer was all-consuming. "Zara, you wouldn't believe the narrow scrapes I've had! A vine snagged me—I swear, it yanked me away from a gravity beam—along with a giant flower—a warm fern—"

"Anika, listen, there's no time—"

Anika knew that, but she couldn't stop herself. She started pacing the walkway, back and forth, back and forth. A part of her recognized the symptoms: fast breathing, twitchiness, an inability to keep still. The other part of her was drowning in the accumulated adrenaline from all those narrow scrapes with death, babbling uncontrollably.

"Zara, so listen, this pet owner whose enclosure I'm in—I think she was some superhero rescuer—there's pics all over of her exploits—she has an orange crest on her head—I thought it was a hat, would you believe that—"

"Team Leader Anika Fong." That was Director Penn—what was he doing on comms? He was probably going to kill her if she got off-world alive—

"So is *this* what flying into missions is like? It's... *intense*!" Amazingly, the grouchy old cat sounded exhilarated for once. "I... finally understand why you disregard orders the way you do!"

"Oh, hi! Penn! It is intense, isn't it? Hahahaha!" Anika was shivering and tearing up now, but she couldn't stop. "Did you know the original caretakers of this planet had orange head-crests? K-406 is *not* its name, what an ugly-sounding name. No, what was the original name? S'ana. Yes, that was it. Anyways, I think the rescuer was half-human. And half S'anan. I'm in the home of a half-human, half-S'anan resident with a classified pet—oh! The pet!"

Anika started searching frantically, kicking newly fallen bricks from her path. The moaning sounds had disappeared. She needed to get to that flyer. The sounds had been coming from there.

"We have to get her to calm down," Ulani's voice came on. "She's been down there too long, and it's affecting her cognitive state—"

Anika kept ranting. "Oh, listen to that, Ulani is going all psychiatrist-science-y—"

"ANIKA! I KNOW YOU'RE FREAKING OUT, BUT SO AM I. LISTEN TO ME! THE VINE *WAS* THE PET. THE GIANT FLOWER? THAT WAS THE PET. THE FERN? ALSO THE PET. IT'S BEEN WITH YOU THE WHOLE TIME!"

Anika stuttered to a standstill. The last brick she'd pulled dropped from limp fingers.

Zara's voice came back on, still shaky, but steadier. "Anika? You heard what I just said?"

Anika gulped some air. "Uh. Yes, Responder Winn. I heard that."

Ulani snickered in the background. "That did da trick, sistah. Good job."

Zara continued, "The animal is a S'anan shapeshifter that can mimic plant-life. It can become a tree, a flower, a vine, whatever. It's very intelligent, Team Leader Fong. *Very* intelligent. Sentient. So if the owner was half S'anan, maybe she knew how to talk to it. And they weren't owner and pet. More like partners. Pals. Buddies."

Anika went back to clearing debris. "I don't speak the S'anan language, though."

Zara sighed. "No. So you're going to have to win its trust. That's very important, Team Leader. The elders of S'ana insist that the creature doesn't go anywhere it doesn't want to. You cannot force it. That's why the owner classified its existence. If you try to force it, you're no better than the ones who pushed the S'anan off-planet."

"So… that's why I haven't died ten times over? It was watching over me?"

"The creature is the very living breath of S'ana. Its instinct is to preserve and protect."

The heartbroken whimper sounded again. "It sounds injured." Anika picked up the stun-pistol she'd dropped. "So, I take it that stunning it is out of the question?"

"Absolutely," Director Penn said. "Tranquilize it. There's no time to do this nicely. It'll be disoriented, but alive—"

There was a quick movement, like Zara had grabbed the transmitter. "NO! You can't stun something that big, Team Leader Fong. Repeat. Do not stun. You have to find the owner. The creature will be loyal to the owner. Speak earnestly. S'anans are sensitive to sound and can tell your true intentions just by listening to the quality of your voice."

Anika saw a form huddling under the flickering lights. It looked like a moss bed, with magenta blooms. "Great, Responder Winn. I'm okay now. I'm approaching the creature."

"Team Leader—" Director Penn's voice sounded, but Anika spoke over him.

"I'm fine. Please stand by." She clicked a button on her belt, and her feed went silent. She lowered her voice as she slowly approached the end of the bay. "Hello?"

The animal didn't run. Anika saw that vines connected from its bear-like body, that those vines crisscrossed the ruined walls and kept going throughout the facility. She'd been passing those growths since she'd entered.

It turned a magenta-speckled head to her and snuffled. Anika slowly reached out her hand. It nuzzled her like a dog, its soft mossy surface feeling a lot like fur. A low whine came again, sad and long.

Anika turned to the crumbled debris the creature refused to leave.

A great pile of bricks covering a person. And sticking from the top, what looked so sorrowfully like an orange hat. All those pictures with this person, and those grateful rescued groups. Come to think of it, the giant plant in each image was growing in each successive picture. They'd traveled the galaxy together, these two friends, and seen and done so much. Now Anika understood. Its heart was broken.

"Oh, pet." She took the warm creature's head in both arms. "I'm so, so sorry."

The animal moaned again, loud and braying. The same sound Anika had heard after she'd first landed. "Pet," she whispered. "I'm a rescuer. Like you. I've come to help. You're in danger if you stay here. The planet is collapsing. We have to go."

She tugged gently, but the great creature refused to budge.

"C'mon. She'd want you to leave. To live."

Anika felt a big leaf, not roughly, push her off. The creature flattened itself into a grassy pelt around the mound that was once its friend.

There was another violent quake, and Anika stumbled. Purple light flickered into the bay. The gravity-inducer had finally broken through the layers of planet. It was time to go.

It can't be forced, Zara had said.

"Are you sure?"

The creature moaned again.

Anika shook her head. She couldn't save everybody. She stepped toward the flyer. It looked virtually undamaged, and its entry-ramp was extended. The rescuer had no doubt been leading her pet here to flee, when the rubble—

The floor split again. Dust spumed in Anika's face.

She felt a crushing sensation that grew with each passing second. Even the air felt heavy.

Why was the dust taking so long to clear? Why wasn't she falling?

Then Anika saw the purple light engulfing her body. *Oh no.*

Her bones crackled and popped, like she was stretching. But this wasn't like normal stretching. Stretching apart, maybe. The purple light kept intensifying, and Anika felt heavier, and heavier, and heavier, and heavier. How long before the gravity ray crushed her into smithereens? Because it felt like it was taking forever. Didn't intense gravity warp space... and time?

Then something crashed onto the gap in the floor, blocking the light. Anika could breathe again. She landed on something mossy.

"Urrrrrrffffffff," the bear-like, tree-like form murmured, carrying Anika up the ramp in a wave of greenery. Together, they swept into the ship, as Anika took in ragged breaths.

⁂

"Ship detected!" Ulani clicked some switches and rustled.

Director Penn snarled. "Team Leader Fong! Is that you?"

Static, then, "Yep! Team Leader Fong here! Got a S'anan Breath of the World aboard. It saved me."

"Received, Team Leader," Ulani said, rapidly tapping the controls. "Time to get the heck away."

This was as good as Zara could tell, with the blindfold wrapped tightly around her head. She let her head rest against her cushion, sighed, and concentrated on not thinking about flames, or burning, or anything fire-related.

⁂

Following Investigative Bud's instructions, they did their best to give the Breath of the World the biggest storage space, but it was obvious it wasn't comfortable. It needed a varied landscape to be truly at home, something like its home on S'ana. And it still mourned its loss.

Breath of the World was a mouthful of a name, but it felt right. Whenever someone spent time around the creature, the phrase just popped into their minds.

Responders Zara and Ulani met Team Leader Anika at the makeshift enclosure, who leaned on a crutch. The gravity beam had broken her ankle before the Breath of the World had rescued her. But despite the tragedy, the Breath of the World had a playful personality. It gamboled and rolled in the storage space as Ulani and Anika tickled its belly and sprayed it with water.

There, the S'anan contingent arrived, led by Investigative Bud. They flowed onto the deck more than walked. The S'anan were a tree-like people with orange-crested crowns.

"I'm sorry about your world," Zara said as she and Investigative Bud watched through a window.

The other S'anans had just entered the playroom. Some of them called out. The Breath of the World flowed and rustled to its feet-roots. It had no mouth or eyes, just magenta flowers, but it looked excited.

It bounded over to the S'anans, forgetting Ulani and Anika.

Watching the scene, Investigative Bud had what Zara thought was a rare smile on his grayish face.

"The Living Breath of the World contains samples of all flora and fauna lifeforms that once walked S'ana. That's why it moves like an animal, yet is still a plant. It is a seed."

Zara blinked. "Wait. So you're saying…"

"Nothing will replace the furthest back S'ana, the previous world, but when it is ready, this younger one will sleep and grow into a new… how did your friend put it? 'Āina?"

Zara nodded. "'Āina is the Native Hawaiian word for… well, you know."

Investigative Bud looked down at Zara. "We do indeed. We have known it far before and will know it far beyond. Our people will thrive again."

And before them, the S'anan embraced their beloved Breath of the World, and for them, it was like a great homecoming.

ABOUT THE AUTHOR

Andrew K. Hoe is a speculative and children's fiction writer based in Hawai'i. His stories appear in *Diabolical Plots*, *Highlights for Children*, and other venues. He hopes he can honor the indigenous peoples who are the true guardians of many of our world's beautiful lands and waters since time immemorial. Their traditions and practices, passed down from generation to generation, create sustainable environments—and we must respect that knowledge.

THOUGHTS ON *BRAVE NEW GIRLS*

"Women scientists come with a variety of abilities and disabilities, but are united in their passion for STEM. Zara may not feel confident because of her mental health struggles, but she's absolutely a scientist who has so much to offer her rescue group. Just as Zara becomes lifelong friends with Anika and Ulani, may you find your own families in science, girl readers!"

Illustration for "Go for Pets" by Kay Wrenn.

light as a feather,
STIFF AS A BOARD

Julie Palomba

LIGHT AS A FEATHER, STIFF AS A BOARD

JULIE PALOMBA

"LET THE TRICK-OR-TREAT CANDY AUCTION begin!" Phoebe declared. She removed her plastic vampire fangs so she could be heard more clearly over the storm roaring outside her bedroom window. "I'll start with an offer of one full-size Baby Ruth for three fun-size Snickers." She plucked the bar from a colorful mound of candies on her shaggy throw rug.

Phoebe surveyed the other two girls sitting in her poster-plastered bedroom, her best friends Shelly Daniels and Lexi Wang. Shelly's costume was the Bride of Frankenstein, and Lexi was Wednesday Addams. Each had their own piles of candy—chock-full of Snickers—dumped upon their sleeping bags.

"Going once..." Phoebe waved the Baby Ruth in the air. The Snickers wrappers glistened in the other piles, taunting her.

"Going twice?"

Shelly feigned gagging. "Baby Ruths are nasty."

Panic surged in Phoebe's chest. Would it be the first year in the history of their annual Halloween slumber party that Phoebe Valdez would be left Snickers-less? As if there wasn't already enough pressure for this night to go perfectly?

Every year since Phoebe could remember, she and her BFFs had had a Halloween tradition. They went trick-or-treating, brought back the loot to one of their houses to sort and trade, then stayed up all night telling spooky stories while wrapped up in their sleeping bags.

But they were eighth-graders now, and the adults answering their knocks had looked at them a bit funny this year. "Aren't you girls a little old to still be trick-or-treating?" their neighbor Mrs. Walton had sneered—as if that was any of her business. But Mrs. Walton had a point. They *were* getting old. In fact, this could be their last year to get away with trick-or-treating, meaning the tradition as they knew it would end. As this year's slumber party hostess, Phoebe was determined to make it a night to remember.

However, the itinerary was already off to a rough start. Their trick-or-treating had been cut short by a downpour. The news was calling it "The Electrical Storm of the Century." But there was still hope for the slumber party portion to turn things around. If only Phoebe could acquire a Snickers, her all-time favorite Halloween candy.

"Going three times!" Phoebe pleaded. "C'mon, girls. You've got, like, a jillion Snickers. I'll even take just one measly, fun-size Snickers!"

Lexi sighed without looking up from scrolling her phone. "That's such a bad trade on your end..." Her scrolling finger paused. "Wait, hold up. Which house gave out full-size bars? I didn't get one!"

"The Agarwals," Shelly replied. She was weaving strands of Lexi's glossy black hair, still damp from the rain, back into the French braid pigtails that were crucial to Lexi's Wednesday Addams costume. "You wouldn't go up to their door because they had massive *fake* spiders dangling from the storm gutters."

Lexi shuddered. "Oh, right. Spiders are where I draw the line. Even with full-size candy bars at stake." She checked her hair in the wall mirror. "But if I were in possession of a full-size chocolate bar, I wouldn't give it up..." She raised her eyebrows at Phoebe in the reflection.

"That's capitalism, baby." Phoebe flipped her blood-red-streaked curls back dramatically. "Simple supply and demand: I really hate Baby Ruths and I really love Snickers, so I'm willing to make a serious deal to get what I want."

"When did you become such a businesswoman?" Lexi teased. "I thought you want to be an electrical engineer when you grow up."

Phoebe shrugged. "I still do. But it helps to know a thing or two about business if I want to market my inventions."

"Well, here's your first marketing lesson," Lexi lectured. "Baby Ruths and Snickers have literally the same ingredients. The difference is just marketing and brand loyalty. Have you even read my Halloween candy conspiracies post on Reddit?"

"Whatever, it tastes different to me... it's a texture thing." Phoebe grimaced. "I suppose next you're gonna say Coke and Pepsi taste the same too?"

"Now those have totally different chemical compositions!" Shelly perked up, her towering black-and-white wig almost tumbling off her head.

"The future chemist has entered the chat," Lexi sang. "Yes, we all remember your award-winning Coke versus Pepsi chemistry experiment at last year's science fair."

Shelly secured the wig back in place. "Just you wait 'til I unveil this year's science fair project. It's my most genius work yet!"

"Well, you certainly look the part of a mad scientist!" Phoebe poked Shelly's wig.

Shelly launched a pillow at Phoebe. Phoebe swept her vampire cape around herself like a shield and hissed. They proceeded to clobber each other with their pillows.

Lexi turned up the volume on her phone, and a drumbeat started to play. "Ahem, ladies! I am over this argument." She rose to her feet and started dancing. "Now, you both know the rule: silence when Queen Bey comes on... *Who run the world?!*"

"Girls!" Phoebe and Shelly chorused.

They all danced until the end of the song, then collapsed back onto their sleeping bags in a fit of giggles.

"Well, you still better watch your back, Shelly," Phoebe panted. "I'm working on a feat of electrical engineering that's gonna blow all of the judges' minds and win *me* the prize this year."

"OMG, show us a preview!" Lexi squealed.

"No, no. It's not ready for showtime yet," Phoebe sighed. "Still some bugs to work out. Can't risk it going up in flames in my bedroom."

Lexi and Shelly glanced at each other. "Flames?!"

"Anywhooo..." Phoebe loved keeping her friends on their toes by dropping a juicy morsel of information, then moving on. "Hey Lexi, why don't you take the Baby Ruth trade, since it's just a conspiracy?"

"Umm, no thanks," Lexi blushed.

Phoebe huffed. The Snickers barter was a lost cause, but there was much more to look forward to on her sleepover itinerary. "Fine, then. Next up is to paint our nails. I've got a new color-changing polish. Shel can explain the chemistry behind it to us."

"Nah, I just got mine done," Shelly replied, fanning out her fingers to show her fresh mani.

"No worries," Phoebe assured herself more so than Shelly. "Onto the next activity then!"

The next tradition was scouring internet forums for new creepypasta stories, seeing who could spook the others the most. Lexi, who was obsessed with urban legends, conspiracy theories, and theoretical physics—basically anything adjacent to formalized gossip—always won.

"Have I read you both the one about the headless woman in white who wanders around with a ghost pet pig?" Lexi asked as she scrolled through Reddit.

"Yep," Phoebe sighed. "Twice."

"Hmm, okay..." Lexi scrolled on. "What about the shape-shifting goat called the Puca?"

The room was silent aside from the aggressively pattering rain on the windowpane.

"Can we do literally anything else?" Shelly groaned.

Phoebe grew nauseous with dread. Was this yet another tradition they were outgrowing? "But we have to tell scary stories on Halloween night. It's on the itinerary!"

Shelly scratched at some crusty fake blood caked on her chin, unaffected by Phoebe's plea.

Phoebe pursed her lips. A lightning streak lit up the window, followed closely by the boom of thunder. Phoebe's eyes lit up. "Aha! Shel, you'll love this fact: did you know that Mary Shelley wrote *Frankenstein* at only nineteen years old, after making it up during a storytelling competition on a stormy night just like this? She was super into science, just like us. She had all these theories about the power of harnessing electricity. And from those ideas, Frankenstein's monster was brought to life... literally!"

"This storm is giving Frankenstein vibes," Lexi chimed in. "Have you no appreciation for your groom, Shel?!" Lexi tugged at Shelly's ruffled bridal gown, and hummed the Wedding March.

Shelly brushed Lexi's hand away, and fixed her gown. "On that note, I think it's time to change into pajamas."

"C'mon, girls! Mary Shelley was an icon of feminism and sci-fi," Phoebe pleaded. "Reading spooky stories tonight is the least we can do to honor her legacy!" Phoebe huffed and refreshed the browser on her own phone, but alas, there were no new stories to be found. They'd really read all the creepypasta stories that existed on the internet. "Maybe we'll just need to make up one oursel—"

A crash of thunder boomed, the loudest one yet. So loud, the house tremored slightly.

"Mwahaha, perfect..." Lexi grinned fiendishly. She cleared her throat. "'Twas a dark and stormy night...'"

A knock rapped on the bedroom door.

They all jumped. Their eyes flashed toward the door as it swung open.

"Mom barging in alert!" Phoebe's mom poked her head into the room. "But I come in peace... with pizza bagels!" She tiptoed sheepishly across the bedroom, navigating the labyrinth of blankets, makeup supplies, and costume accessories.

She placed the sizzling tray on the candy-sorting rug. "I figured you should fuel up on something other than sweets. Am I interrupting any juicy gossip?"

"Nope, quite the opposite actually," Shelly replied. "We're so bored out of our minds that we're arguing about Gothic literature. Pizza bagels very much welcome." She popped one in her mouth.

"Bored at the annual Halloween slumber party?" Mom put her hands on her hips. "I find that hard to believe. Each year, I hear you girls up all night giggling away." She sighed. "I can't tell you three enough about how happy your moms and I are that you're keeping up this tradition. When we were little girls, we'd stay up all night sharing spooky stories and urban legends."

"I agree with you wholeheartedly, Mom!" Phoebe nudged Shelly. "You see? Slumber parties are for spooky stories."

"But we've read every single legend on the internet!" Shelly nudged Phoebe back.

Phoebe's mom shook her head and chuckled. "It may be hard for you girls to imagine, but we didn't have the internet or cell phones when we were your age. We had to make up games to entertain ourselves. And, of course, there were the classics everyone played. Oh, what was that one called…" She stroked her chin. "Aha, yes, 'Light as a Feather, Stiff as a Board.' Do kids still play that these days?"

The girls exchanged puzzled glances. Phoebe's forehead burned with embarrassment. Her mom could be so cheugy sometimes.

"Nope, don't think we know that one," Shelly replied.

"Light as a what now?" Lexi asked.

"Ugh, we got such a hoot out of that one. Cackling in a circle on the floor like we were a little coven of witches performing a seance… but just beware you don't go and conjure up Bloody Mary, though." Mom made a spooky expression. "Then you'll really have trouble. You girls must have heard about Bloody Mary, right?"

More confused glances. "I think I read about her on a creepypasta thread once," Lexi offered.

"Creepy what now?" Phoebe's mom frowned.

"Think of it as the 2024 version of sharing urban legends at an internet-wide slumber party," Phoebe explained.

"Ugh, you girls really do rely too much on the internet. What fun is it to be a kid these days? Doing nothing but staring at one screen or another."

Phoebe scowled.

Mom scowled back. "Well, I should get out of your hair." She flashed a pained smile. "If you girls need anything, just wake me. I hope this storm ends soon."

"I don't!" Lexi exclaimed. "It's the perfect setting to tell spooky stories… boOoOo—"

"Thanks for the pizza bagels, Mom," Phoebe cut in, shoving a bagel into Lexi's mouth. "We should get to eating them before the cheese gets all gummy."

"Yeah, thanks, Ms. V," Lexi and Shelly mumbled through mouthfuls of pizza bagel.

Phoebe's mom slipped out of the room with a wave. The door clicked shut.

Lexi tapped away on her cell. "Wait, what was that lady's name that your mom said? Scary Mary?"

"Bloody. Bloody Mary," Shelly answered.

Phoebe shuddered. "So morbid."

"Aha! Now I'm getting search results. There are tons of creepypastas about her. Here's what Snopes has to say: 'Attempting to summon Bloody Mary in a mirror is a classic urban legend turned slumber party game…'"

Phoebe gazed into the mirror hanging on her bedroom wall and gulped.

Shelly let out a long yawn.

"Oh, no, no! You are not allowed to get sleepy already!" Phoebe protested. "It's slumber party law: we're supposed to stay up all night gossiping and giving each other makeovers or whatever…"

Lexi looked up from her phone. "It's only 9:30 P.M. What are we, kindergarteners?"

"Sorry, I didn't realize the sleep police were on patrol." Shelly rubbed her belly. A splat of pizza oil ran down her white gown. "I'm full of warm cheesy pizza bagels, and it's making me sleepy."

Phoebe started to freak out internally. The party was so boring that one of her guests was dozing off. It couldn't be a night to remember if her guests weren't conscious.

"Well then maybe we should spice this party up a bit; get active." Lexi shimmied. "Let's try one of Phoebe's mom's slumber party games!"

Thank God for Lexi, Phoebe thought.

"Fine, but just not Bloody Mary, please," Shelly grumbled.

Phoebe nodded eagerly. "I'm in! But what—"

Lexi raised a finger. "Hold that thought. Your mom mentioned some game called…" She tapped away on her phone. "Aha, found it: '"Light as a Feather, Stiff as a Board" is a common slumber party game. One player lies on the floor "stiff as a board," while the rest of the players huddle around, each placing two fingers, palms up, beneath the lying player. They all chant "light as a feather, stiff as a board,'" until the player becomes "light as a feather," magically levitating off the ground.'"

"It's not gonna work," Shelly interrupted. "The trick only works because the player's body weight is distributed amongst a group of people. We'd need a lot more than two of us."

"Oooor it's the power of the supernatural," Lexi countered. She wriggled her finger in the air. "OoOoOo—" In perfect timing, a crash of thunder rattled the house again.

Shelly glared. "It's just not physically possible. At least not with the gravity conditions of our Earth."

Lexi rolled her eyes. "Shel, please take your lab coat off for just one night and go with it. It's fun! Vintage eighties fun!"

"They probably still thought the Earth was flat back in the eighties," Shelly snapped back.

"Some Boomers still do," Lexi jabbed.

"Anywhooo," Phoebe continued. "Let's just give it a try. Better than sitting here popping our zits all night."

"Rude!" Shelly scolded, covering a ripe pimple on her cheek.

"And Shelly the Skeptic can be the test subject!" Phoebe cheered.

Shelly let out another yawn and stretched her arms above her head. "Ugh, fine—even though it's not gonna work."

"And then you can tell us '*told ya so!*'" Lexi poked.

The girls studied the Wikihow directions on Lexi's phone and mimicked the illustrations. Shelly lay flat on the ground, belly up, arms crossed upon her chest, and closed her eyes. Phoebe and Lexi sat cross-legged on either side of her. They placed each of their index and middle fingers underneath Shelly.

"Ready?" Lexi grinned.

Shelly gave a thumbs-up. Phoebe nodded.

Lexi cleared her throat and squeezed her eyes shut. She led the chant: "Light as a feather, stiff as a board..."

Phoebe and Shelly joined in: "Light as a feather, stiff as a board... Light as a feather... stiff as a board!" They braced themselves. The words hung in the air.

Phoebe was the first to peek her eyes open. Shelly was still lying flat on the floor. She was stiff as a board, but still not quite as light as a feather.

"Is it working?" Lexi asked, cautiously fluttering her eyelids open.

"Nope," Phoebe sighed. Her heart sank.

"We must be missing some detail of the ritual." Lexi slipped her arms out from beneath Shelly and grabbed her phone. She scrolled through the instructions again. "Hmm, we're doing everything just like it says. I don't understand..."

Shelly's eyes popped open. "Do I get to say 'I told ya so' yet?"

"Not so fast!" Phoebe blurted. The words had come out before Phoebe could really think things through. But she had to save the sinking ship that was this slumber party. "What Shelly said earlier just gave me an idea. One that won't rely on superstition or googling internet forums to get Shelly to levitate."

Shelly sat up tall. "You've got my attention..."

"What if I told you we have our own magical powers..." Phoebe paused for dramatic effect.

Lexi leaned in closer.

Shelly groaned, and slumped back down. "Attention lost..."

"What if that magic is science?!" Phoebe sprang to her feet and ran to her closet.

Shelly jerked back up. "Attention back!"

As Phoebe tugged her closet door open, sweaters and tennis balls and a few burnt-out light bulbs tumbled out. "Shelly said levitation is impossible 'with the gravity conditions of our Earth.' But that's not entirely true..." She rummaged through her closet. "Remember how last month in science class we learned about electromagnetism? And how maglev trains and hoverboards rise and levitate by using electromagnets to counter the downward force of gravity?"

Shelly and Lexi nodded.

"Well, ever since then I've wanted a hoverboard sooo badly. Not those lame ones with wheels... a real, *Back to the Future 2*-style levitating hoverboard. It's like skateboarding on air!" Phoebe swooned. "I asked for one for my birthday, but my parents said that very few prototypes exist, and they're way too expensive and dangerous."

Phoebe wrestled a device that looked like a snowboard out from the closet. An avalanche of clothes tumbled down upon her. She shook a rogue sweater off her head. "So I thought to myself, 'hey, I'm an engineer, I'll try building one myself.'"

The slick, metallic body of the board glinted as she twirled it on its end. It stood almost as tall as her. "The science of it is actually pretty simple. You can make a basic version out of hardware store parts. So I asked for a few heavy-duty magnets and battery packs for my birthday instead... and voila." She ran her finger along the edge of the board.

"Right, electromagnets... a totally normal birthday gift for an eighth-grader,"

Shelly scoffed. "Did you also have Bunsen burners and a spectrometer on the wish list?"

"Ignoring you," Phoebe scowled. "Anyway, spoiler alert—this hoverboard is my science fair project. I've built a few prototypes. But this is my latest model." She laid the hoverboard on an empty patch of floor and turned it over. Bunches of copper wire were attached to the bottom of the metal body, where a skateboard's wheel decks would have been. The copper wire connected two saucer-sized magnets at each end of the board to a massive battery pack in the middle.

They all took it in for a moment with awe. It was like something out of a sci-fi movie.

"It's giving scientific pioneer!" Lexi gushed.

"So back to the levitating matter at hand," Phoebe continued. "My idea is that Shelly lies on top of the board. When I turn on the batteries, it activates the electromagnets hidden under the base. The magnetic metal in the board will repel the force of the electromagnets, causing a reaction of anti-gravity that will lift the hoverboard—and Shelly on top of it—up off the ground. As the magnetic forces balance out with the force of gravity, the board will remain still, hovering above the ground. She will literally be levitating, as light as a feather!"

"Oh my gosh, that's brilliant, Pheeb!" Shelly gasped. "Let's try!"

"Watch out, world," Lexi proclaimed. "This is not your mother's slumber party. This is how the STEM squad does it!"

"OMG, Lexi. Please tell me you're not livestreaming this..." Phoebe groaned. She scowled into the lens of Lexi's phone camera, pointed at Phoebe holding her hoverboard.

Lexi panned her phone camera in selfie mode around the bedroom. "C'mon, just a quick behind-the-scenes slumber party update for my followers. They're asking if the ritual worked!"

Phoebe glared and shielded the hoverboard. "This is top-secret science fair material. One of your followers could steal my invention!"

"Ugh, fine!" Lexi tossed her phone onto her sleeping bag.

"Wait, Pheeb, didn't you say there were still bugs to work out with your project?" Shelly stammered, twirling the snaking coils between her fingers. "Are we sure it will be safe?"

Phoebe tinkered with a connection point between the magnet and one of the copper wires. Shelly was right. The device was probably not ready for showtime. Dangerous, even. But desperate times called for desperate measures. This might be the only chance for something legendary to happen tonight—to make it a night to remember. "Umm, I'm sure it will be fine. I've tested this one a bunch of times, and it hasn't blown up like the previous models." Phoebe glanced up at a wide-eyed Shelly and paused mid-twist of the wire. "Do you doubt my craftsmanship?" She shooed Shelly's curious hand away.

"N-no ma'am." Shelly detangled her fingers from the copper coils.

"But hey, Lexi, go fetch the fire extinguisher under my desk," Phoebe giggled nervously. "Just a precaution."

Phoebe flipped the board back over, right side up, and patted the top. "All ready for ya, Shel."

Shelly climbed on the hoverboard and laid down belly-up.

Phoebe steadied her finger on the switch on the underside of the board. She inhaled deeply. "Ready, girls?"

Shelly crossed her arms tight to her chest and squeezed her eyes shut. She gulped.

Lexi grasped the fire extinguisher handle and aimed it toward the hoverboard, at the ready.

"Liftoff in three... two..." The counting competed with the sound of rain pounding on the windowpane. "One... activating!" Phoebe flipped the switch. The hoverboard whirred loudly to life.

Shelly's body shook as the competing forces jolted and jostled the board. Her arms shot down to grip the edges of the board.

"Light as a feather, stiff as a board," Phoebe chanted.

Lexi joined in, "Light as a feather, stiff as a board!"

The hoverboard slowly rose, wobbly at first. Then it stabilized. It hovered in midair about a foot off of the ground.

"It's alive!" Phoebe rejoiced. "My creation works!"

"Shelly, you're levitating light as a feather!" Lexi shouted. "What does it feel like?"

"It feels like I'm riding a drone or a hummingbird or something! It's awesom—"

A burst of lightning illuminated the room bright as midday.

The light refracted on the wall mirror. Phoebe and Lexi shielded their eyes from the blinding reflection. A sharp zap of electricity surged and sizzled. A shriek rang out. A crash of thunder roared.

Then there was silence.

Phoebe opened her eyes to complete darkness. She smelled smoke. She felt around the floor for her cell phone. Once she snatched it up in her trembling palms, she flicked on the flashlight. The light beam rippled and dissipated in a thick cloud of smoke before her. "Fire extinguisher!" she cried, followed by a fit of coughing.

Lexi sprayed furiously at the smoke cloud. Fanning away the lingering haze, Phoebe aimed the phone flashlight at the scene of the accident and braced herself to assess the damage. Only Shelly's white-streaked wig remained where she and the hoverboard had previously lay.

"Where's Shelly?" Lexi gasped.

"And my hoverboard!" Phoebe cried.

The two girls frantically scanned the smoggy room with their phone light beams.

"Hey! Where'd you all go?" Shelly's voice called faintly. "Is the hoverboard alright?"

"Shelly, where the heck are you?" Lexi called back.

Phoebe's flashlight flitted about, searching for the direction of the voice. "Did you go on a bathroom run? And where's my hoverboard?!"

"What are you talking about? You're the ones who bolted." Shelly's voice rose in panic. "I'm laying right here, next to the hoverboard. I took a bit of a crash landing off of it. And I hate to break it to you, Pheeb, but it's totally fried."

Shelly's voice sounded as if it were in the room, yet also distant somehow. And there was still the fact of the matter that she and the hoverboard were nowhere to be seen.

"Umm, no you're not," Phoebe quivered. Her flashlight beam hit the mirror and gleamed back, and Phoebe froze. Something unexpected in its reflection caught her eye. "Umm, Lex. Take a look at the mirror..." She inched toward it warily. "Am I delusional, or are you seeing what I'm seeing?"

"Ahhhhh!!" Lexi shrieked.

Taking it as confirmation, Phoebe screamed too.

"What's wrong?" Shelly's voice cried. "Is Bloody Mary in the mirror? I don't see her!"

"No it's worse, Shelly..." Phoebe inhaled sharply. "We see *your* reflection in the mirror."

"Ha ha ha, very funny..." Shelly deadpanned. "But that's kinda how mirrors work, no?"

"Sure, but not when the object reflected isn't physically *here in the room with us...*" Phoebe marched over to the spot in the room where Shelly's reflection showed her to be standing.

Lexi approached the mirror and stroked the glass where it reflected Shelly's face. "Girl, can't you see? You're like... on the other side of the mirror!"

"What the... How?" Shelly's reflected nose pressed against the glass. "Girls, that's not physically possible. A mirror is just a sheet of glass with a coating of silver or aluminum on the back that makes it reflective. There's no *other side*..." Shelly tapped the glass and jerked back. "Ouch!" A shock of pulsating blue electricity ran up her finger. "OMG, what's going on? Ouch!"

"Well, coincidentally, silver and aluminum are great conductors of electricity." Phoebe lifted the mirror and inspected the backside coating.

"Hey, put me back, I can't see you anymore!" Shelly yelled.

"Hmph." Phoebe placed the mirror back, unsatisfied.

"That's better," Shelly exhaled. She tried to smooth her hair down. "Ouch!" She wrested her shocked fingers from her wavering tendrils of hair. The whole mane stood up on end with static electricity, as if she'd stuck her finger in a socket.

Phoebe choked back a laugh. "A mirror would be the strongest conductor for electricity to converge upon in this room. That and the hoverboard. Maybe that's the connection."

"Well, on a positive note, Shelly, you don't even need the Bride of Frankenstein wig to pull off your costume anymore." Lexi flashed a pained smile.

Reflection Shelly's eyebrows furrowed. "I *so* wish I could clobber you with a pillow right now, Lexi Wang! Ahhhhhh!" She pounded on the glass. Sparks flew from her fists. "Ouch! Ouch! Ouch!"

"I *so* shouldn't have encouraged this stupid game!" Lexi cried.

"No, it's all my fault!" Phoebe sobbed. "I put us all in danger because I just wanted this party to be unforgettable!"

"Girls, girls!" Phoebe's mom burst into the room. "Are you all okay? That crash of thunder nearly gave me a heart attack. Then I heard you girls shouting."

Phoebe and Lexi dove into their sleeping bags.

"Sorry, Ms. V, that was my bad. The thunder was so scary I screamed," Lexi explained, clutching the blanket up to her face and shivering.

"But we're fine, Mom," Phoebe assured. "Thanks for checking on us."

"Well, I'm glad. But it does appear the power got knocked out." She flicked the light switch a few times. "If it doesn't come back on in a few, I can turn on the generator in the garage. It should have enough gas left to get us through the night."

"That's all right, Mom. We're about to go to sleep anyway. No need for light. You can go back to bed." Phoebe snuggled in her sleeping bag and yawned.

Phoebe's mom turned to leave the room, then did a double-take. "Wait, where's Shelly? In the bathroom?"

Phoebe and Lexi nodded in unison.

"Let me go make sure she's okay—"

"No, I'll do it!" Lexi blurted. "I'm supposed to check on her in a minute anyway. She mentioned being afraid that Bloody Mary might get her in the bathroom mirror."

Phoebe shot a death glare at Lexi.

"Oh, you girls are too funny. That legend used to freak me out too. I still avoid looking in the bathroom mirror at night." Mom shuddered.

Lexi and Phoebe giggled in nervous agreement.

"Well, okay then. You just come tap me awake if there are any more problems. Good night!" Her slippered feet shuffled back down the hall, and the bedroom door clicked shut.

Phoebe ran her fingers through her hair. "What are we going to do? How are we supposed to get Shelly and my hoverboard back? I don't have time to build a whole new one before the fair! And obvi, I can't lose one of my BFFs… of course…"

"Deep breaths, Pheeb, deep breaths." Lexi raised and lowered her hands like a conductor guiding Phoebe's breathing.

"Hey, where did you go?" Shelly's voice trailed from afar. "Heeelp meee!"

Lexi and Phoebe hopped out of their sleeping bags and rushed back to the mirror.

"What happened?" Shelly asked breathlessly. "I thought you left me for dead."

"We would never! You're our BFF," Lexi assured.

"My mom came to check on us because the power is out," Phoebe explained. "It must have been that huge lightning strike."

"You think that had something to do with… *this*?" Lexi gestured at Shelly's reflection.

"I mean, she is glowing…" Phoebe studied Shelly's reflection. "There's also a buzzing sound coming from the mirror. She almost looks like a hologram."

"I'm what?!" Shelly patted around her face and body.

"OMG!" Lexi squealed. "You were electrified, just like Frankenstein's monster!"

"Or electromagnetized like the magnets in my hoverboard," Phoebe hypothesized, her voice trembling. "But why would that make her and the hoverboard visible in the mirror, but invisible to us in real life?"

"Wait! I actually have a theory this time…" Lexi announced. "Isn't it true that our human eyes can only see a small portion of the whole electromagnetic spectrum?"

"Mhmm." Phoebe pursed her lips.

"Just like we can only see a portion of the universe. Dare I say, the multiverse. Of course, it's all theoretical physics. But the theory states that there are multiple universes—–or alternate planes. Some physicists even think that one could travel to an alternate plane in the multiverse, if given enough energetic power to be propelled there."

Phoebe hung onto each word, trying to process it all.

"The Earth is like a giant magnet, and Phoebe's hoverboard showed us the powerful reaction that is created when a magnet is electrified," Lexi continued. "You may call me a conspiracy theorist, but I hypothesize that this crazy electrical storm temporarily messed with the Earth's electromagnetic field. The electrical energy generated by the lightning strike, converging with Shelly on the hoverboard, catapulted her into an alternate plane aboard the hoverboard. That's how we can be in the same place as Shelly now, but not see it or know it. She is on an alternate plane."

Phoebe stared at Lexi with her jaw agape. Shelly did the same in the mirror.

Lexi plucked a Snickers from the rug and unwrapped it. "You know, in Pagan folklore, it's believed that on the night of the Samhain festival—the ancient version of Halloween—the portal to other worlds opened. So that would make tonight a perfect moment for this to happen." She popped the candy in her mouth. "Coincidence? I think not."

Phoebe opened her mouth to speak, but nothing came out.

Lexi curtsied. "Thanks for coming to my TED Talk."

Shelly applauded in the mirror, sending electric shocks into the air.

"Okay, but how does that result in her being trapped in a mirror?" Phoebe asked.

"She's not trapped *in* the mirror, I don't think," Lexi hypothesized. "The electromagnetized mirror just happens to be a way that we can see the alternate plane."

"Lex, if you know so much about the topic, then you can probably figure out a solution, right?" Phoebe encouraged.

"Yeah, what the heck are we supposed to do?" Shelly exclaimed. "Just casually manipulate Earth's magnetic field again? Hope that lightning strikes me and the hoverboard twice?"

"Well, considering there's a whole expression about lightning never striking twice in the same place, that seems pretty statistically unlikely..." Phoebe lamented.

They stood there in silence for a few moments. In fact, it was too silent.

Phoebe rushed over to the window and opened the curtain. Outside, the night was still. She gazed up at a cloudless, inky black sky, lit by a plump full moon. The storm had passed. "Ladies, we've got a problem." Phoebe kept her gaze out the window. "The storm is over."

"No, that can't be possible!" Lexi swiped open her phone and tapped and swiped some more. "Oh."

"Oh what?" Shelly moved closer to the mirror. "Show me! What are you looking at?"

"The weather app says clear skies for the rest of the night." Lexi raised her screen to the mirror for Shelly to see. "And a news alert says most of the state lost power. Could be hours before the power grid is back up."

"Well that's just great!" Shelly shrieked. "First, I was zapped into an alternate dimension, and now the lightning that sent me here is gone. I'm gonna be stuck forever!" She pounded on the mirror. "Worst slumber party ever!"

The words were a gut punch to Phoebe.

"Shelly, don't panic." Lexi paced. "Let's think about this rationally. Like scientists. Right?"

"How can we not panic?" Shelly shrieked. "Without electricity, I'm doomed!"

"Way to keep things positive, Shel," Lexi snapped. "I'm trying to defuse the situation, and you're detonating a bomb of negativity!"

"Can you two stop arguing for just a single second?" Phoebe yelled. "I might have an idea, but I'm trying to figure out what it will take for it to work."

"OMG, that's great, what is it?" Lexi asked.

"Well, Shelly said that without the lightning, she's doomed, right?" Phoebe started.

Lexi shook her head. "Right. Yep. Totally doomed—"

"Wrong!" Phoebe interjected. "That's actually a fallacy. It's not actual lightning that we need. We just need to generate and conduct enough electric charge to mimic the reaction the lightning caused to my hoverboard."

Shelly snorted. "You're suggesting we can just create lightning levels of energy in a teenager's bedroom? We're not Zeus."

"We don't necessarily need lightning-level wattage," Lexi countered. "Just whatever the minimum threshold is to zap a person across alternate planes."

"Well that sounds... hopeful?" Shelly snarked. "Buuuut, there isn't exactly a mathematical theorem calculating the energy required to zap humans across the multiverse, is there?"

"And the batteries that powered my hoverboard are fried," Phoebe sighed. "Plus, the power grid is down for the entire state. So we're still doomed for tonight at least…"

"Actually," Lexi cut in, "*that* is a fallacy."

"How?" Phoebe asked. "Those are the literal facts of the situation."

"Pheeb, what did your mom say after the power went out? That if it didn't come back on soon…"

"The generator!" they squealed in unison.

"There's a generator?" Shelly exclaimed.

"Yep! In the garage," Phoebe explained. "A super-duper heavy-duty one. My parents bought it before Superstorm Sandy. It works by turning mechanical energy into an electrical energy output. It powered our whole house for weeks!"

"Genius!" Shelly cried. "That might just work!"

"Okay, I have a plan," Phoebe declared. "Shel, you're gonna carry the hoverboard out to the garage in your, umm, plane. We'll meet down there, and I'll explain to you how to hook the hoverboard up to the generator. Maybe if we turn the generator on in both dimensions and double the wattage in that physical space, the energy will be amplified enough to converge and transport you back to this plane."

"Sounds like a plan," Shelly agreed. "See you down there."

Lexi and Phoebe raced down the hall soundlessly past Phoebe's mom's room. They tiptoed down the creaky stairs, down another hall, and out through the laundry room to the garage.

Phoebe scanned the dark, chilly, cavernous room. It was a fairly bare garage, with a work bench on one wall and a shelving unit stocked with Costco-sized packs of cleaning supplies and cereal boxes on the opposite wall. Phoebe pointed her phone flashlight at a corner across the room. "I think the generator is over there." The red and black metallic box glimmered in the light beam.

They cautiously approached and sat before it.

Phoebe inspected the sticker on its side. *Heavy Duty Generator. Peak Wattage: 10,000.*

"Hopefully that's enough wattage," Lexi whispered.

They sat there for a few moments in silence.

"Shelly, are you here yet?" Lexi called out to the space around them, her voice echoing off the bare concrete walls. "Did you get lost?"

A cricket chirped from some crevice in the room.

"We didn't really think this through, did we?" Phoebe sighed. "How will we communicate with Shelly without the mirror?"

Lexi's cell pinged in her pocket. She pulled it out and swiped on the notification.

"Seriously, Lex. Is this an appropriate time to check Insta?" Phoebe's eyes darted down to Lexi's screen.

Lexi beamed. "Why yes, in fact, because I just got a notification that Shelly requested to join my Live!" Lexi clicked on the stream.

"Going Live in an alternate plane? How the..."

"Oh, thank God," Shelly's voice sighed in relief through the phone speaker. Her video showed that she, too, was standing in the garage. "Lexi, thank you for being so addicted to your phone and social media. I panicked and thought maybe I could call you. That's when I saw Lexi's livestream notification from earlier. You never ended your Live, ya dingbat!"

Lexi blushed.

A few viewers popped in and out of the Live and left comments.

@Taliabell499: OMG the annual Halloween sleepover. Wish I could make it this year [frowny face]. Have so much fun! [heart emoji]

@Alliecat2004: OMG you girls are too funny. Shelly, why are you glowing like that?

Lexi started to type.

"Lexi, focus!" Shelly snapped. "Show me where the generator is."

"It's that big metal machine in the corner by the workbench. See it?" Lexi panned the phone's view to show Shelly.

Phoebe and Lexi watched along as Shelly fumbled around with the phone in one hand. With her other hand, she set down the hoverboard beside the generator.

Phoebe spoke into the phone receiver. "Hey Shel, you'll also need some electrical tape to secure the connection. It's in my dad's workbench right over..." Phoebe turned Lexi's phone to show her. She watched Shelly retrieve it. "There, yup... in the top drawer. Bingo. And let's have the fire extinguisher handy again—for obvious reasons. It's mounted on the wall over there."

Shelly returned to the generator with her supplies.

"All right, Shelly, here's what you have to do," Phoebe instructed. "We need to connect an electricity source to the magnets on the board in order to create an electromagnetic charge. See those copper wires on the bottom of the board? They connect each of the magnets to the battery packs. In our scenario, the generator will be our new battery. So, disconnect the ends of the wires that attach to the battery packs, but leave the ends attached to the magnets as-is."

Shelly angled her phone camera view so that Phoebe and Lexi could watch her. She carefully uncoiled the copper wiring with her other hand and raised the frayed ends in the air. "Check!"

"Perfect!" Phoebe praised. "Now, we want to connect those free ends to an electrical source that actually works. Enter our nifty generator. You should see an outlet port on the side of the generator, kinda like a wall outlet." Phoebe grabbed Lexi's phone and pointed it close up to the outlet.

"Found it," Shelly confirmed.

"Good! Now, you're going to thread the copper wire into the outlet hole and tape it down with the electrical tape. But *do not* touch the copper wires once we turn the generator on, unless you wanna become fried chicken, that is. This whole makeshift setup is super unsafe. But desperate times call for desperate measures."

Phoebe and Lexi watched Shelly set up the electrical connection through the livestream. She smoothed down the electrical tape over the wires shoved into the outlet. She yanked on the wires to test the tape's hold.

Phoebe squinted at the view on the tiny screen. "Looks good as far as I can tell."

"Roger that."

"Now, let's crank this thing up and pray it works." Phoebe gulped. *Please work, science.* "Let's see, where's the switch…" She searched around the sides. "Aha! Here we go. See it, Shel? To the right of the outlet."

Shelly lay down on the hoverboard and reached for the switch. With the outstretched tippy-tip of her finger, she flicked it on. She waved at the phone screen. "Ready for blast-off! Hopefully…"

The two generators creaked. The motors kicked in. They rumbled to life, humming in harmony. On Shelly's plane, ten thousand watts coursed through the copper wires connecting the generator to the hoverboard. Ten thousand watts magnetized the homemade electromagnets. Ten thousand watts propelled the hoverboard, and Shelly atop it, slowly but surely up off the concrete floor of the Valdez family garage, in some alternate plane of the multiverse.

The hoverboard settled into equilibrium. Ten thousand watts cranked in the Valdez family garage, where Phoebe and Lexi sat desperately hoping for their friend to return.

Twenty thousand watts converged across the multiverse.

"You doing ok, Shelly?" Lexi shouted into the phone over the ruckus of humming and buzzing.

"I'm floating!" Shelly cheered. "It's the most incredible feeling!" Shelly's livestream flashed to a view of the rumbling generator. From it dangled the copper wires, dancing with the pulses of electricity. "But nothing is happening yet to send me back home—" Sparks popped from the generator outlet.

Phoebe, watching through the phone, saw the problem immediately. The vibration of the generator was jostling the copper wires. Each tug on the electrical tape loosened its hold, compromising the connection and flow of the electricity between them.

"Shelly! Shelly!" Phoebe called. "The tape's not gonna hold. Show me a closer-up view."

Shelly's view zoomed in on the outlet: another dance of the wires, another tug of the tape. The connection was more and more precarious. If the electrical current cut off, the hoverboard would short out again, or maybe it would even break the generator.

"Houston, we do indeed have a problem!" Shelly shouted. "But I can fix it!"

Phoebe watched the stream as Shelly's hand reached out for the tape, which was hanging by its last edge of adhesive. The trembling fingers avoided the tangle of scalding hot wires, and wrestled with the exposed edge of tape flapping off. Reaching her arm with all her might was just barely enough for Shelly to smooth the tape back down over the outlet.

But then her finger slipped. The phone's view jerked down.

Zappp!

Shelly's livestream blacked out.

Phoebe tapped on the screen, refreshing the feed. "Shelly! Are you there? Do you copy?"

The generator inexplicably went up in smoke.

"Fire extinguisher!" Lexi screamed, swiftly grabbing the can from the wall and spraying it wildly at the smoke, in an unfortunate case of deja vu.

Silence fell as Lexi tossed the empty canister to the floor with a *ting*.

As the smoke thinned, a shadow rustled beside the smoldering generator. Phoebe shined the phone flashlight upon it, and caught a glint of metal.

The faint voice of Shelly responded through the haze, "Copy that." The words echoed through Lexi's phone speaker.

"Shelly!" Phoebe and Lexi raced over to the hoverboard and embraced the crumpled, burnt-smelling mass of their friend.

"OMG, are you okay?" Lexi fanned the smoke from Shelly's face.

"I think so…" Shelly smoothed out her staticky hair, still sticking straight out on end. "Just a little flambéed."

"Girls! What's going on here?" Phoebe's mom rushed through the door of the garage. "If you needed to turn on the generator, you should have gotten an adult to do it. You could've burned the house down!"

Phoebe tried to casually shield the hoverboard from her mom's view. "I'm so sorry, Mom. We thought we could handle it ourselves."

Mom sighed as she surveyed the room, caked with fire extinguisher foam. "We'll clean this up in the morning. You girls get back to bed. Now!" She pointed to the door. "Wait, what's that snowboard-like contraption?"

But the girls were already running off.

Phoebe closed her bedroom door and caught her breath.

Shelly collapsed down onto her sleeping bag and blew the singed hair out of her eyes. Phoebe and Lexi collapsed down beside her. They lay in silence for a while, just staring at the ceiling.

"Now what?" Shelly whispered.

"Umm, IDK." Lexi looked at her cell. "It's only 11:30 P.M. We could try to summon Bloody Mary next?"

"No!" Phoebe and Shelly shouted in unison.

Lexi chuckled. "True, I think that's enough shenanigans for this year's slumber party. It will go down as one to remember, that's for sure."

"The one where we proved the multiverse theory of quantum physics!" Phoebe beamed.

"Too bad there's no proof…" Shelly murmured. "We could've won a Nobel Prize with such a discovery. Would've made getting electrocuted twice sorta worth it." She picked up a few Snickers from her candy pile, and tossed one to Phoebe. "Here, consider it a thank-you gift."

Phoebe smiled wistfully and unwrapped the candy. As the nougaty chocolate melted on her tongue, she felt assured that at least some Halloween traditions—and best friends—weren't going anywhere. And so what if her prospects of winning the science fair were blown up… literally. There would always be next year's competition—another tradition to look forward to.

Ding!

Lexi's phone lit up with an Instagram notification. Her eyes narrowed as she read it. "Umm, speaking of which…" Lexi extended the phone out for Phoebe and Shelly to read:

> *@NASA: Hi @Lexigirl15, it seems your livestream went quite viral. We were tagged over 20,000 times. Please contact us. We'd like to invite you and your friends for an interview at our campus.*

The girls locked eyes and squealed.

"Oh, we're totally gonna win the science fair this year!" Phoebe grinned.

THOUGHTS ON *BRAVE NEW GIRLS*

"Despite getting A's in math and science throughout school, I determined my identity pretty early on in life as 'not a STEM person.' Anytime I did feel a strong connection when learning a concept in STEM, I wrote it off as a fluke. Sure, I liked reading and watching sci-fi, but that was different, I told myself. When I had to actually study the subjects, the anxiety crept in, and a little voice in my head would whisper, 'this isn't for you.' I had already relegated myself to my 'not-a-STEM-person' identity, after all. Looking back now, I resent falling into this fallacy of identity. My goal in writing stories that incorporate STEM concepts is to dispel the misconception that a girl's identity must be a binary choice of 'I am or am not a STEM person.' Rather, an interest in STEM can form a piece of identity for any girl—no matter how big or small that piece is. Such knowledge is a relevant life skill that will surely come in handy… even if the reader never finds themself needing to use engineering during the electrical storm of the century!"

ABOUT THE AUTHOR

Julie Palomba is a middle-grade and YA writer living in New York City. By day, she works as a digital producer for an education tech company that creates immersive K-12 curriculums for schools. She also volunteers as an 826NYC mentor, helping kids unlock their inner storytellers. She holds a degree in English Literature and Creative Writing from the University of Pennsylvania, where she was first inspired by her "Penn-gineer" dormmates to dive into STEM themes for her stories. Her goal as an author is to incorporate educational themes in engaging and relatable stories for kids and teens. When she's not writing, you can probably find her at the Tompkins Square dog park with her shorkie, Lucy. Otherwise, she's OOO, racking up countries on her travel bucket list—57 countries and counting!

Illustration for "Light as a Feather, Stiff as a Board" by Ben Falco.

LIMINAL SPACE

HJ FARR

LIMINAL SPACE

HJ FARR

R AEA HAD ALWAYS THOUGHT THAT flying through space would be far more exciting than it turned out to be.

Sure, it had been wild when the whole ground rumbled beneath her feet and an entire spaceship had landed in her family's backyard, the metallic sound of the flooding rain against it unlike anything she had ever heard (and, from what little her eyes could make out, unlike anything she or her family had ever seen). The footsteps of the four different aliens had sounded thrilling as they'd made their way down the ramp and introduced themselves as members of the Interplanetary Rescue Fleet. And, of course, packing up had given her stomach such butterflies. Even agreeing to spend an unknown amount of time in an enclosed structure with her little brother, Jer, had the potential to be adventurous if they were *in space*.

But now that it had been nearly a year, Raea was basically bored of the whole trip.

The halls of the *Nimrerer*, the Galaxy-Class X04-1 ship they now resided in, were second nature to her feet. Every wall and pipe she had followed from start to finish. Multiple times.

Even the aliens seemed a little mundane to her now. Captain Mira, a Vameerian, loomed less dauntingly tall, their small horns on opposite sides of their forehead seemed less sharp, and even their footsteps seemed less clangy and loud and ominous (except when they approached right when Raea was about to go somewhere she shouldn't be). First Mate T, a P10 (at least that's how it always sounded to Raea), and all his long flowing hair that grew from every inch of his stocky body, seemed fairly banal now. The Medic, Col, a Raf-yite with extra digits on each hand, seemed more boring than enticingly stoic…

It was really only Engineer Dua who continued to capture Raea's attention. And that was probably more to do with where Dua worked—deep in the depths of the ship, tinkering like Raea used to in the family garage back on Earth, her dad teaching her with gentle hands how to use every single tool, how to hold a screwdriver, what size washer goes with what, how to dismantle something and put it back together, and even create something better than what they had started with.

Dua, a small Gru with slightly scaly skin, let Raea explore every inch of the Engineering floor (even after Captain Mira told them both it was too dangerous to have a teenager touching such important pieces of this older-model ship, which was chugging its way back to the United Planetary Rescue Fleet's headquarters).

Even the concept of having no faster-than-light travel had originally sounded great to Raea: more opportunity to meet other aliens! All the newer X-5s and beyond were sleek and small and fast (according to Dua), so they could only house one rescued family at a time. But the *Nimrerer* had the capacity for ten whole families, even with the skeleton crew of four. So they took their time coasting between galaxies, searching for dying planets (like Earth) and potential life signs, which the ship would automatically detect, veering off course to rescue the inhabitants. It had sounded so exciting!

But after ten and a half months, and apparently only halfway to what her parents said would become their new home, Raea was *boooored*. No extra alien families had joined them. She wasn't allowed to go onto the bridge. She'd recently lost the privilege of exploring the other living quarters (after a bit of a kerfuffle involving the comm systems and Jer's favorite roaring dinosaur toy).

Even sneaking into Engineering had started to lose its luster. Dua was beginning to stress about potential mechanical problems. Apparently this particular model of ship relied on regular gravity changes to help the different systems work together. But rather than explain to Raea what the exact problem was and how they could fix it together without landing, Dua just worried herself into standoffishness.

So it was decided (not by Raea, but by all the adults on the ship) that it was simply "too dangerous" for her to do anything other than play hide-and-seek with her little brother (who Raea thought should be getting a little old for such games at five-and-three-quarters).

It was during one such game, while Jer was hiding underneath their parents' bed (Raea could hear him giggling, so she made a big show of looking in the laundry box, the closet, even under the sheets of the bed), when an alarm started blaring. Not a big, scream-y, scary noise like a fire alarm, but a constant warning tone, continuing for a full minute. Then the automated ship's voice announced, "Proximity to rescue, changing course," and Raea felt the whole ship clunk out of one autopilot direction and into another.

Captain Mira had mentioned this possibility, but also insisted that any direction change wouldn't be noticeable. But Raea felt it, and was so excited by the prospect of something new happening that she ran out into the hall, forgetting her ban from the bridge, forgetting even her brother waiting for her under their parents' bed. Until he screamed.

Raea skidded to a stop as the whole ship seemed to do the same, and then went completely silent. Her brother's scream echoed in the midst of the sudden quiet of every other hum that filled the *Nimrerer*. No buzz of electricity, no circulating air blowing in her face, even the momentum beneath her feet seemed to slow—she knew something was wrong. So, she reluctantly backtracked to the quarters and pulled Jer out from under the bed.

"What's wrong, doofus?"

Jer sobbed into Raea's embrace. "Everything's dark. It's too dark, Ray-Ray. I wish we were home."

Raea took a moment to feel just a little bad about calling her brother a doofus, and to glance around the room. While usually her blurry eyes couldn't make out much more than a few fuzzy, shadowy blobs here and there, Jer was right: she could now see absolutely nothing.

"It's gonna be okay, Jer, you're gonna be okay. Let's go find Mom."

Raea heard Jer sniff uncertainly. "But how?"

Raea leaned in close, knowing that now was the time to be the superhero sister Jer thought she was. "We're going to use everything but our eyes."

The trembling child in her arms seemed to calm with curiosity. "But how?" he repeated in a whisper.

Raea straightened up and tried to turn him around. "You know where the bed is, right?" She felt his head nod as he remained burrowed into her middle. "And the door is on the other side of the bed from here, so if we keep our hands on the side of the headboard..." Raea took her brother's hand and placed it on the minimalist headboard. They both took small steps towards the other side, and let go when the headboard ended. "Now one, two, three steps, and here's the door." This time, Jer's hand went out without her leading.

"Cool." She could almost hear the familiar giggle back in his voice. So far, so good.

"Next: walls. If you turn right and let your right hand trail on the wall, you can follow it through all the turns and curves. All the other living quarters branch out left. The right side is consistent..." She talked as she traced the familiar cold metal and slightly warmer pipes of fiber-optic electricity running through every inch of the *Nimrerer*. She explained as she took small step after small step, her brother not letting go of her shirt with his left hand. "The right side is consistent, until..." she prompted.

"The corner!"

"Yep, the corner." Raea's hand stopped when she knew it would change from the smooth surface to the textured metal that marked the beginning of the common area. "Where do you think Mom is?"

Jer took a moment, his sniffles not quite subsided, but calming with each passing moment. "I think… the plant room."

Raea nodded to herself and said, "Yeah, I think so, too. So that means we have to go across the middle of the common area."

"But there's no wall in the middle!"

"No, but if we start with our backs to the corner and walk directly across, we won't hit any tables or chairs, and that's exactly where the hall to the bio and tech quarter starts. And I bet you anything Dad is in Engineering right now."

Jer took the deepest breath Raea had ever heard from his tiny lungs and said, "Okay. Get into position?"

Raea leaned her back against where the frame and the wall met, imagining the large room: kitchen, table, chairs on the right, softer places to lounge and converse on the left. The center was empty in at least a five-foot radius, sometimes more if Captain Mira and Medic Col remembered to tuck in their chairs after mealtime. She put her hands on her little brother's shoulders and placed him right in front of her own body. "In position. Don't think, and don't try to see, just walk forward."

They walked. They walked with purpose, and with each step she could feel Jer getting more and more confident. Raea barely needed to direct his body, and then their feet found the hallway.

"Did you hear it?" Raea asked.

"The steps sound different here." Jer had been paying attention with his senses, and Raea was thankful for the complete darkness hiding her beaming face—she didn't want to give her brother a big head. He still had a lot to learn about life, but at least he picked things up quickly.

"Yep. The common area is dampened by storage underneath. Now we're on the open layered hallways. Upstairs and downstairs. It echoes. We can even tell when we're near a room when the echoes start bouncing off the thick door instead of the walls."

Both siblings walked with conviction to the end of the hallway, where the door to the bio-room, a makeshift greenhouse/growing lab their mother had created, loomed. Knowing the rules, but figuring the emergency was a legitimate excuse for not following them exactly, Raea knocked at the door. But she didn't wait for an answer before pulling it open.

"Mom?" they both called out.

"Jer? Raea? Is that you?" Raea knew her mom well enough to hear the hidden panic in her voice. "Don't let the door close; I think some automations have shut off with the rest of the ship."

Raea dutifully grabbed the stool, which often served as her seat while she listened to her mom explain all the plant experiments, and lodged it between the heavy door and its frame. Jer bounced up and down beside her and shouted, "Mommy, Ray-Ray got us here using our hands and our ears!"

"Oh yeah? Is that how you're going to get me out of here?" Raea could hear her mom as she approached, methodically stepping between all the grow boxes and specialized lamps.

Carefully choosing her words, Raea responded as kindly as she could, "I think you and Jer should stay here. Whatever's happening is probably going to be fixable in Engineering, and I'll be able to get there much faster by myself." She waited a half-second for any protest on either person's part, but when none came, she breathed a sigh of relief. "Dad's in Engineering, yeah?"

Raea's mother answered in the affirmative. "We walked over from lunch about an hour and a half ago." Raea heard and then felt her mother finally get to her. Her mother's strong hands rested on her shoulders, smelling of dirt and fresh-grown vegetables. "Please be careful, my little love." And Raea felt a gentle kiss on her forehead.

"I always try to be!" And before either her mother or brother could combat that statement, she rushed past the heavy metal door, grabbed the railing exactly five steps to the left of the garden room, clanged down all twenty-six steps, and followed the long hallway until it opened up. The echoes changed as the walls and ceiling widened.

The large space marking the unofficial entrance to Engineering surrounded her. She knew Dua's office was to her left, the controls and physical tools were stored to her right, and the engine core that should have been glowing purple, bright enough for even her eyes to see, towered directly in front of her. But everything remained completely dark.

From below the core, the sounds of clangs and shuffling caught Raea's attention. "Dad?" she called out as her steps slowed.

"Raea?" Her father's soft voice emerged from the tiny access chamber beneath the core. "How did you get down here?"

"I walked," Raea replied, unable to keep the sass out of her voice. She shook her head, knowing this was not the time for jokes. "Is Dua down there?"

"I'm over here," called Dua from the large supply closet. And then came the sounds of dropping metal, desperate scrambling, and a *thunk* of head on wall. "Crapperjacks. Oh no... Ow!"

"Hold on, Dua," Raea called out, as she followed the ridges in the floor, over to where the engineer was haphazardly smacking the floor as she tried to grab at fallen supplies.

Raea could hear the panic setting into Dua's voice as she said, "I guess I really should have organized this thing... then maybe I'd know where everything is. Captain Mira is going to be so mad... if we all survive this."

"What do we need?" Raea knelt to the ground and started feeling the different tools for size and shape and temperature of metal.

There was only a half-second of hesitation from Dua, but true to their friendship, she didn't doubt this barely-fourteen-year-old would be able to help in whatever way she could. "Fifteen chrome washers, standard size; the small soldering iron; a couple of screwdrivers; and at least three lengths of the fiber-optic cabling that's rated for zero gravity, though more would be better... oh, and a flashlight would be fantastic, but I think Col took mine as a prank like a year ago... the backup generator usually kicks in and gives us emergency lights and partial nav, but the connections are all bunk, and I think if the generator isn't working, then life support is out, and I have no idea how to deal with all this when I can't even figure out what cabling is what, and I... wait, is this everything?"

"Except for the flashlight and the cables. I'm still finding those."

As Dua had panic-ranted, Raea had reached inside the big bucket of washers and identified size and material based on touch, found the smallest soldering iron exactly where Dua tended to leave it out (in the little basket on the outside of the cabinet door that was likely placed there to hold keys of some kind), extracted her and Dua's favorite screwdrivers out from exactly where she had placed them last time she had been allowed to tinker, and grabbed one more for luck from the fallen pile of stuff on the ground. She had a feeling Dua was right about Col and the flashlight, but at least she could find the fiber-optic cables.

Dua stood, dumbfounded for a moment, hands full of washers and screwdrivers and a tiny soldering iron. "How in the world are you going to find the cabling?"

Raea smiled to herself as she continued to sift through the cables. "I'll let you in on a little secret," she said, and paused to sniff the edge of a cable, "fiber-optics smell kind of like my childhood. I could pick them out of anywhere." She pulled out one, two, three, then four, then five, and finally six from the very back of the cabinet, checking each time that they were double the length of her own wingspan and had the tiny tape marking on either end that she had been told read "0 grav."

"I'll carry these. Now follow me." Raea led the still-dumbfounded Dua beneath the core, assuming correctly that this was where the issue had started.

The work was slow and grueling, as only one person could fit directly under the core at one time. Dua knew exactly what needed to be done to get emergency power back, but wasn't used to navigating all the complex wires and screws and safety valves without sight. And as they worked, it became increasingly obvious that the disconnect between the energy core and ship's controls had, in fact, disconnected life support as well.

Raea's father reassuringly gave both engineers words of wisdom, and prods to keep going, even as their breaths shallowed and the shivers started. Dua was affected first, then Raea and her father, making the fine-tuning of soldering nearly impossible. But they still worked and worked and worked.

Finally, Raea's dad tried for the ninth time to throw the hard reset switch, which was hidden behind glass in the crevasse leading to the tiny workstation Dua and Raea had been sharing for over two hours. And Raea saw a faint purple glow begin above her, heard the *chnk chnk chnk* of the lights coming on, and felt the rush of fresh oxygen breeze past her face and fill her lungs. As she tasted the purified air, she could hear the clanging steps of their captain approaching.

But Captain Mira did not seem angry when they arrived in Engineering. Raea tried to stand as straight as she could, but she was still so cold, and feeling a little faint. Captain Mira did something Raea never thought possible—they led Raea to Dua's office chair, sat her down, knelt directly in front of her, and hugged her!

"I had a feeling it would be you saving the day."

Raea opened her mouth multiple times before she was able to squeak out, "But… but you said I wasn't allowed in Engineering?"

"We all say things we regret—you'll learn that when you're older. For now, I have to be thankful you *didn't* heed my warnings." Captain Mira bowed their head with respect. "Thank you, Raea Malton, for saving my ship."

"I mean… it's my home now, for better or worse. For boring or exciting."

"Well," started Captain Mira, a sly smile entering their tone, "things are about to get a whole lot more interesting here. The computer picked up life signs of a few families still on a planet a couple days' travel from here. And from what I saw before the change in navigation jostled the connectors loose, some of them seem to be about your age."

Excitement flooded Raea's body, but before she got too excited, the captain's words echoed in her head. "Wait. How did you know it was the connectors and the change in nav?"

Captain Mira stood and gently touched Raea's forehead. "Every captain has to come from somewhere, and I happen to come from this exact Engineering room." Their footsteps clunked away, until they turned around at the door. Raea heard the captain's clothes rustle as their hand lifted, and she somehow knew they were touching the frame. "This ship is pretty old, and needs a little love and attention. Do you think you could balance being a Junior Engineer, as well as an ambassador to the new families coming aboard?"

Raea broke into the biggest grin of her life. Without thinking, she blurted out, "After months of doing nothing, I would be happy with five million somethings!" and then, thinking better of her words, she very seriously stood up straight and said, "I'll do my absolute best, Captain Mira."

"I know you will," Captain Mira said, turning away and clunking back up the steps.

Raea walked to the doorway and placed her hand where the captain's had just been, the heat of their hand not yet faded from the cold metal of the ship. "I guess you are my home now. So please, no more scares!"

As she walked out of the office, she could hear Captain Mira already explaining to Engineer Dua what duties a Junior Engineer would have.

And, although Raea was looking forward to it, she was glad to have a couple of days before things got too exciting on the *Nimrerer*.

THOUGHTS ON *BRAVE NEW GIRLS*

"With a spouse who is also a gender-minority in STEM, I've had a lot of opportunities to re-think my own perceptions and prejudices within the past eleven years of our relationship. Kip has taught me through their own passion, and through helping me gain my own experience, that STEM is inherently creative. I am forever grateful to my spouse for showing me how utterly cool STEM is, not only so I could perceive the world in a more open and creative light, but also so I could contribute to this wonderful (and wonderfully important) anthology!"

ABOUT THE AUTHOR

HJ Farr (they/them) is an actor/writer/aerialist originally from Cleveland, Ohio, who found a home in NYC after a slight (six-year) detour in Madison, Wisconsin.

With a lifetime of training in Musical Theatre Performance and their nose always in some book, HJ constantly made up stories as a child, but this is their very first published fiction work! In addition to acting and training aerial circus, HJ also writes poetry, sews, and collects various other hobbies. "HJ loves Kip!"

Illustration for "Liminal Space" by Adriano Moraes.

Lady Verdant: Hero Knight of Mara Villa

JR Rustrian

LADY VERDANT: HERO KNIGHT OF MARA VILLA

J.R. RUSTRIAN

"NEXT!"

Agnes Alvarez fumbled with her documents as the clerk's raspy voice echoed through the Department of Chivalry's lobby. She stepped forward, nearly tripping over her own feet, and placed the stack of crumpled papers on the counter. The clerk loudly chewed a piece of bubblegum as she watched with disinterested eyes. The name on her tag showed "Julia," and she had clearly been at this for far too long.

"Purpose?" the clerk asked.

"Registration! My name is Agnes Alvarez and I—"

"Do you have all the required paperwork, including certification of completion of required combat and engineering classes, list of equipment, and liability insurance?"

"Yes, it's all here. I just finished my courses last week," Agnes stated.

"Uh-huh," Julia said, typing, not giving Agnes the courtesy of her gaze. "Okay, Agnes Alvarez, rookie Hero Knight permit with the proper documentation… says here you're sixteen. Isn't that a little young for a Hero Knight?"

"Y-yeah, I suppose so," Agnes said as she presented her with a piece of paper, "but I got a waiver from City Hall signed by my parents."

Julia snatched the waiver and continued typing, much to Agnes's growing dismay. The anxiety clawed at her, and so she turned her attention to her wrist-mounted computer, an invention of her own design, complete with police blotter, frequency tracker, and full video display. Agnes swiped on the glass, eagerly hacking the channels for any signs of trouble, like she had dozens of times before. Her heart sank when the search results turned up nothing.

"Presentation of armor, weapons, and/or gadgets," Julia said.

Agnes obliged, and pulled out an old steel broadsword with an ornate bronze basket hilt, a small iron shield called a buckler, and a brown, homemade grapple gun with a hook at the end. She placed it all on the counter with a loud clang and crossed her hands.

"A grapple gun? Haven't seen those in years," Julia said.

"Made it myself. Also made my wrist-mounted computer and my armor, which is made up of nanomesh fiber—"

"Uh-huh. I get it. I'm going to need a title of nobility to process your permit."

Agnes smiled. She'd been waiting for this part her entire life. Entire Hero Knight careers had been made based upon nailing the perfect alias. A good one had to be simple to remember and roll off the tongue, but a legendary name was one that you couldn't imagine never existing.

"Green Guardian!" Agnes said with excitement.

"He was killed in battle fifteen years ago. Try another," said Julia.

"Emerald Guardian?"

"Move away from the 'Guardians,' honey. They've all been taken."

"Green Enforcer?"

Julia shook her head. Agnes shifted nervously in her own armor, having settled on her favorite color long ago. The pressure of the perfect name was overwhelming. She scratched the back of her head, trying to throw off the weary gazes of dozens of potential Hero Knights still waiting their turn.

"How about… Lady…Verdant?" Agnes said, bracing herself for a rejection.

Julia turned her eyes to the computer screen. "All right, it's available. Congratulations, Lady Verdant, you're a Hero Knight now, pending final approval of equipment by the city council of Mara Villa," Julia said, handing Agnes back her equipment and a certificate of licensure. "Make sure to submit a recent picture online. Next!"

Agnes suppressed a smile and stepped away from the counter. Excitement welled up inside of her. She crossed the crowded lobby, at first strolling casually as she dodged city workers, civilians, and iron-clad Hero Knights. Then, the smile exploded across her face. The stroll increased into a power-walk, then into a jog, before Agnes burst into a full sprint. She blasted into the cafeteria, nearly crashing into a cook before excitement overtook her.

"I DID IT!" she screamed at the top of her lungs. The cafeteria went dead silent as each person dropped what they were doing to stare at Agnes, including her best friend, Indy. Agnes waved sheepishly, blushing bright red as she began to cross the silent cafeteria, feeling like an amoeba underneath a microscope.

Indy, trying her best not to laugh, waved Agnes over to take a seat. "By the looks of it, I'm having the privilege of meeting Mara Villa's newest Hero Knight! Congrats, Green Guardian!"

"Uh, yeah, that name was taken, so I had to go with 'Lady Verdant,'" Agnes said.

"Lady Verdant? Hm. I kinda like it. It sounds royal, like you're the princess of Mara Villa or something."

Agnes chuckled, always keen to listen to her best friend of over ten years. Independence "Indy" Martinez was only about a year older than Agnes, and had been adventuring for several months now. She'd taken on the moniker "Indy Indigo," a name reflected in the color of her secondhand plate armor. Indy had seen her fair share of action in those few short months, and she always was eager to offer her bestie all the advice she could. Agnes relished the advice, but rather preferred the stories of bank robberies, car chases, and building fires, of which there were only a few.

"I'd rather be a Hero Knight than a princess. A defender of the innocent. A friend to the people. Just like—"

"Like Miss Golden?" Indy asked.

A wide smile crept across Agnes's face. *Like Miss Golden.*

"Yes! Imagine being a guardian of the city like her. They'd enshrine your name in lights on La Mancha Square and build a statue in your honor," Agnes said with vigor.

"It also helps that she has three million followers on social media and dozens of sponsorships. I saw half of the adventurers here wearing some of her fashion line. Speaking of which, how's your online presence?"

Agnes groaned. "I really don't think it's for me. I get why Miss Golden does it. She lets people know she's out there protecting them, but I just hate posting selfies."

"Then how are you going to become a famous Hero Knight?"

"By adventuring! If only I had the opportunity to pick Miss Golden's brain for just a few minutes, I could learn a lifetime's worth of wisdom."

"Well, Lady Verdant, now's your chance. She's here, and it looks like she's getting a salad."

Agnes perked up as she heard the gasps and cheers of the various armored adventurers in the cafeteria. She turned quickly, almost knocking the table over as she laid eyes on the splendor of her hero.

Miss Golden. Hero Knight.

The Hero Knight.

Time seemed to slow as Miss Golden entered the cafeteria to the cheers of the assembled crowd. Legions of adoring fans flocked to her, kept at bay by the many assistants and bodyguards surrounding her. She smiled and waved, livestreaming herself mingling with the crowd on her smartphone. Agnes stared at her idol, utterly starstruck, and observed the way her blond hair flowed, the way her jewel-embedded sword hung from her belt, and just the perfect posture she seemed to possess. Miss Golden shined with a regal radiance few others could dream about, let alone possess.

"I'm going," Agnes said as she fixed and adjusted her armor. "How do I look?"

"Like a crazed fangirl. Are you sure? Look at her entourage. I'd be surprised if you got within five feet of her."

"Too late now! Wish me luck!"

Agnes snaked through the hordes of onlookers, her heart pumping as she inched closer. It was like approaching a demigod, an image made more apparent by Miss Golden's sterling golden plate armor and hand-sewn cape, intricately crafted by the finest armorers in the world. Many had compared her to King Arthur walking the earth again, but even Arthur didn't have a social media team as robust as hers.

As Agnes neared Miss Golden's entourage, excitement overtook her. Miss Golden was tall and statuesque, blue-eyed and beautiful with an amazing smile. The way she moved across the cafeteria reminded Agnes of the grace and athleticism of a ballerina. Agnes stopped only a few feet away, right next to her group of big, burly bodyguards. The way they stood resembled the walls of a fortress.

"Miss Golden!" Agnes cried out, planning to breach the walls of the fortress. Miss Golden continued to livestream, ignoring her cries. Agnes spied an opening between her bodyguards and quickly slipped through. She stopped Miss Golden in her tracks, and Miss Golden eyed Agnes with surprise and confusion.

"Miss Golden! My name is Agnes! They call me Lady Verdant!" Agnes said.

"Yeah... good for you," Miss Golden said, eyeing her with indignation. "Nice armor."

Agnes's heart fluttered. "Thank you! I made it myself. I integrated nanomesh technology into the seams, so it reflects any damage taken outward with a working output of eighty percent! It was hard work, but I eventually got the wattage down well. You see, I just became licensed today, and I thought—"

Miss Golden's face perked up. "Did you say you just got licensed?"

"Uh, yeah. I went to the counter and—"

Before she knew it, Agnes was pulled into a close embrace, as Miss Golden held up her smartphone and snapped a photo of the two, with Agnes giving an awkward smile.

"Good pic for the feed," she said, typing away on her phone. "I'll caption it, 'Miss Golden meets and encourages brand new Hero Knights.' Thanks, Green Suit."

Agnes was shoved aside by the strong arm of one of the bodyguards, as Miss Golden continued through the cafeteria, waving and snapping photos of herself, while her golden cape waved majestically behind her.

Agnes stood there, feeling like a five-year-old caught coloring on the walls. Shame overcame her, and she found herself longing for the embarrassment of screaming in a crowded cafeteria again. It was much more preferable to being dissed by her idol. The moment replayed itself in her mind as she searched for where she had gone wrong. Maybe she'd come on too strong, Agnes pondered, or she hadn't properly introduced herself.

"That was rude," said Indy, snapping Agnes out of her thoughts.

"It's okay. I'm sure Miss Golden has very important things to attend to right now," Agnes said. "Besides, there will be other opportunities when we are out in the field, right?"

Indy frowned. "Let's hope so."

In the bright June sunlight, Agnes couldn't keep her eyes off her wrist computer's screen. She'd programmed it to go red and sound a notification the moment it detected even the smallest of emergencies. At first, she'd expected at least two notifications a day, then at least one, and then maybe one every three days.

After two weeks, barely one had sounded, and that one was just a convenience store robbery. By the time Agnes had arrived, ten Hero Knights had already converged.

Full of energy, Agnes found herself patrolling the city of Mara Villa, taking in its sights and sounds, and waiting for something to happen. Anticipation turned into frustration, and frustration turned into anxiety.

On one of her daily patrols, she found a group of idle Hero Knights milling about on a street corner, laughing and gossiping. Agnes frowned. She remembered hearing stories of Hero Knights turning to villainy because the money was better.

She turned away and found a park bench to sit on. The lure of the computer was too much to resist. Agnes checked the police bands, the civilian frequencies, and the news reports. Nothing indicated any sort of trouble. Just another quiet day in the wonder-filled world of Mara Villa. A world where Agnes's dream slipped further and further away.

She sat there for half an hour before Indy joined her, bringing Agnes some slight joy on a day which should've been full of adventures.

"How's your patrol?" Indy asked.

"Bleh," Agnes grunted.

"That bad, huh?"

They sat in a brief silence. Agnes fanned herself with her green tricorn hat and regretted adding an emerald-hued cape to her armor. The duo sat there, watching joggers and cyclists go by. Several of them gave Agnes a strange and subtle sneer, and it was then she realized that not everybody trusted guardians in armor.

"Indy, have you ever felt guilty about wanting something bad to happen?" asked Agnes.

Indy chuckled and nodded. "I don't think you're a true Hero Knight until you get those feelings."

Agnes frowned. "Does that make me a bad person?"

"Of course not," said Indy. "It makes you aware of what's right and wrong. Don't worry, honey, you'll get your chance, and when it comes, I trust you'll make the right decision."

Leave it to Indy to make her feel better, Agnes thought. Indy possessed not only an infinite capacity for selflessness that Agnes tried to emulate, but a severe amount of humbleness. Indy often let others take credit for resolving situations. Agnes shook her head, secretly praying that Indy would, for once, take her spot in the limelight.

They turned into a bustling, vibrant neighborhood, full of people enjoying their day, when a loud alarm sent a chill up Agnes's spine. Her eyes darted to her computer, and she spied an unfamiliar blue screen. Agnes arched an eyebrow and tapped on her screen.

"What is it?" asked Indy.

"A powerful network signal. It looks like an automated robot's signal, but I've never seen one this strange or this powerful."

"Where's it coming from?"

Just as Agnes pointed toward a building across the street, the roof blasted apart in a massive explosion. Flaming shards of wood and concrete rained down upon the streets. Agnes and Indy dove for cover underneath an overhang. The sounds of people screaming and cars smashing into one another echoed throughout the neighborhood. Agnes covered her head, fear and adrenaline coursing through her veins.

The panicked cries of civilians were replaced with the sounds of machinery and metal grinding against brick. Agnes peeked out from the overhang and spotted a machine she'd seen before. That everybody had seen before.

The machine resembled a horrifying cross between a robot and a spider, with eight mechanical legs twisting and turning as it grasped onto the side of the ruined building, crushing the brick and mortar with three sharp iron claws at the ends of each leg. The limbs connected to the main body, a shifting mass of iron and rubber-coated wires, huffing and puffing powerful jets of steam as it moved to the adjacent building. Nothing about the machine indicated anything remotely human, except for a crane near the front, which carried the human-looking head of Professor Kahill Marron.

Agnes's eyes widened at the sight of Mara Villa's premier supervillain crawling a few yards away. News reports had mentioned the shimmering metallic body, the talon-like claws, and the massive tangle of technology that made up his torso, but they'd said nothing of his eyes, if they could be called that. They glowed a fiery red, mechanical and artificial, but still hinting at life behind them. If Marron was fully machine, then whose life was it?

"What now?" asked Indy.

Agnes, acting on instinct, rose to her feet and unsheathed her sword. Her heart was racing at the sheer turn of events unfolding in front of her. This was it. Finally, she'd prove herself.

"We do our jobs, Indy. We get up there and take him down!" cried Agnes, raising her sword upward.

"Hopefully we can do it before your idol does it. Somehow, she got the drop on Marron." Indy said, staring at the building.

Agnes, puzzled, craned her head to look up at the roof above them and spotted the familiar golden hue of Miss Golden, standing majestically like a queen atop the building, flanked by three camera drones. She held her short sword aloft with her right hand, while her left tightly grasped her golden shield. Professor Marron turned to face Miss Golden and grunted, his eyes locked right on her.

"Miss Golden," the machine said with a raspy, metallic voice. "There's no possible way you can stop me this time."

"That's what you think, Marron. I won't let you hurt anybody else!" cried Miss Golden. She blasted out a wire from her grapple gun and glided like a gilded angel across the street. She immediately leaped onto Professor Marron and plunged her sword into one of his spidery limbs. He groaned in pain and tumbled backward, taking Miss Golden along with him.

"One has to wonder how she's always the one to show up when he's around," Indy said. "It feels like she always has the jump on the major villains."

"She's a famous Hero Knight. She probably has some sort of advanced tech that we don't know about," Agnes answered. "Whatever the case is, we need to go help her. Weapons ready!"

"But Miss Golden has it covered."

Agnes shook her head. "Are you kidding? This is our moment to show everybody what we've got! You take the back, I'll head up, and we'll surround him. Got it?"

Indy, hesitation on her face, dashed down the street. Agnes pointed her grapple gun up at the building and propelled herself up in mere seconds, landing hard on the unstable rooftop. There, she spotted Miss Golden slicing off tiny bits of metal and wire from the massive robotic body.

Agnes shuddered with excitement. This was the moment she'd been waiting for her whole life. She raised her sword and buckler high into the sky and dashed toward the rampaging Professor. With each step, the rooftop trembled and crumbled as the damaged brick cracked underneath her feet. Agnes spied a crack between two iron plates and, with little hesitation, plunged her sword deep into the machine.

The entire struggle stopped dead in its tracks. Miss Golden, hanging on for dear life to Marron's thorax, slowly and methodically turned her confused eyes to glance down at Agnes. A scowl crawled across her face before turning to concern.

"No, you don't know what you're doing!" Miss Golden cried.

Seizing the opportunity, Marron threw Miss Golden off like a bucking bronco, crashing her into an air-conditioning unit. Agnes removed her sword and swung it at the machine, hitting nothing but air. A mechanical arm came out from the left, wrapping its cold metal around her, and slammed her into the crumbling brick roof.

Agnes struggled to get free, reaching for her thrown sword, which lay only a few precious inches out of her reach. Professor Marron approached her with furious eyes, scanning every part of her like a computer scanning for a virus. He frowned and clenched his claw, crushing Agnes.

"Interesting. A nanomesh weave reacting to external stimuli... like an electronic Kevlar. Advanced craftsmanship for a young one like yourself," he said.

Agnes shuddered. Fear gripped her tighter than his claws. She closed her eyes.

"You're afraid? You should be," he said, as he loosened his grip. "But don't worry, little one, I'm not going to waste my time on you."

Agnes opened her eyes, meeting his softening red ones. "You... aren't?"

"You're not worth it. Just a little girl playing knight."

Marron released his grip and retreated down the building just as Indy approached the scene. Agnes rose to her feet and dusted herself off with an audible sigh.

"What happened?" asked Indy.

"I couldn't wait. I jumped the gun," answered Agnes. A low groan sounded from a pile of twisted metal a few feet away. Agnes suddenly remembered Miss Golden and dashed over to her, digging through the twisted metal and helping her hero to her feet.

"I'm so sorry!" Agnes said. "Are you okay? Marron escaped! We damaged him, though. Maybe we can track him down somehow!"

She watched Miss Golden, wide-eyed and out of breath, survey the scene. After a brief moment of silence, Miss Golden turned her gaze upon Agnes and snarled.

"Stop the stream!" roared Miss Golden. She grabbed Agnes by the collar and slammed her into a brick wall.

"What in the hell were you thinking? How dare you step on my fight? I had over six thousand people tuning in just now, and you ruined all of it!"

Agnes watched the anger boil in Miss Golden's eyes. She trembled at first, confused at her intensity, but then the words rang inside her head. Six thousand people tuning in? There was something just petty about it.

Miss Golden cocked her head. "Wait... you're that green girl from the cafeteria. But you're just a newbie!"

Agnes smiled awkwardly. "Yeah, that's me."

"You nearly got me killed, green girl. Do you even have any experience outside playing around with tools?"

"Well... n-no..."

"Then hear it from me, newbie," Miss Golden said, letting go of Agnes. "You are *not* cut out for this. You are a *bad* Hero Knight."

Agnes's heart shattered.

Miss Golden turned to leave, her cape swatting Agnes in the face. "People don't want to see some nobody pretending to be something they're not. Do everybody a favor and invent yourself a brain, will you?"

Agnes, deep in a daze, could barely see Miss Golden take off from the rooftop. She felt her armor tighten around her body. Breathing became difficult. Her legs gave out, and she fell sideways into Indy's arms.

"Agnes... oh God, I'm so sorry," Indy said.

The tears started falling by themselves. The words continued to echo inside Agnes's head. *You are not cut out for this. You are a bad Hero Knight.* They hurt more than anything else Agnes had ever experienced. She'd embarrassed herself in front of Miss Golden. Maybe there was a way to make it up to her and prove she was worthy.

"I need to find her," Agnes said through her sobs.

"What? No, Agnes, you need to call it a day," Indy said.

Agnes freed herself from Indy's grasp and stood at the edge of the rooftop. "I'll admit that I messed this one up, but if only she could see what I can really do, then Miss Golden wouldn't think I'm some poser," she said, taking ahold of her grapple gun.

"And what are you going to do? This is a really bad idea," Indy pleaded with her. "Why does it matter so much what Miss Golden thinks of you?"

"Because! Because. Because she's strong and powerful and heroic."

"And you think you aren't?"

Agnes sighed. She glanced back at her friend and saw the hurt on Indy's face. Part of Agnes wanted to stay, but the overwhelming urge to find Miss Golden was too much to ignore.

"You'll see. Come to my apartment tonight, and I'll let you know what happens."

The grapple gun fired its claw across the street and latched onto an antenna. With a strong leap, Lady Verdant swooped off into the dusk.

As marvelous as Mara Villa was during the day, certain parts were downright dreary and scary as soon as the sun set. Few people ever traveled up to Ponte Norte during the dark hours without having a very specific reason, and even fewer Hero Knights patrolled there without having extensive backup, as one wearing brightly colored armor and expertly crafted weapons often seemed quite an attractive target.

None of this mattered to Agnes as she wandered the dark, foreboding, derelict remains of a once-great city. Mara Villa had been built on the burnt remnants of Aztec homes, palaces, temples, colonial churches, and neighborhoods. These places now served as the signposts of Mara Villa's seedier areas.

She walked alongside stone buildings, nervous yet determined. It wasn't too difficult to narrow down Miss Golden's approximate location. Her last social media posts had taken place in the retail section of Downtown, where she'd visited all the best fashion boutiques. The rest had been left to Agnes's wrist computer, which had pinged Miss Golden's cell phone signals and used triangulation to place her somewhere in this neighborhood.

Pieces of trash littered the cracked and neglected sidewalks. Boarded-up windows were an omnipresent sight among the decayed ruins. Agnes glanced down an alleyway, spying a mother hunkering near a small, makeshift fire with her two small children, one a toddler and the other just a baby. Agnes and the mother locked eyes for a moment. Instinctively, Agnes reached into her pocket, pulled out a few coins, and tossed them her way. The mother nodded and smiled.

Agnes continued on, nearing an abandoned foundry destroyed long ago in a fire. There wasn't anybody nearby, and Agnes briefly considered turning away, before a shadow near the foundry caught her eye. A blond woman in a large, beige trench coat and wide-brimmed hat. The woman stopped near a small door briefly to see if she was being followed, then opened it and closed it behind her.

When Agnes reached the door, it was locked tight. She backed up, surveying the scene, until she realized that the rafters overlooking the foundry were wide open. Agnes blasted the grapple gun, attaching the hook to a sturdy railing, and swung herself up to a high vantage point. A bright light was lit near the very center of the production floor, where she spied the woman in the trench coat taking off the hat, spilling Miss Golden's radiant hair across her shoulders.

There she is, thought Agnes, *but what is she doing all the way out here?* A million scenarios filled her head. *The foundry is her secret lair where she bases her fight against evil from, or she's here to meet with a secret league of Hero Knights from another city, or it's a place where she's working on some prototypes for new armors and weapons.*

Then, Agnes felt her arm vibrate. She looked down to see the screen on her wrist computer flash red. She immediately checked it out and froze. The signal was identical to the one she'd captured earlier. A chill went up her spine. For a brief moment, Agnes tried to rationalize it away, but the more she investigated the signal, the more it became clear that it could only have come from one source.

A loud stomp shook the foundry. The terrifying buzz of electrical and mechanical horror signaled the arrival of Professor Marron, marching his way into the abandoned foundry without a care in the world. He circled Miss Golden, who stood stoically defiant in his presence.

Agnes smiled. Finally, she would see the ultimate showdown between Miss Golden and the villainous Marron. Years of on-again off-again battles would culminate here in this derelict foundry, and how lucky was Agnes that she would be the only witness! She stood by and waited for somebody to make the first move.

Instead, Miss Golden reached into her coat pocket and pulled out a small remote. Instantly, Professor Marron stopped cold and kneeled. Miss Golden confidently approached him and tapped his face with the remote. He sneered at her with cold eyes.

"Good boy," she said to him. "We need to plan for our next little dance."

"How much humiliation must I endure before you free me from this enslavement?" he asked, keeping his eyes square on Miss Golden.

"Don't get lippy with me, robot." She scowled. "You're lucky that I saved your CPU from our little fight atop the Quetzal Building, or else you'd be scrap metal."

Agnes's heart stopped cold. Air refused to enter her lungs. Her legs collapsed from underneath her. It wasn't true, she told herself. Miss Golden couldn't be working with the enemy. Agnes gripped onto the railing with such strength, she nearly ripped it off its hinges.

"We need something big," pondered Miss Golden. "Something with lots of destruction and dozens of eyes on it. Like a hurricane. No, that's silly. A fire?"

"Too unwieldy," said Marron. "A bomb would be more precise."

"Yes! A bomb! Somewhere visible, too, where we can get millions streaming at once. So many eyes that it'll crash the internet! I'm thinking… the Department of Chivalry."

Marron arched an eyebrow. "Why there?"

"Too many heroes are trying to take up the spotlight these days. Let's face it, I'll be taking out the trash."

"And they call me maniacal."

Miss Golden pressed a button on her remote, and together they moved off toward the opposite side of the foundry. Agnes followed silently from the rafters, straining to hear their conversation.

"We plant a bomb there, then you make your appearance, thrashing like a madman," Miss Golden said. "I'll come in, we fight, and right before the bomb goes off, you throw me into a nearby ditch. I think it's going to be our best work ever."

Agnes shook her head, unable to rid herself of the words she was hearing. *No. Not Miss Golden. Professor Marron must've corrupted her or implanted a cybernetic chip into her brain.*

Anger rose through her. She wanted desperately to go down there, take Marron out, and rescue Miss Golden from his clutches, but she knew she was no match for him. She took a deep breath and exhaled, accidentally knocking over a glass bottle. Agnes reached out to catch it, but missed, sending the bottle crashing to the floor below.

"We aren't alone..." Marron said. The machine leaped onto the ruined ceiling and scrambled across it. Agnes ran across the rafters toward the corner, and slid down a support beam just as Marron came crashing over. She scrambled to her feet and dashed as fast as she could down the darkened street. Her heart pumped a mile a minute. She let her feet take over, not wanting to think about what had just happened.

She turned back to the foundry and locked eyes with Miss Golden, watching from the entrance without a care in the world. Miss Golden gave a cursory smile before disappearing back inside.

Agnes ran as fast as her legs could take her down the darkened city streets, dodging traffic and colliding into pedestrians. She could hardly see through her tear-filled eyes, let alone navigate a city nightscape. The shadows seemed to cave in on her, and she couldn't shake off the heartbreak. Upon reaching her apartment, she stopped to catch her breath.

The stairs wound up for an eternity. The muscles in her legs burned and yearned for a rest. Agnes stumbled into her apartment like a mad woman and slammed the door behind her. There was no sign of her parents at all, leaving it empty and a bit unnerving. She strolled past the living room, placing her sword and buckler on the couch, before storming off to her room and dropping onto her bed.

Miss Golden's picture lay front and center in her room, an old reminder of who she'd aspired to be. Agnes stumbled over to the picture and eyed it. Miss Golden's immaculate smile beamed down at her, doing nothing now but filling Agnes with sadness.

"How could you?" Agnes violently punched the picture square in the face, before breaking down into tears at the foot of the image.

A knock startled Agnes. She rose to her feet and stumbled over to the front door, remembering that she'd invited Indy over earlier that day. She breathed a sigh of relief, needing her company right now. They'd probably eat bad food and watch a movie to take her mind off everything. How would Indy react to the news of what she'd found out about Miss Golden?

Agnes whipped open the door, expecting to see her friend, only to find the perfect form of Miss Golden standing in her doorway. She smiled confidently, her hands gripping a small blue purse, which paired well with her expensive-looking blue dress.

"Hello, Agnes," Miss Golden said. "We need to talk. May I come in?"

Agnes stood there, frozen. Every nerve in her body screamed for her to slam the door shut and hide in the closet. Miss Golden's gaze was friendly and affable, but there indeed was something else behind it. Agnes's grip on the door nearly tore the frame off.

"Agnes?" Miss Golden prompted her. Agnes, too scared to utter a word, nodded and stepped out of the way.

Miss Golden entered and glanced around, careful not to touch anything that might even have a hint of common folk. "Cute little place, Agnes. I can call you Agnes, right? You can call me Rachel. 'Miss Golden' is a bit too formal, but if you prefer, I can call you Lady Verdant."

"How do you know my name?" Agnes asked.

"Information is easily accessible these days, Agnes Alvarez. Sixteen years old, Latina, and living in Mara Villa. You went to Ruiz Elementary, spent middle school at Shurman, and then graduated from Perez High School. Did you know that I went there too?"

Agnes gulped as Miss Golden wandered the apartment and eventually poked her head into Agnes's room.

Miss Golden spied the picture of herself on the wall. She smiled, pointed at it, and approached the trembling Agnes. "I know you're a fan of me. You have been since I started, right? You've liked every one of my photos since I started posting on social media. You're even a part of my fan club."

"Y-yeah, that's, um, ahem, that's right." Agnes suddenly remembered she was drenched in sweat and covered in dust.

"Let's get to the point then," Miss Golden said, crossing her arms. "You and I saw different things. It would be very bad for me if you, oh, I don't know, started spouting some crazy idea that maybe, just maybe, Mara Villa's greatest hero was in league with its greatest villain. Nobody would believe it, of course, but I like to cover my bases."

"What are you getting at?" Agnes asked meekly.

"What I'm getting at is that I can make this whole Hero Knight thing much, much easier for you, darling."

Miss Golden smiled softly. She carefully approached Agnes and placed her hands on her cheeks and neck, bringing her in close. Agnes's heart fluttered, despite the burning desire to scream at her.

"How would you like to be my sidekick? Hm? Think about it. Millions of followers, tons of sponsorships, with truckloads of money flowing in. Top-of-the-line fashion? It's yours. Spacious townhome on La Paz Avenue? Why settle for one?"

Miss Golden grinned as Agnes became putty in her hands. The thought of literally becoming a legendary hero overnight was almost too much to resist. Agnes raised up her hands to meet Miss Golden's. They were calloused, yet soft and warm. She wanted so badly to say yes.

Then, thoughts of the Department exploding intruded. Her brain screamed at her heart to get lost. Hundreds of innocent Hero Knights hurt. A tear streamed down her face. Agnes remembered pondering why some Hero Knights turned bad, and realized how easy it was to do it.

Agnes pushed Miss Golden's hands away. "It's everything I've ever dreamed of, Rachel, but I just can't shake the memory of you and Professor Marron scheming together. I mean, blowing up the Department just to get some likes? It's... it's... too... villainous."

Miss Golden arched an eyebrow, confused. "You're saying no? Even after I offered you everything?"

"It's not yours to offer or take. It's ours to protect. You have to somehow still believe that, right? Please don't go through with it. I believe you're still a great Hero Knight, deep down inside."

"I *am* a great Hero Knight. Don't you ever forget who you're talking to!" Miss Golden snarled.

Agnes backed away, her heart breaking once again. Her fear was gone, now replaced with disappointment.

Miss Golden composed herself. "Forgive me, Agnes. I lost my cool there for a second. Are you sure you won't change your mind?"

Agnes shook her head. "Sorry, I just can't let it go. It's not what a great Hero Knight would do."

Miss Golden nodded and strolled over to the door. "You know, Agnes, I hope for your sake you stay quiet, because this Hero Knight business... it can be quite dangerous. Anything can happen at any time. Take care of yourself." She slammed the door behind her, leaving Agnes in the quiet solitude of her own apartment.

She stood there, quaking and short of breath, attempting to process what exactly had taken place. Those ominous words still rang with force in her mind. *Anything can happen at any time.* Was it a warning? Some sort of threat? Agnes felt the pangs of exhaustion ring through her body, and so she wandered to the window.

The city lights twinkled against the night sky, so majestic and peaceful. She longed for some semblance of peace now. The adventure had been here, in her apartment, but not in the way she'd expected. Agnes shook her head and stared at two small red lights off in the distance, content to get lost in the beauty of the night skyline.

Then, out of the corner of her eye, her wrist computer buzzed and beeped with the familiar red warning. Agnes's heart stopped. She craned her head back to the window and found the red lights had grown in size, burning with an intense fury. Agnes dove to the floor just as Professor Marron smashed through the window, skidding to a halt in her kitchen. He looked around like an eagle scanning for its prey, before settling his gaze right on Agnes.

"Poor choice you made, child. Now I have to kill you," he said in that disturbing electronic voice. One of his many arms shot at Agnes like a spear. She instantly reacted, reached for her sword, and sliced off the hand. Professor Marron recoiled in pain. Sensing her chance, she bolted for her bedroom.

Marron smashed his way in, sending splinters of plywood and paint flying everywhere. He snarled and reached down for her. Agnes rolled across the floor and stabbed Marron in the chest. He screamed, stumbled back, and crashed through the front wall of the apartment. Agnes made for the fire escape and slid down to the street below.

She hid in the alleyway, looking from the shadows at her destroyed home. Marron peeked his head out, searching for Agnes. His eyes glowed red with anger and frustration. Police sirens echoed in the distance.

"Don't even think about showing up at the Department, girl. You'll pay dearly for it," he said, as he jumped down to the adjacent building and scurried away.

Agnes shivered with exhilaration and fear. She looked at her surroundings, trying to focus and figure out her next move. Professor Marron was too much to handle on her own. She needed her friend, and needed her now. Indy would be on her way here, and she would obviously be taking Obregon Avenue.

Using her sneaking instincts, Agnes made her way down the darkened, dangerous streets.

Agnes kept to herself as she silently strolled down the busy and bustling avenue. People, as they usually were, had their noses buried in their smartphones. As she passed an intersection, the first ding popped into her ears, then the second, and soon she heard a whole multitude of cell phone dings. Each person suddenly became aware of her presence.

A quick search on her computer revealed the reason:

Hero Knight Betrays City, Assists Prof. Marron in Attacking Miss Golden.

A rookie Hero Knight using the moniker "Lady Verdant" was seen teaming up with Prof. Marron in attacking and nearly killing famed Hero Knight Miss Golden.

Agnes quickly swiped the article away, unable to read any more. More and more eyes locked in on her, quickly followed by pointing and gawking. She jogged down the street, avoiding the gazes, and soon quickened to a sprint. Along the way, she spotted a group of Hero Knights, each of whom had their noses buried in their phones. One of them, a shorter man in gray armor, happened to glance up briefly and caught sight of Agnes. He squinted, as if struggling to remember where he recognized her from.

Agnes turned away from the group, ducking her head, trying desperately not to attract unwanted attention. She decided to turn into an alleyway, walking through it, crossing the street, and slipping into another alley, working hard to stay off the main boulevards. As she turned into yet another alley, she felt a hand grab her and push her up against the wall. Agnes stared into the wide, concerned eyes of Indy.

"Is it true?" asked Indy.

Agnes quickly shook her head. "Of course not!"

"Don't lie to me. I've known you for over ten years."

"I didn't do it, Indy!"

Indy released her grip, turned away, and whimpered, trying her best to hold back frustrated tears. She turned back with a scowl and pointed a finger at Agnes.

"Are you a villain?" Indy asked.

"How could you even ask me that?"

"Answer the question!"

"No! I'm not a villain, Indy. You know me. Please, you know I'm not a villain!" Agnes said through sobs. "Not a villain… I'm just a bad Hero Knight."

She fell to her knees, letting the tears stream. Indy quickly bundled her up in a tight hug, which Agnes desperately reciprocated.

"You're not a bad Hero Knight, Agnes. You're the most dedicated out of all of us," Indy said softly. "I believe you didn't do it. I just needed to hear it from you."

They let go of one another and smiled. Agnes patted Indy on the shoulder and chuckled. Leave it to Indy to make her feel better.

She sighed as the memories of Miss Golden's plans entered her head. "Oh, God, we need to move. Miss Golden and Professor Marron are going to blow up the Department of Chivalry. I just don't know when."

"The Department? Wait a second..." Indy said as she pulled out her smartphone. Agnes watched her swipe. Indy stopped and placed her hand to her mouth.

"What is it?"

"Look!"

Indy's smartphone glowed with a smiling picture of Miss Golden, followed by an ominous caption:

I'll be reporting to the Department of Chivalry today at 8 A.M, and I'll be signing free autographs all day! Hope my fellow Hero Knights can make it!

"Oh, no," Agnes said. "It's happening soon. We've got to go!"

"How are they going to do it?" Indy asked.

"I'll explain on the way!"

Agnes dashed down the street, leaving her fear and despair behind, replacing it with a new objective: Stop Miss Golden at all costs.

Dozens of Hero Knights had already arrived by the time Agnes and Indy made it to the Department. They milled about outside in the sunlight, some on their phones, others practicing their combat skills. Each one of them was surely eager for a chance to meet Miss Golden.

Yesterday, I would've been one of them, Agnes realized. She stuck to the trees nearby, her notoriety still very high from last night. Everything so far seemed rather normal, but it would explode as soon as Miss Golden arrived. Agnes kneeled behind a tree and sighed. Fatigue inched away at her. She shook her head. It was too late to feel tired now.

A luxury limousine pulled up to the front entrance. Wasting no time, Miss Golden exited the car, waving and smiling at the gathering crowds of Hero Knights. She quickly disappeared inside, flanked by her bodyguards and admiring onlookers.

Agnes and her friend snuck up to the side of the building. "We need to find those bombs. Indy, you take the front, and I'll take the high ground. If I remember the layout well enough, they'll be posted toward the middle. Good luck."

Indy nodded and dashed off toward the main entrance. Agnes grappled herself up and searched the roof for anything out of the ordinary. Seconds turned into precious minutes.

Just as Agnes was beginning to panic, she spied a small metal sphere jutting out against the Department's glass dome. Agnes grabbed it, eyeing the large, pulsating red light on its axis, and pressed down on her wrist computer.

"Found mine. It's remote-activated on a specific frequency," Agnes said. "How're you doing?"

"Negative on my end," Indy chimed in.

"Keep looking. I'll try to defuse it before I come down there."

Agnes's celebration lasted only a brief moment, as her wrist computer buzzed and flashed red once again. She turned around and stared directly into the snarling face of Professor Marron. He crawled closer, keeping several of his clawed arms raised and ready to attack.

"For some reason, I knew you'd be here, little worm," he said.

Agnes quickly hid the bomb, clipping it onto her belt behind her. "I can't let you go through with this, Marron. We can figure this out if we just talk about it."

"Ha! There's nothing to talk about. This is what she wants, and it's going to be what she gets," Marron said as he stomped toward the glass dome.

"No, wait! What if I can free you? I'm positive she's hidden a command-and-control module on you. If you tell me where to find the bombs, I promise you, I'll find it and destroy it."

Marron stopped cold. For the briefest of moments, the machine turned to look at her. The red in his eyes disappeared, replaced with almost-human pupils. They were sad, tired, and full of confusion, as if he was wondering how he was still stuck in this situation. He then shook his head and turned back toward the glass.

"The bombs will go off in a few minutes. Do yourself a favor and run as fast as you can," he said, placing his claws on the glass. "Consider this a mercy."

He smashed through the glass, flying down to the surprised screams of the gathered heroes. Agnes fired her grapple gun, attaching it onto Marron's thorax. The force of his entrance violently pulled Agnes, slamming her into one of the dome's support beams. She fell several dozen feet, crashed onto Marron's back, and finally bounced off to the hard, glass-strewn linoleum floor.

A loud gasp echoed from the gathered crowd. Agnes, pain wracking her body, stumbled to her feet. She realized she was in the middle of the lobby, surrounded by Miss Golden, Professor Marron, and the scores of Hero Knights.

"It's that green girl! She's working for the Professor!" a voice called out from the crowd.

"Don't let her hurt Miss Golden!" another called.

"You brought your little enforcer, Marron?" Miss Golden yelled, raising her sword. "Everybody, get them!"

A knight in high-tech pink armor dove at Agnes. She jumped out of the way, only to be met with another in beige armor swinging their ax. Agnes parried with her buckler and knocked that knight away. She ran across the lobby, looking back to see Marron engaging a large swarm of Hero Knights.

Another group cut her off from the cafeteria. One of them rushed her, nearly knocking her off her feet before sliding to the left. A burly knight crashed his hammer down right next to her. Agnes dodged to the side and knocked the knight's hammer away with her sword.

"Agnes! I found the bomb!" Indy cried as she rushed into the fray. She held the pulsating sphere up with her hands. The assembled knights cried out in fear and rushed toward the exits.

"What do we do with them?"

"Give them to me. Get everyone else out. I'll dispose of them," Agnes said.

"And what about... him?" Indy said, pointing at Marron.

Agnes raised her sword. "It's time I slay the dragon."

Indy scrambled out with the group. Agnes and Marron circled each other like two duelists sizing each other up. She breathed heavily, her lungs working overtime. Sweat poured down her face, and her legs ached and burned. Her body yearned for rest, but she ignored it and placed her right foot out, balancing her weight onto her left.

"You've made a grave mistake, little one," he said. "Give me those bombs and I won't have to eviscerate you."

"Marron... it's not too late to surrender," Agnes said.

He snarled and swiped his claws at her. Agnes ducked and swung hard, slicing off his arm near the joint. Marron howled in pain, stepping back. Agnes took the chance and plunged the sword deep into his abdomen, slicing through the wires and pieces of silicon which sustained his vitals. Agnes cut deep and retracted her sword.

Marron swung his arm at her. Agnes dodged, dashed down the corridor, and dove into a supply closet. The machine stomped through the corridor, missing her by several feet before skittering away. Agnes fumbled with the bombs. She stared at them as they glowed in the dark, her arms trembling in fear. An idea popped into her head. These things were designed to be activated at the most precise moment. Miss Golden wouldn't have it any other way. Agnes typed as fast as she possibly could on her wrist computer. If Marron had made the bombs, there was a possibility that they shared similar frequencies.

Just as Agnes finished hacking the explosives, Marron's claw smashed into the closet, pulled her out, and slammed her into the floor. The mechanical arm squeezed tightly. Agnes beat down on Marron's limb, trying to free herself to no avail. Marron raised his other limb and revealed a long, sharp knife.

"The armor is impressive, little worm. I'm sure it'll withstand the blade," he said, inching the knife closer to her face. "But steel still cuts through flesh like butter."

Agnes reached for her belt and unclipped the bombs. She clutched them tightly and shoved them deep into the sword wound. Marron, shocked and confused, loosened his grip, enabling Agnes to grab her sword and slice off Marron's limb.

"Argh! Get them out!" he cried, desperately reaching for the bombs.

"You're welcome!" Agnes cried as she pressed down hard on her computer. The explosion ripped through the Department, reducing the entire lobby to rubble as the roof caved in and support columns collapsed in on themselves. Small fires raged around the lobby by the time Agnes crawled out from the pieces of the destroyed wall.

Marron's wrecked body lay torn asunder, covered in broken pylons and pieces of rebar. Sparks shot out from his machine parts as the whirs and hums of failing circuits slowly faded away. He glanced around and finally spotted Agnes. The look of confusion on his face turned into pure anger.

"Finish me off, then," he said. "Make a name for yourself as the one who finally killed the great Professor Kahill Marron."

Agnes shook her head and raised her sword at Marron. She plunged it into a compartment next to his head. With great effort, she pried the cover off, revealing a pulsating red light connected to several circuits. Agnes ripped the light out and crushed it beneath her boot.

"No, Marron," she said, walking away, "I'd rather be known as the one who saved you."

Pity washed over Agnes as she stared at the incapacitated machine. Mara Villa's most powerful threat was now just a pile of scrap iron and overheated silicon. Agnes was wondering what to do with him, when a sword sliced through his internal components. She stumbled back and watched as Miss Golden retracted her sword, sneering at Marron's idle body.

"Pathetic. Didn't put up as much of a fight as when I placed the controller module on him." Miss Golden scowled.

"I was going to help him!" Agnes cried.

Miss Golden squinted in confusion and pointed her sword at her. "You know, you've caused me a lot of trouble today. I've lost thousands of potential followers and millions in revenue because of your antics."

Agnes saw the growing anger and frustration behind the bright blue eyes she'd once admired. Fear invaded her body. She wanted so badly to run away, leave everything behind for Miss Golden to clean up. There'd be a way for Miss Golden to spin it, Agnes then realized. She'd profit from this and get away with nearly destroying Mara Villa's protection from outside threats.

An idea popped into her head. Agnes reached down for her sword, secretly pressing a small button on her computer as she did, unsheathed her weapon, and raised it at Miss Golden.

"You're... really going to try to fight me?!" Miss Golden chuckled loudly. "A little piece of nothing thinks they can take me on? Who do you think you even are?"

"My name is Lady Verdant," Agnes said confidently, "and I am a Hero Knight of Mara Villa."

Agnes stepped back just as Miss Golden lunged at her. She parried with her sword and buckler, and swung down at Miss Golden. With a quick flick of her wrist, Miss Golden dodged to the side and kicked Agnes back. They eyed each other again and raised themselves into an *en garde* position.

It was Agnes who attacked first, thrusting forward, before Miss Golden dodged, swung her sword low, and sliced into Agnes's side, cutting a deep gash into her armor and her abdomen. Agnes howled and keeled over, grasping her wound. She felt the warm rush of blood.

Miss Golden, not content with finally landing a blow, stomped over to her and cut through Agnes's left leg, driving her sword deep into the linoleum floor. Agnes cried out in pain. She attempted to crawl away, only to be stopped by Miss Golden clamping her knee onto her chest. Agnes struggled to breathe. Pain wracked her body as she struggled to free herself.

"Remind me again what your name was? Oh, that's right. Nobody cares," Miss Golden growled. "And now, you're going to die as a nobody."

Agnes reached out with her hand, trying desperately to choke out some words.

"What was that?" Miss Golden asked.

"L-l-liveeeee...sssssstreaaammm..." Agnes managed to get out.

"Livestream?" Miss Golden said. She looked behind her, and was met with a multitude of Hero Knights and civilians livestreaming the duel with their phones. Miss Golden stood up, keeping her sword pointed at Agnes, and sighed.

"Thank goodness you guys are here. I captured Lady Verdant! She was the one who masterminded the attack on the Department."

The crowd stood there, still filming. Indy shook her head in disapproval.

"Well?" Miss Golden said, growing indignant. "Somebody arrest her!"

They didn't move an inch. Agnes, bleeding and out of breath, stumbled to her feet and snatched Miss Golden's sword away.

"When I said livestream, Rachel, I meant *my* livestream," Agnes explained, raising her wrist computer. "Indy, you do the honors."

"With pleasure, Lady Verdant," Indy said, putting Miss Golden in binds. "Rachel Willoughby, as a representative of the Department of Chivalry, I hereby put you under arrest."

"No, stop it! Let me go!" Miss Golden cried as she was led out of the building by other Hero Knights. "Please, I'll do anything! Stop!"

Agnes could feel nothing but pity at the scrutiny Miss Golden was about to face. Compared to her, Agnes thought she was getting off rather easy.

Then, pain overtook her, and she collapsed backward onto a broken table. Her body cried out in pain and fatigue. Agnes felt the lure of sleepiness overtake her.

"Are you okay, sweetie?" Indy asked her.

Agnes only mustered a thumbs-up before drifting off to sleep.

In the days following the destruction of the Department of Chivalry building, the full extent of Miss Golden's plan was revealed to the general public. People commented that they had never seen a harder fall from grace in all their lives. Miss Golden had her detractors, sure, but even the most hardcore of her haters still felt a twinge of depression. If somebody like her could get corrupted, then who else?

Miss Golden would spend the next fifty years behind bars, unable to even post a single sentence from her prison cell. As for Professor Marron, he'd survived the battle at the building and Miss Golden's final blow. He wound up imprisoned in an air-gapped cyber prison, free to move about his tiny digital space, surviving on drip-fed information about the outside world.

It was more than Agnes Alvarez could have hoped for. He was a mastermind, a cunning villain, and a monster, of course, but still a victim of Miss Golden's drive to stay relevant.

Agnes wouldn't stay idle for long. After her release from the hospital, she enjoyed an increase in notoriety: some good, as she'd been the one to foil Miss Golden's plot, and some bad, as some Hero Knights derided her for robbing them of the city's hero.

Agnes limped down the street in full dress armor, followed by her best friend Indy Indigo. Merchants, delivery people, and random passersby would cry out, "Hello, My Lady!" as a sign of recognition. She'd smile and wave back, happy they weren't waving to Agnes Alvarez, but to Lady Verdant, Hero Knight of Mara Villa.

THOUGHTS ON *BRAVE NEW GIRLS*

"I look back at all the wonderful stories that have been featured over the years with a smile. There are so many different tales that girls can read and find somebody who they can identify with, and hopefully be inspired to go on and do great things. We need to keep pushing those boundaries and keep reaching for the stars, for our daughters, our nieces, our sisters, and anybody else we want to see succeed. I hope I have played but a small part in that."

ABOUT THE AUTHOR

J.R. Rustrian is an author of speculative fiction who lives and works in Southern California. When not writing, you can find him playing video games, cooking, and enjoying the outdoors. He is incredibly proud of being featured in this year's *Brave New Girls,* and can't wait for what next year might bring.

Illustration for "Lady Verdant: Hero Knight of Mara Villa" by Harley Scroggins.

Researching the Behavior and Habits of Terrestrial Exoplanet Fauna

By
Jeanne
Kramer-Smyth

RESEARCHING THE BEHAVIOR AND HABITS OF TERRESTRIAL EXOPLANET FAUNA

JEANNE KRAMER-SMYTH

MY NEW PURPLE IRIDESCENT BOOTS extended halfway up my calf. I could hardly wait to see how the colors might change in natural sunlight. We rarely got to order custom clothing at Magellan Transstellar Boarding School, but our official field trip to the terrestrial exoplanet JP-2056387-h warranted special equipment.

"We'll be doing real research on a planet whose records are incomplete! Scientists will use our samples and data!" Hayden had lobbied as we walked our usual loop through the gardens, sharing snacks. Her short hair was hot pink, and she wore a color-coordinated pink jumpsuit. New boots hadn't been Hayden's first selling point, but it probably should have been! She always preferred wearing a single color—she said it made it easier to get dressed in the morning.

"Sounds dangerous." I ate one pretzel and passed the bag to Jay. I hated sounding afraid, but I also wasn't sure I wanted to go somewhere that might not be safe.

"I bet we'd have to get authorized on a bunch of new equipment." Jay made it sound like that would be a good thing, before he poured the rest of the pretzels directly into his mouth.

"Come on, Alice," Lee encouraged me, "it must not be too dangerous, or they wouldn't let a team of high schoolers land there. Plus, Dr. Tracey already agreed to be our chaperone." Lee knew she was one of my favorite teachers. She was cheerful and smart and treated her students like peers.

"Come on, Alice." Jay joined the chorus. "You know you don't want to go on some other field trip without us." He shoved the empty pretzel bag in his pocket and took my hand in his. "Please?" He stopped walking, kneeling on his long legs so our eyes would be on the same level.

Jay didn't want to go without me. I already knew that. He would go on whatever other field trip I picked—but then he would miss out on getting his hands-on experience with all that equipment.

"Fine." It was hard to see Jay looking so hopeful and say no. I mustered a smile. "I'm in, as long as you promise to share the snacks."

Jay laughed and nodded, jumping back up to his feet. Lee, not as tall as Jay but broader through the shoulder, gave Jay a high-five over my head.

Hayden whooped and skipped ahead, spinning to face us, and called, "I'll go tell Dr. Tracey!"

The month of prep went fast. We had so much to do—and all on top of our regular classes. I started to get excited. We got to put in print requests for our special field trip clothing.

Jay got his wish. We spent hours working through course modules on all the new gear we might need to use on the trip. Everyone did the training on the popup survival shelters, but each of us got to choose a different set of the science equipment coming with us. I picked the nano-sampling tools for plants and soil. Lee trained on piloting the low-flying drones used for mapping. Hayden was excited to get her hands on some new data processing programs. Of course, Jay chose to train on every system in the drop ship. We actually had to bring him food because he kept forgetting to eat. He even did some practice take-offs and landings—in case of an emergency.

The large transport ship swallowed up our drop ship, along with the rest of the supplies and deliveries slated for its route. We were just one stop along the way.

We had gone through a simulation at school of what the drop ship would feel like, but plummeting down to the surface of JP-2056387-h was so much more intense. I felt like I was being devoured by a mountain! Our harnesses held us in place in our well-cushioned seats, but they couldn't absorb all the vibrations.

I was so glad when we reached the surface. I'd read about earthquakes—and I imagined that the sense of stillness I felt was akin to someone adjusting after riding out a massive quake.

Dr. Tracey ran one final scan to confirm that the air outside was fine for us to breathe and that the gravity was at a safe level, before opening the hatch.

I'd been on lots of different planets before, but this was my first undeveloped one. It was very different to just step out of your vessel onto bare ground. Usually, we landed at a port, all built out with concrete and steel. Sometimes, there were elaborate glass terminals that let you see the landscape, but even then, it was a long walk before you were at a park or nature preserve.

Here, we stepped out of the drop ship directly onto a small plateau covered with rocks. The sky stretched forever in all directions, until it met mountains on one side and a broad river valley on the other. A light breeze carried strange new scents to us—distinctly flowers and leaves, but remixed somehow from those I had smelled before.

The sky was greenish-gray, and the local system's sun was a bright white blur high in the sky. Dr. Tracey surveyed the landscape. Tall and tidy, even fresh off our drop ship, her long gray braids shone in the odd light. She doled out things to carry to our campsite, and led us down the hill, along the river, and into the woods. The trees were tall and had very straight trunks, bursting into a canopy of leaves that shielded us from the sunshine as we walked.

We finally made it to a clearing with enough space for our camp. This would be our home for the next week, until the transport ship returned to pick us up. I wasn't used to feeling so disconnected. Usually, I had every person I knew in the universe just a message away.

As dusk fell, we worked on the shelter Jay and Lee were going to share, bolting it to the ground in case of wind. Hayden and Lee were arguing about how far away to put Hayden's and my shelter when I heard a strange sound. A peculiar rumbling and grinding vibration rolling toward us from deeper in the woods.

"What is that..." And then the clearing was full of moving shapes. Large and loud and fast. I saw horns and felt fur brush past me.

"Into the shelter!" yelled Dr. Tracey, waving us toward the structure we had just put up.

We huddled inside, away from the soft walls. The entire thing shook as the large shadows jostled past it. Periodically, the entire pack of whatever they were growled and hooted, enveloping us in sound. It felt like we were in there for so long, but I think the whole thing was over in under five minutes.

Dr. Tracey checked the clearing before she let us out. There was still dust in the air from all the creatures stampeding through the space that was supposed to be our home for the next week. Jay knelt on the ground and traced deep gouges that hadn't been there five minutes ago.

"What are they?" I sat beside him, trying to see what he saw.

"Claw marks," Jay said softly, "I think?"

Each gouge was nearly a foot long, deeper at one end than the other. Everyone else walked over and stared over our shoulders for a moment.

"I don't want us here if they come back!" Dr. Tracey hustled us all back to the drop ship.

The local fauna (a.k.a. "the immense stampeding creatures with shockingly sharp claws") that had emerged at dusk were not supposed to be here. How had the Magellan Transstellar Boarding School scouting team missed something so crucial? Had they failed to understand this planet's seasons? Had these huge creatures been hibernating during the scouting cycle?

Whatever the origin of the mistake, THAT was definitely not the place for us to set up camp.

"Get inside, and stay put. I'm going to go get the shelter modules before those creatures come back and destroy them." Dr. Tracey rarely used her stern teacher voice, but she used it now as she pulled a weapon out of a cabinet and a headlamp from the supplies.

"I can help carry them." Lee actually started to follow her.

"Stay here." This time, Dr. Tracey added a glare I had rarely seen her use. "Monitor the radio." She pointed to a panel near the door, and waved a hand radio before shoving it into her pocket.

Lee stayed. I didn't like the idea of Dr. Tracey out there alone either, especially as the sky grew darker, but she was the grownup. She disappeared over the edge of the plateau, and the four of us clambered back into the ship.

"I guess we could sleep on the floor"—I stood by the radio panel and looked around—"but there isn't much room. The seats don't recline."

"Let's run some fresh scans." Jay was already at the large wall display, tapping on the screen to bring up the maps the scout team had provided us. "Maybe we can find someplace to move to. The transport ship won't be back for a full week."

"What's the range on the drop ship's scanners?" Hayden shifted to watch the screen.

They spent a while reviewing their fresh scans, identifying three possible new landing locations still in the geographic zones we were meant to gather samples from.

"The creatures are back!" Dr. Tracey's voice came over the radio, loud and panicked. "They're back and have me surrounded!"

With that, the radio crackled and went silent.

"Dr. Tracey?" I tried to remember the way I was supposed to talk on the radio, but right then none of that seemed to matter. "Are you okay? What should we do?"

But she didn't answer. It took maybe thirty seconds for us to dole out headlamps and pull more weapons from the locker. I found myself holding a defensive stunner. They were easy to use, but I had no idea if they would do anything to a massive alien animal.

We set out, following the same route as we had only a few hours ago. We had just found the river when a flare exploded loud and bright above the trees. We wanted to run, but finding our way in the dark wasn't easy.

I thought that the clearing had to be just ahead when the screaming began. It was awful. Heart-wrenching and terrifying. A sound unlike any I'd ever heard— like from a horror movie, not reality.

Lee's long legs brought him to Dr. Tracey before the rest of us could even see the clearing. The flare's explosion must have scared the animals away. By the time my short legs and I caught up, the creatures were gone. For now.

There was too much blood. More blood than I had ever seen outside of a science lab video. It was bright and scattered across the ground. The air smelled metallic. And of fear.

Dr. Tracey was conscious, but so pale, and obviously trying to put on a brave face for us. Lee and Jay slung their weapons on their backs, and each put one of our teacher's arms over a shoulder. They walked her back toward the shuttle as fast as they could. I raced ahead of them while Hayden guarded our backs.

First, I found the first-aid kit. It had all the basics for minor injuries. Bandages, burn ointment, slings, and a dozen fluid packs for treating dehydration. It even included all the things you would need to give a blood transfusion. If one of us had been a medic, maybe we could have treated her wounds with what was in this kit. But none of us were trained on anything beyond the most basic first aid.

Next, I found the manual for the on-ship bio-suspension pod. Holding my breath, I flipped the thick plastic pages and read as fast as I could. The passage I needed was near the end, but it explained how the pod could be used to stabilize someone with an injury for brief transit to proper medical care.

Lee scooped Dr. Tracey up in his arms and whisked her through the doorway. He set her down as gently as he could into one of the seats. I ignored the blood and the gashes and the panicked look in Dr. Tracey's eyes.

"I think the BioPod is the best bet." I gestured to the pod compartment at the back of the vessel. "The manual says it works best without bandages in the way."

"Do we need to take off her clothes?" Jay asked awkwardly, shuffling away from the possibility that he would have to help do such a thing.

"Yes," said Hayden, as she set down her weapon and pulled the external hatch closed. "You and Lee get back to figuring out where else we might set up camp."

They left fast. I avoided looking at the bloody footprints that Lee left as he went.

"I can help." I approached Dr. Tracey. "We need to get your clothes off, ma'am. I am so sorry, but none of us are medics, and the BioPod should stabilize you until the ship comes to pick us up."

She nodded, trying to take off her jacket. Her hands shook too hard, and the blood made everything slippery. Hayden and I managed to strip her down to her underwear before half-dragging her back to the BioPod. Somehow, we got her inside.

"I trust you four," she said before the pod closed over her face. "Take care of each other."

With a click and a soft whir, the BioPod engaged, automatically hooking up her veins and arteries to the pod's internal systems for monitoring. The display showed a reassuring set of health markers. Dr. Tracey was safe. For now.

It was a strange night. We ate some protein bars that we found on the ship and took turns watching the unchanging life stats on the BioPod display. Jay found a new location that was still in the sampling zone. It had no reports of native fauna from the scouts, and the scans that he ran all night showed nothing alarming.

I slept in my drop ship seat, but not well. All was still when I woke up—confused until I remembered enough to be scared again. Hayden convinced us we should go back to our original campsite one final time, in daylight, to retrieve the shelter modules. We dug through the weapons locker until we found the largest weapons that we had been trained on.

In under an hour, we walked there, packed everything up, ignored the claw marks and blood on the ground, and dragged it all back to the landing site.

We all breathed a collective sigh of relief when Jay successfully launched and navigated the drop ship to the new spot, an entire continent away from our original site. It took five hours to get there, flying over mountains and a large body of water.

I walked the perimeter of our new campsite for a third time. It felt practical. Useful. It helped me not think every second about how to make sure we all survived this trip. The spot Jay had found us had enough room by the ship to set up the shelter modules. None of us wanted to sleep too far from Dr. Tracey, but Jay and Lee were both so tall that sleeping on the floor inside the ship just wasn't feasible. And neither of them had managed more than a cat nap last night while trying to sleep in the seats.

Hayden swore she had a plan. Jay and Lee were digging through every storage compartment of the drop ship, taking stock, while Hayden had set up a command center just outside the BioPod.

"Come on the field trip, Alice," I muttered to myself. "It will be fun, Alice. We'll get to see someplace most people never get to go. It'll be a break from school." I resisted counting my steps as I stalked the path I had plotted. It was just far enough from our landing spot to be worth guarding, and just close enough that I could still see the ship with every step.

School and the transport ship all felt absurdly far away. Here and now was all that mattered. And finding a way home without Dr. Tracey to guide us. The transport ship would come back to get us in seven days. But they would look in the wrong place, at least to start. And the BioPods were really only meant for long journeys—they didn't actually do any healing, so who knew what state Dr. Tracey would be in when we were found?

My purple boots still felt strange. They were well-suited to the irregular surface of this planet. The necessary ankle support made them much taller than anything I'd worn at school, where all the surfaces were smooth and flat. This planet's surface crunched underfoot. Some parts of the perimeter path sloped up, while others sloped down. With each lap, it felt more like an obstacle course I was practicing, and less like I was guarding anything or anyone.

I completed the third lap and went to find Lee.

"Can you program a drone to be our sentry?" I found Lee and Jay with stacks of mysterious containers they had pulled from the drop ship's storage. "Could it alert us if it saw a large animal or a big group of moving things?"

"Huh." Lee's hands stopped moving as he stared off into the middle distance. "Yeah, I don't see why not."

"I've been walking a perimeter, but I don't think I would spot anything in time to help."

"No, no." Lee shook his head. "A drone is perfect for this job." I gave him a hand up from his spot on the floor.

I left him to his drones and found Hayden still sitting on the floor by the BioPod that held Dr. Tracey, an extra-large tablet on her lap.

"Come look." Hayden patted the floor beside her.

"What have you found?" I leaned against the wall and slid down until I was just to her left.

"Well"—she tipped her tablet so I could see it—"we have plenty of food and water."

"That sounds good."

"It is definitely in the 'good news'"—she made air quotes—"column."

"Which means there is a 'bad news' column." I air-quoted back.

"Well, Dr. Tracey"—Hayden tapped on the door to the BioPod over her head—"is counting on us to get her to medical help as soon as possible, but the transport ship isn't due back for a week."

"Can't we call it back early somehow?"

"There is a radio on this drop ship, but it is short range. It's only meant for us to use during our work here on the planet."

"Can we boost the signal somehow?"

"Maybe you and Jay can try and figure that out?"

"I'll bug him when he's done with his inventory. What other ideas do you have?"

"If we can't boost the radio we have, maybe we can build something we can put out into orbit?"

"You want to build a communications satellite?"

"And launch it," added Hayden.

"Build and launch a communications satellite?" I repeated.

"Yes." Hayden brandished her confident smile.

"And I'm assuming we can't steal parts from the drop ship to build it?"

"That would probably be smart, since the fastest way back up the gravity well to the transport ship is back the way we came."

"Let's go find Lee. I asked him to rig one of his drones as a sentry. And Jay is probably done with his inventory by now."

It didn't take long to gather outside the drop ship. Lee launched the sentry drone, and I breathed a huge sigh of relief.

"Great idea, Alice," said Jay, eyes on the drone as it started its first circuit.

"Thanks. I just didn't know what I was going to do if I saw something anyway. This way, we'll have some warning, and time to decide how to defend ourselves."

"Now that we are safe," Hayden pronounced, "we need to figure out if we can get someone to pick us up early. I'm worried that Dr. Tracey's injuries are too severe for the BioPod to keep her stable for a full week."

"She wants us to build and launch a communications satellite!" I blurted.

Lee and Jay laughed until they saw that Hayden was serious.

"A drone I can manage." Lee gestured to the one he had just launched. "But a satellite?"

"It would need special shielding," said Jay, "even if we could get it off the ground."

"And if we got it off the ground and it didn't burn up on its way through the atmosphere"—I counted on my fingers—"we would need the communications part to actually send a message far enough that anyone would notice."

"Well, what do you want us to do?" Hayden threw up her hands. "Just wait and hope Dr. Tracey doesn't die?"

"I'm more worried about the transport finding us now that we are so far away from where we're supposed to be."

"Both of those are real problems." Jay moved between us, then pulled us both into a hug. "She's going to be okay. We'll figure this out."

"Let's set up the shelters and eat a real meal," suggested Lee. "I bet we'll think more clearly once we have some food and take a nap. Those seats in the drop ship were not conducive to restful sleep last night."

"I'm amazed you slept at all!" I answered from the middle of our group hug. "I'm the smallest, and it definitely wasn't comfortable, even for me."

Jay waved Lee toward us. We opened the circle and pulled him into the hug. We cried a little, and then ended up laughing when Lee used his arms around all of us to tip us a bit from side to side. The sort of laughter that comes from being too tired and hungry, but still with people you trust.

We split up and set up the shelters—one for Lee and Jay, and one for Hayden and me. Side-by-side and only a few feet from the drop ship. Then Lee figured out how to set up the portable kitchen and surprised us with a hot lunch. The sun was high, and the breeze was light. This location smelled different than the first one, which, given the scary creatures over there, was quite reassuring.

With full stomachs, we went back to planning. I turned the largest screen in the drop ship into a brainstorming board.

"I think we have three possible scenarios." I used a stylus on the touch surface of the massive screen to make a list. "We wait for the transport ship and hope they find us. We find a way to call them back faster. We wait for the transport ship and come up with a way to help them find us faster."

"I love Hayden's idea about a communications satellite," said Jay, "but I don't think we have the raw materials, or things we can safely scavenge from the ship, to build something like that. And even if we did, it would probably take longer than the week we have to wait anyway."

"Darn," said Hayden, folding her arms and sighing.

"Could we go back to the old site?" I wrote *fly back* with a question mark and turned to check with Jay. "Right before the transport ship is scheduled to arrive?"

"Umm." He looked a bit sheepish. "Not enough fuel for that. I made sure we have enough to get back up to where the transport can grab us, but I really wanted to make sure we were very far away from those creatures."

"Ah." I turned back to look at my list. "So no flying back." I crossed out *fly back?* and stared at my list.

"Won't they just scan the planet for us?" asked Lee.

"Probably." Jay shrugged. "They'll try. But our little spot here is so far from where we were supposed to be."

"There has to be an emergency beacon on this thing." Hayden gestured to Jay. "Didn't they train you on that?"

"I don't remember anything about a beacon." Jay stepped over to one of the terminals with keyboards and started tapping. "I'll look. Keep going, and I'll let you know if I find something."

"Okay." I wrote *emergency beacon* with a question mark.

"If we're going to stay the whole week anyway, we should at least collect samples for the scientists," said Lee.

Hayden perked up a bit at that. "I like that idea, since we don't have to spend a week trying to build a satellite." She winked at me.

I felt this wash of relief. I hadn't realized how stressed I'd been that Hayden's idea hadn't been feasible.

"Right." I wrote *build a satellite* and then crossed it out. "No satellite building."

The BioPod started beeping. I shoved the stylus in my pocket as we all raced over to stare at the BioPod's readout.

There were a few numbers flashing red, and an alarming line of text looping: *INJURY DETECTED. TRANSFER SUBJECT TO MEDICAL POD ASAP.*

"It just figured it out?" I asked, pushing the *ACKNOWLEDGE* button and silencing the alarm. "Dr. Tracey has been in there for hours."

"I don't know how these things actually work inside," said Lee, "and none of us got actual training on it, right?" He looked around at all of us.

We all shook our heads.

"I read the instructions." I pulled the binder back out to show them all. "But there isn't a lot in here beyond how to put someone in and take someone out."

"I wonder what else I have in my own library." Hayden turned her tablet back on and settled into her seat. "I have so much saved on here—let me look."

"You think you have information about this BioPod on your tablet?"

"Not specifically." Hayden shook her head. "No. Of course not. But maybe I have info about how BioPods work—or a research paper about how they hope to improve them."

"Wow!" Lee was suddenly digging in his bag. "I've got so much archived on here." He pulled his laptop out with a flourish. "Who knows what might be able to help?"

I left the two of them with their noses deep in their devices. Jay was still hunting for the beacon we were counting on. So I went back to the big screen and switched it to a search interface.

The drop ship had a very extensive library to support the planned sampling mission we were on. Videos and diagrams and how-to guides about how to use every sampling kit on board, and then some. The next library I found was actually about servicing the drop ship itself. If we had to make any repairs, it had everything we needed, including instructions about how to find or 3-D print a wide range of tools. It was in this section that I finally found the BioPod documentation. With a cheer of victory, I expanded the listings to fill the wall and worked my way through my discovery.

It was definitely not intended as a medical bay. It couldn't even apply first aid. But what it could do was accept inputs, like fluids and liquid food, to sustain someone for more than a day.

"Hayden," I called, "do you have the full suite of nano-programming libraries on your tablet?" Maybe the nano dust—tiny particles that can be programmed to do all sorts of different things—could help?

She came over to the huge display, trying to make sense of the wall of file listings, paused videos, and diagrams. "What are you trying to do?"

"Well, I brought six full nano dust kits—in case there was something interesting we could do with it here. And I have my favorite programming suites on my computer, but not the full catalog of libraries. More libraries would let me code them to do more different things."

"I have a few, but not everything. Lee?" Hayden called. "Do you have nano-programming libraries in your archives?"

He joined us at the display, followed by Jay, who had gotten curious about what we were all up to. "I have lots of things on there. I would have to dig once you explain what you're trying to do."

"So," I turned to their hopeful faces, "I have six sets of my nano-dust with me. Each container of the dust-sized particles can be programmed to do virtually anything. Most of what you guys have seen the nano-dust do is visual. Floating lights turning on and off and changing color. But nano-dust can do lots of other things—including medical stuff."

"We can give Dr. Tracey nano first aid?" Jay's eyes were wide, and he sounded excited.

"Maybe? But we could also make things worse? We aren't doctors."

"True," agreed Lee, "but the warnings from the BioPod make it sound like attempting first aid might be better than doing nothing but waiting and hoping."

I had everyone load all the nano-coding libraries they could find into a coding space I set up on the drop ship's server. It was hard to not get distracted by all the different things I could do, but the BioPod I could see in my peripheral vision helped keep me focused.

Hayden and Lee dug through the BioPod's manuals until they worked out how to give Dr. Tracey fluids from our big first aid kit, using one of the ports below the display. Jay figured out that there was an emergency beacon that should at least enable the transport ship to look at the right continent.

Lee made us all stop and eat as dusk fell. I went back to work, coding and running simulations, until Jay dragged me outside to see the stars and the two moons high in the sky. I thought I would never fall asleep, my mind buzzing with ideas for the code, but it had been a very long day. Had we really only landed on this planet yesterday?

I fell asleep amazed at that thought, and woke up to the smell of breakfast. Did they make me pancakes?

Yes, they did! Lee gave me a huge stack, with butter and syrup. I inhaled it even faster than Jay normally would. Everyone was impressed.

My first attempt at code that would turn the dust into something that could heal a wound was done and downloaded into my first canister of nano-dust before lunch. As I was about to cut my arm to test it, Jay stopped me and stepped in as my guinea pig. It was a small cut, but it did bleed. I poured some of the dust on his cut, and we all watched, holding our breaths.

"It tickles," said Jay.

"Don't touch it!" I grabbed his other hand.

We kept watching. But it never did more than tickle him. The blood dried, and the cut scabbed over, but it wasn't healed the way I had hoped. Alpha versions of anything usually needed a lot more work.

Version Two took another three hours of coding and importing two new libraries. One added clearer instructions for micro-stitching torn or cut skin. The other consumed dried blood to make sure we could see it was working.

Jay was less happy to cut himself a second time—but the new version worked! The second cut rapidly became a small, smooth scar. Then it kept going. It removed all the dried blood from the first cut—and its scab, making it bleed again. Just as Jay was starting to freak out about it, the nano-dust kept going and sealed the original cut too.

I wiped off his arm with a version of liquid soap that I had turned into a nano-deactivation fluid with my third batch of nano-dust. That made sure that everything from my healing dust would stop trying to fix things.

A full day had passed since Dr. Tracey had been attacked. Hayden kept administering fluids to the BioPod, but her vital signs continued to drop. With my fourth batch of nano-dust, I knew we could handle all the open wounds, but what about the blood she'd already lost?

"How do we figure out Dr. Tracey's blood type? Do you all know your blood types?" My out-of-context question caught everyone off guard. "I think she is going to need a transfusion once all her wounds are healed."

"I don't remember mine." Jay shrugged. "Anyone else?"

None of us knew.

"That is private health data," Hayden said. "It is going to be very locked down in the drop ship's systems—if it's there at all."

"My turn," said Lee. He pulled some cables out of his bag and opened his laptop again. Lee's mom was a famous ambassador, and he had bounced around from school to school before finding his home at Magellan. He had learned lots of hacking techniques along the way. He'd sworn he usually only used them to get him access to stuff that he would eventually get access to anyway—he was just impatient.

He hard-wired himself into the dashboard of the drop ship and sat in the pilot's chair to do his work. Hayden, Jay, and I cooked dinner, and by the time it was ready, he reappeared, ready to eat.

"Ok. Hayden is type A positive. Alice is B positive. Jay's A negative." He pointed to us each in turn. "And I'm O negative."

"What type is Dr. Tracey?" I asked.

"I couldn't get into her medical records. Teacher records are harder to hack."

"So, now what?" asked Jay.

"Now, you figure out how to take my blood to give to her." He pointed at himself. "O negative is the universal donor. It doesn't matter what type she is."

We hugged and danced around before eating our food too quickly. It was dusk again when we finished.

The transfusion kit included for first aid was scary to contemplate, mostly consisting of tubes and bags and a few needles. It turned out that the transfusion would be easy—we had all the right tools, and Hayden had discovered that the BioPod had a transfusion port next to the fluids port. So, with Lee's arm standing by, we were ready.

Getting my coded nano-healing paste into the BioPod and onto our teacher's skin was hard. We didn't want to wake her up or take her out of the pod, but it wasn't designed to permit the application of anything to the skin.

I had to add another component to the code. Instead of applying the nano-paste to the skin, I had to figure out a way to get the paste to apply itself and stay on the outside of the body. The first batch of the self-applying paste, using canister four, was almost perfect. I had only forgotten to include sensors to make it be drawn to the smell of skin and blood, and avoid inanimate surfaces.

Batch five worked exactly the way we needed it to. This time, Hayden offered up her arm for testing. She sat in her seat on the drop ship, her arm bleeding from a small cut. I put a dollop of the paste from batch five on her shoulder, where it met the plastic of the chair. The paste avoided the chair and moved down her arm to heal the cut. Once the cut was healed, it continued to wander across Hayden's skin, until it encountered her clothing. She was especially brave when I put a tiny bit on her cheek to make sure it stayed out of her eyes, nose, and mouth, but it did. I think it actually healed a small cut she had been picking at on her neck!

So, we had everything we needed. All that was left was to put our plan into action. Jay agreed to monitor the ship's systems and make sure that we didn't trigger any alarms. Lee sat on the floor next to the pod, ready to donate his blood.

I used the emergency lever to open the BioPod's hood. A blaring alarm went off. I ignored it. The smells of blood and sweat rose up out of the pod. I ignored them too.

As quickly as I could, I scooped some of batch five onto a few parts of Dr. Tracey's body, trying to get places near the worst of her wounds. One scoop on her left arm, one on her right. Another larger one on her stomach. And one more on each of her legs. It took less than a minute, and then the hood was back down, and the terrifying sights and smells of our teacher were locked away again behind the cool smooth surface of the hood.

I went back to the large display wall, patching into the few cameras inside the pod. Hayden got Lee hooked up to donate his blood, using the BioPod's indicators to make sure we didn't take too much. We needed to heal Dr. Tracey, not hurt Lee.

The nano-dust moved so much more slowly than I wanted it to, but it did move. It slid across her skin, until it encountered the gashes and bites from the huge creatures that had cornered her at our first campsite. It took longer to heal them than it had taken to heal the superficial cuts we had tested with, but I had expected that. As the wounds closed and Lee's blood began to replace what Dr. Tracey had lost, her stats got better. Her blood pressure rose out of the danger zone. Her breathing became more regular. Her limbs relaxed.

I couldn't stop watching, until it looked like everything was as healed as it was going to be. I had made sure that my code forced healing from the deepest part of a cut outward to the surface of the skin, so when all that was left were scars, I knew batch five had done as much as it could.

And then we woke her up. We had argued about it for a long time while we waited for the healing to be done, but we finally agreed that we could always put her back under sedation if she was in too much pain or something, but she was the adult. She would want to be back out in the world and able to help us as soon as she could be.

We let the BioPod do it, with its guided sequences of tests and gentle administration of sedation counteragents.

"Are we still on the planet?" she asked as we wrapped a blanket around her. We helped her out of the BioPod and into a seat. She was looking at her skin, trying to find the wounds she remembered receiving. I used my nano-deactivation fluid to clean the paste off her skin and disposed of it into one of the empty canisters.

"Yes," I answered. "I coded the nano-dust to heal you so we could wake you up."

"Amazing," Dr. Tracey said softly, running her hands over her new scars.

"What blood type are you?" asked Lee.

"B negative. Why?"

"Ah, ha! Good thing we gave you my blood. I'm O negative. Universal donor," Lee said proudly, pointing to the small bandage in the crook of his elbow.

"You gave me a transfusion?"

"Yes," I said. "You lost a lot of blood, so just healing your wounds wasn't enough. And the BioPod kept saying alarming things about transferring you to a medical bay. But we didn't have a medical bay. So we did this instead," I finished in a rush.

"Of course, you might have other injuries. Broken bones?" said Hayden. "Or internal injuries? Did they run into you or crush you?"

"No. Just fangs and claws. And then I managed to get the flare to go off, and I guess that scared them away."

We'd done it. She was awake and talking to us, and we hadn't had to spend a week worrying that she was slowly dying in that pod.

She hugged us each gently, looking into our faces one by one and telling us we had done such a good job.

Jay and Lee set up her shelter, so she could sleep in an actual bed. The two moons crested the horizon just in time to cast a beautiful silvery glow over our late-night meal.

We spent the rest of our time on JP-2056387-h collecting all the data and samples that we could, while conspiring to keep Dr. Tracey from working too hard. We took turns "spontaneously volunteering" to be her assistant.

I used my last batch of nano-dust to create an illuminated circle around our camp for the transport ship to see. The emergency beacon would probably have been enough, but I wanted to make sure they found us quickly. I remembered reading about people stranded on an island on Earth creating a signal fire to get the attention of passing ships.

Batch six was our signal fire.

After we returned to Magellan, I kept wearing my purple boots. I didn't really need them. The Magellan space station's corridors were flat and even and smooth. Even the paths in the central gardens were absolutely flat.

But they were the most fantastic shiny purple. I put matching beads in my hair. Purple was definitely my favorite color now.

Dr. Tracey thought my nano-healing paste should be standard issue for field trips, but it needed a lot more official testing by scientists with actual medical training.

And the creatures that had attacked our camp and Dr. Tracey? They were usually totally docile and calm. Our first campsite had been less than a five-minute walk from their nesting grounds.

Now, the scientists knew which one week a year was their breeding season.

THOUGHTS ON *BRAVE NEW GIRLS*

"Growing up, I happily missed the memo that math and science were for boys. I was on the math team and I cloned carrots for a science fair project. I hope that seeing tenacious, smart, clever girls solving problems and saving the day with STEM will broadcast that STEM is for girls too."

ABOUT THE AUTHOR

Jeanne Kramer-Smyth (she/her) has been writing since she first got her hands on a typewriter at age nine. She is an archivist by day, and a writer, photographer, and fan of board games by night. She lives in Maryland with her husband, son, and two cats. You can learn more about her at https://www.jeannekramersmyth.com/.

Illustration for "Researching the Behavior and Habits of Terrestrial Exoplanet Fauna" by Kay Wrenn.

GIRLS RULE THE THE SOLARPUNK WORLD!

IRA NAYMAN

GIRLS RULE THE SOLARPUNK WORLD!

IRA NAYMAN

Meanwhile, in a universe 2,137 90-degree angles to the right and 150 90-degree angles inward…

"YOU CAN'T DO THAT!" EDDY27 barked.

"But… but… but… but… science!" Jennifer protested.

"Will science save you if the Council—if your gene mother—finds out what you're doing?"

"Science can do a lot of things," Jennifer stated, although not as definitively as she would have liked.

"You worry too much," FLO14 purred.

"Thank you," Jennifer said, appreciating the support.

"We're not the ones who are going to get in trouble if this little science experiment goes sideways," FLO14 finished her thought, then licked the back of her leg.

FLO14 (short for Feline Lingual Oddity) and EDDY27 (short for Edified Dog Doing Yoga) were descendants of the pets who had been modified during the Genetics Debacle Era (not to be confused with the Artificial-Intelligence-Enhanced Robot Pet Era, which was a completely different Debacle). Not only did they have opposable thumbs (forcing their humans to hide the treats so they didn't open the bags and gorge themselves on tasty goodness) and enhanced intellects (now, cats can solve complex mathematical equations in their heads—they just can't be bothered to; maybe after they take a nap—no promises), but their vocal apparatuses had been modified so that they could talk (boy, did people have their motivations wrong, as humanity quickly discovered to its embarrassment).

FLO14, a Persian cat, sounded like an eternally aggrieved Shakespearean actor. Bulldog EDDY27 was so enthusiastic that he always sounded like he wanted to lick the whole world.

Jennifer Gudrundottir gave them a side-eyed look. Jennifer was famous for the breadth and depth of her looks. This look said: *Oh, hush, you two. I have important work to do here, and there's no room for doubters. Say another word, and there will be no treats tonight!*

FLO14 harrumphed but did not say another word. EDDY27 shook his head sadly but was already salivating at the mere mention of treats in a look, so he did not say another word either.

When she was four years old, Jennifer had been introduced to the scientific method:

THE SCIENTIFIC METHOD

1. Observate of the natural world

2. Develop a hypothesis that explains the observations

3. Design an experiment to test the hypothesis

4. Experiment either contradicts the hypothesis, in which case a new hypothesis must be formulated that better explains the observations, or confirms the hypothesis, in which case, party!

She immediately fell in love with it. Using the scientific method, you could explain anything! When Jennifer was six, she observed that Helen Amydottir hadn't come to her birthday party. Jennifer hypothesized that it was because Helen was jealous that Jennifer was learning her studies faster and getting better grades than her. So, party! Not, as it happened, because Jennifer was correct: Helen hadn't come to her party because she had a wicked bad cold, and her birth mother didn't want her to give it to anybody else. But, birthday, so party anyway.

Today, Jennifer faced a problem that was a little trickier.

1. OBSERVATION: Jennifer's gene mother, Gudrun, had been… weird lately. Like the time Jennifer had come home with a B in her botany exam. She'd been expecting fireworks. A major explosion like: "That's the best you can do? Jennifer Gudrundottir, you're a crushing disappointment to me!" Or something really colorful like: "Goddess dammit, Jennifer! How do you ever expect to take my place if you get marks as poor as these!" Instead, Mama Gudrun came up with something of a dud: "Oh. Well, I'm sure you

tried your best. Maybe you'll do better next time." *Who are you and what have you done with my gene mother?!!!!!*

2. HYPOTHESIS: Mama Gudrun's work for the Council of Three was making her weird. She was spending more and more time in Council meetings, and when she came home, she seemed tired. Okay, Mama Gudrun was ancient—she was almost forty!—so that might have had something to do with it. Still. More than tired, she looked... defeated. Jennifer found that fact scarier than stories of The Fall (or The Collapse or The Great and Terrible Bad Thing We Did to Ourselves and The Planet, depending on which of her mothers was telling the story).

3. EXPERIMENT: Break into her office and look at videos of Council meetings to see what had happened that was making Mama Gudrun so upset.

Jennifer had kludged together a makeshift device for bypassing the security on the door to her mother's office. It would trick the sensor by the side of the door into thinking that her mother had put her eye to it. Jennifer had taken the faceplate off the sensor and attached wires from the kludge to wires inside the security device. It should open the door any second now.

Any second now.

Gudrun Eleanoradottir had been chosen by the people to sit on the Council of Three. She had no aspirations to be the Presidentess, also known as the Council of One; she was allergic to criticism, which made her break out in anger. She had been promoted to the Council of Three, the body which set priorities for the community, because of her stellar work on the Council of Twelve, the body which passed rules, allotted resources, and set the direction for the community. Smart enough to be an engineer/seamstress/farmer/opera singer (with so few people left alive, everybody was obligated to multitask), she had avoided sitting on the Council of One Hundred Sixty-Four, which was where troublemakers were put to keep them busy, while people who cared about the community did the actual job of running it.

Jennifer had known that something was wrong, terribly, terribly wrong, for weeks, but whenever she'd asked about it, her gene mother had sighed and told her she would understand when she grew up. So unfair! Jennifer was plenty grown up—she was almost fifteen!

The last time Mama Gudrun had used the "you'll understand when you're grown up" line on her, Jennifer had stomped off to her room in a huff. When she calmed down, she realized her behavior might have proven her mother's point, but she would never have admitted it. Not admitting things was, she thought, very adult of her.

In any case, Jennifer knew that if she didn't take matters into her own—

BEEP! A red light on the sensor turned green, and the door to the office quietly whooshed open.

"Apparently, I *can* do this," Jennifer gloated, as she disconnected the kludge wires and screwed the sensor's faceplate back in place.

"You *know* that's not what we were objecting to!" FLO14, grooming accomplished and sitting regally by Jennifer's side, pointed out.

"Did you say something about treats?" EDDY27 asked, his tail wagging furiously, his drool puddling on the wooden floor.

FLO14 rolled her eyes. "Do try to pay attention to what's important!" she admonished the cuddly canine.

Ignoring them, Jennifer walked into the room, making a beeline for the desk on which her mother's comm sat. On those rare occasions when she had been invited into the room, she'd inched in with awe and respect (but mostly awe). There was an impressionistic tapestry of a busy city street on one wall, which always made Jennifer feel like she had missed out on something special, even though she couldn't really say what it was (or make out many of its details). On the opposite wall was a bookcase full of yellowing tomes by long-dead authors. The desk was a solid piece of wood. Everything in the room screamed, "Respect me!" and Jennifer had always obeyed.

But not today. Today, she was on a mission. A SCIENCE mission. How important was the mission? When she opened her gene mother's comm, she didn't check the email to see if there was anything about her, but searched for a folder of videos instead. *That* was how seriously she took SCIENCE!

When she found the folder with videos of meetings of the Council of Three, Jennifer opened the one that had the most recent timestamp: three days ago. The meeting was held around the kitchen table of Roseanne Rosannadannadottir, who was the current Presidentess. (The Council of Twelve met in Carlotta Tzipporahdottir's barn, which looked surprisingly comfortable, with the members lounging on hay bales or sitting on milking stools. The Council of One Hundred Sixty-Four met virtually by comm.)

"Okay, I've almost got this set up..." Jennifer heard Roseanne Rosannadannadottir say over a murkily dark screen. Then, the woman backed away, removing her hand from in front of the camera lens, and Jennifer could make out the warm kitchen, with its wooden cabinets, wood-burning stove, and steel sink (because wood can only do so much in life). Hung on a peg by the door which led out of the building was a pair of aviator goggles.

Gudrun Eleanoradottir sat so straight in her chair at the table that you would be forgiven for thinking her spine was a ruler. On her face was the stern expression she always wore, an expression that said she had judged you and found you wanting before she had even met you. The black braids of hair that fell on either side of her face reminded people of columns in ancient Greek buildings. On the table in front of her was a cup expelling a gentle mist.

Roseanne Rosannadannadottir walked over to the table and sat opposite Jennifer's gene mother. The Presidentess of the Council of Three was just over four feet tall, with shaggy brown hair that seemed to add another foot and a half to her height. Her brown eyes and thin lips were surrounded by the crinkle of crepe paper, a sure sign that she loved to laugh. Next to the cup on the table in front of her was a gavel, lest anybody forget her position.

Hermione Fumikodottir was just thirty-two, one of the youngest members of the community to ever be chosen to sit on the Council of Three. Her acute awareness of this fact showed in the way she bit her full lower lip, or nervously ran her hand through her short blond hair, or burned her palate because she tried drinking the tea without letting it cool down. She sat between the two older women, her eyes ping-ponging from one to the other.

"We have to deal with—" Hermione Fumikodottir started.

"We absolutely will." Roseanne Rosannadannadottir cut her off. "But we have to start the meeting before we can have discussions. Roberta's rules, you understand."

Hermione Fumikodottir lowered her head as the Presidentess took a long, satisfying sip of tea from her mug. When she was done, she put it down and banged the gavel on the table. "I now call this meeting of the Council of Three to order."

"As I was saying," Hermione Fumikodottir looked up to continue, "we must deal with the—"

"Now, now," Roseanne Rosannadannadottir interrupted again. "Hermione, you know we have an agenda. We must follow the agenda, or all will be chaos. And if recent history is our guide, we certainly do not want that."

Chastened, the younger Council member put her hands around her cup and stared deeply into it. "Now, under old business, we start with the matter of the maximal distribution of seeds to ensure enough crops to last us the winter. As you may recall, Eileen Edwidgedottir has complained that..."

Jennifer was not interested in the maximal distribution of seeds, or what Eileen Edwidgedottir had to say about it, so she fast-forwarded the video. Jennifer giggled—as they always did, the figures on the screen looked like they were puppets being controlled by a particularly inept puppeteer. When she noticed that her gene mother looked very angry, she dropped back into play mode.

"...doing the best I can!" Gudrun Eleanoradottir was shouting. "This is a delicate matter—I can't just walk up to members of the community and ask, 'Are you stealing power from the grid?'"

"Why not?" Hermione Fumikodottir hotly retorted. "Your 'gentle inquiries' haven't gotten us anywhere!"

"You know why not!" Gudrun Eleanoradottir shouted back. "It will divide the community if members start to question whether their neighbor is stealing power from them!"

Roseanne Rosannadannadottir pounded the table with the gavel. Jennifer made time stand still (okay, she paused the video, but she preferred to think of it her way). Somebody in the community stealing power from the grid? That was unheard of. Most buildings were constructed with solar panels, which produced a majority of the power they needed. This was augmented by the wind turbines that had been built by the lake. Their output was transmitted by power lines to the community, where it was distributed to members on an as-needed basis. If somebody was draining the power without approval—it was unthinkable!

But the Council of Three was thinking it. And now, so was Jennifer. She thought:

1. OBSERVATION: Power is being drained from the grid without Council of Twelve approval.

2. HYPOTHESIS: There must be a leak in the transmission lines. Maybe one was cut by a storm or something.

Jennifer started the recording again. Once the tumult had died down, Roseanne Rosannadannadottir stated, "We've already been through this. We are not receiving the amount of electricity that the wind turbines should be generating at this time of year. System checks have shown that the structural integrity of the system is intact." (*Okay, scratch that hypothesis.*) "I'm afraid that, unless a member of the Council has any other ideas, we have to assume that somebody has found a way to tap into the transmission lines and… steal electricity from the community."

Jennifer paused the video again. *I have a better idea!* her brain screamed. *I have lots of better ideas! It could be—I mean, it has to be that—it can't be that somebody is stealing! There has to be another reason! There has to be—*

"I must say I'm not surprised, but I am disappointed."

Don't turn around! Don't turn around! This isn't happening if you don't turn around to face it. Whatever you do, DON'T TURN AROUND!

Jennifer turned around.

Gudrun Eleanoradottir stood in the doorway of the room, hands on her hips, severe expression on her lips. More severe than usual, I mean. "Apparently, I—"

["You injected a personal comment into the narrative, dear," a warm voice stated. "I really think it's about time you introduced yourself."

Mooooooooooooom!

"Don't take that tone of voice with me, young Omniscient Narrator! I may have retired when I had you, but my work lives on in libraries all over the world! The position is a great honor, but it comes with great responsibilities."

Argh! So embarrassing! Fiiiiiiiiiiiiiiiiine! Hi. I'll be your Omniscient Narrator for today's adventure. My every word will be analyzed, so no pressure. There. Introduction over. Can we please get back to the story, now?

"We'll talk later, dear."

Aaaaaaargh!]

"Apparently, I am going to have to reconsider the security of my office." The tone of Mama Gudrun's voice matched her lip expression. Lipression.

"You-were-so-sad-and-I-wanted-to-find-out-why," Jennifer explained in a rush. "Somebody stealing electricity from the power grid is bad—worse than bad! I wanna help if I can—I have a lot of ideas about—"

Gudrun Eleanoradottir held up a hand to stop the flow of words, and Jennifer stopped saying them. "Go to your room, child. In the morning, we'll talk about your punishment."

Jennifer rushed out of the room. EDDY27 followed, head down, tail between his legs. FLO14 strutted out. Cats know no shame.

After breakfast the next morning, Jennifer stood in front of a modified electric bicycle that had been rolled out of a shed at the back of her house. A large-wheeled triangular platform was attached at the rear of the vehicle. It was made up of three compartments which contained: food and water; tools and a first aid kit; and an engine and an electric battery that stored energy. Laid over the triangle were solar panels that fed into the battery. Welded onto either side of the bike was a pet car.

The engine ran quietly—with nary a chitty, let alone two, and the only bang being if you accidentally drove it into a wall. It achieved a maximum speed of a whopping five kilometers per hour if you ensured the battery was charged. If the battery wasn't charged, it still had pedals, although given all the extra weight it carried, anybody who rode it would quickly wish their journey was downhill all the way.

Jennifer and her gene mother stood by the vehicle. "For your punishment—" Gudrun Eleanoradottir began.

"Could we call it… an extra credit research assignment?" Jennifer interrupted to suggest.

"For your *punishment*," Gudrun Eleanoradottir insisted (*I'm going to think of it as an extra credit research assignment*, Jennifer thought), "You must go to each of three sets of coordinates which I have sent to your comm, and write a report about what you find there."

That's observating! Jennifer thought. *I know how to do that!* Out loud, she said, as emotionless as she could, "Oh. Okay. I guess I can do that."

Gudrun Eleanoradottir held out her hand. "You mustn't forget to wear these." Jennifer looked at what her mother was offering. Goggles. GOGGLES?

"Moooooooooooooom!" Jennifer complained. "What do I need these for? Kamikaze ladybugs?"

"Jennifer!" her mother sternly advised. "The first rule of lab work is safety! Just like you wouldn't mix chemicals in a beaker without protecting your face, you shouldn't go out without protecting your face. PUT. THESE. ON."

Grumbling, Jennifer put on the goggles. They always itched where the rubber met her skin—ew! She settled into the seat of the electric bike.

"Road trip!" EDDY27 zealously cried, as he jumped into the right sidecar of the bike. His rapidly wagging tail thumped rhythmically on the back of his seat. It wasn't exactly Taylor Swiftdottir, but it wasn't entirely unpleasant.

Poised and dignified, FLO14 jumped into the other sidecar and phlumphed onto the seat with a contented purr.

"Do not tarry," Mama Gudrun advised. "If you go straight to the coordinates and record your observations, you should be back by sundown. Go straight to the coordinates. Be back by sundown."

"Will do," Jennifer assured her.

It was Mama Gudrun's turn to feel unassured.

Jennifer placed her comm in the holder between the handlebars of the electric bicycle, and fed the first coordinates into the LPS (Local Positioning System), which gave her a route to follow to the location. Then, she pressed the switch on the handlebars and turned on the bike's engine. Saluting her gene mother with two fingers, Jennifer went off.

As soon as her gene mother was out of sight, Jennifer pulled the goggles up so they rested on top of her head, and told her companions, "Okay, while we're out here, keep your eyes peeled for anybody who might be stealing power from the grid."

"There's nobody out here," FLO14 stated, with all the confidence of the species she was patterned after.

"That's why we have to observe really, really closely!" Jennifer responded.

"But... that's not what your mother told us to do," EDDY27 whined. Even though his voice was digitally constructed, the fear of being referred to as a bad dog clearly came through.

"For Mama Gudrun, this may be a dreary punishment," Jennifer enthused, "but, for us, it's an opportunity to do some serious SCIENCE!"

She quickly made her way through farmland, where everybody now lived, south into the city of Toronto. The concrete roads were broken apart and buckled in places, with plants and flowers growing out of the cracks. Jennifer had to concentrate on the road to make sure she dodged the dodgy bits.

Once inside the city, she drove past houses without roofs, windows, or, in some cases, one or more walls (improbably, only brick chimneys seemed to have been left largely unscathed, although many tilted Tower-of-Pisa-like). It was as if she were driving through a mouth full of teeth that hadn't been brushed in many years.

Grass grew wild in front yards. In the ruins of one house, Jennifer could just make out the decaying remains of a metallic orb that she conjectured had been a satellite.

Ah. Civilization.

Jennifer had only ever been to the city a couple of times on class field trips, and only three or four blocks inside the city's limits. If she had thought about it, it would have occurred to her that Mama Gudrun had placed a lot of faith in her ability to navigate deep into Toronto on her own. Mostly, though, she thought of what could be draining the power lines of electricity. And goggles.

A few minutes later, as they passed a two-story stone house (which, unlike the houses around it, wouldn't fall to ruins for another thousand years—say what you will, but you can't beat natural materials), Jennifer asked, "Do you think they were happy?"

"Think who was happy, dear?" FLO14 wanted clarification.

"The people who lived in these houses."

"Oh, yes, yes, yes, yes, yes," EDDY27 responded. "I bet they were the happiest happy people full of happiness in the whole happy world!"

FLO14 shook her head. "You'll have to forgive him," she said. "He was clearly dropped on his head as a puppy."

"It didn't hurt," EDDY27 cheerfully assured her.

A few moments of embarrassed silence passed before FLO14 offered the opinion: "If they were happy, would they have made the world into this?"

This time, the silence lasted for several minutes.

43.7254° N, 79.4522° W

Eventually, they came upon a large paved-over area in front of a vast two-story building. "Whoa," Jennifer said, as she stopped the electric bike and took the structure in. She had never seen anything so big.

She drove around the building, both to get a sense of its size and to find ways of getting into it. Eventually, she discovered what once must have been a large glass facade, which was now a gaping hole that allowed Jennifer to drive right into the building. Convenient!

She drove past a tall staircase; the central stairs were flanked by two thinner sets of mechanical stairs. Jennifer recognized them from old videos as escalators, although they hadn't… escalated… for over a century. So, basically, stairs with treads?

To either side of the broad hallway down which Jennifer drove the electric bicycle were rooms piled on top of each other, many of which now housed nests of mice or other small creatures, but the roof largely gaped open two tall stories above them.

As she took it all in, Jennifer wondered, "What was this place?"

"Isn't it obvious?" FLO14 replied. "This was once a zoo."

"A zoo?" Jennifer gave her cat a sidelong glance that clearly communicated skepticism.

"Absolutely!" FLO14 stuck out her chin; she was nothing if not convinced of her omniscience. "All these rooms were cages." After a couple of seconds, she added, "Do you have a better idea?"

Jennifer opened an app on her comm and tried to search the internet to find out what the building had been. Unfortunately, while the satellite system was largely intact, some had fallen to Earth, leaving gaps in coverage, and she was currently in one. All she got for her troubles was the swirly blue circle of limbo. Frustrated, she gave up and closed the app.

"Well, I think this must have once been a place of worship," she said.

"A place of worship?" FLO14 scoffed.

"Don't scoff!" Jennifer admonished her pet. "I was taught that, in medieval times, people built huge churches, often the biggest and most ornate structures in their cities. This has got to be the biggest structure for miles—it could be some kind of church!"

If a cat could lick its paw and pat down the fur on its head dubiously, FLO14 did so.

(When Jennifer got home and did research for her report for Mama Gudrun, she would discover that the building had been a shopping mall called Yorkdale. So, she hadn't been far off.)

They continued driving through the building. They passed a pair of deer munching on vines, which appeared to have grown up the side of what remained of a counter. The deer looked up at the bicycle warily, but didn't bolt. Over a century of not interacting with humans could make you forget how much of your enemy they were.

Turning a corner, Jennifer stopped the bike as they came across a half-dozen cats with mangy, matted fur, their tails standing straight up, like flagpoles without the regional pride. The largest, an orange tabby with a furless patch on its back, stood at the front of the pack, hissing louder than a balloon rapidly losing its air.

"Can I bark at them?" EDDY27 eagerly asked, his tail swishing this way and that, his tongue lolling out of his mouth. "Can I? Can I? Can I? Please, please, please, can I bark at them?"

"They are my kinfolk," FLO14 distastefully responded. "Allow me to deal with them."

FLO14 jumped out of her sidecar, gracefully landing nearby, and strutted up to within a couple of feet of the orange tabby. "Hello," she said. "It is my distinct pleasure to—"

The orange tabby, claws out, swiped at FLO14 with a mighty hiss. She jumped back. "Now, now," she chastised. "There is no need for violence. We are all felines here!"

The orange tabby clearly had other ideas. It sprang at FLO14, who reflexively swatted the feral cat away. (Out of the corner of her eye, Jennifer could see a pair of rats in the distance, looking on with astonishment and what might have been approval.) The orange tabby tumbled away before righting itself. Back arched, tail straight, claws out, the feral cat yowled its anger.

FLO14 looked at it for a moment, then made a hacking sound which was, for her, a sigh. She turned back to the bike and said, "This is so tedious. Edward, do your thing."

As the cat leaped into her sidecar, EDDY27 energetically jumped out of his and barked enthusiastically. The cat pack scattered, returning to the shadows of the rooms around them.

The dog returned to his sidecar and shook himself in satisfaction. "You have to let loose once in a while to remind yourself of what you are truly capable of," he commented to the air.

"Okay, I think I've seen enough," Jennifer said. "Think we should move to the next destination?"

FLO14 had closed her eyes; she might have been taking a well-deserved nap. EDDY27, all barked out, lay in his sidecar, panting.

"I'll take that as a yes," Jennifer said to herself. She turned the bike around and retraced her path to the entrance of the building. This time, she had her comm in her hand (the other on the steering wheel) and recorded what she had found.

Jennifer wanted to point out to FLO14 that if these animals had survived in the world without people, perhaps something else could have, something that sucked electricity out of the grid. She was tempted to wake FLO14 up to tell her. How many times had the feline woken her up by tap-dancing on her bladder just to get some attention? Jennifer realized, though, that momentarily being proven right would not be as satisfying as basking in the warm glow of correctitude all the way to their next destination.

Jennifer enjoyed the basking.

As they drove through the city, the houses gave way to buildings where porches had been replaced by burned-out signs—stores? Then, neighborhoods with a mix of houses and definitely stores.

What the city lacked was people. Jennifer hadn't seen any videos set in Toronto (although she had seen her share of scenes shot in Toronto, it was just called a different name—some places have no pride!), but she had seen enough crowd scenes to know that there was something terribly sad about the depopulated city.

Eventually, she electric-bicycled down a street lined with trees. Her destination was a small, squat building that teemed with plant life.

43.6683° N, 79.3999° W

The front of the building was divided more or less in half. On the left, you had metal doors with the glass blown out. In front of that half, close to the street, was a concrete slab, out of which stuck a metal rod that may have once held a sign... or a flag... or the start of a clothesline.

On the right was a brick wall with a small window of glass blown out. (Are you sensing a theme here? Because Jennifer certainly was!) Above that was a red logo, in which the letters "TTC" could be made out. A rusty canopy with a lot of small holes eaten into it covered some of the sidewalk in front of the structure.

Jennifer stopped the electric bike in front of the building, and got off the seat. As FLO14 and EDDY27 got out of the sidecars, there was a sound she hadn't heard since the start of the journey: silence. She strained her ears, really worked them hard, but she couldn't make out anything.

She was about to mention this when something cawed loudly overhead. Jennifer jumped. After that, she could make out the occasional yowl of a cat or howl of a coyote in the distance.

At least, she hoped they were in the distance.

Jennifer finally commented to FLO14 and EDDY27, who were waiting patiently on either side of her, "I... I'll bet this building was homely even before The Great Messed-Up Thing That Happened." (Oh, yeah. I forgot that's what some people called the cataclysm that befell humanity. Sorry about that. I don't know where Jennifer could have got it from!)

"Oh, so you're an architecture critic now?" FLO14 commented, but without much bite, suggesting that she agreed with the assessment.

Jennifer ignored her. She had to shimmy sideways to get through the thin opening to the building. Not being over-endowed with physical grace, it was quite awkward—pretend you didn't see it.

Inside the building were six turnstiles, divided by a rotting structure that may have been a booth of some kind. Another booth along the right wall was equally decayed.

"Hunh," she hunhed. Jennifer tried turning the handles of a couple of the turnstiles, but they were rusted in place. Reluctantly, she clambered over one. That's probably an image you'll have trouble getting out of your imagination—try to replace it with something from your happy place and get past it.

Immediately in front of her were two staircases: a normal one and, to its left, one with treads. She looked down, but could only see about ten feet, at which point the stairs were filled with murky water. Jennifer took the comm out of the pocket she'd placed it in when she'd gotten off the bike, and fired it up.

"What are you doing?" FLO14 asked.

"Looking up what this place used to be," Jennifer told her, intently watching the screen of the comm boot up.

"Where's the science in that?" FLO14 coolly objected.

Jennifer thought about this for a moment. If you believed in the scientific method, you had to be a problem-solver. Solving problems is what science is all about. You have to problem solve.

Just as the opening screen with the icons for all her apps came to life, Jennifer shut off her comm. "You're right," she said. "Let's think this through."

The girl observed the water for a couple of minutes. "Okay," she finally said, "these stairs must lead to an underground tunnel. So. Hypothesis: People built this tunnel in order to have a place to live while The Great Messed-Up Thing That Happened was occurring on the surface."

"Good guess," FLO14 encouraged her.

"But am I right?" Jennifer demanded.

"Yes, oh, yes you are!" EDDY27 enthused, his tail wagging this way and that like a drumstick. "You're right! You're right! You're soooooo right!"

"And you're wrong," FLO14 contradicted him. More or less.

"Hunh?" Jennifer sounded as confused as EDDY27 looked.

"Yes, during The Fall, some people sought refuge in the tunnels," FLO14 explained. She had never been comfortable with the phrase The Great Messed-Up Thing That Happened—she was old-fashioned that way. "But they were soon chased back up out of the tunnels when the water level in them rose. But the important thing is: That's not what the tunnels were built for."

"How do you know this?" Jennifer challenged her.

FLO14 imperiously stuck her chin out. "I was on the comm one day looking at different bird species. You know how one thing leads to another on the internet. Before I knew it, I was looking at the tunnel system under the city. They did some weird blapblap back in the day."

"I was looking for dog treats," EDDY27 bashfully admitted, looking expectantly at his human.

Okay, Jennifer thought, nodding to herself. *Let's observe and see what we can hypothesize.* She looked into the stagnant, algae-filled water. That wasn't much to work with. So, she turned back to the small room at the top of the stairs. Jennifer focused on the turnstiles.

"Okay," she hypothesized (it wasn't repetition because nobody could hear her thoughts), "these were probably here to regulate who could come in and out. So, maybe this was some kind of… underground prison?"

"Correct purpose," FLO14 responded, her impassive face giving away nothing. "Wrong end."

Jennifer continued cogitating. "Maybe people had to… pay to get in?" she tentatively suggested. The village where she lived had an informal barter economy, so they didn't use money, but she had watched enough old videos with her emotional support mother Heather Heatherdottir that she understood some of the basics of how the world had worked before The Great Messed-Up Thing That Happened. A lot of girls had no interest in learning about the past, but Jennifer believed that understanding the past might help to better understand the present, an only partially-plausible hypothesis that emotional support mother Heather did nothing to dissuade her from.

"Getting close!" EDDY27 enthused encouragingly.

"Okay, so, if people paid to get in here, it must have been for something that they wanted," Jennifer reasoned. "Could this have been… a video theater?"

FLO14 made that noise that could have been a laugh, could have been the onset of a nasty hairball. Hard to tell, really.

Jennifer was offended. "Hey, I'm trying!" she huffed, planting her feet and putting her hands on her hips. "It's hard to develop a working hypothesis without enough observavtable facts!"

FLO14 considered this and eventually hinted, "This isn't the only building like it in the city. There are another sixty-five or seventy."

"Are they connected?" Jennifer surmised/asked. Surmasked.

FLO14 nodded.

"So, were they some kind of… transportation network?"

"Oh, good! Oh, good! Oh, good!" EDDY27 jumped up and put his forepaws on Jennifer's shoulders. "You figured it out!" Then, he licked her face with fire hose intensity.

"This was known as a subway," FLO14 informed Jennifer, as the girl tried to get EDDY27's paws off her and stop the slobbery onslaught. "It ran from the lake to just about where we live now, and across Toronto from end-to-end. At its height of popularity, it carried hundreds of thousands of people a day."

Jennifer was finally able to get EDDY27 to stand down. "Pah pafft bleh!" she said, spitting doggy slobber out of her mouth. *This would never have happened when the dogs were electric*, she thought. *Though, with my luck, I probably would have been shocked by sparks!* Then, she wiped her mouth with the sleeve of her shirt and surmasked, "And they used it to visit friends and family who didn't live near them?"

Jennifer knew *some* of the basics of how the world had worked before The Great Messed-Up Thing That Happened, but by no means all of them. She had never seen a video that took place in a shopping mall, for example, so she had no idea what they were. Another gap in her cinematic education had to do with the need for transit systems. She lived in a village where everything and everybody was within walking distance or a short bike ride of each other. The idea that you would have to travel an hour to get to work was as natural to her as singing the song of Blutorian fluffenvargel. (It was completely alien, is what I'm saying.)

"Sure," FLO14 told her. "Let's go with that."

Pleased with herself, Jennifer took out her comm and shot video of the sub-a-way (she may not have heard it exactly right—you may recall she was kind of busy at the time), spending a lot of time on the water-filled tunnel and the turnstiles. When she was satisfied that she had enough, she climbed back over the turnstiles, out of the room, and onto her electric bike, the dog and the cat dutifully following.

"One more stop!" Jennifer exulted. She considered pulling the goggles over her eyes, but decided not to spoil her enjoyment of the moment and engaged the engine and started to drive.

As they drove further into the core of the city, the buildings grew taller and taller, which gave them more options for falling apart. In one case, the sixth floor of a building must have collapsed, strewing rubble onto the roof of the building to its left; the spaces between the buildings filled with it, rubble spilling onto the street in front of them (requiring riding the bike on the opposite sidewalk). All that remained above were bars that went up another four or five floors.

In another case, she encountered the rubble first, then had to maneuver around it for five blocks before she came to the hole in the ground where a building had once stood (and another four blocks beyond); the other buildings in area were ten to fifteen stories tall, so she figured that one must have been as well.

Then there was the block of buildings that had been burned down. Only the charred remains of walls indicated that anything had been there.

Eventually, they arrived at their final destination.

43.6426° N, 79.3871° W

"That's tall," Jennifer said, the awe in her voice powerful enough to fuel her electric bike for three-and-a-half days.

"One thousand, eight hundred fifteen feet," FLO14 confirmed.

"So unfair," Jennifer muttered.

"So you keep saying," FLO14 purred in her most infuriatingly calm voice.

"Oh, boy! Oh, boy! Oh, boy!" EDDY27 enthused. "Can you imagine the game of fetch we could have with that thing?!"

Jennifer and FLO14 turned their gazes away from the structure and looked at EDDY27. As was his way, he panted and drooled, oblivious to their attention.

The electric bike was parked in front of a structure made up of tall pillars of concrete, now heavily pitted and bleached white. Ivy had slowly crept more than twenty feet up it. Over a thousand feet above them, the pillars held up a platform, into and out of which birds flew. A single steel spire, tipping precariously, poked out of the top of the platform. They were close enough to Lake Ontario that areas of the sky were dense with seagulls.

"It was called the CN Tower," FLO14 stated.

"What did that stand for?" Jennifer asked. "Crane Neck Tower?"

"Catnip Now Tower?" FLO14 suggested.

"Completely Nutty Tower?"

"Couldn't Name Tower?"

"Cocoa Nuts Tower?" EDDY27 offered.

FLO14 closed her eyes and shook her head. Jennifer sighed. Eventually, FLO14 said, "This was the third-tallest free-standing structure in the world at the time when… such things stopped mattering."

"Now, it's the third-tallest free-standing bird stand in the wor—" Jennifer began to point out when something splatted on EDDY27's head. Something white and unpleasant. Having a pretty good idea of what it was from its odor, the enhanced dog barked angrily at the sky.

"More like the third-tallest free-standing poop machine in the world!" FLO14 asserted.

Eventually, EDDY27 barked himself out. Then, he panted himself out. When he was back to his usual goofy self, he good-naturedly recited, "My name is Ozymandias, King of Kings. Look on my works, ye Mighty, and despair. Yep. Yep. Yep. Yep. Yep. Look and despair. Un hunh!"

"Where is that from?" Jennifer asked.

"A poem that was read to me when I was a puppy," EDDY27 answered. "I can recite the whole thing to you when we get back home."

"Hunh!" FLO14 snorted. Elegantly, but still snortily. "It's easy to forget he has a genetically enhanced super-intelligence when most of the time he acts like such a dog!"

As if to prove her point, EDDY27 tried to lick the bird poop off the top of his head. Not only was his tongue not long enough, but *ooh, gross!* Before he could paw the poop off (and lick it off his paw—*double gross with an added helping of disgusting!*), Jennifer got some napkins out of the bike and cleaned him off as best she could, promising to give him a proper bath when they got home.

"That was the lesson my gene mother wanted me to learn from this homework assignment, wasn't it?" Jennifer asked as she finished cleaning EDDY27.

"What lesson?" FLO14 encouraged her.

"Not to get too full of myself," Jennifer cogitated. She waved a hand, which took in not only the tower, but the steel struts to their right that had once been an aquarium, the vast concrete oval without a roof that had once been a sports stadium, and the dilapidated skyscrapers that had contributed to the skyline behind them. "The people who created these things must have thought they would last forever. Like Ozzy Man Diss."

"Ozymandias," EDDY27 corrected her.

"Yeah," Jennifer took it in stride. "That guy. The lesson is: Don't be like him."

"Good conclusion, dear," FLO14 said. If Jennifer caught the hint of, "I got there five minutes after we entered the zoo, but so glad you finally caught up with me" in her voice, the girl chose to ignore it.

The three looked at the decaying tableau, following their own thoughts. (EDDY27's consisted mostly of dog treats, and FLO14's had a lot to do with belly rubs, but who are we to say that, for them, that wasn't profound?)

A couple of minutes later, EDDY27 started barking. Loudly barking. Really putting some lung power into it.

"What is it, boy?" Jennifer asked, petting him on the head. "What are you looking at?"

"Other dogs," EDDY27 told her, and resumed barking.

"But that's not possible!" Jennifer blurted.

EDDY27 stopped barking and looked at her. He turned his head to the side for a moment, then, straightening up, asked, "Why not?"

"Uh... uh... because..." Jennifer mumbled. How could she explain to him that domesticated dogs had not adapted to living without masters as well as domesticated cats had? (As any cat companion could tell you, they were only ever domesticated on sufferance.)

"Because all of the dogs who lived before we were created have gone to heaven," FLO14 told him as gently as she was able.

EDDY27 thought about this for a moment, then responded, "Really? Oh, boy! Oh, boy! Oh, boy!" He licked Jennifer's face. She ruffled his chin. Then he stopped and cocked his head again. "But if they're not dogs," he asked, "what are those things near the wind machine thingie?"

Jennifer and FLO14 turned their attention toward one of the wind turbines that existed at the edge of the rising waters of Lake Ontario. Reluctantly, Jennifer pulled the goggles down over her eyes and adjusted the focal length of the lenses. They could do that. Sure enough, animals that looked like dogs were standing next to the wind turbine. Their entire attention was trained on it.

Jennifer smiled. "That," she said, "is proof."

Oh, umm, hello. It's me, the Omniscient Narrator, again. I don't know if I should be saying this, but I'm really proud of Jennifer. She rocks. And this was quite the adventure she's been on. I'm so happy I was the one who got to tell it.

I just… I'm new at this, and I'm trying my best. If I missed a detail, or used a metaphor that wasn't perfect, we all have a lot to learn in the beginning. ALL OF US. Right? Right. So, um, anyway, why don't we—why don't we get back to the story? Okay? Okay.

Jennifer rode her electric bicycle at top speed straight home. When she got there, she, FLO14, and EDDY27 ran into Gudrun's room. They found Jennifer's gene mother knitting a sweater as she listened to her comm read a Council of Three research paper on stabilizing global temperatures. When Jennifer burst in and breathlessly explained what she had discovered, Gudrun put the knitting aside and paused her comm.

"So, you're telling me," she said, incredulous, "that energy is being drained out of the system by robot dogs?"

"Yep. Un hunh. That's right," EDDY27 said, his tail wagging furiously. "That's exactly what Jennifer was telling you. Because all the flesh-and-blood dogs went to heaven. Yes, they did! Oh, yes, they did!"

Gudrun shook her head. "FLO?" she demanded.

"As usual, my canine friend has fixated on the wrong thing," FLO14 quietly, calmly responded. "However, I can confirm that Jennifer's conclusion is correct: robot dogs are responsible for the energy drainage."

"But how is that possible?" Gudrun asked. "We assumed that, left to fend for themselves, they would have all ceased to exist decades ago!"

"They were created with cords that allowed them to plug into the energy grid to recharge," Jennifer told her. "When they were released into the wild, some of them must have figured out how to adapt the cords to be able to suck energy out of the system without a plug."

"Do you have proof of this?"

"Do I have proof? Do I ever!" Jennifer proudly showed her gene mother video she had taken of the dogs around the base of the wind turbine before she'd left. "So, you see? No member of the community has been stealing electricity from the grid! They've all been good!"

"Jennifer Gudrunsdottir, this is very helpful. I shall bring this to the attention of the Council of Three at once. Thank you," Gudrun said, the hardness in her voice softened slightly. Then, she harrumphed and said, "Have you completed your field report?"

"What? I—but—I just got ho—didn't you just say—" Jennifer sputtered.

"Your punishment for breaking into my office must be completed," Gudrun commanded. "Go to your room and start your report. Once I have straightened this out with the Council of Three, I will start making dinner. Now, go."

Jennifer looked at Gudrun. Then, she looked at FLO14, who gently shook her head. Defeated, she said, "Yes, mother."

But as Jennifer trudged to her room (having missed seeing Mama Gudrun's lips tick ever-so-slightly upward), she smiled to herself and thought, *The future is now, and a girl can do anything she puts her mind to!*

THOUGHTS ON *BRAVE NEW GIRLS*

"When I first considered braving *Brave New Girls*, I had intended to write a single story that spanned three different universes, each representing a different subgenre of sci-fi, with three different heroines who used three different areas of STEM to solve their problems. Unfortunately (in a sense), the first segment came in at over 7,000 words, and the limit for *Brave New Girls* was 10,000 words! What to do? What to do? The only reasonable thing I could do: I split the story into its three component parts and submitted them separately to different volumes of the series.

"Words cannot express the gratitude that I have toward Paige and Mary for accepting all three parts of the story, allowing me to contribute thrice to this fantastic project. I imagine mothers sharing these books with their daughters and, when they grow up, them sharing the books with the next generation of girls. May *Brave New Girls* inspire girls to become scientists for many generations to come!"

ABOUT THE AUTHOR

Ira Nayman writes humorous speculative fiction. He has had eight novels and over 30 short stories published. He was also the editor of *Amazing Stories* magazine for three years. *The Dance*, his first anthology as editor, was published in 2024.

Illustration for "Girls Rule the Solarpunk World!" by Jarod Marchand.

JUPITER JIGSAW

BY KRIS KATZEN

JUPITER JIGSAW

KRIS KATZEN

"You want me to what?" Standing up from the conference table, Kasey Trung closed her laptop with slow, deliberate care as she mentally replayed what Professor Wolfmother had just said to her.

The exam over, Wolfmother stood in front of the conference room's now-open doorway. Behind him, the window on the other side of the corridor showed one of her favorite views from the Jovian colony. The colorful swirls of red, orange, and yellow—along with streaks of other colors—of Jupiter filled the window. Despite the profound beauty, Wolfmother glowered, completely oblivious to it.

Kasey still questioned whether or not she'd heard him correctly. With the test over, her mind had already switched gears to an impending crisis. The Bastet University computer system had somehow lost all her project work—due in two days. Kasey kept backups—tons of backups—so the work remained intact. But if the computer had lost it once, it could lose it again. She needed to figure out *why* her uploads had vanished. Otherwise, it could tank her grade.

Not to mention, she needed to solve the problem *before* the trips she'd scheduled to each of the Galilean moons to gather data for her potential *next* project.

Standing at his full rangy height, Professor Wolfmother loomed over her and looked down his nose at her. Kasey could avoid taking his classes, but somehow he seemed to proctor an awful lot of exams. Long black hair hung in a single thick braid halfway down his back. His narrow face wore its usual expression of petulant contempt, but his dark eyes betrayed a glimmer of malicious glee. "It is customary for Ph.D. students to teach." He stated the obvious in his default tone, intractable and smug.

Kasey questioned how someone could project petulance *and* smugness simultaneously, but Wolfmother managed the feat.

The rest of the students scooted out, many shooting her quick, surreptitious looks of sympathy—one, a look of disdain. They gave Wolfmother as wide a berth as possible—meaning, not much. The conference room, with its single table, held only ten people. The lack of windows made it seem even smaller.

Mostly in their early- to mid-twenties, not counting two even older than that, the other students—finally—mostly ignored that Kasey had just turned seventeen. They did still tease her good-naturedly about the shimmering silver streaks in her otherwise jet-black hair.

"It's customary for *Teaching Assistants* to teach, and to have plenty of time to prepare. *Research Assisantss*, not so much." Especially not brand new RAs, Kasey thought, as she—with *great* effort—kept her reply mild. She didn't exactly manage respectful, but civil she could do. A shame, actually. From what she'd heard and seen, Wolfmother knew physics *really* well. If only he knew how to teach.

"We're talking about an entry-level computer programming class. I trust you're familiar with the material."

"I skipped all the entry-level classes." The words escaped before Kasey's brain caught up with her mouth. At least she hadn't blurted out that she'd skipped practically all the undergraduate classes, too.

Wolfmother's heavy brows drew together in a deep scowl, and his normally reddish skin deepened in color from the angry flush. "I have no doubt you'll manage somehow. Tomorrow. 13:30 hours. Auditorium 13."

That room held two hundred people. Likely anywhere from five to fifty would show up in person. However, up to five hundred more could attend remotely. No problem. Even five hundred only amounted to a tiny percentage of the largest group Kasey had ever spoken in front of.

"Professor, this is just one time, right? I have my own RA duties, and my studies. I can't add teaching." Her mind already raced ahead to what she would do for the two-hour session. One, she could manage. More, not so much. RAs didn't add teaching schedules to their workloads. The day simply didn't contain enough hours for that. Plus, the computer problem still weighed heavily on her.

Wolfmother pressed his lips tightly together, then relented. "Yes, Ms. Trung. Professor Lanai's baby came early. Professor Samuelson can't get back from Saturn in time to cover this one class."

Relieved, Kasey beamed. "Her baby came! That's wonderful!" She tucked the thin laptop under her arm and slid her hand-held into her jacket pocket. "Have a good day, Professor."

Two hundred people? A full auditorium? Unheard of—according to hearsay, of course—but Kasey could only go by second-hand information. An occasional outburst of laughter or raised voices punctuated the otherwise soft, steady hum of conversation filling the room. Well, the room was not quite full yet. Scanning the lecture hall that sloped down to the podium and table at the front, Kasey spotted a handful of empty seats scattered about.

Lucky for the students still trickling in. With ten minutes remaining till class time, Kasey heard a few exclamations or mutterings of shock and annoyance from the newer arrivals. No one paid her any attention while she lurked beside one of the three double doors in the back.

No one, until one older man came in the far door. Tall, blond, with a slight curl to his short hair, and kind of handsome in a dad sort of way, he moved with far more purpose than everyone else strolling in. At least thirty—to her eye—he saw her and did a subtle double take. The man didn't break stride as he walked past her, but Kasey swore he gave a barely-perceptible nod and locked eyes with her in the briefest moment of acknowledgment. The vivid green color of his eyes reminded Kasey of one of her mother's favorite jade figurines. Kasey's gaze followed him as he took an empty seat in the front row, way off to the side.

Hmm. He carried no laptop, or any computer accessory that she'd seen, although he could easily have a handheld if his dark gray jacket or trousers had pockets. Then again, that didn't mean much. Any registered student could watch the recording of the lecture any time.

Facilitating that recording, fellow RA Sammy sat at the table up front, his bald head bowed over a keyboard. Kasey liked Sammy a lot. He always grinned, his beaming smile lighting up his dark face. Kasey couldn't remember ever seeing anything less than a smile on his face, even if it sometimes became a distracted half-smile as he pondered some particularly stubborn computer problem. Sammy also monitored the online chat feed, and would relay any incoming questions to Kasey at the appropriate breaks in the class.

With five minutes to go, Kasey joined him at the front of the auditorium.

"Hey, Sammy."

"Hey, Kase!" He tore his attention from the computer and held up a fist to bump. "What the heck?" The fist-bump turned into a gesture at the audience. "Online queue is full, too. Everyone wants to see the celebrity just back from being Guest of Honor and Keynote Speaker at one of the biggest conferences in the solar system."

"Yeah, yeah." She pretended irritation at his good-natured teasing, but couldn't hold back a laugh and a big grin of her own. "We'll see what they all say *after* class."

After studying Professor Lanai's syllabus, Kasey had decided she'd recap the first quarter of the semester during the first thirty minutes. After that, she'd take questions and see how long that lasted. Lots of students wouldn't ask teachers questions, for any number of reasons. Kasey figured they'd be less intimidated by someone their own age.

She'd use what remained of the two hours to start the next topic on the syllabus.

Ignoring the podium, Kasey boosted herself up to sit on the table and called the class to attention.

"Very nicely done. I've never heard algorithms explained quite that way before." The words came from behind Kasey.

Kasey thanked Sammy again and fist-bumped him one more time, before turning toward the smooth baritone voice. She knew even before looking she'd see the older guy from her class.

Sure enough, the older guy wearing the dark gray jacket and pants and a white turtleneck stood there.

"Thanks." Kasey picked up her laptop and tablet. Her handheld vibrated in the pocket of her slacks, but that could wait a moment. Probably her friends confirming the pizza plans for later that day. "You an official observer, or just curious?"

Probably the first. Random people were not supposed to—not allowed to, in fact—wander into classes. Sometimes faculty did, but Kasey had never seen this guy before.

"Both, actually. Apologies. I'm Derek Weiss." He held out his hand. "The Professor needs to see you in her office right now."

"Now?" Kasey frowned, nearly forgetting to return the handshake. That sounded bad. *The Professor*, to anyone studying the computer sciences, meant the head of the whole department, Mara Kiyashko. She rarely summoned people, and *never*—so far as Kasey knew—did so by sending a live person as a messenger. But—he'd waited until *after* class to tell her? So, urgent but not *urgent*? That made no sense.

Curiosity mixed with a faint sense of dread. The sooner she found out, the better.

"Thank you, Derek. Ms. Trung, very nice job with the class." The Professor stood as Kasey knocked on the doorframe then entered the elegantly spartan office.

Department Chair Professor Kiyashko's deep, melodious voice belied her willowy frame. Kasey always thought the timbre matched far better to a much huskier person. With her flowing black hair and deeply bronzed skin, the professor cut a very non-professorial figure.

Kiyashko gestured to the two chairs—fancy anti-grav models that hovered next to the desk—then sat back down in her own traditional seat. It should have looked out of place in the otherwise high-tech room, yet somehow didn't. The desk itself appeared to be a sheet of clear glass on four fancy golden metallic legs. Kasey knew better, and recognized it as a huge touch-screen computer interface. The clear wall behind the desk revealed Jupiter, with all its glorious bands of color. Bare dove-gray walls flanked either side, and the last wall gave a view of the department's lobby area, with assorted tables and chairs. Faculty offices surrounded it, most with transparent walls that gave a clear look inside.

"Thanks, Professor." Kasey took a seat. To her surprise, Derek Weiss dropped into the other one.

"Computer, privacy mode," Kiyashko said, the welcoming smile fading from her face. "Do Not Disturb." Her office door slid shut, and the interior wall turned dove gray.

Kasey's anxiety grew. *What the heck?* "Professor, did something happen? Is my family okay?" No idea where *that* came from, but clearly something seriously wrong was going on.

"Oh, my, yes!" Kiyashko looked startled, then apologetic. "They're fine. This is a computer issue."

Kasey took a huge breath of relief as the professor continued.

Now chagrin and irritation mingled into the woman's expression. "The University hired a consultant to test our computer's security so we could shore up any potential weaknesses. He—Dr. Weiss," Kiyashko gave a slight nod in his direction, "managed to breach the system in some unexpected ways. He was actually in the process of backing out, and restoring all the original code in preparation for us fixing it, when you ran your retrieval script." One eyebrow raised slightly.

Ah. Kasey flushed. Her attempt at finding her lost data hadn't *exactly* been hacking, but it had skated perilously close. "And that messed up one of the reboot points?" She made the question a statement.

"It basically took a jigsaw to my program and the entire database," Dr. Weiss confirmed.

Kasey had no clue what a jigsaw was, but from his grim tone and this whole context, she understood his meaning just fine. *Definitely not good.* "Why aren't the backups an option?"

Dr. Weiss let out a whistle of surprise. Kiyashko's mouth compressed into a tight line as she skewered him with a sharp look that to Kasey read—somehow—as "I told you so" unless her ego was reading too much into it.

Dr. Weiss ignored the Professor and regarded Kasey with renewed interest. "Okay, that's impressive." But then annoyance replaced the admiration in his voice. "My program found a vulnerability with retrieving the backups. We get everything back or nothing back."

"That means the entire semester is basically lost for everyone except those—rare—few who make non-network backups." Kiyashko's scowl deepened. "Not to mention faculty will lose work going back years, if not decades."

Kasey winced. Even worse than—

The room plunged into total blackness.

Kasey yelped as her chair crashed to the floor. She heard the simultaneous *bang!*—accompanied by a loud grunt—as the other chair lost power as well. None of that mattered, though. She shouted, "The backups!" even before the words fully formed in her head.

Evidently, Dr. Weiss realized it instantly as well. Light flared as his handheld (either shielded or previously powered down—Kasey kept one of each) came on, illuminating his face with weird blue light, as he half sat up where he'd sprawled on the floor. "Pull the plug, Sara! Sara, pull the plug! Don't let the system power on!"

"Sheeeesh, Derek, don't launch yourself out of orbit!" A woman's drawl crackled over Dr. Weiss's device. "It's fine. I already made sure."

The lights came on in time for Kasey to see him flop back on the floor in relief. "Thanks, Sara." He clicked the handheld off.

Ever since the first attack months ago by "loyalists" attempting to assert Earth's authority over the entire solar system by setting off a major electromagnetic pulse, the Jovian colonists had worked diligently, and as quickly as possible, to protect the electronics, starting with the most delicate and vulnerable. First priority: protective shielding and the gravity generators, because without them, *everything* would go kerfluey. Second: hospitals and communications. Third: life support, including air and waste recycling, temperature regulators, matter converters, and the like.

They'd checked those three priorities off the list, but plenty more tasks remained, like protecting university computers—and floating chairs.

"Are you both all right?" Kiyashko asked as Kasey and Dr. Weiss climbed to their feet.

Kasey nodded. The chair had basically cushioned her landing, although her backside ached slightly.

"Yes. Fine. Thanks." But even as he spoke, he rubbed his left hip. "I'm sorry, Mara. I don't think we can get any of it back."

The Professor let out a half-sigh/half-growl, then fixed her gaze with guarded and very determined optimism on Kasey.

Yeah, no pressure.

Kasey did *not* want to make any promises she couldn't keep. "Can I see your code?"

Dr. Weiss handed her his tablet, not stating the obvious. This kind of hack would be thousands of lines of code.

Knowing exactly what signposts she wanted to find, Kasey studied some sections, scrolled more swiftly through others. The methodology and patterns began to look ever-so-slightly familiar. She gasped, stealing the quickest glance at Dr. Weiss, then turned her full attention back to the computer code.

"I take it I've just been recognized," he said, a wry smile on his face.

She gave a quick nod but didn't shift her focus. Her whole life she'd pretty much avoided the shadowy underworld of hackers. Even so, anyone with any level of expertise and interest remained at least peripherally aware of trends—and of certain famous, or infamous, characters. She knew that code! That style, rather, thanks to an old cybersecurity report her mother—a.k.a. the Most Esteemed Governor of the whole colony—had shown her.

Notorious over a decade ago, someone named WhiteGhost, a mostly White Hat—a lawbreaker who fancied themself one of the good guys— had displayed a knack for harmless yet very public mischief. He'd once programmed an army of nanodrones to plant holographic microprojectors at every single window of the university HJO (high Jovian orbit) space station and then activated them in the middle of the "night."

A handful of people, due to insomnia or night jobs or whatever, had seen them activate. But for the most part, everyone awoke to see Saturn outside instead of Jupiter. They never did find all the projectors—or hadn't yet. Once in a while, the view outside a random window would change to Saturn, or Mars, or Neptune. Once it even changed to an ocean, with merpeople cavorting outside and happily waving or flipping their tails at onlookers.

The merpeople had been Kasey's favorites. She had always suspected that

WhiteGhost had periodically replaced some projectors. And now WhiteGhost, Dr. Weiss, was helping the university—until Kasey had scrambled his program.

"Ha! Found it!" Her exclamation made both adults jump. Working rapidly, she highlighted sections of code, then handed the tablet back to Dr. Weiss. "What do you think?"

He studied it for so long, scrolling back and forth so slowly and methodically, that Kasey's heart sank. She must have missed something, or misread something. The silence grew unbearable, but she forced herself not to break it.

Her shoulders slumped, and she mentally reviewed her idea and the code, trying to think of a better solution. Of one that would actually work.

Then Dr. Weiss caught his breath, and one corner of his mouth twitched. A moment later the corner quirked upward. Ever so gradually, a smile spread across his face, until he grinned from ear to ear.

He looked at her in amazement. "I think you did it. A remote forced boot. But how do—?"

"A tandem hack. *Two* remote boots at the same time."

"Of course." He dove back into the code for another few minutes. A few times, he pointed to something and asked, "Why?" and she explained. Once she realized he'd found something she *had* overlooked, and she tweaked her original plan.

"Mara, you're a genius." He hugged her. The Professor raised an eyebrow. "Because you surround yourself with geniuses, of course." He winked at Kasey. "Come on, kid, let's go save the semester and make a whole lot of professors *really* happy—even though they'll likely never know."

He strode so swiftly through the dove-gray halls that she had to half-jog to keep up. She wasn't short by any means, but nor was she overly tall, which made keeping up with his long strides a challenge.

She followed him into the elevator and heaved a huge breath of relief.

"Sorry," he said, but she waved it off.

"We can link in with our handhelds, right? Load the code and have them generate the power and force the boot?" She had never examined the university mainframe in person, only ever accessed it wirelessly. As good as the network was—and it was *really* good—it was no longer state-of-the-art. Bastet, the main colony in LJO (low Jovian orbit), had the most state-of-the-art equipment. Kasey credited her mother, who was not only the governor but also an esteemed scientist, and her engineering prodigy sister (not that Kasey'd ever tell her that), for the continuous progress.

"That should work, yes."

A stout woman with dark hair and heavy glasses—Sara, no doubt—met them as soon as they entered the computer room. Gleaming white walls set it apart from the rest of the space station, aside from the fourth wall that was the computer itself. It mostly looked like a frosted window: opaque, but still showing their reflections. In addition to touch interfaces, the computer had several integrated terminals, and a few wireless ones as well.

Dr. Weiss gave Sara his handheld, which he'd somehow managed to program as he'd rushed down the halls.

"Nice." She handed it back. "Very nice. Pleasure to meet you, Kasey. I'm Sara."

"Hi, Sara." Kasey shook her hand. The woman didn't look familiar. Then again, neither had Dr. Weiss. "Are you with the university?"

"Not me. Cargo pilot."

"Oh. Cool." A cargo pilot who clearly knew enough about computers to grasp what Dr. Weiss had shown her. But Kasey could delve into that later.

The butterflies went nuts in Kasey's stomach. She had every confidence in her solution—and Dr. Weiss and, apparently, Sara did too.

But that didn't mean everything would go smoothly.

Kasey *really* didn't want to obliterate a semester's worth of work for the students. And even worse would be wrecking the staffs' projects.

She and Dr. Weiss turned off their devices, then plugged them into the mainframe. If this went wrong... The greatest breakthroughs often came from correcting mistakes. This was so *not* the time for that. They didn't have the luxury of repeated attempts. It would be a lot harder to reassemble all the data—if they could at all—than to avoid losing it in the first place.

"Ready?" Dr. Weiss asked.

Kasey squared her shoulders and forced a confidence she didn't feel at the moment. "Definitely."

It worked.

Two hours later, Kasey laughed with delight and overwhelming relief. Dr. Weiss caught Sara in his arms and danced her around the room.

"Great job." Then he gave Kasey a quick fatherly hug and a light kiss on the top of her head. "Seriously. I didn't think it could be done. Thank you."

Kasey grinned. "You're welcome." She savored the praise and the sense of triumph. She'd never considered herself particularly needy, but she still happily accepted positive reinforcement. She'd also noticed some intriguing twists and details in his code she could likely make good use of in the future.

Plus, mystery solved! Bug eliminated! Now she didn't need to worry about the university losing her homework! Or about canceling her trip! Bring on Ganymede, Io, Callisto, and Europa!

ABOUT THE AUTHOR

Kris Katzen composed her first novel—seven handwritten pages! Complete with cover and table of contents!—at age seven, and hasn't stopped writing since. Bilingual thanks to living in Germany, Kris has worked as a translator and interpreter, and enjoys studying history and architecture. Kris's credits include "Kaboom Ka-Bye," the lead story in the *Shadowrun* sourcebook *Seattle 2072*; the novels *Curai'Nal*, *Escapes!*, and *A Little Piece of Home*; and numerous short stories. Most importantly—especially according to them—she dotes on her astronomically adorable feline kids. Visit Kris at BluetrixBooks.com for more information.

THOUGHTS ON *BRAVE NEW GIRLS*

"I'm thrilled and privileged that *Brave New Girls* includes another story of mine. Girls need all the encouragement they can get that, yes, science is for girls, and it's totally okay for them to pursue it. This is an important collection of action-packed tales for young girls (see it, be it!), but people also need to give this awesomely fun anthology to little boys, to normalize the idea for them at a young age that science is for everyone. It's not a boys' club, or weird for girls to like it; it is cool for girls to be interested, and they can excel at it."

Illustration for "Jupiter Jigsaw" by R.M. Nielsen.

The Owl and the Rabbit

Brad Jurn

THE OWL AND THE RABBIT

BRAD JURN

Elena should have been focused on the cadence of her run instead of the various paths her mind was running. One path led to her robotics workbench at home and the incomplete project sitting on it. The other led to her surroundings: dark, save for some streetlights, and in a part of town not far from where one of her teammates had gone missing. The last path led to her Mamita, who would be furious if she knew her teenaged daughter was out getting her morning run in at 4:15 A.M. In light of recent events, it wasn't a safe time to be out.

Her pace quickened as her anxiety increased. Cadence became irrelevant as she passed 4:20 minutes per mile. These morning runs always gave her the edge when it came to after-school practice. Just as late-night hours in her workshop did, putting together bionic assemblages for her robotics class.

Running and robots were her two passions. And they complemented each other, as the running stimulated her creative thinking. She had always been good at running track and field, and if Coach Sheridan had his way, he'd have her on the bus going to Eugene, Oregon next week for the Olympic Trials.

The idea of qualifying for the Olympic Games greatly appealed to her. Unfortunately, there was another bus leaving her school that very same weekend. One that would take her robotics class to Dallas, Texas, to compete in the VEX Robotics World Championship. Elena was a valuable part of the Bionics Team, and they needed her.

The day when she'd have to choose between buses was coming, sooner rather than later. She would soon have to pick one of two options career-wise: going for the Olympic gold or applying for the BioEngineering Scholars Program at Berkeley. Of course, there was always the *third* option of doing neither, and continuing her job at Shop N Save so she could take care of her mother.

Before she could ponder any further, the piercing shriek of an owl echoed into the night sky. Her heart rate increased, and her pace accelerated. She looked around the peaceful neighborhood, but saw nothing except slumbering suburban homes and their porch lights. Before her heart rate could return to a more rhythmic pace, another nocturnal scream sounded off. This animal's cry was unfamiliar at first, and then it dawned on her that she'd heard it before: a mother rabbit, which no doubt had just lost a baby to the now-triumphant owl.

Elena's heart sank in sadness at the early morning act of predation. *Poor little bunny,* she thought as she tried to find some meaning in the carnivorous act. *Well, I guess that's nature's way of keeping balance.*

The melancholy of the morning run soon came to an end as Elena rounded the curb into her cul-de-sac. A light illuminated a window in her and her mother's modest pale-blue home.

"Crap! Mamita's up!" Elena huffed, as she placed her hands on her knees and caught her breath. *Maybe she's just going to the bathroom.*

Elena was disappointed as she stood straight up again and saw the light still on. She immediately started to think of responses to what would no doubt be a lengthy interrogation.

She took a moment to steady her breath, then entered the front breezeway and took her shoes off. She looked up to see that her mother had blocked the entrance with her wheelchair.

The older woman had curly salt-and-pepper hair and wore a green nightgown. Her squinting eyes peered at her daughter behind thick bifocal glasses. "Baby, what are you doing out this early?" she asked, disappointment echoing in her words. "What happened to 'no runs before sunrise'?"

Elena spread her arms defensively. "I wanted to get it done so I could work on my project before school!"

Her mother tried to cover up the tremor in her right hand by balling it into a fist. "Why would you go out this early after what happened to your friend?"

Elena spread her arms even wider. "I told you—she probably got into it with her dad and went to stay at her aunt's."

Mamita squinted an eye at her. "And what about all those UFO sightings around town? That's *three* sightings in *three* weeks, and here you are out at four A.M.!"

"Mamita… UFOs, *really*? You're watching too much TV. Turn off the news already!"

"Still, being out at four A.M. in this part of town isn't any place for a teenaged girl."

Elena ignored the chastising and took a step forward. "Okay, fine, *I promise*… no more morning runs." She tilted her head forward sarcastically.

Mamita begrudgingly grabbed her wheels and backed out of the doorway. "Okay. It just worries me sick when you're out in the dark, that's all. Remember, you're all I got. Well, you and Aunt Rosa."

Elena walked into the kitchen. "Aunt Rosa doesn't count. That woman gets lost in her own house." Elena laughed as she looked at the small Cuban flag hanging on the wall. The flag reminded her she was home, no matter which country the little banner hung in. "I'm hitting the shower, then my work bench."

"Okay. Hey, what's that you got stowed away in the crate that says 'Project X'?" Mamita asked as she followed behind Elena.

Elena turned to face her. "What are you doing snooping in my workshop, Mamita?"

Mamita spread her arms defensively. "I was looking for dirty socks! You know how you leave laundry everywhere!"

Elena shook her head and continued to the bathroom. "Whatever. Any excuse to snoop. You *love* to snoop."

"I *love* getting the laundry done."

Elena took a sharp right down the hallway and returned with a small sign in her hand. She held it up and displayed it in front of her mother. "See this? It says—"

"'Project X… KEEP OUT.' Yeah, I see it every time I go in your workshop to collect dirty socks." Mamita smiled.

"Tell you what," Elena offered. "I won't go running in the dark anymore if *you* promise to stay out of my workshop."

"Works for me," Mamita agreed as she rested her hands on her lap.

"Okay, I'm going to hit the shower. Why don't you get back to bed, Mamita?"

"You going to tell me what Project X is?"

Elena gave her mother a determined smile over her shoulder. "No, I'm going to *show you*… if I ever get it working."

Mamita started to wheel herself to her little bedroom. "You will. My baby gets everything working."

Elena's determined smile turned sad as she watched. She never offered to help her mother into bed, as she knew the prideful woman would scorn at such assistance. Nonetheless, she always felt a twinge of sadness for her when she struggled through even the simplest of tasks. Her sorrow had gotten worse lately, as it was becoming obvious that her mother's paraplegia was starting to spread. They both knew that without proper treatment, the immobility that ravaged the lower part of her body would soon wreak havoc on the top as well.

Elena skipped the shower and headed directly to her workshop.

Elena entered Coach Sheridan's office, and he looked up from his paperwork with a smile. Most people were intimidated by Sheridan. He was well known for being by-the-book and disciplined. He demanded perfection from his women's track team, and often presented it.

His office was immaculate and tidy, and trophies adorned his shelves. He always wore a gray silk shirt with pressed black pants, and his salt-and-pepper hair was cut high in a brush cut, giving every impression of an authoritarian. But Elena had come to know him as an encouraging mentor who recognized and appreciated her hard work.

"Elena! Did you have a good weekend?"

"Yeah. I got a couple of really good runs in, both under 2:20." She rested her hands on the chair in front of his desk.

"Good," Sheridan replied as he stood up. "The extra training is doing your endurance wonders. I'm still amazed by how you broke your record time at practice Friday. But I want you to rest up and recover for a few days before trials."

A nervous knot tied in Elena's stomach. *Do I dare tell him I'm thinking about ditching the Olympic Trials for the Robotics Championship?* She looked up at her coach with a fake smile. "Too bad the Robotics Championship is the same weekend as the trials."

"Yeah," Sheridan laughed. "But you know how important this opportunity is for you. Besides, you'll be representing your team."

But what about my Robotics team? Elena looked nervously at the floor. She suddenly looked up with a smile, remembering why she had paid the coach a visit. "Oh, I forgot to tell you, I'm doing a bionics demonstration for my Robotics class this afternoon. I'd really like you to see what I've built!"

Sheridan laughed again. "So *that's* what they're prepping the auditorium for. Okay, I'll see what I can do."

Sheridan's attitude toward robotics had always bothered Elena. She knew he considered it a frivolous waste of her time. But as a member of the Bionics Team, she was part of an elite group among her Robotics class. And she was ready to show Coach Sheridan—*and* the Varsity Football Team—just *how* elite.

Elena watched the sweat glisten on Tommy Walter's forehead as he let out an exasperated grunt. The two-hundred-and-fifty-pound linebacker didn't typically exert this much strain in an arm-wrestling match, especially against a girl. But Elena wasn't about to back down—not with her arm encased in a bionic exoskeleton. The lean mechanical arm—composed of carbon fiber, metal, and elastic—was attached to Elena's body by a wraparound apparatus across her chest. She had full confidence in the gears and servos as they whirled and hummed for more power.

The mechanical appendage slowly started to push Tommy's arm toward the table. The auditorium roared with cheers from not only the Robotics class, but also the football team.

"Don't let her beat you, Tommy!" a rowdy quarterback called out. "You'll never live it down!"

The obnoxious jeers only egged Elena to dig deeper. She twisted her body as actuators and sensors converted her movements into mechanical force. The bionic arm pushed the linebacker's hand until it was inches from the table, and Elena saw bewilderment in his bulging eyes. She curled her wrist and brought her opponent's arm up a few inches before she finally slammed his hand to the touchpad. The auditorium roared with applause from both sides.

Tommy pulled his arm away from the robotic hand and rubbed it.

"Are you okay?" Elena asked.

"Yeah, I just can't believe that thing's so powerful."

Elena swung the arm in front of her as she opened and closed her fist repeatedly. "I have a force sensor in my palm that sends electromyography signals up and down the arm, giving me just the right amount of torque." She smiled at Tommy. "I was starting to worry you might drain my battery."

The linebacker shook his head and perked his eyebrows. "Wow," he said in a low voice, as he retreated into a sea of varsity jerseys.

Robotics teacher Mr. McDowell looked at his stopwatch as he approached the victorious teen. "One minute, thirty-three seconds. That's pretty impressive," he said as he looked at Elena.

She regarded the bionic hand with admiration. "Yeah. I thought I'd take him down quicker."

"Do you have the torque actuator turned to the maximum setting?"

"No."

"Good for him." He watched the football players exit the auditorium.

"Mr. McDowell?" Elena said inquisitively. "Did you see Coach Sheridan come in?"

He looked back and forth. "No. But I wasn't paying too much attention to who was here."

She looked toward the main entrance with sadness, and her victory was quickly forgotten.

▄▖▄▖▄▖▄▖

Elena tiptoed into her house with a huge duffel bag tucked under her arm. She had almost succeeded in smuggling the secret contraband to her room when the familiar noise of Mamita's wheelchair sounded in the bathroom.

"I hear you sneaking, Elena. Those old floorboards tell no lies."

Elena finished her approach to her bedroom on flat feet as she looked back over her shoulder. "Wasn't sure if you were sleeping or not."

"Why would I be sleeping in the bathroom?" Mamita deadpanned as she entered the hallway.

"Mamita, you fell asleep once at the fireworks!" Elena said as she walked into her bedroom.

"Get out of those sweaty track clothes and hit the shower," Mamita called out. "Aunt Rosa's cooking Ropa Vieja, and I don't want to be late! What'd you smuggle now? More stuff for Project X?"

"Maaaybe," Elena said, certain Mamita would be able to hear the smile in her voice.

"I can't wait to see what you're cooking up! But I know it's a secret. I know because all your laundry has been accounted for. So, there's really no reason to go snooping in your bedroom, is there?"

"Nope, there isn't." Elena dropped her duffel bag and picked up the stack of neatly folded clothes on her bed. She sniffed the clean laundry as she exited her room and joined Mamita in the hallway. "These clothes smell *so* good. You do such a good job keeping up with my laundry."

"Well, I've got to do something while you're out there running around and tinkering with robots all day. What's that team you're on called again? The Probiotics Team?"

"*Bionics* Team," Elena laughed.

"Oh, oh, okay." Mamita flung her arms up in frustration. "Well, I don't know the names of all these teams you're on. I lose track. Speaking of which, how are you doing on your big decision?" Mamita turned her wheelchair to face her daughter for an answer.

Elena stood in silence for a moment, holding her laundry while looking at the floor. "I know I have a good shot at making the Olympic Team. But placing at Robotics Championship might help me get into the Scholars Program at Berkeley. Coach Sheridan seems to think there is only *one* choice."

"Yeah, but it's not his choice to make… it's yours. And remember, a career in bioengineering could open the door to *so many* different opportunities for you." Mamita paused for a moment, then looked at the floor as she slowly shook her head. "I'm just afraid you're going to have regret, no matter what bus you get on."

"I know. Coach Sheridan makes a good point though—that going to the Olympics is a once-in-a-lifetime opportunity."

Mamita looked up to Elena. "Yeah, but what if you get hurt? What if you lose? What if you *don't* qualify? You have to consider what's best for the long haul ahead."

"True." Elena looked at the picture on the wall under the Cuban flag. "I just love running so much."

"So run!" Mamita exclaimed. "But don't run for Sheridan, or for me, or for that picture on the wall—run for *you*!" She folded her arms on her lap and leaned forward. "You need to learn how to *balance* your passions."

Elena continued to stare blankly at the black-and-white photo. It was encased in an imitation gold frame and featured a young couple sitting close together in a convertible. They both had gleaming smiles and held a baby in their arms. "Why would I run for them? They're dead."

"Oh, no, they're *not* dead," Mamita said defiantly. "They're very much alive in my heart, as I'm sure they are in yours. Otherwise, you wouldn't be standing there gawking at that picture, looking for guidance. And I know for a fact that they would want you to follow *your* heart, not someone else's."

Elena looked down at Mamita. "You don't like Coach Sheridan, do you?"

Mamita looked forward and averted eye contact. "Well, I only met him that one time at your track meet." She paused for a moment, then looked up at her daughter with determined resolve. "I don't think he has your best interests at heart. I think he sees you, and the rest of the girls, as *objects*. Objects he can groom to achieve *his* goals. There's a *detachment* to him that I can't figure out, and I don't like it when I can't figure people out. So, no… no, I don't like him. Sorry."

"Wow," Elena said, with a sarcastic grunt. "He's been like a…"

"…a father you never had. I know. But a *good* father would want his daughter to follow *her* heart, not his."

"Coach Sheridan just tries to bring out the best in people."

"A little too hard, if you ask me."

"And I feel that if I don't go to trials, I'll be letting him down."

"What about letting *yourself* down?" Mamita looked back up at her daughter. A silence lingered in the air for a moment before she continued. "I know Sheridan has spent a lot of time training you to be the perfect athlete, but *you've* spent a lot of time in that little workshop of yours building... *whatever*. And you know what I see every time you come out of there?" Tears started to fill Elena's eyes as Mamita continued. "I see a huge smile on your face. I see a teenaged girl gleaming with excitement, like when you won that robotics competition!" She grabbed Elena's arm and shook it. "I see a happy girl in her happy spot! So, you'd better sit down and have a long talk with yourself before you decide what bus you're going to get on."

Mamita let go of Elena's arm and started to wheel herself into the living room. "Now, I'm going to catch a few minutes of *Judge Jorge* while you take a shower. Make it snappy... Aunt Rosa doesn't like it when we're late for dinner!"

Elena looked at the picture on the wall one more time before heading to the bathroom, this time with a heartfelt smile.

Mamita snored in a peaceful slumber as Elena watched her from the bedroom door. The extra helpings of Aunt Rosa's Ropa Vieja—as well as the late-night conversation—had really tired the woman out. Elena would have no problem sneaking out for a midnight run tonight.

I just want to get it over with, she thought to herself as she slid the black-and-gold varsity jacket over her shoulders. She shoved a heavy-duty flashlight up one of her sleeves in case she had to blind, or perhaps *club*, any potential abductors. There was no way she was going to become a statistic.

The newly lubricated front door didn't make so much as a creak or squeak as she slipped through it and out into the night. The prospect of getting back in time to make some adjustments to Project X before school fueled Elena's run.

As she cleared her second mile, a smile crept across her face, as the endorphins started to surge. Giddy anticipation started to overcome her as the physical exertion stimulated her divergent thinking. Solutions to programming errors that hadn't been there before now began to resolve themselves in her head. *I need to start bringing a pad of paper and pen.*

A low rumbling sounded from above.

She looked up. A low-flying craft descended from the moonlit sky. *The airport's on the other side of town... There shouldn't be anything flying this low over here in the burbs.*

A pulsating current swept through the air as the craft continued its descent. Elena's run slowed to a jog. The tailwind pushed her forward, and she stumbled.

Trees and bushes swayed back and forth as Elena came to a stop. She strained her eyes and tried to make out what it was.

The craft was hexagonal in shape, with dark red lights running along the bottom—too dark to be navigational lights. It was unlike anything she'd seen before.

Probably some experimental military craft. Elena followed the craft's trajectory, and watched as it decelerated and started to land in the subdivision just ahead of her. Goosebumps covered her body when she realized that the craft had landed on Feltch Street, a cul-de-sac that corresponded with her running route.

She started to jog toward the cul-de-sac, anxious to see just *what* had landed in the neighborhood ahead. But before she could advance any further, a scream from up ahead caused her to come to an abrupt stop. She stood there, panting, listening, waiting. The low rumbling of the unidentified craft soon drowned out the sound of her heart pounding. Trash, broken tree limbs, and leaves blew in Elena's direction as the craft ascended back into the night sky.

Elena was sure she made record time running back home.

Elena entered her normally noisy first-hour science class to low murmurs and whispers. Small groups of students conversed in gossipy tones, while the teacher, Mr. Sanchez, talked on his cell phone in what was obviously *not* a social call. She took her seat, and the always-chatty Emily Perez turned to her abruptly.

"Did you hear about Jennifer Smith?" she asked with wide eyes.

"No."

"Apparently, she was taken from her home last night." Emily looked over her shoulder quickly and then continued. "Her parents woke up to her screaming, and when they went up to her room, she was gone!"

Emily was cut off by an abrupt "Ahem" from Mr. Sanchez. The students all straightened in their seats and faced forward.

"As many of you know by now, another student has been taken from their home and is now missing." He slowly scanned the classroom and cleared his throat before continuing. "I want you all to please, *please* be careful after dark. Make sure you and your family are locking doors, leaving on lights, and taking the necessary precautions to ensure your home's safety." He looked down at his desk and composed himself. "Police and faculty are doing all they can to determine the whereabouts of Jennifer Smith."

Emily quickly turned to see Elena's reaction. Elena just stared ahead, bug-eyed.

"Jennifer's the leader of the swim team. *Another* varsity athlete," Elena said, more to herself than Emily. What was even more shocking to Elena was that she knew exactly where Jennifer Smith lived: *Feltch Street.*

‖ıl‖‖ıl‖‖ıl‖‖ıl‖

Coach Sheridan had an open-door policy with all his students and athletes—something Elena had always admired about him. The door to his office had been removed long ago, and windows surrounded Sheridan's office, giving it an air of open approachability. But approaching him today was something Elena was dreading. Especially with what she had to tell him. She knocked on the steel door frame, which was painted the school colors: black and gold.

"What are you knocking for?" Sheridan said with a smile. "Come in, Elena."

She entered his office and rested her hands on the chair in front of his desk. "Hi, Coach." She looked to the ground.

"What's wrong?" He shuffled through the papers on his desk. "Up late *tinkering* for your robot class?"

His backhanded use of the word *tinkering* hurt. Elena put a little anger behind *her* words. "No, no, actually I was out *running.*"

Sheridan stopped shuffling and looked up. "Oh. How was your time?" he asked eagerly.

"I wasn't timing myself. I was running because I enjoy it. It clears my head."

Sheridan shook his head and let out a giggle. "Well… okay. At least you got a workout in. But you might want to focus more on your pacing and repetitions instead of just 'clearing your head.' The trials are this weekend."

"Yeah… about that." Elena looked out the window.

"That reminds me," Sheridan interrupted. He sprang from his desk and raised a hand. "Wait here, I've got something for you." He quickly went to the back of his office and pulled a brown box out of a locker. He brought it back and handed it to Elena with a gleeful smile. "Sorry, I didn't have time to wrap it."

Elena's already strained nerves tensed even more. She knew what was in the box. She opened it and found the brightest neon-orange track spikes a star runner could wear. She just stared at them, speechless.

"Well? What do you think?" Sheridan asked. "They're a lot like the ones you had, just brand new."

She looked up at him with a forced smile. "These are *really* great, Coach. But I won't be needing them. We already won state finals."

Sheridan laughed in disbelief. "They're for the *trials* this weekend, remember? You really *did* put in a long night!"

Elena tried to divert the conversation. "So did Jennifer Smith... did you hear about her?"

Sheridan's tone became serious, and he nodded while looking at the floor. "I did. How unfortunate. Hopefully the police will turn something up." He looked back up at Elena. "You might want to try those on."

Elena looked at the shoes in the box. "Coach, I'm not going to the trials."

Sheridan's eyes widened. "WHAT?! What are you talking about?"

Elena looked up at him. "I've decided to attend the Robotics Championship in Texas and support my team."

Sheridan's face turned grave. "What about your *team* you'd be representing at the Olympics? What about the *team* you just won the state finals with—"

"—one of whom is still missing," Elena cut in. "Any word on Lisa's whereabouts?"

"The police are doing everything they can," he said dismissively. "You'd be doing her *and* your team a huge disservice by not going." He paused for a moment and stared at Elena in disbelief. He then sat back down at his desk and started checking over paperwork again. "You know, I've often seen my athletes as strong, healthy flowers just getting ready to bloom. And it's my job to help them bloom to their full potential... *before* they start to wilt."

"I can bloom in other ways, Coach. And I've chosen to do that with bionics."

He looked up. "Yes, but your body and its abilities aren't going to last you forever. You need to utilize your potential while you're still young." He looked down at his papers again. "You can tinker with toys *after* you've achieved your athletic potential."

Elena felt like she'd been punched in the gut, and for the first time ever, she felt anger toward her mentor. "I wouldn't be *'tinkering with toys.'* I'd be designing neural prostheses that help people with neurological disorders, creating artificial limbs for combat veterans and people with birth defects." She raised her chin proudly, and Sheridan finally looked up at her. "A career in biomedical engineering isn't about *'tinkering with toys.'* It's about improving peoples' lives."

"But that will still be there *after* you've won the gold." Sheridan furrowed his brows. "You need to learn *balance.*"

"I *need* to do what makes me happy," Elena said with defiance. "Working with bionics is like working on a crossword puzzle you never want to put down because you enjoy the challenge." Saying those words invigorated Elena, and she was glad she'd spoken them.

She set the track spikes on the chair.

Sheridan looked up. "Take those home with you. When you're done working on *puzzles*—try them on." He looked back at his paperwork. "The bus will be leaving Friday night at 7 P.M. sharp."

"Coach... I've made up my mind." She turned to leave his office. She stopped at the doorway and looked back. "And by the way, Lisa was more than just a teammate... she was a *friend*." She exited the office quickly, not wanting to hear Sheridan's response.

Friday came, and Elena was glad the long, stressful week was coming to a close. She came home with another duffel bag full of hardware under her arm.

"Whatcha got now? More parts for Project X?" Mamita greeted her daughter in the kitchen. "You must be building a car back there."

Elena unslung the bag and held it in front of her. "These are more donations from the hospital: a few servo motors and some microcontrollers. They might come in handy for us at the robotics competition this weekend."

Mamita folded her arms on her lap and looked at her daughter proudly. "I've got all your laundry done and ready for you to pack. I also baked—"

"—oatmeal cookies!" Elena interrupted. "I can smell them! My team will love them!" She leaned over and hugged her mother.

"Aunt Rosa wants to make you a send-off meal tonight. She wanted to know what you'd like her to make?"

Elena shook her head. "Honestly, I just want pizza or something easy."

Mamita nodded. "Okay, I'll call and tell her. You go get packed for tomorrow."

Elena retreated back to her workshop with a giddy smile on her face.

Elena and her mother returned home just after 6:00 P.M., so Elena could finish preparing for her trip.

"I ate too much," Mamita said as Elena wheeled her into the house.

"That pizza hit the spot, and Aunt Rosa didn't seem to mind us bailing on her early." Elena shut the front door behind her.

"Oh, I'm going to hear about it tomorrow, trust me. You heard what she said about 'looking after me while you're gone,' like I'm some kind of invalid or something!"

Elena smiled. "No! What she said was that she'd be *checking in* on you, that's all. Besides, it doesn't hurt to have someone to keep you company."

Mamita turned to face her daughter. "I love my sister, but she's a snoopy gossip queen."

Elena grinned. "Hmm. That sounds familiar."

"That reminds me, have you heard from that coach of yours since you set him straight?"

Elena looked to the floor and shook her head. "No... I didn't see him the rest of the week." She looked up at her mother with a sarcastic smile. "But I stayed clear of his office, if you know what I mean."

Mamita shook her head. "It's too bad. Some coaches get way too wrapped up in their students and try to live their lives *through* them."

Elena nodded in agreement. "Being in track was still an awesome experience, one I'll never forget."

"I just hope they find those missing students," Mamita said sadly.

A sudden knock at the door made both women jump. They weren't used to having visitors. They looked at each other, and Elena went and opened it.

She was shocked when she saw Coach Sheridan standing in the doorway. "Coach! What are *you* doing here?"

He regarded her with a wry smile. "Are you ready to go, Elena?" He glanced over Elena's shoulder and nodded toward Mamita, then looked back to Elena—who just stood there looking at him blankly. "I brought your shoes."

He pulled a cylindrical object out of his front pocket. The cylinder was black and looked like a canister of pepper spray. He held up the cylinder and depressed the top with his thumb. It started beeping and emitted a dark crimson glow. "The bus is on its way," Sheridan said with a toothy grin as he shook the cylinder toward Elena.

Mamita quickly wheeled her chair around Elena to confront him. "Didn't my daughter tell you she wasn't going on that bus of yours?"

Elena held up a hand toward Mamita. "I got this, Mamita." She crossed her arms and looked at Sheridan. "Coach, I already told you I made up my mind. Did you think I was joking?"

"I think you're being silly." Sheridan gave a condescending smile. He took a step toward Elena, and she stepped back. "Why don't you go pack your bags quickly so we can get going."

"Hey!" Mamita called out. "Why don't *you* get out of my house!" She wheeled closer to Sheridan and reached out to grab his arm, while he swatted at her like she was a fly.

His backhand sent the older woman toppling over, along with her wheelchair.

"MAMITA!" Elena screamed as she ran to her mother's side. She looked up at Sheridan with bug eyes. "Coach! What the heck are you doing?!"

Sheridan just narrowed his eyes and folded his arms. "Go pack your bags."

"*No!* I don't know what's gotten into you, but you're *not* the man I thought you were." Elena looked to see that her mother had crawled out of the kitchen and down the hallway. Elena stood up straight and balled her fists. "You're crazy! *Really* crazy! How *dare* you come into my house and hit my mother! GET OUT!"

"We need you, Elena. The *team* needs you. Do you know how much time I've invested in you? Now, you're coming with me."

The house started to shake and vibrate suddenly. At first, Elena thought it was the rumbling of a seismic tremor, but she could see from over the coach's shoulder that the wind had picked up outside, and debris was flying everywhere.

Terror filled the teen when she recognized the droning hum as the unidentified craft she had seen on Feltch Street. She looked from it to the cylinder in Sheridan's hand, and a realization hit her.

It's a remote... that craft is landing in front of my house. It's... my coach's. She stared at the man she'd once looked up to, with bewildered eyes.

The electricity of the house surged, making the lights flicker. And the dark red lights from the craft filled the street.

Sheridan ignored everything that was going on around him and stared at Elena with narrowed eyes. "Do you know the *one* thing I'm good at? Finding and grooming the strongest, most robust youths, and giving them a proper cause."

Elena slowly backed up until she hit the kitchen counter. She thought her heart was going to pound out of her chest as she covered her mouth with her palm and glared at Sheridan in disbelief.

"Oh my God... oh my God..." Elena murmured over and over. *All this time, all the training, the mentorship... a lie.*

Elena hadn't felt this much shock and disbelief since the day Mamita had told her how her parents had died in a car accident when she was a baby. That was the day she'd found out her *Mamita* was actually her *Abuela:* her grandmother.

Sheridan continued his rant. "You're going to help our cause, and your planet won't miss you one bit."

What... MY planet?

"There are too many of your kind as it is—your race needs *balance*," Sheridan stated.

Tears started to fill Elena's eyes as one horrible truth hit her after another. She closed her eyes tight and hoped that when she opened them, she'd be in her bed waking from a nightmare. Not only was Sheridan *not* the man she thought he was, but he was also *not of this world*!

Her fear turned to rage as she thought of her missing teammates. "YOU took those girls!"

Sheridan smiled. "I put them to good use." He stepped toward Elena, and she sidestepped into the living room. "Now, pack a bag while you still can. You've got work to do."

"Where?" Elena demanded.

Sheridan let out an evil laugh. He looked up, then back to Elena. "You'll see."

His expression went blank as he suddenly jolted forward and fell face down in front of Elena. The familiar sound of motorized bionics filled Elena's ears, and she felt relief when she saw Mamita's foot hit the kitchen floor with a heavy thump. She looked up. Mamita stood in front of her, with all her lower extremities encased in a bionic exoskeleton.

"Stay away from my daughter, you creep!" Mamita yelled. She flung the upper part of the exoskeleton at Elena with a grunt. "Here! Put it on before he gets up!"

Elena quickly scooped up the suit and wrapped it around her torso. She slid her arms into the exoskeleton and secured the apparatus by fastening a buckle at the center of her chest. She then reached over her shoulder and slapped the power button on her back, and the suit came to life.

Sheridan brought up both of his arms and slammed his fists into the ground, as if he were doing a push-up.

Mamita took a couple of heavy steps toward Sheridan and pointed at him. "Don't let him get up!"

Elena raised a bionic fist and brought it down like a jackhammer onto Sheridan's head. His face slammed into the kitchen floor and made a small crater, which sent cracks in every direction on the linoleum. Orange and yellow sparks erupted from under Sheridan's face. Elena looked up at her mother, whose expression was aghast with horror.

She pointed to Sheridan. "That ain't no man! Hit him again!"

Elena raised her bionic fist once more, but before she could bring it down, Sheridan slapped her legs out from underneath her with a simple swipe of his hand. She landed on her side, but quickly recovered as Sheridan pushed himself up and started to stand. Elena helped him the rest of the way up by uppercutting him in the chin. His head snapped back as sparks erupted from his mouth, eyes, and ears. He staggered a couple of feet, only to be jolted forward by another kick from Mamita.

Elena cocked her arm back and balled a fist as the robotic monstrosity staggered in her direction. She exerted all the myoelectrical force she could and slammed the bionic fist into Sheridan's chest. The blow sent him crashing into the kitchen stove.

"My stove!" Mamita hollered as she spread her arms in disbelief.

Sheridan sat on the kitchen floor with his back against the now-destroyed stove. His head hung forward, with sparks raining from his mouth and eyes.

Mamita pointed to him and looked at Elena. "You ever see a robot like that before?!"

"Uh… NO." Elena stared at Sheridan with wide eyes. She snapped out of her reverie and looked to her mother. "Mamita! The cops!"

"I already called them—they're on their way." She looked out the door. "I wonder if there are any more of these things in that ship out there."

Almost on cue, the hatch of the ship opened up slightly, allowing dark red light out.

"Mamita, look!"

Mamita looked back to Elena, who was pointing at Sheridan. The sparks had stopped trickling from the robotic man, and now a yellow light blinked intermittently from his eye sockets and ears. Each blink was accompanied by a low beep. His head slowly started to rise, and the blinking yellow light flashed around the kitchen.

"Look out!" Mamita grabbed her daughter's arm.

They both took a couple of steps back, as Sheridan slowly leaned forward and sat upright for a moment. The flashing yellow light and beeping continued, as Sheridan came to his feet in a trance-like manner. Elena gave him a wide berth as he turned toward the front door and started to walk out like a possessed zombie.

The door to the ship slowly lowered as Sheridan walked toward it. Red light from the craft flooded the street, and silhouetted bodies started to make their way down the platform.

Mamita looked to Elena as they stood in the doorway. "Uh-oh. I think we're in trouble."

Both mother and daughter were startled when a voice from the ship cried out, "Elena!"

One of the silhouetted figures ran the rest of the way down the platform, past Sheridan and onto the street. It was a blond, teenaged girl wearing a dirty gray jumpsuit that looked something like a prison uniform.

"Lisa!" Elena called out.

The two teens embraced in the middle of the street, and Elena looked up to see four other teens approaching as Sheridan entered the ship. Lisa broke the embrace and held out her arm for Jennifer Smith. Jennifer joined the bittersweet reunion and started to sob.

"Are you both okay?" Elena asked.

"We're fine," Lisa answered. "Just hungry." She gestured to a stocky teen who approached them. "This is Andras. He's from Hungary." She then pointed to an Asian teen who had her hair pulled back in a tight ponytail. "And this is Mikayla, from Singapore."

Mamita approached the group. Some of them took note of her bionic leggings. She pointed to the last teen, who seemed too shy to approach the others. "Who's that? Is he okay?"

Jennifer spoke up. "He's fine, just a little shy."

"What's that blue stuff all over his face?" Mamita asked.

The teens all smiled at each other. "That's Zelnoy," Lisa answered. "And that blue stuff is... *his face.*"

"Are there more of those bots like Sheridan on that ship?" Elena asked.

"No, there's only one bot for every ship," Jennifer said. "They're programmed to return to their ship when they're deactivated. And the weird handcuffs we were wearing just fell off." She rubbed her wrists. "It looks like those bionic arms of yours did the trick!"

Lisa turned to Elena. "They're called *Seekers*. Programmed robots used to gather a slave labor force for a race known as the..." The group all looked to Zelnoy.

"Garlanize," the shy teen answered, in a strange accent.

Elena inquired further. "Where did they take you?"

Jennifer explained, "They have these portals up in orbit, kind of like a mirror you can step through. When the ship flies through the portal, you're *instantly* in another galaxy."

"And then the ship sets down on this huge asteroid with breathable domes," Lisa added with terror in her eyes. "It's filled with workers digging some kind of ore that gives their ships power."

"Why don't they just put their bots to work?" Elena asked.

"There's a gritty dust in the ore that messes with their circuitry," Jennifer added before she started to cough. She hocked up a black loogie and spit it on the ground. "See." She pointed to the black goo on the pavement. "That's what we've been breathing all week."

Lisa patted Elena on the shoulder. "The Garlanize don't make their bots as good as you do, Elena. That's why they need the strong, athletic types like us."

Elena returned the compliment with a smile.

Mamita stared at the teenager with the blue face. She slowly raised a finger toward him. "You mean he's an…"

Elena quickly pushed Mamita's hand down. "Mamita, stop it!" She looked to the others. "Have any of you been injured or hurt?"

"No," Jennifer answered. "Like Lisa said, we're just hungry."

Andras pointed to the ship. "That food on that ship… *not good*," he said in a thick accent.

The hatch to the ship suddenly started to close. A startled Zelnoy quickly joined the others as the ship started to hum to life.

"Everyone, get inside!" Elena cried out. The ship started to blow debris everywhere, and the sound of police sirens could be heard in the distance.

The teens all filed into the little house, followed by Elena and Mamita. Elena stopped in the doorway and watched the ship as it quickly ascended into the sky.

Jennifer rested her chin on Elena's shoulder and watched with her. "Zelnoy said the ships are programmed to return to their base once a Seeker's been deactivated. Wherever that is."

"I can't believe that… *thing* was our coach," Elena said sadly.

"That *thing* would have worked us all to death. You should have seen some of the teens on that rock. They were totally worn out."

Mamita snapped the girls out of their reverie. "First things first! You kids call your parents and let them know you're okay." She grabbed her cellphone from atop the microwave. "Then go ahead and raid the fridge." She looked to Zelnoy, then to her cellphone, then back to Zelnoy. "I might need some help reaching *your* folks, son."

Elena approached her mother and looked at her new legs with a smile. "So, how do you like them?"

Mamita looked down at the bionic wonder her legs were encased in, then back up at her daughter. "So, is *this* Project X?"

"Yup!"

"And when exactly *were* you planning on telling me about it?"

"Like you didn't already *know*, Ms. Snoops-A-Lot!"

Mamita spread her arms defensively. "I can't tell one of your contraptions from the other."

"I wanted to try out my *contraption* at the Robotics Championship before revealing it to you, Mamita. Now I won't have to worry about you so much if I get accepted to Berkeley."

Mamita looked down at her new legs again as she hobbled from one to the other. "I don't think getting into Berkeley is going to be a problem." She looked up and pointed at Zelnoy, who was munching on an oatmeal cookie. "Now, explaining him to the cops… that might be a problem."

THOUGHTS ON *BRAVE NEW GIRLS*

"I think it's very important for any girl going into STEM to remember the word 'balance.' Don't let the passion and drive for your career make you lose sight of who you are as a person. Everyone has passions and hobbies they like to indulge in from time to time. These hobbies and diversions can stimulate creative thinking, which you can later apply to your respective STEM field. So go hiking, skateboarding, or learn a musical instrument. Find the proper balance between personal and professional life so that they rejuvenate one another!"

ABOUT THE AUTHOR

Brad Jurn is an office furniture manufacturer who moonlights as a sci-fi author. His love for science fiction began at age four, when his parents took him to see *Star Wars*. At the age of fourteen, he became a Trekkie, and has been a fan of the *Star Trek* franchise ever since. Brad began his writing career by writing a pulp masked-hero story titled "The Brick." When he's not making office furniture, Brad enjoys reading, writing, drawing, and spending time with his cat, Elsa.

Illustration for "The Owl and the Rabbit" by Harley Scroggins.

A Girl and Her Cyberdog

by Phil Margolies

A GIRL AND HER CYBERDOG

PHIL MARGOLIES

WHEN VIC WAS TEN, SHE'D loved the nighttime darkness. Unlike the Earth of her parents, the planet they'd named "Ellison" had no moon, few clouds, and only the trees and animals the pioneers had brought or bred. Under the shield of stars, Vic and her dog, Buddy, lingered outside after sunset, enveloped in the whir of the atmosphere generators creating breathable air.

Nowadays, five years after the Disaster, Vic didn't fear the darkness, but she was rightfully wary of it.

Nowadays, she didn't linger after dark when she wasn't scavenging tech, because there were things outside worse than the Ellison-bred insects, the croaks of frogs, and the chirps of birds. Like escaped cherbals the size of capybaras, with the attitude of starving alligators.

Nowadays, when the bugs and frogs and birds fell silent, that meant danger.

The living sounds fell silent now. Vic crouched behind the melted stub of a light post. Beside her, Bud growled. Vic shushed him. She heard nothing. Bud stilled, ears up, the antenna that served as his tail at attention.

They were kilometers beyond the "safe zone" around Phoenix, the renamed settlement where they lived. There were hundreds of cherbals in the wild, at least. And a dozen rovers. They hadn't encountered any, but the autonomous patrol bots Phoenix sent roving were near-silent. After a moment, Bud nuzzled her knee, his sign that everything was all right.

Like Bud, a few of the other pet dogs and cats had survived the Disaster. Unfortunately, so had the cherbals. What had her dad said about why the pioneers had brought the cherbals as meat animals? *Even with all the facts, people don't always make smart decisions.*

Some of their decisions had been wise, though. The pioneer's charter, she'd learned in school, contained a provision that if there'd been existing life on Ellison, they wouldn't have even landed. The pioneers hadn't found any native life. The planet, or at least the area they'd settled, was basically lifeless desert they'd made bloom over the last twenty years.

Vic sniffled. The night was colder than it should have been. She brushed snot away with the back of her hand. They wouldn't have been out here if the last of their spare control panel circuits hadn't proven beyond her repair skills. And it wouldn't have been the last if she hadn't cannibalized two others to fix the ambulator for Bud's back right leg.

Now they had to trek further than ever before, five kilometers to the ruins of the Cordwain, the main settlement on Ellison.

Vic rubbed the snot off on her pants. Her hand came back dirtier. She had wipes in the pack attached to Bud's harness, but those were for emergencies. Instead, she tore a leaf from a nearby eucalyptus tree and cleaned her hand the best she could.

So far, they hadn't run into anyone or anything since they'd snuck out of Phoenix long after nightfall, to wind through what was becoming a forest of eucalyptus, ash, and pepper trees between Phoenix and Cordwain. She wished she still had her night goggles, but she'd used them when she had to fix Bud's cybernetic eye. In the starlight, she could make out pools of shadow lying within craters, between them and the building whose name had been "Academy," but only the letters "Acmy" remained above the half-collapsed entrance. The building had been their objective, but it was still too dark to do anything but hide and wait until almost dawn.

Fortunately, days and nights weren't as long on Ellison as her parents told her they'd been on Earth. She'd been so focused on finishing up her duties and sneaking the both of them out that she hadn't paid enough attention to the time. Bud had tried to warn her, but she'd dismissed his comments as kvetching.

Vic scratched Bud's neck. Of all his petting spots, that was his favorite. The insects and frogs took up their chattering again. Vic and Bud settled in to wait.

The first time she'd been to the Cordwain before it had been destroyed, was thanks to her parents' work. Her dad had been a veterinarian and farming expert, and her mom an electrical engineer. They'd taken five-year-old Victoria, as she was then known, with them for a month-long visit. The second time was two years before the Disaster, when her mom spent months in Cordwain teaching mechanical engineering at the Academy as part of a failed solidarity effort, before the pioneers in Cordwain and their settlement completely stopped talking to each other, because of political and other disagreements.

The disputes on how to govern Ellison and what kind of society to build felt ridiculous after the Disaster, but they'd led to her parents and dozens of others establishing their own separate settlement. And that, ironically, had led to many of them surviving after the Disaster killed everyone in Cordwain.

Vic's stomach pinched, and not from hunger, though she hadn't eaten in hours. More memories flooded her.

The initial Disaster had struck when Vic was ten. A coronal mass ejection—a C-6 on the Carrington scale, her mom had said—punched through the planet's atmosphere. The blast of solar plasma created the most beautiful and long-lasting auroras Vic had ever seen, but destroyed the atmosphere generators and every other piece of terraforming technology. Her mom and the other techs scavenged what they could and got one generator semi-functional.

They might have been okay had the second part of the Disaster not shattered any hope beyond bare survival.

Even a C-6 CME shouldn't have taken out the space elevator connecting Cordwain to the orbiting ship that had brought her parents' generation to Ellison. But it had. The crashing elevator destroyed Cordwain and devastated her own settlement. Still, the survivors persevered, renaming their settlement "Phoenix" as they struggled to rebuild. They had no other option. Without the elevator and the orbital ship, there was no chance of rescue or return to Earth.

She and her parents had survived the Disaster. Buddy lived as well, though he was badly injured. Despite her pleas, her parents had focused on the injured people, and only turned their skills to Buddy when it was too late to make him whole. Between her parents and with Vic's help, they saved Buddy. Renamed Bud, his back legs were mechanical now, one of his eyes cybernetic, and his tail an antenna covered in fake fur. At her urging, her parents had given Bud a voxbox that translated a limited set of his thoughts into words. He was still Bud, though, even if he was half mechanical and cybernetic.

A year after the Disaster, another had struck, this time a virus, apparently carried by the cherbals. Vic had gotten sick but survived, unlike her parents and forty others in Phoenix.

Bud growled, quiet and low, then tugged Vic's sleeve.

"Hey," she said, pulling away. "Stop."

"Rover," Bud said, in a voice so low, Vic strained to understand him.

The night fell unnervingly quiet. Bud's ears perked. Vic flattened against the ground. She knew that distant buzz, moving closer.

A rover.

Bud pressed against her. The rover, a gumdrop-shaped robot as big as Vic, rumbled into sight, starlight revealing its outline. A fat vine tangled one of its steering fans, but the security bot trudged on. In addition to hunting cherbals, the rovers were programmed to recover anyone that slipped off or got lost. Vic swallowed. Getting in trouble for sneaking out again was as much a worry as being ushered back before she'd scavenged the tech.

The rover's spotlight flashed over their heads. Vic held her breath. Bud panted silently. The light swung all the way around. Vic stifled a gasp as it swept inside the Acmy building. Movement!

Someone—or something—was in there.

She listened, but heard neither sound nor scurry from a person or an animal. The spotlight brightened as the rover focused on the debris inside the building, then flicked off so it could scan in infrared. The moment it did, the sounds of small feet came rushing through the debris to her left. The rover's spotlight snapped back on. Vic's heart thrummed. Three cherbals dashed into the ruins of another building. The rover took off after them.

Vic waited until she couldn't hear the rover or the cherbals, then let out the breath she'd been holding. She tapped her watch to wake it, then scrolled to the mapping app. The map in the watch showed her their track from Phoenix to Cordwain. She enabled the scanner so it would layer in the debris around them, and she could finally see more than dark shadows, as the first hints of pre-dawn light glowed along the eastern horizon.

She scratched the fur beneath Bud's harness, thinking about how she'd built and coded a tracker for Bud so she could locate him, and he her, if they were ever separated. His version sent subtle twinges to his shoulders through his harness, to guide him to her. Hers simply mapped his path on her app. Without working GPS satellites or communication towers, the devices could only track each other over short distances, a kilometer at most.

Vic popped to her feet. "Come on, Bud. Stay close."

"Always," he replied. They headed, cautiously, for the Acmy building. Bud growled as they reached the entrance. Vic froze. Bud padded forward, ears back, tail straight up. He was so protective, and yet, she couldn't imagine him hurting even a frog.

"Person," Bud said. "Hiding."

Vic couldn't see anyone, but then she didn't have Bud's infrared vision. So the rover *had* detected someone. The bot's limited processor hadn't considered them as much a threat as the cherbals. Could she take the same chance?

She had a knife in the toolkit on her belt, but that was for whittling and prying tech out. She drew it anyway.

"Small girl," Bud said.

"Are you sure?"

Bud quirked his head. "Sure as can be. It a girl."

Vic pressed her lips. Her last tweak of the voxbox code had made Bud sound more human. It didn't work flawlessly, but the inconsistency in the language made her feel sad. As if there was some secret her parents hadn't revealed before they'd died. She shook her head. Those were thoughts for when she was back at Phoenix.

"Hi there," she called out before she could think better of it. "Hey."

Bud had said "girl" and not "woman." Vic imagined some six-year-old with pigtails cowering behind a mound of broken lab equipment. In the minimal light, she couldn't separate the shadow of the mound from the surrounding debris. Bud seemed to read her mind. His cybernetic eye flickered on, casting a red cone of light on the mound so as not to ruin their night vision.

The gasp from behind the pile wasn't one of a six-year-old.

"Come on out," Vic said. "I won't hurt you."

The knife twisted in her hand. Keeping it out felt like calling her words a lie. Sheathing it felt like the kind of over-trusting that used to get her in trouble. Swallowing her concerns, she slid the knife back into her toolkit.

Bud circled to the right, disappearing behind the mound. Vic tensed, expecting to hear a scream or see the girl leap out. Nothing happened. Slivers of the red light from Bud's cybernetic eye shone through gaps in the mound, but not enough for Vic to see by. Bud gave a quiet bark. Vic jumped. So did the girl, right into the open.

She was a shadow against dark, but from the shape and size, she was a head shorter and slighter than Vic. Bud rounded the girl, his eye casting a dim red glow on her. Vic was half-right. The girl was maybe twelve, maybe ten. A ponytail, tied tight, slung over her shoulder. She half-crouched, her breath coming fast and sharp, eyes pinched in terror.

"It's okay," Vic said. The fear didn't waver as the girl stepped backward toward the darkness. Bud's head swiveled to follow her and keep her in the light.

The girl swallowed a gasp as she stumbled into what had been a chair.

"Watch out—" Vic called as the girl tumbled backward. Vic darted forward and pulled the girl to her feet. They stared at each other for a moment, then at Vic's hands gripping the girl's forearms. Vic let go and stepped back as the girl opened her mouth to scream. The girl's expression changed from panic to confusion. With Bud's light still on both of them, the girl studied Vic.

"You're not—" The girl sucked in a breath. "You're not from Kansas. Are you a stray?"

The girl's eyes widened, and she went pale, like she was about to faint. Vic caught her as her legs buckled, and eased her to the ground. Bud trotted over. Vic popped open Bud's pack and pulled out a container of water. She handed it to the girl.

The girl drank three deep gulps before thrusting the container to arm's length. Her breaths came rapidly, like Bud's panting after a run.

"It's water," Vic said.

The girl looked uncertain, then licked her lips. She took another tentative sip, then a longer one.

"Thank you," she said.

"You're welcome."

They watched each other silently, neither sure of what to say. *Was* the girl alone? Vic didn't hear anything but bugs and frogs, most of them outside the ruined Acmy building. The girl obviously wasn't from Phoenix. Vic clearly wasn't from Cordwain. Which meant… there were survivors in Cordwain after all! But how?

Realization clicked, like a mechanical circuit making an obvious but missed connection. Other survivors. Other people. Things to trade. People, maybe families to reunite. Her heart thumped with excitement.

"So," Vic began, "you said 'a stray'? And Kansas? You mean Cordwain?"

The girl handed the container back to Vic. "Yeah, you're definitely not from Kansas if you don't know the name." The girl let out a long uncertain breath.

The girl. She had to have a name.

"I'm Vic." She gestured to Bud. "This is Bud. What's your name?"

"Quill."

The light in Bud's eye rounded and dulled, giving the two girls enough to see by, but not projecting into the distance.

"His eye!" Quill gasped, reaching.

"Don't poke Bud eye," Bud said, backing away.

Quill gasped and scrambled backward. Vic dropped to a crouch and held up her hands. "It's okay."

"How?" Panic resurfaced in Quill's voice. "Is there someone with you?"

"No, just me and Bud." Vic pulled Bud next to her. She tapped the voxbox around his throat. "It's a voxbox. It translates for him."

Quill relaxed but didn't come closer. "We don't have voxboxes after the Disaster. We have telephones. And why would you put one on a dog?"

Vic touched the scruff of Bud's neck to caution him not to respond. He made a low rumble anyway.

"Telephones?" Vic asked, ignoring Quill's question. She'd heard of that old Earth-based tech from her parents, but she'd only seen them in history vids.

"Yeah." Quill's confusion returned. Then her eyes brightened. "How does a stray have so much tech? And for a dog?"

"I'm not stray," Bud said, his voice fierce.

"We're not strays," Vic answered. Whatever a stray was. "I'm from Phoenix. The other settlement."

The girl turned white as sand in the sun. "Other pioneers survived?"

"Yes," Bud said. "Obviously. You not smart as Vic smart."

"Bud," Vic chastised him. "Apologize."

"No."

"Bud." She reached down to scratch Bud's neck, but he shied away from her. "Sorry, buddy. Here." She held out a treat. He snatched it from her hand without hesitation. She set a hand on his back as he chomped.

Quill watched, eyes wide in fascination.

"Now, Bud. Apologize."

Bud's expression was severe, but he said, "Sorry," to Quill.

"So the people of Cordwain. In Kansas?"

Quill's eyes welled with sadness. "Not everyone. But a lot of people."

"I'm sorry." Vic looked away again as if to give Quill privacy. No shadows moved. She couldn't hear the rover or the cherbals. Bud stood by her side, his tongue lolling and his tail at rest. So nothing out there meant danger. "What *are* you doing out here by yourself at night?"

Quill looked amused. "I always forget when it's night up here. But I like listening to the sounds of the real outside, not recordings. And I can get away from the Rules for a while."

The way Quill said "rules," it sounded like a word with a capital *R*. Vic started to ask about that when Bud's ears perked. He issued a low growl. Vic's words caught in her throat. She listened. And heard the sound, too. The rover was coming back.

Quill's exhale wasn't panic, but it wasn't exactly not. "I need to go."

She popped to her feet and made her way into the dark toward the back of the Acmy building. Vic followed. Quill paused and looked back, concerned and confused.

"I want to come with you. To Kansas."

"No," Bud said. "No Kansas."

"We have to go, Bud."

"No." He paused, but not long enough for Vic to question him. The light from his cybereye blinked off. "Not Kansas. Get tech. Go home."

Vic glanced the way they'd come. They were kilometers away from Phoenix, with at least one rover around, and who knew how many cherbals? She shook her head. Whatever, whoever was in Kansas, it was the closer and safer destination. And she was curious as could be.

"Come on, Bud."

He didn't move.

The sound of movement made her turn. Quill was gone. Vic's heart choked her.

"Come on," Quill called from the darkness.

"No come," Bud said. "Go."

Vic frowned. As much as she looked after him, Bud was *her* guardian too. She hated using a command on him, but his willfulness was causing problems. "Buddy, come."

Ears flat, tail down, Buddy trotted after her through a gap in the half-standing side wall of the Acmy building.

"This way," Quill said, and picked her way through the debris-strewn yard as nimbly as if she had Bud's cybereye. A well-known path, Vic thought, recalling her own routes into and out of Phoenix, that she could navigate with her eyes closed.

Starlight lit a metal pillar at the far edge of the ruined settlement. Twice as tall as Vic and maybe six meters across, it stood like a cap on an underground bottle. Quill skirted it. Bud issued a low growl as they passed.

"That was the main entrance to Kansas," Quill whispered when they were beyond it. "We can't go that way."

A hundred meters onward, Quill stopped in a tangle of brush. A vent slanted into the ground, steep enough that they'd have to crab-walk down it, but not so steep that they'd slide. Vic glanced at Bud. There was no way his front paws could stop him against the slick metal, but his mechanical back legs were perfectly adept. Still, Vic would stay in front of him.

"No," Bud said. "I'm not going."

"Bud, you can't stay here by yourself."

"No. Bud Vic not go. Go home."

Quill looked from Vic to Bud and back again.

"Bud," Vic said with a measured tone. "I'm going. You can't stay here alone."

"No. We go home I say."

Vic drew in a breath. A cyclical argument served no purpose. The breeze stirred around her. The sounds of night animals kept a constant murmur. No threats right now, but she had to see Kansas. There were other survivors! Why couldn't Bud understand that?

Because he's a dog. She answered her own question. With mechanical and cyber enhancements, but still a dog. He stared at her with firm, decisive eyes.

Something in her mind snapped. "You stay here, then. I'm going with Quill."

The shaft led to an empty instarete-walled room at the bottom. Vic had expected… she wasn't sure. Her annoyance faded, and wariness reasserted itself. She always had a plan, but now her mind reeled. She'd been so thrilled at the thought of finding other survivors, she hadn't constructed a plan on what to do, or how to get out. She glanced back up the shaft, but all she could see was darkness. Not even the reassuring glow of Bud's eye.

Guilt swirled her stomach, but she wasn't going to go back up yet.

At the bottom of the shaft was a giant fan. Quill grabbed the frame around it with both hands. The hinges groaned. "Don't worry. It doesn't work. But I keep it in place in case anyone remembers this room. And to keep the cherbals from getting in." She latched it. "I found a dead one once at the bottom when I swung it open."

Vic grimaced. She'd learned on the way down the shaft that Quill was in fact only ten, and as adventurous as Vic had been at her age.

Quill crossed to what looked like an ill-fitted door and grabbed the handle.

"Hold on," Vic said, "what's out there?"

Quill looked at her oddly. "Kansas."

"I know, but what's the plan?" Quill's expression didn't change. Vic sighed. "Where are we going? In Kansas."

"To the Bureau," Quill responded, as if the answer should have been obvious. Before Vic could ask what "the Bureau" was, Quill went on. "It's like the town hall for Topeka. That's our town, really more a neighborhood, in Kansas, which is really a bunch of neighborhoods. Well, they call them neighborhoods, but it's all the same houses all together. The adults all make a big deal about calling different groups of houses 'towns.' Anyway, my dads should be at the Topeka Bureau of Community Affairs. They'll know what to do next."

Vic rubbed her wrists, working the ache out of them. Her fingers latched onto her watch. She didn't have Bud's sense of direction, but she had her watch, with its mapping and tracking functions. While she didn't have a map of Kansas, the apps could still run a virtual string along whatever route they took. If she got lost, all she had to do was find some place she'd been and follow it back to the air vent room.

Quill slid the door open. Vic had tried not to imagine what Kansas would look like, so she wouldn't prejudice herself. She'd failed in that, picturing a kilometer-long space beneath a vaulted ceiling a couple meters over her, stuffed with random useless junk and trash, wandering animals, and haggard-looking people. Like Phoenix, but underground.

She wasn't prepared for how wrong she'd been.

Kansas was a natural cave, far longer than it was wide. A high ceiling gave it the appearance of an even larger space. Bright but scattered light came from a glowing ball on the cave's roof. A fake sun? What shocked Vic more were the houses. Set along well-marked streets, the houses resembled less the homes the pioneers had built on the surface. They appeared more like the ones people had lived in back on Earth. Staring at them sucked the air from Vic's lungs. People had come all this way to remake what they'd left behind.

That had been part of the disagreements which had led the people of Phoenix to establish a separate settlement in the first place.

"They began building Kansas after the landing," Quill said, as if giving a history lesson. "In case something like what happened, happened. When the space elevator collapsed, it blocked off the other part of the cavern." Quill gestured below and behind them. It took Vic a moment to understand they were making their way down a rockfall. Quill continued, "Don't worry, these rocks are stable. I come up here all the time, even if I'm not going out. Nobody comes here but me, so it's a good place to get away from everyone. Anyway, the damage was light in this cavern. And we're building new 'towns' at the far end where there's space."

At the bottom, Quill led her along on a narrow path between the last row of houses and the cave wall. The younger girl ran her fingers across the top of a fence made of short white posts and rails. Vic knit her eyebrows. The fence wouldn't keep anything in or out. She glanced back and realized she hadn't noticed the dozen or more they'd passed.

Quill turned down a street, and then another, and another. She stopped in front of a squat white building beside a large square of the mossy grass Phoenix had given up on cultivating. Vic whistled, low enough that Quill wouldn't hear her. Maintaining the green underground—not to mention the artificial sun—must have taken significant resources.

Quill opened a plexi door labeled with TOPEKA, KANSAS, BUREAU OF COMMUNITY AFFAIRS, and strode inside. Vic followed.

"Hey, Lew, where's my dads?" Quill called to a boy seated behind a counter. He was maybe a few years older than Vic, and looked equal parts bored and annoyed.

Lew bounced a mop of brown hair across his face, neither clearing his view nor obscuring it more. "How should I know? I'm busy, can't you see?"

As best Vic could tell, Lew hadn't been doing a single thing besides glowering at the universe for sticking him behind the counter. Snappish as he was, she empathized. She hated busy duties when there was important work to do.

"Real busy," Quill muttered. "Where's June?"

"You forget the Council's celebrating Wichita today?" came a voice from the opened door behind Lew. Vic couldn't see anyone, but the voice sounded like a version of Lew's.

"New 'town' at the far end of Kansas," Quill whispered to Vic.

"Everyone's supposed to be there," Lew said, with the satisfaction of someone who'd gotten out of it. "Except Councilors' spawn, who get to pretend they're important by managing the Bureau offices. Right, Ari?" Those last words, he said over his shoulder to the open door. Through it, Vic saw an office and a desk, but not who sat there.

"You're the only one who's *not* busy," came a gruff answer from inside the office.

"I *am* busy. Who wants to listen to boring speeches?" Lew jerked a thumb toward the hall. "June's pretending she's busy in your Papi's office."

"Wait here," Quill said before she darted down the hall.

"You can take a seat, uh, I guess I forgot your name," Lew said with dutiful disinterest, as he waved toward a bench against the wall.

Vic stayed on her feet. She pulled her composure together. "I'm Vic."

Lew looked up, confused. "Do I know anyone named Vic? Do you go by another name? Vicky? Victoria? Victory? Vinny?"

"No, just Vic."

Vic bounced from one foot to the other, desperate to ask him a million questions. Instead, she stuck her hands in her pockets. Her fingers wrapped around the electro-whistle she'd built for signaling Bud. Would it work with her down here? She figured it might, but would Bud be able to get down here and find her? A weight grew in her chest. Even if he could, he didn't want to. And it wouldn't be safe for him.

The sound of running water from down the hall grabbed her attention. Lew's gaze followed hers.

"There's a second toilet if you need," he said.

She shook her head, though she had to go a little. Even more, she wanted to inspect the toilet and its plumbing, and see how the Cordwainers—*Kansans*—made all this work. Surely, their tech had been knocked out by the coronal mass ejection too. Had they somehow shielded their tech in the cavern? She looked up, wondering if there was some massive Faraday cage surrounding the cavern. And if so, how could the people of Kansas have built it without anyone in Phoenix knowing?

Lew followed her eyes again. "There's something on the ceiling?"

"No."

Lew shrugged. "Well, I'm busy then." He got busy doing nothing. Vic's sympathy for him drained away.

The sound of Quill knocking on a door echoed from down the hall. "June!" Her tone was annoyed, not concerned or scared.

A creak followed, and then Quill's voice came again, low enough that Vic couldn't tell what she'd said. A moment later, Quill stepped back into view, followed by June. About Vic's age, June was taller and leaner than Quill, though the curve of her face and angle of her nose gave away that they were related. Older sister?

June narrowed her eyes, assessing Vic. "You're not from Kansas."

The words were flat, accusatory.

The weight in Vic's chest exploded into shards.

"You got to stop bringing strays back, Quill," Lew said.

Vic's hand fell to her side, where Bud should have been. A pit opened in her stomach, and the shards fell, cutting her on the way down. Bud had been right. She shouldn't have come.

"She's not a stray, Lew," Quill huffed. "She's *from* the other settlement."

"She can't be from the other settlement," Lew said, "because that would mean—"

Ari stepped through the door behind Lew. Where Lew was pale, as if he'd been underground for years, Ari looked as if he'd spent his time out in the sun. Vic noted their similar features as well. Brothers?

He stared at Vic, his eyes unable to decide between squinting or going wide. "Lew, there's five hundred people in all of Kansas and, what, fifty our age?"

Lew coughed in offense. "Fifty peoples' names are a lot to remember."

Ari scoffed, never taking his focus off Vic. "What are you doing here? Phoenix and Kansas had an agreement. You leave us alone; we leave you alone."

"That was before the Disaster," Vic said.

Lew smirked. "Yeah, but the *new* agreement after the Disaster said it more—"

"What new agreement?" June's tone was angry and incredulous.

Ari glared at Lew. "There's no 'new' agreement."

"We overheard our parents talking about it," Lew said, with the confidence of pride in knowing and revealing a secret. "The Council decided not to tell anyone."

"Shut up, sit down, and go back to pretending to be busy," Ari snapped at his brother. Lew closed his mouth, crossed his arms, and stayed on his feet.

"We *knew* they survived?" June's glower demanded Ari answer.

Vic tried to speak, but her mouth was dry. Not only did the leaders of Phoenix know the Cordwainers had survived in Kansas, but they'd been in contact! And kept it secret. And the people of Kansas knew about Phoenix.

"We're not supposed to know," said Ari, still glaring at Lew. He turned to June. "You think *I* was going to tell you? We'd get beat. You know the Rules."

Doubt about everything spiraled through Vic. What else had the leaders of Phoenix kept to themselves? She had to get out of Kansas. She had to get back to Bud. Back to Phoenix. "Why keep it a secret?"

She didn't realize she'd spoken the thought aloud until June repeated her words to Ari.

Ari shifted.

"Yeah, why?" Lew said, crossing his arms and cocking his eyebrows at his brother. "Because they destroyed the elevator? That's why we didn't let them down here, is what mom said."

The accusation took Vic aback. "We did not! It was—" She couldn't blame the flare, but what other explanation was there? "*You* destroyed the elevator, not the CME."

Ari responded with a strangled laugh. "Why would we destroy the only way to get back to Earth?"

"Then why build this..." She gestured around them.

"Because of the solar flares. You all helped us build the Faraday cage in the other cavern before the falling space elevator destroyed it. You people chose to leave and set up your own settlement, so you could all be free and not be responsible and follow rules and all. And you took all but two atmo gens and the spare parts."

Vic blinked. How had she not been aware of *any* of this?

"And all the dogs, too," Lew chimed in, his face as red as Ari's. "Left us with a handful of cats. Like cats catch cherbals?"

"She brought her dog with her, too," Quill interjected, with the excited hope of someone trying to make peace. "His name's Bud, and he's got cyber and mech parts. He's really—"

Vic's heart dropped into the pool of shards in her gut.

June's eyes went wide. "Cyber?"

"We need that tech," Lew said to Ari.

"Everybody knows that, Lew." Ari looked to June. "You let the Council know about her and the dog. I'm going to find that dog."

He shoved past Vic. Vic was so stunned, she didn't think to grab for him until he was out the door. His head whipped left and right, then he darted left.

She had to go after him. She had to get to Bud first. June moved between her and the door, blocking her way. Her expression was as furious as Ari's had been when Lew had spilled the secret about the agreement. "I'm going to talk to our dads and the Council about this," she said to Quill, then pointed to Lew. "You keep both of them here until we get back."

Unlike Ari, she ran off down the street to the right.

"Hey," Lew called as Vic stepped toward the door. Quill grabbed her sleeve. Vic shook her off.

"I'm sorry," Quill said. "I shouldn't have said anything about Bud."

"No, you shouldn't have," Vic snapped.

Quill's eyes welled with tears. She rushed past Vic and down a different street than Ari or June. Vic started for the door.

"Hey, don't, don't follow her, please," Lew said. "I can't chase after you. I gotta stay here."

Vic raced after Quill.

Minutes later, huffing at an intersection, Vic paused and looked around. She hadn't seen or heard Quill. She hadn't seen or heard *anyone*. None of this seemed familiar, but at the same time, it all did. All the houses, all the yards in Topeka looked identical. Bland boxes capped with angled roofs (why, when it clearly didn't rain down here?), and grassy front yards surrounded by waist-high white fences. Each street had a distinctive name, but she hadn't been paying attention to the street signs when she and Quill had walked to the Bureau. A sour taste coated her throat.

Vic spun around, searching for *something* familiar.

"Hey, what are you doing out here?" came June's voice. Vic glanced over her shoulder. June was walking toward her, her face flushed. "Where's Quill?"

"She ran after Ari," Vic answered before she could think better of it.

"Which way did she go?"

Vic stared at her. Why did June expect *her* to know? "Shouldn't you know?"

"I know she gets out through an air duct, but..." June shook her head. "I don't know which one or where it is."

June's worried expression called back a memory for Vic. The days after the Disaster, when everyone was in a panic, and all Vic wanted was Buddy, but she couldn't find him, and no one, not even her parents, seemed to care or prioritize him. He was her constant companion, the closest thing she had to a sibling.

"Did you tell your Council about me and Bud?"

"I got halfway there and then..." June took a calming breath. "They'd told us no one in the other settlement survived. A team went there and found it destroyed. Did you know about this 'new agreement'?"

Vic knew a team from Phoenix had found Cordwain destroyed, and dozens of bodies. They'd said—claimed—everyone else had fled into the elevator to get to the ship, and had been killed when the elevator fell. "They lied to us, too, apparently."

June nodded. "This makes me wonder what else they lied about. But I want to confront my dads first by themselves. So, I went back to the Bureau, and it was just Lew, and he said you ran after Quill. If the Council finds out she's been going outside..."

Vic didn't care about *that* now. "If she leads Ari or them to Bud..."

"She wouldn't do that," June said with defensive certainty. "On purpose," she added, in response to Vic's seething expression.

Vic swallowed a snide response. June's face was pure worry, the same feeling Vic had for Bud. Empathy overrode Vic's anger. She didn't trust June, but she could work with her to get back to Bud. And find Quill.

That left the problem of finding the vent when she hadn't paid attention when they'd—

She tapped her watch. She *hadn't* paid attention to their path, because her watch had done it for her. She called up the path they'd taken. The app hadn't added the houses and roads to the map because she hadn't turned on monitoring, but that didn't matter. A bright red line showed the route she and Quill had followed. All they had to do was get to it. And not get caught on the way.

A palette of yellow and orange lit the horizon as Vic and June reached the surface. Animal sounds fell silent. They crouched in the brush around the air shaft to get their bearings. In the dawn light, everything looked different. What had been a settlement of over eight hundred people and one hundred buildings was a mess of instarete, plexi, and smashed or burned-out vehicles. A few structures were partially intact, especially those furthest from the staggered line of broken cylindrical segments that had formed the space elevator.

"Can you call your dog?" June asked, her voice hushed.

Vic shook her head. She *could*, but she didn't want to. What if there was a rover nearby? Or cherbals? Or what if a party from Topeka had come out another way? Her gaze swept the ruins of Cordwain, looking for—*There! The Acmy building!*

She pointed. "That's where Bud and I ran into Quill. He probably went back there."

"We call that the Acmy because some of the letters are missing."

Vic laughed. "That's what I called it when I saw that."

"Come on," June said. "I bet if he's there, so's Quill." They snuck forward, staying low. The sounds of wildlife rose and fell as they passed. Nothing artificial or human startled them. They paused halfway to the Acmy building, and watched for Bud and Quill, and anything—or anyone—else.

Bud's whine cut through the hesitant silence.

Vic leaped up and ran toward the sound of his pain, dodging scattered brown masses on the ground. Bud lay on his side, surrounded by the rubble inside the Acmy. His back right leg splayed at an unnatural angle. Bite marks ran up his left front leg to a gouge in his shoulder. Deep scratches cut his side beneath matted fur. One ear was bent and bloody. His mouth was smeared red.

"Vic. Cherbals," he said between pants. "Quill."

June slid over the debris, landing beside Vic. "Quill!" She darted beyond them and dropped to her knees beside Quill, dirt-covered, panic-eyed, curled into a ball against the remains of a table. "Are you hurt?"

Quill shook her head, then threw her arms around her sister and burst into sobs.

"Bud. Pro—protect. Quill."

Vic found a spot on his head that was barely dirty and uninjured. She lay one hand there while the other pulled bandages and medicine from Bud's pack. It had been torn from his harness, but was still within arm's reach.

"What happened?" Vic asked, as much to Quill as to Bud.

Quill's lips moved, but Vic couldn't hear her.

"It's okay," June said, still holding her sister.

It's not okay, Vic thought, as she fed Bud a chewable pain tablet, then started applying antibiotic ointments to his wounds.

"Cherbals," Quill said.

Vic thought about the three or four brown-and-blood-red masses she'd dodged. Dead cherbals. She shivered as she dabbed Bud's leg. Her focus shifted to his broken mechanical leg. She whistled. The lower ambulator was broken, again, and worse, the wires that connected it to the knee actuator were chewed through. She wouldn't be able to fix the leg until they got back to Phoenix. And she still hadn't found the parts for the ambulator. Scratches raked across his other mechanical leg, but it moved as she watched. Vic's shoulders relaxed a little. She'd worry about his cyber and mechanical parts once she got his physical wounds tended.

"Bud find tech when Vic gone. Then I came here, back. Wait for you," he said, his whining diminishing and his pants easing. His words barely registered. "Hear Quill. See Quill. Cherbals attack Quill."

June startled, but Quill held her arm and explained about Bud's voxbox.

Vic glanced over. The two sisters sat side-by-side against the table, June's arm around Quill's shoulders, Quill leaning hard against her. The fear in her eyes was gone, replaced by worry and exhaustion.

"They chased me after I came back up," Quill said. "I've only seen one or two at a time before, but there were five, maybe six. I'm so sorry I told them about Bud."

"It's okay," June repeated.

It wasn't, and it wasn't June's place to tell Quill it was. Vic let her annoyance go with a breath. They could talk about that when Bud was patched up.

"I screamed. I shouldn't have, but Bud came. I think he was waiting here. There were so many of them, but he fought them and kept them off me. Is he going to be okay?"

I hope so. Vic thought he would be, but she wanted to get a better look at him in full daylight with her dad's vet equipment once they got back to Phoenix. Too many thoughts crashed into her. She pinched her eyes shut. Getting back in the daylight with Bud injured. Sneaking, if they could, back into Phoenix. The secret agreement between the leaders of Phoenix and Kansas. Who did she have to tell? Who could she trust?

She shook off the thoughts and opened her eyes. She'd have to deal with all that—so would June and Quill, she realized—but *after* she tended to Bud.

Quill sobbed. "Oh, Bud. I'm so sorry."

Vic looked at her and June, confused. Belatedly, she realized Quill had taken the shake of her head to mean Bud wouldn't be okay. "No, he'll be okay," Vic said. "But I've got to get him back home."

June bit her lip. Her eyebrows furrowed. Her expression was one of internal debate. "I don't know anything about mechanics or electronics, but do you need help carrying him?"

Vic didn't want to say yes, but her aching shoulders and back argued otherwise. "Well, if you know where I can find the right tech to fix Bud's leg or build a canine wheelchair…"

"Is there anything you can use in that pile?" June pointed to the jumble of wires, controls, and other assorted tech near her and Bud. Vic blinked and remembered what Bud had said. *Bud find tech when Vic gone.*

Vic leaned close to his face. "You found all this, buddy?"

"Bud find tech while Vic gone. Bud is good boy."

Vic worked through the pile he'd made. Sure enough, he'd found the things they'd been looking for. Vic sighed with relief. The training she'd done with him to identify all manner of tech for them to scavenge had paid off.

"You are a good boy," she said. Bud wagged his tail and tried to roll to his stomach. "Easy, boy."

Vic cleaned the dirt out of his good mechanical leg, finding one cable damaged. She dug through the tech he'd gathered and found what she needed. She spliced in the new cable, then tested the leg by scratching a sweet spot on Bud's belly. He kicked with no trouble.

Bud struggled to get up. "Not yet, we can wait a little," Vic said. She wasn't sure they could, but the sun was fully up now. No one had come up after them, but that didn't mean they couldn't at any given moment.

"We go," Bud said.

"Your dog's right," June said. "Are you sure you don't need help?"

Vic shook her head. "I can take care of him. You and Quill have a lot to deal with here."

June's relieved look didn't last long as she took in what Vic meant.

"Yeah," she said, squeezing Quill's shoulder. Her face took on a severe expression. "So do you."

June pushed to her feet and pulled Quill up. With Vic's help, Bud worked to his feet. The front two worked fine, as did the back one that Vic had been able to repair. The other back right wasn't functional at all. He'd have to get by on three legs, unless she could fashion a canine wheelchair from whatever scraps she could find.

"Thank you," Vic said. She wanted to say more, but held back. Maybe she'd be able to fully trust Quill and June someday. She hoped so. Maybe the remaining people on Ellison would learn to work and live together again. Maybe they'd battle each other until they were all gone. If the budding friendship between the three girls was an indication, the survivors of Phoenix and Kansas *could* find ways to help each other. They had come from the same colony ship after all, and they were all stranded on the same planet. If Vic had to pick between doubt and hope, she'd choose the latter. As long as Bud was with her, that was always the best bet.

Quill let go of her sister and waved. "Bye, Bud."

"Bye, Quill," Bud said.

"Can I hug you, Bud?"

Bud's happy pant and Vic's nod were all the permission Quill needed.

"Thank you for protecting my sister," June said to Bud. She scratched the same spot on his head that Vic had earlier. "Even at the cost of…"

"I protect my human, and her friends."

"Do you know what love is?" Quill asked Bud.

"Sure I know. A dog loves his girl." He nuzzled Vic's knee.

Vic stroked his neck. "And a girl loves her dog."

THOUGHTS ON *BRAVE NEW GIRLS*

"Amazing is considered a far better state than normal. What's truly amazing is when what is seen as special and unique becomes the norm. There are far more girls in STEM than there used to be. That is a good thing. As even more girls enter STEM fields, the diversity of perspectives and ideas grow, leading to a normal that's more powerful than the time when having a few girls in those fields was seen as both amazing and sufficient."

ABOUT THE AUTHOR

Phil Margolies has loved reading and writing since before he co-created a publishing company in fourth grade. In high school, sarcastic but supportive friends encouraged him to combine his love of science fiction TV shows and writing. He has been writing stories ever since. He mainly writes science fiction and fantasy, but dabbles in horror, slipstream, mainstream, mystery, and literary fiction. His short stories have appeared in *Curiosities*, *Brave New Girls*, *The Worlds of Science Fiction, Fantasy & Horror*, *Perihelion SF*, and *The Big Book of New Short Horror*, among others. He's kept grounded by his artistic wife, awesome daughter, pair of skittish rescue dogs, and now a wacky puppy. He's on Twitter/X and Bluesky as @philmargolies far more often than he's on his website, philmargolies.com.

Illustration for "A Girl and Her Cyberdog" by Ann Piesen.

Gaia: The Legend Of the Moldavite Stone

by Denise Sutton

Gaia: The Legend of the Moldavite Stone

Denise Sutton

"ANOTHER STUDENT HAS GONE MISSING."

"Is that all, Professor?"

"Headmistress Cypress, with all due respect, she's the third one this year, and it's only May! Usually, three to four students disappear per year. Isn't that alarming?" The professor raised her brow and stared at the Headmistress.

"No. Students always leave us. That is no secret. They either get homesick, feel this education is too stressful and break under pressure, or run away in the name of some boy they fell desperately in love with over at the military academy." Cypress sighed. "I would not be too worried, Professor."

"Headmistress, you forgot one vital reason for their departure."

"Ah, yes. The Moldavite Stone," Cypress almost giggled. "Professor, if a student decides to seek out the Stone, she is not one we need to worry about."

"Why's that, Headmistress?" The professor stared at her.

"Those who go for the Stone either want to claim it for themselves, or distribute its powers to norms who did not receive its gifts." Cypress paused. "If it is the latter, I would not mind getting more students to teach. If it is the former, we would not want a student like that anyway."

The professor gasped.

"Tell me, Professor, would you want a power-hungry pistol loaded with unhinged and unpredictable energy roaming these halls?"

The professor shook her head no.

"I did not think so."

"But Headmistress Cypress," the professor looked up at her superior, "what if the student seeks to destroy the Moldavite Stone?"

The Headmistress grinned. "I do not believe that will be an issue. Now, please, return to your class, and instruct these children on how to be the best contributors to Gaia this world has ever seen."

The professor nodded, took a breath, then said, "Will do, Headmistress Cypress." She turned around and gracefully left the office.

·ılııtl·ılııtl·ılııtl·ılııtl

"Hey, Wren, did you hear?"

Of course I had. I just didn't want to respond. But my sister was not having it. She kept giving me those big brown puppy-dog eyes. I bit. "Hear what, Willow?"

"Another girl went missing. I think it's Scarlett. You know, the really tall, skinny one with the dark green eyes and the long wavy red hair. Talk about growing into your name, huh?"

Scarlett. Yes, I knew her. She was the one who just loved to pick on me. Kind of hard to miss her either way. Physically, she was rather giant-like, but in a Greek-goddess kind of way. Personality, 100% ogre.

"She's the girl that always has amazing clothes, jewelry, handbags, and, oh my goodness, her shoes! Servants at her beck and call. She gets anything she wants, no effort or knowledge required. Must be nice, but I wouldn't trade my brain for her brands."

My little sister would keep going and going without any regard to the other party in the conversation. I had to stop her before she dictated a novel.

"Willow… Willow! Breathe between sentences. Yes, I know Scarlett, and yes, I did hear she wasn't at roll call this morning. But honestly, I don't care. She is a total bully. Good riddance."

"Most Fire elementals are," Willow interrupted.

I nodded in agreement. "True, they do think that they are better than everyone else. Personally, I don't get it. I mean, they can light a fire, big deal. A candle can do that."

Willow laughed so hard that her soda burst out of her nose.

"Gross!" shouted Diana from nearby. "DelRio, try to eat your lunch like a person, not a plant." She tossed her blonde hair behind her shoulder and walked away.

That doesn't even make any sense. Those girls just loved insults that came with a dig at your element. Especially if you were anything but Fire. Willow didn't care. She had me, and I had her. We didn't need anyone else.

"Those Fires are all flame and no brain!" she yelled out.

My smile reached both my ears. "Willow, you are the best sister ever!" I was blessed with a sister that I actually liked. Loving was easy when you were family, but liking was an entirely different story. Willow was three years younger than me, so it helped that we were close in age. Easier to relate to, you know.

It also helped that we were the younger two of our family. Our three older brothers, Westley, Wallace, and William, were at the military academy. Like most boys, when they'd turned fifteen, they'd gotten the gift of strength or elemental control, and went to study to become soldiers for Gaia's army.

That was their school. This was ours: The National School for Girls. Kind of on the nose, but I appreciated the simplicity of the name. Some referred to it as a finishing school.

When girls reached the age of eleven, they either got their powers or remained a norm. Norms stayed home and helped the family cook and clean, with the occasional gardening thrown in. Of course, they were homeschooled to the high standard that Gaia's regime demanded, but it was not the same as a finishing education. I felt kind of bad for those girls and boys who didn't get gifts, but I was sure on some level they were happy to lead simple home lives.

Girls who got powers, like me and Willow, automatically went to NSG, where we were taught to sharpen and strengthen our powers. We mainly learned to control them, so that they could be used to better Gaia. The boys were the protectors, and we were the caretakers.

Ever since our people had landed here ages ago, Gaia had been rumored to give off some kind of atmospheric effect that altered our DNA. It was the sole explanation we'd had for developing powers, until researchers found no known cause after testing the planet's air, water, and soil. Shortly after, the discovery of the Moldavite Stone came to light. It was theorized to be the battery that charged Gaia's inhabitants, and had been the accepted truth ever since.

I got the power of Air. Not the most popular one—kind of the least, actually—but it was better than nothing. Willow, on the other hand, got Earth. I'd put it at one level above Air, even though in reality, the opposite was true. That was a little inside joke I kept to myself. It was odd for sisters to get different powers, but we didn't let that bother us. We were the DelRio sisters first, elementals second.

And that held true anywhere, anytime. Even at school, where there was an unwritten rule of division, exclusivity, and social hierarchy, we remained united. Basically, different elements didn't mix or mingle. But my sister and I didn't care. Sure, we got the regular disapproving stares, odd facial expressions, unintelligible insults, and, my personal favorite, the unoriginal physical acts of bullying. You know, nothing too big that it could be noticed, more like simple collisions in the hallway, or "bumping" our books to the ground.

But truthfully, it did sting, no matter how thick our skin was. Which was why I didn't mind when Scarlett, one of the biggest bullies, went missing. After all, there was only so much a fifteen-year-old could take. As for my sister, Willow was one strong twelve-year-old. She was forever the optimistic, sunny, and funny sister she'd always been.

"Wren! Wren!" Willow screamed at me.

"Sorry, what were you saying?"

"Just that I managed to blow some dirt onto Diana's designer short skirt. But she walked away too quickly for us to truly enjoy that moment."

"Awesome! She's gonna freak out when she stops looking at her face in the mirror long enough to notice."

"Good one." She laughed.

I loved to make her laugh. She always did it for me.

Then, Willow looked down at her half-eaten, soda-sprayed lunch. She seemed five years older at that moment.

"What is it, Willow?"

"I'm just worried. I know it's only my second year, but these disappearances don't sit right with me."

"Scarlett? You're worried about Scarlett?" I almost yelled.

"No, Wren. Not just her. All of us. Who's to say who'll be next to vanish?"

"They didn't vanish. They chose to leave. Completely voluntary, no foul play whatsoever. Only themselves to blame!" I was starting to get a little angry.

"Yes, I know they did. I get that. But where are they now? Why haven't the others returned?"

I took a deep breath to calm myself. "Students leave the school for many reasons. The first is that they miss home, so clearly, they wouldn't want to come back. The second is the pressure of the classes and coursework. If they couldn't handle that and ran away, I'm sure they wouldn't have a change of heart and return. The third, and my personal favorite, is that they met some army hunk over at the military academy on one of our school trips, and ditched to be with him."

Willow's cheeks turned rosy pink. I couldn't remember any other time she'd ever blushed like that. Perhaps this was the first time? Wow, she really was growing up. I continued, "And as for that, I don't expect her to come back here if she made a life with her boyfriend."

Willow nodded, then stared deeply into my eyes and asked, "But what about the girls who go after the Moldavite Stone? None of them ever came back, and I'm pretty sure no one ever reached it, since there have been no announcements or changes of any kind in Gaia."

She was a bright one, my Willow. So I figured honesty was the best play here.

"I don't know. Best case scenario, they failed, and were too embarrassed to come back to school."

"I guess. But wouldn't they have returned home? And if so, wouldn't their families have notified Headmistress Cypress?"

So logical. "Yes, but maybe their families would be ashamed as well, no?"

Willow rocked her head from side to side. In Willow-talk, that meant my answer made sense, but did not satisfy her. "How about we investigate?"

"Investigate?"

"Yeah, Wren, let's get down to the truth of all this. I know we can do it together. Plus, it could be fun! Besides, what else are we doing here?"

"We're in school, Willow. We are supposed to be learning stuff."

"I haven't learned anything new in months. I feel like I'm still using training wheels."

Okay, she got me there. Our classes were kind of lame.

"I'm not saying to skip class," she continued. "I am just suggesting a new after-school activity."

It did sound cool. "I'm in! We'll do it together, though, okay?"

"Of course, sis. I'm going to need your Air powers to cool me down when I get too sweaty from all the rigorous detective work."

"Ha, ha, Willow, very funny," I mocked. "So when should we start?"

"There's no time like the present."

Geez, what have I gotten myself into?

"We've been at this for weeks!" I whined. "I can't find any other book in this library that even mentions the Moldavite Stone. It seems *The History of the National School for Girls: A Detailed Account of the School's Foundation* is the only text that does it. Published recently, but again, slim pickings here."

"Written by the school's administration," Willow added.

It was odd. "Okay, lil sis. I jumped up, using all the pep I had left in me. "What do we know about the Stone so far?"

Willow opened the book and read aloud, "'The Moldavite Stone is a unique and powerful source of recyclable energy. It is a massive monolith-type structure that absorbs the power from its environment and projects it throughout the atmosphere. Those who inhabit Gaia are bathed in this filtered energy. Therefore, they have Gaian particles in their systems, which grant some of them powers. The chosen males and females get their powers at age fifteen and eleven respectively. These powers are either increased strength, or elemental powers: Fire, Water, Earth, or Air.

"'If a person were ever to absorb all of the Stone's energy, they would become all-powerful, a luminary. In that case, all of those who already possessed special powers would be stripped of them in that instant. However, if they choose to, the possessor of the Stone would be able to transfer or project some or all of their power to others.

"'The Moldavite Stone is said to be housed somewhere in the western region of Gaia. Seekers beware: the Stone itself is as perilous as the path toward it.'"

Willow stopped and closed the book, clutching it to her chest.

"Now, why in the world would they mention where to find that thing, if it's so dangerous?" I asked sharply.

"To be thorough?" Willow joked.

Okay, so we don't know much, I thought. *But that doesn't mean this information won't be helpful.*

So, supposedly, the Stone was a steady source of energy. Without access to it, hypothetically, we would all lose our gifts—maybe for a little while, maybe forever. As scary as that sounded, maybe we could find a way to block the Stone's energy, leaving only us powerless. We couldn't risk hurting anyone else, or letting anyone know what we were up to. But if we managed to shield ourselves from the Stone's energy, then at least we could confirm its existence.

Now, how can we do that? Underground? Nah, not strong enough. Armor? No, but that would be cool to wear for fun. Come on, think, Wren... think. Wait a minute! I got it!

"Did a lightbulb just go off in your head without me, Wren?" Willow asked, all excited.

"Yes, I have an idea."

"I'm listening," she said, with her big brown eyes as wide as I had ever seen them.

"The fallout bunker!"

"Huh? I don't follow where your brain is roaming. Please elaborate."

"Every building has a fallout bunker, in case of yet another nuclear war. We are very good at learning from previous mistakes. Unfortunately, we still repeat them sometimes."

"Yes, I get that, but what does protection from a nuclear bomb have to do with finding the Moldavite Stone?"

"Before physically finding it, we need to prove it exists in the first place. So, if we can lock ourselves in the bunker, it'll shield us from the Stone's energy, which supposedly feeds us our elemental power."

"How exactly would that work?"

"Well, the bunker is lined with lead, which protects against radiation. But it's also a Faraday cage, which means it blocks electronic signals, waves, and pulses. We don't know what kind of energy is emitted from the Stone, but one of those should cover it."

Willow shrugged, accepting my explanation.

I guess if something is said with enough confidence, it becomes more believable. I continued, "Once inside, if our powers drain or dwindle, we can be a little more sure that the Stone is out there somewhere, and then we can continue our search for it with more confidence. If, however, our powers remain fully intact and operating at one hundred percent capacity, maybe then the Stone is just a story."

Willow nodded in agreement. Her feet began moving to the beat of a marching routine.

"I can see that you are ready to test out that theory. But I'm not sure what will happen. There is a chance that our powers could be lost forever. Are you truly okay with that? I could go in by myself."

Willow looked directly at me and said, "Don't you dare. I'll always have you, sis. That's all I really need."

My eyes began to water.

Willow took my hand, squeezed it tight, and shouted, "TO THE BUNKER!"

ılııl.ılııl.ılııl.ılııl.

It wasn't so impressive, but a fallout bunker shouldn't be judged by its beauty. We both peeked inside. The bunker had two doors, one in the front and one at the rear of the room, a solid floor, and no windows.

"Geez, you'd think they'd spring for a sofa or something," Willow joked. "Not even a chair in sight. How is anyone going to be comfortable while awaiting a deadly nuclear bomb?"

"Maybe they wanted to fit more people?" I guessed.

"I can't believe you're defending a bunker."

Me neither. "Someone's got to," I said. "Okay, moment of truth. Let's go in and shut the doors, and then test our powers and see if we've still got 'em." I winked.

"Oh, that's how we do it?"

"Stop making fun of me. I just like to explain things. You know that. It calms me when I'm nervous."

Willow hugged me right then and said, "Love you for that, sis."

I took her hand, and we walked into the dark, dusty room together, closing the door behind us. It was a bit scary, so neither of us let go, even as we reached the very center.

And there we stood. Two sisters holding hands in the middle of an empty fallout bunker. Nothing happened. We looked at each other and knew neither of us felt any different.

"Maybe it takes time?" she asked.

So we waited a little longer just in case.

"Okay, maybe we should try using our powers now," Willow suggested. "I'm getting bored."

I started to panic. What if our powers didn't work? What if we never got them back? Would Willow ever forgive me for robbing her of her gift?

Willow turned to me and said, "Don't worry. Whatever happens, we are in this together."

With that, she gave me the courage to try. And I did. I closed my eyes, believing that would help me concentrate, and summoned my inner Element. But something about it felt amplified. Like it was one thousand times stronger than I was used to. It felt incredible, until I realized Willow had let go of my hand. My confusion was muffled by how exhilarating it all felt. I couldn't wait to describe it to Willow.

Willow?

Willow!

The feeling disappeared. All feelings did. I knew she was here; I sensed her shape in the air. She was lying motionless on the cold bunker floor.

"WILLOW!" I yelled. "What happened?" I dropped to her side and frantically shook her whole body. "Do you hear me? It's Wren. Wake up!" I began to cry.

Please come back. I need you. You promised me I'd have you forever. Us together. Always. I held her hand as tightly as I could. I didn't care if I bruised it.

Suddenly, that feeling came through me again, but this time I felt it being channeled through my right hand and into hers.

Willow jumped up, gasping for air.

"Oh, Willow! Oh, thank heavens!" I hugged her so tight, I might have cracked her rib.

"I... can't... breathe... Wren..."

I quickly released her.

"Are you okay? What happened?"

"Geez, let the oxygen get to my brain so I can formulate a coherent sentence."

I gave her a few minutes of my silence. I think my constant staring finally got her to start talking again.

"I can't explain it, but I'll try. What I remember last is holding your hand, and both of us getting ready to summon our powers. Then," she looked at me, somewhat scared, "I felt like all the air was being sucked right out of me."

"You're saying I did that to you?" I teared up.

"Well, there's no one else here, silly Wren." She smiled.

I got angry, mostly at myself. "I appreciate what you're trying to do, but the fact is that I hurt you, and I don't know how it happened, or what I could do to prevent it from happening again!" She stood there, looking at me. "You should be scared of me!" I added.

"No, I'm only scared of losing you! I know you didn't do it on purpose," she said.

"Never! I would never hurt you like this! I love you more than anything in this world!"

"See? That's all I need. Okay, so let's think. All we did was hold hands, which we've done many, many, many times before. The only difference is…" She gulped.

"The bunker," we said in unison.

"But how does that make sense?" Willow thought aloud.

"One minute, let me think," I said. The wheels in my head began to turn. I saw from the corner of my eye that my sister was stepping away from me, giving me space so I could concentrate.

Okay. Focus, Wren. What's different about being in a bunker? It's secluded. It's quiet. It blocks everything out. Nothing can come in. No distractions… maybe it gave us the ability to focus more? Really hone in on our elemental gifts? But that can't be the only thing!

"Did you get anywhere with your thinking?"

"Just need a little more time, Willow. I'm not there yet." *Okay, let's get back on track. Wait, maybe it's not just the bunker. Maybe it's the both of us, together. We never held hands while summoning our elements before. We mostly practice in class, and those are divided. Fire, Water, Earth, and Air almost never interact on the grounds. That has to be it!*

I quickly turned to her to share my theory.

But before I could get a word out, she cheered, "I can tell you got it now!"

I nodded. "Maybe, but we need to test it to be sure."

"Um, I'd rather not. In case you didn't notice, the last time didn't end so well for me."

"No. Not here. It's too dangerous. But I do have a hypothesis."

"Theory, hypothesis... care to share it with the class, Wren?" She smiled at me.

"I think that when we held hands and attempted to use our powers together, it made the effects stronger. Huh, the whole was greater than the sum of its parts! I finally get what that old philosopher was trying to say. And I think that it could be applied to numerous fields of study. Anyways, that, coupled with the 'blank page' atmosphere of the fallout bunker, made our powers peak. A double whammy! Well, my powers to be exact, but I think that's only because I tried my gifts before you did. Maybe next time we do something like this, we'll time it better..."

"Yeah, we didn't really plan it right, and I still feel the whammy," Willow jumped in. "My head hurts a bit from hitting the bunker floor. I think it knocked my brain back into place, so all good here."

That's my Willow. Sense of humor fully intact, even after that nasty ordeal. "So, here's what I want to do."

"Hold hands outside the bunker and try powering up?"

I tilted my head in surprise.

"It's an obvious next step." She grinned.

"Very good, lil sis. We can try that when you are ready. I want you to recover from that fall first."

"I'd call it a trust exercise without a partner."

I looked all around the bunker, then back at my sister, and said, "But one thing is becoming a bit clearer."

"And what's that?"

"The Moldavite Stone might not exist. Think about it. It's supposed to give off energy that fuels our power, right?"

"Right."

"The bunker blocks that energy from reaching us. In theory, we shouldn't have been able to power up inside it. But we did. If the Stone does or ever did exist, it is not responsible for our gifts. We need to dig a little deeper into this, and I think I know how."

<hr>

"What do you mean, you sensed my shape in the fallout bunker?"

"It's hard to describe, but I was aware of everything around me, because the air framed everything. Does that make any sense?"

"Help me out a bit more."

"To put it simply, I can make out anything the air touches, sorta like a radar, but only if my elemental power reaches the height it did when I was holding hands with you in the bunker."

"So, you need me and some quiet to boost your powers, and then you can make out anything surrounded by air?"

"Yup! And I believe I can absorb or extract air, as well as expel it."

"Yes, Wren. You *are* an excellent fan when I need you to be, but wow! Now you're a vacuum, too?"

We both laughed at that.

"But we need to hold hands for it to work," I added.

"That should be very easy," Willow said. "I have two right here." She raised both of her hands in the air and wiggled them.

"I love you, lil sis."

"I know."

"So, now that we know that you are a human tracking device, leaf blower, and portable vacuum/Grim Reaper, but only with MY helping hands... how does that help us with our investigation?" Willow asked, sporting that goofy smile of hers.

"Hey! It helped you find your backpack last Thursday, didn't it?"

"Not fair! It was under your bed!"

"And what about your toothbrush, Willow?"

"You did that on purpose to further prove your bloodhound skills. Just another experiment. I always keep my toothbrush in that orange cup by the sink." She'd gotten me there.

"Willow, what I'm trying to get at is that I'm pretty sure that with your help, I can use my new Air-power-on-steroids to search the western region and see if I can locate the Moldavite Stone... remotely, of course. The missing girls might be tougher, since I have no idea where they might be. They could be anywhere or nowhere. There are too many variables to consider. I think locating the Stone is the next best step."

"But that area is huge! How will you know what to look for?"

"Great question. Before I start my 'Air search,' I need to do some research on the topographic maps of the western region. I need to familiarize myself with the area on the 2-D paper map first. Luckily it's mostly desert, so finding this massive monolith-type stone should be easy enough. But I need to make sure. Just think, if it's so big, how come no one has ever seen it? Yes, you can blame the dangerous terrain, but I got a hunch that there's more to it. And now that I can search for it without physically traveling to its domain, we can finally get some answers. Then we can tell Headmistress Cypress."

I couldn't mess this up. I wouldn't. I needed to use these heightened powers for good.

Willow waved me out of my trance.

"Yes, sis?" I whispered.

"Headmistress Cypress... isn't she the one who wrote that book, the only book that mentions the Moldavite Stone? Why not just ask her point-blank?"

"We have no guarantee she will be honest. We need to have solid proof first. Physical proof that something—or nothing—exists in the western region. Only then will we have a leg to stand on. Think of it as our insurance policy."

I grabbed Willow's hand, then grabbed the book. Together in the black of night, we went to the library to get the maps we needed. The only light was the one within us, as we hoped our efforts wouldn't be in vain.

"Hey, think of the bright side. At least you'll ace Geography this year."

"Of the western region." She chuckled, then stuck her tongue out at me. "You were right, it's all just desert."

My tired eyes met hers, and I saw a map of Gaia streamed across her face. "I'm calling it, Willow. We have our answer. I've conducted my 'Air search' seven times already, and everything I've sensed matches perfectly with the map of Gaia." I slumped my shoulders. "Given what happened in the bunker two weeks ago, and the fact that I can't see or sense any difference in Gaia's terrain, I fear there is only one conclusion: the Moldavite Stone does not exist."

Willow let out a deep breath. "We need to go to Cypress. She must have lied. Why write about a power source that doesn't exist? What is she hiding? She's just plain weird. The lady doesn't use contractions, like at all! That alone screams villain. Or at the very least, it's a red flag, no?"

Suddenly, the thought dawned on me: *What if SHE is behind all the disappearances? What if SHE can't be trusted? What if SHE is the enemy? Then I'm about to lead my little sister right into a dangerous trap. I can't.*

"Wren, oh, no you don't. I know that look! You are *not* leaving me behind and going to Cypress alone. And before you open your mouth, I *do* know the risks, and I'm willing to face them head-on, just like you. I chose to go through this with you, remember? Together always!" She started to tear up a bit. I hugged her, again, probably tighter than I should have.

"Willow, you've helped me since this all started, and you *will* stand with me when this all ends. Together. Always."

"That's what I just said. But wow, that was easy. I didn't have to give you fake crocodile tears, grovel, or pull out my personal best… the sad puppy-dog eyes."

"And thank heavens for that. You know I can't resist that face."

She giggled, then added, "My true and ultimate power."

"And what Cypress doesn't know is that if she tries any funny business, I will literally suck all the oxygen out of her lungs. But I need your helping hands."

"Oh yeah, I forgot you could do that."

"Me too, it's new." I winked. "Okay, let's get some rest. Tomorrow, we pay Headmistress Cypress a visit."

"You and me," Willow added. "Don't let me sleep in. Promise you'll wake me. PROMISE!"

I nodded. "I promise."

She got up from my bed and used her elemental Earth power to block the only door to our room with a bunch of thorny vines. "I don't trust you."

"I'm wounded," I said dramatically, as I raised my right hand across my forehead for emphasis.

"Well, you will be if you try to leave without me. These thorns are extra sharp." She pointed to the tooth-like buds on her new security measure.

"Just go to sleep. We need to be rested if we're going to take on Cypress."

"Bring it! She doesn't scare me. I've got you!"

"And I've got you."

Willow turned the lights off, and we both laid down in our soft, warm beds for a much-needed and well-deserved sleep.

*. *. *. *.

"Willow! Willow! Wake up!"

"Is it time to storm the castle?" She yawned so loudly, she could have woken up our next-door neighbor.

"No. It's still nighttime."

"So why the heck are you trying to wake me up?"

"Another girl! Another girl is heading off the grounds. I see it… no, I sense it with my Air powers. I have a lock on her location right now." It was kind of like I was an ocean, and anyone who passed through me left waves.

She shot up at that. "What? You can do that alone now? I thought you needed to hold my hand for your power to be amplified?"

"I don't understand it either. Maybe it's like training wheels, and now that I practiced enough, I can ride my elemental two-wheeler?"

She looked confused.

"I guess once I unlocked it and practiced a few times, it got easier and easier for me to do. It just flows out of me… the elevated power comes more naturally to me now. I have you to thank for it."

"You're welcome. Now, just focus on this girl. Do you know who she is?"

"No, I don't think I can do that. But I do know that she left through the front gates!"

"And you'd think there would be an increase in security measures after all the other disappearances. Geez, where does all our tuition money go?"

"Willow, you're not getting it! I can track her. I can 'Air-track' her, I mean. We can finally know what happens to these kids."

Willow smiled at that. "And stop anyone else from disappearing ever again." I nodded along as she continued, "Wren, we can save the school! We can be heroes! We can finally be…" She stared directly at me before finishing her sentence with, "…popular."

We both laughed so hard at that. "It's good to know we have our priorities straight, huh?"

"Yup. Together forever, sis."

It was about time to put an end to this mystery.

Sitting on my bed, with my sister beside me, I Air-tracked the girl for about forty-five minutes as she went out toward the western region. She was without a doubt heading for the infamous Moldavite Stone. *Infamous. Ha! More like imaginary!*

I kept bouncing a bit more with every step she took. Willow, happily, didn't mind nor comment. Deep down, we were both nervous and excited. She probably was annoyed at my fidgeting, but kept quiet because she knew I had to focus. The last thing I wanted was to suddenly lose track of this girl. *This* was our only real lead. Both of us knew how important it was to get it right. We were scared. There was no question about it as the room remained silent and still.

Five, ten, fifteen minutes later, and still nothing. I began to think that she'd walk forever, deeper and deeper into the desert area, when, out of nowhere, four large figures cornered her. I had probably focused all my attention on her, and had nothing left to track anyone else.

'Willow! She's not alone!" I screamed. "They've got her!"

"Who's got her?"

"I'm not sure. From what I can tell, they seem to be men. Very large men."

"Like giants?"

"No, just really tall and muscular. She's like a tiny mouse next to them. I can sense her struggling. She may be smaller, but she's a fighter. The air around them is chaotic, like a tornado."

"What else can you sense?" She grabbed hold of my hand, thinking it would help.

It did. "AHH! They're armed. Those irregular shapes must be weapons."

"Unless we're in the middle of an alien invasion," Willow only half-joked.

"No, Willow. They're humans all right. *That* I can tell for sure. And only Gaian military personnel are allowed to carry weapons. So what we know so far is that four armed military men kidnapped this girl as she was heading toward the fictional Stone's suspected location. Now, though, they are changing course. They are taking her slightly north."

"Don't lose her, Wren, this is it!" She gripped my hand even tighter.

No pressure, I thought to myself. "Okay, okay. They are still headed north."

"Just keep up with them. They may lead us to some of the other missing students."

Maybe. I followed the group for about twenty minutes until they finally stopped by a barren field. My powers had never had this range before. It was her. It had to be her.

"Nothing, Willow. They stopped in front of nothing." Willow's shoulders slumped. "Wait, wait! One of the men is kneeling on the ground. Oh my gosh! I think he's opening a patch of land. I can feel it making a slight wave in the air around it."

"You use water references a lot for an Air elemental."

"Oh, hush, Willow. Let me focus." The man opened the hidden door in the ground and rested it on the patch of land behind it. The girl was then shoved inside. This time, she showed no sign of a struggle. No doubt the guns erased any feelings of bravery. "Okay, she was pushed underground."

"Any idea what's down there?"

"If that door stays open long enough, I think I can peek inside. I need more air to travel through to do it. Come on, come on." My chances were slim, but I'd faced worse odds before. An idea popped into my head. I could create a gust of wind and direct it toward the door. Then maybe, just maybe, it would be harder for them to close it. Simple physics. I just needed to delay them a bit.

I closed my eyes, took both of Wren's hands in mine, and tapped into my inner elemental powers. I could feel the air shifting. "Faster, faster," I mouthed.

I felt the men wobble, and a slight grin formed on my face.

Willow started cheering. "You've got this, Wren! Be the best blow dryer you can be." The air traveled down into the hidden underground room.

Yes! Now, to have a look. "Willow, it's not a room at all, it's a prison." I knew I only had a few more seconds to "look around." *Focus. Focus.*

I forced my wind to hit every corner. I had to manipulate it more so that I could collect the information I needed. I couldn't just wait for everyone to move. I pushed and pulled the air so much down there, it could have been mistaken for a hurricane.

What I learned in those fifteen seconds was enough to head to Cypress. I exhaled, knowing I had done the absolute best that I could.

"Did you get it?"

"Oh, I got it!" I let go of her hands.

"Care to share?"

I inhaled deeply through my nose, held it for three seconds, then released the breath through my mouth—a great calming technique I'd learned at NSG. Unfortunately, it wasn't too much help today. "Six people are being held captive down there… in a cage of some sort."

Willow gasped, then smiled. "But that's good news, sis. You found them."

That was her, always seeing the bright side. "True. But now, students or not, we gotta rescue them!"

"Off to Cypress. She's the only one that can give us any answers, and boy, for her sake, I hope that they are the right ones." She pounded her right fist into her left hand.

I looked at Willow, then faced the door of our bedroom. "She'd better, or I'll vacuum the very life out of her."

"And I'll help!"

"Knock, knock!" Willow shouted as she banged on Headmistress Cypress's office door. Her bedchambers and office were adjoining rooms, so finding her at night was no big quest.

"You know, you don't have to say 'knock, knock' when you knock." I grinned.

"Yeah, I know, but it's more effective, don't you think?"

I couldn't help but laugh at that.

Footsteps approached the door. "See?" Willow turned to face me. "You can't argue with the results."

"Wasn't planning on it."

Headmistress Cypress pulled her heavy mahogany door wide open. "Who dares disturb me at this hour?" She looked down at the two of us.

Cypress was a tower at 6'3". Her very being demanded obedience. Her silver hair was usually pulled back in a sleek and tight bun, but not this morning. We'd definitely caught her off-guard… and way too early. Her hair draped over her broad shoulders.

She began to lean her slender figure toward us, no doubt trying to intimidate us even more. "Students? What on great green Gaia are you doing out of your dorms this early? Instruction does not start for another four hours!"

"Great, that gives us plenty of time to chat," Willow said, folding her arms across her chest.

Cypress tilted her head in frustration, but her eyes widened. No doubt she was curious. "About what? What could possibly warrant such an out-of-line and intrusive visit to my office?"

There was no holding back now. "The Moldavite Stone doesn't exist. P.S., we believe a girl was abducted last night while in search of it. P.P.S., we found other kids caged in an underground prison." My eyes became mere slits on my face as I spoke.

Cypress tried to keep her voice calm, but I could tell she was holding back rage. "How dare you barge—"

"Oh, stop!" Willow interrupted her. "Save it for someone who cares. We are here for the truth, and you are the next piece of the puzzle. What do you know about the Stone?"

Headmistress Cypress's jaw fell to the floor. It was clear that no one had ever spoken to her that way before. Cypress backed away from the door, taking a few steps into her office. She gestured for us to follow her in.

"Just so you know, Headmistress, I wouldn't try anything funny. My sis here learned some new tricks that I don't think you'd want to see. Trust me on that one." Willow's left eyebrow lifted slightly higher than her right as she said it.

"I would never dream of harming an elemental. Especially a student under my watch."

"So speak up, and let's not let anyone else get kidnapped at gunpoint over a fake rock."

Cypress froze at that. We all stood there, silently waiting for someone to talk or make a sound… anything. Willow and I could tell she was shaken up. We looked at each other, and made a silent agreement to wait for our Headmistress to start moving again before either of us did.

Finally she said, "What do you mean by 'gunpoint'?"

"Oh, that got your attention."

I quickly hushed my sister. This wasn't the time for backtalk. "Headmistress, full disclosure, my Air-powers have been heightened, thanks to a little experiment my sis and I conducted in the school's bunker recently. I now have the ability to make out figures and objects that are surrounded by air, as well as track them if needed."

Cypress nodded at me, but remained quiet.

"Last night, I felt a girl leave school grounds and head west toward the area that is suspected to house the Moldavite Stone."

Willow rolled her eyes behind me and added, "Which doesn't exist."

"Willow! We'll get to that part," I interjected. "Anyway, this girl was then grabbed by four armed military men. She was carried north for a while, only to end up being shoved into an underground, hidden prison, which housed six others. We have no proof these are NSG students, but they do need saving nonetheless."

Cypress hastened to her desk, picked up the phone, and started dialing. Suddenly, a deep, raspy voice came through the speakerphone. "Headmistress? What can I do for you this morning?"

"General Gafferty, I am sorry to cut through the small talk, but do you by any chance know anything about armed men abducting elementals?"

"Who told you?"

"So it is true?" she gasped. "Are you involved in the disappearances of my students?"

"Absolutely not, Headmistress. And I am cut deeply by your lack of trust in me. We have worked together for decades."

Decades? I thought.

"In these times, given what has happened before, and what could be happening now, I just want my students safe."

"You and me both, Headmistress. We do not want another war. We only want our people to be safe and for Gaia to remain intact. No one wants another migration… or eradication," he added somberly.

"Agreed, General. So please, enlighten me on what you know about the situation at hand."

Willow and I just listened and stood as still as possible, as the conversation went back and forth.

"We got wind of this radical group a few months ago. At first, we thought it was just rumors, but decided to do our due diligence. I wanted to keep our intelligence efforts quiet, in an attempt to handle the situation without tipping the group off or causing panic amongst the masses. Unfortunately, we have yet to locate these rogues. They are elusive, crafty, and tactical. Because their 'attacks' are few and scattered, we cannot seem to pinpoint their base of operations—"

"That's because it's underground!" I shouted to make sure he heard me.

"Is that true, Headmistress?"

"I have reason to believe it is, General," Cypress said.

"Hmm, that does explain a lot. Does that student know its exact location?"

Headmistress Cypress looked at me, awaiting confirmation, and I nodded. "That is a positive as well."

"Finally, we can end this."

"And rescue my elementals in the process. But, General, do you know who these men are?"

The other end of the phone went silent for a few seconds. The General let out a deep breath. "They are former students from our military academy. Apparently, some soldiers grew resentful that they did not get elemental powers. Yes, they had strength, but for them it was not enough. That fueled jealousy, coupled with the influence of some norms who were angry that they received nothing at all. The jealousy grew to a fierce hatred. That toxic bubbling of animosity finally pushed them over the edge, and they began to lash out at elementals. Their plan only solidified when they discovered that a few times a year, elementals leave your school's protection with their sights set on finding the Moldavite Stone."

"Which doesn't even exist, by the way. Did you know that too?" Willow yelled.

"Ah, I see your girls are learning quite more than we ever expected, Headmistress," the General replied. Willow and I low-fived each other. We'd been right all along. This was the validation we were looking for. All of our time researching hadn't been in vain. The Moldavite Stone had never existed. *I knew it!*

General Gafferty still had more to say, but wow, was this satisfying. The question remained: why had Headmistress Cypress made the Stone up? We'd grill her later. The priority was saving those prisoners.

"Now that the four of us are all on the same page, there is no need to be coy. Where was I? Oh, yes, so, when they found out their prey was making the hunt much easier to accomplish, they saw it as a sign to finally mobilize. They began to abduct these 'nomadic gifts,' as they were. It was an added plus when they realized the school was not too alarmed at the disappearances, and didn't even have any plans to organize a search party. For these radicals, it could not have been easier if the elementals had been dropped at their doorstep."

"I see your point, General. No need to harp on it. What I would like to know is, what do they do to those that they kidnap? What is their endgame?"

"Sadly, Headmistress, that I do not know. I am just glad that your informant there said that they were alive. It is better than I had imagined."

"Of course, you are correct," Cypress added.

"But now that we have their whereabouts and more or less a proof of life, we can go in there and get them out."

"Again, agreed, General."

"Headmistress, I will gather a team, brief them, and await our map, as well as the green light from you. Please make haste. Every second counts in these types of situations, and we cannot waste time that we do not have. We do not know their plan. And with individuals such as these, harsh decisions can be made in an instant."

"I will contact you again as soon as I have the information you requested. Thank you for your service, General Gafferty. But above all, thank you for your loyalty. I am ashamed to admit that I ever doubted you, even for a moment."

"Fear changes even the friendliest to foes."

"Clever, General, but fear wanes and loyalty always shines through." I swore I could hear him smile through the phone. "Bye for now, General."

And with that, Headmistress Cypress ended the call. She then turned to Willow and me, who had been marveling over the new revelations, and rejoicing in our hypothesis having been confirmed.

"Elementals, I can see that you already possess many pieces of this puzzle, and no doubt have gained a few more this very morning, having listened to my conversation with the General. There is clearly a lot to discuss, but for the sake of those held captive, we need to act quickly. Please." She looked directly at me now. "Give me the location of their base so that we can rescue them."

I knew she was right, so I gave her the coordinates without any hesitation, and with as much detail as I could muster. Thankfully, I had the map of the western region of Gaia permanently seared in my brain.

"But promise," I added, "once they are safe, that you will explain all of this to us. We've earned that much."

Cypress nodded. "I promise. And at that time, you need to explain to me how you went primal."

Primal? I thought to myself. *So that's what it's called. Cool.* "As long as my sister Willow can be there too. She's a big part of it."

"Deal," Cypress answered.

"Deal."

★★★★

"We have them! And to confirm, they are indeed all elementals from your institution!"

Cypress's shoulders dropped two full inches, as if she could finally breathe fully once she heard General Gafferty's news. The update came only a few hours after our last discussion. Willow and I had decided to stick around the Headmistress's office rather than attend our first and second period classes. Who were we kidding? Our lectures didn't hold as much excitement as playing a crucial role in a rescue mission.

"Excellent, General Gafferty. Thank you for your service." The Headmistress regained her authoritative facial expressions and tone.

"The girls will be tended to immediately. Then, once they are physically and mentally fit, they will be debriefed. Afterward, we will send them right back to NSG."

But didn't they all run away from here to begin with? I thought.

"As expected. When the students return here, I promise as headmistress of this fine facility to rebuild our broken bridge of trust. I want them to feel safe and wanted here, no matter what transpired before."

"So poetic," Willow whispered to me. I chuckled, probably a little too loud.

"Is there something wrong, Miss DelRio?" Cypress glared at me. *Yup, definitely too loud.*

This was my opening, so I took it. "Actually, now that all is... better, we'd like to clear the air a bit." Willow couldn't help but smirk at that Air elemental reference. "Our insight helped bring our classmates to safety, and capture some rebels. Now, it's time for the two of you to hold up your end of our bargain. Tell us exactly what's going on."

The General let out a *harumph* sound, then said, "Headmistress Cypress, would you care to start? I will chime in if necessary."

Willow and I sat down on a nearby couch, crossed our legs, and put our hands nicely in our laps, as if ready for story time. My sister and I were big on the theatrics.

Cypress got the hint, and began speaking calmly yet arrogantly. "First off, I would like to say that I am thankful for the part that both of you played in the safe return of our fellow elementals. Gratitude is not an emotion that I readily exhibit, nor typically have a reason for showing, especially to those inferior to me. So this is quite an honor."

"That is true," the General interjected.

Wow, I just realized that the General also doesn't use contractions. No wonder they get along.

"Secondly," Cypress continued, "I would like to keep this little speech as short and concise as possible—"

Try using contractions, then, I joked to myself.

"—as I am certain you two already know most of it. You are just in need of some minor details to help paint the full picture. Plus, we still have quite a bit of aggravating work that needs to be done regarding this matter."

My sister and I exchanged glances.

The Headmistress inhaled deeply before beginning again, but to her credit, she got right to the point, as promised. "The Moldavite Stone is a lie. I made it up with the intention, at first, to test the character of the students admitted into my school. The power-hungry would be dealt with, the explorers would be scolded, and the charitable would be lectured on how the norms could not be gifted powers, as they are innate. So are the rules of Gaia.

"Over time, a fear slowly grew within me as I watched Gaia's resources dwindle. To the naked, inexperienced eye, there was no great devastating change. But for me, having lived through many worlds and many generations, under many aliases, I was beginning to see hints of overpopulation, environmental pollution, natural resource depletion, animal migration, and climate change. It always starts the same way. In one hundred years' time, Gaia would end like all the other earths before it. Gone forever."

How old is she? I thought to myself. She noticed we were confused and began again.

"I swore when we landed here that this time would be different. We colonized this uninhabited alien planet, now called Gaia, to better our people's chance of survival against foreign invaders. Our home, Astra, was destroyed by humans. At first they wanted to coexist, and we welcomed them, though they were laying waste to our resources. But they quickly became threatened by us and deemed us their enemy.

"While fleeing Freia, our most recent home, due to planet implosion, we chanced upon Gaia. It was a place that we later learned has almost the exact same makeup as Astra. *How fortuitous,* we thought. Better yet, the planet did not appear on any map, radar, or sonar.

"Our scout ship's engines were failing, and we crashed here. Much of our crew perished on impact. The General and I were the only two completely unharmed, due to our experimentation with Chemical XXVI, which turned us immortal but caused us to lose our powers. We believed Gaia could restore the greatness that Astra had once been. And when our younger population were granted the gifts of strength and of the elements, I was convinced we would be restored to our former glory.

"Evolution was kind to us. Gaia was kind to us. As a people, we could not fail now that we were blessed again, and I had a concrete chance to keep my oath. So, I opened a school to guide these young students on a path that would help them master their powers. One day, they would be able to feed Gaia if needed. Restore what one day might be depleting. Give back what we take every day by living on this planet. That was something we should have done with Astra."

"And I agreed to design curriculums to train the boys and girls who were gifted with superhuman strength," General Gafferty interrupted, "because I know that strength means nothing without control. The body is a lame weapon without a sound mind. Over at the Academy, we teach those kids battle tactics and training exercises, sure. But our main focus is on mental health and civil responsibility. I cannot tell you how many soldiers we prevented from succumbing to the twin poisons of greed and entitlement, which spring from limitless power. It is a slippery slope, to say the least. I mean, if these students are the strongest, should they not rule all?

"Add the fact that they fear, one day, elementals might turn on them. Strength is all well and good, but it is nothing compared to the wrath of what can be unleashed by the powers of Earth, Air, Fire, and Water. The soldiers we fought today were lost to us for that very reason. They saw what their peers could do, and feared the possibilities. We do not want another civil war."

"Take comfort in the fact that we are not, and never will be, your enemy, General," Cypress said.

"And I echo that, Headmistress. But these are young, powerful, impulsive, and impressionable children that we are dealing with. We cannot toss their fears aside. We need to acknowledge them, and then steer these kids down the right path with truth and logic. If not, we risk another catastrophic, world-ending war."

"Pass, doesn't sound fun to me," Willow chimed in.

I thought she just wanted to be a part of the conversation, as did I, so I added, quite snarkily, "I echo that." She smiled at me.

The General ignored us and continued, "And that is why we teach our soldiers that we are all vital to Gaia's survival. If they see that we are truly one people, no matter our abilities, their doubts and fears will subside. Our goals are the same, and that is to preserve and protect our home and our people."

"I could not agree with you more, General, which is why the purpose of the Moldavite Stone shifted to a recruiting mission."

Willow and I both tilted our heads, confused by what Cypress meant. *Recruiting for what? Why didn't they just tell us that our people inherently possessed these powers?*

"As I alluded to before, the Stone was originally meant to test character and loyalty to our home and people. However, over the past two decades or so, more and more of our children were not gifted powers. The General and I were concerned that this might lead to the end of our people. So we decided to experiment on a select few with gifts, to see if we could recreate those gifts somehow. The elementals that fled our facility were apprehended, safely, and brought to a sister facility of mine, about twenty miles east of here, for testing. It was a pilot program of sorts."

"So runaways became guinea pigs?" I growled.

"Do calm down, Miss DelRio. No one was injured, and when we realized our efforts were for naught, we focused on trying to turn them primal. That means we tried to make their powers stronger, so that we could replenish Gaia faster if necessary. But nothing worked."

I was shocked. "So, basically, you're telling me I accomplished in a few weeks what you couldn't do for years?" I was trying not to be so smug about it, but I couldn't help but be proud of myself, and feel a little sad for the Headmistress.

She glared at me, clearly annoyed and frustrated, but held her tongue.

The General seemed to sense the tension, and chose to help the conversation along. "I, too, am eager to hear how you went primal, Miss... DelRio, is it? It could mean our home's survival." He was the buffer in a very stuffy atmosphere.

The ball was in my court now. I had the power—literally. The key to the secret they were searching for. I had the chance to ensure that Gaia lived forever. It was my home—the only one I knew, at least. I couldn't lose it. And if I could save it, and everyone on it, including my sister, then there was really only one thing to do.

"Headmistress Cypress, General Gafferty, I'd be happy to share what I know, as long as you promise to use that information to adopt a new methodology of teaching elementals and soldiers. And please stop using us as lab rats."

"If it produces the desired results, I am in agreement," the General answered. The Headmistress just nodded.

"But let's have some extra safeguards thrown in, because you might not get the control you want right away," Willow jumped in. "Believe me, I am proof that we need training wheels before we can ride that bike." She winked at me.

For the next half-hour or so, I told the story of what had happened the night we went to the fallout bunker, and how I nearly killed, then revived my sister. After we were all caught up on why and how this happened, we needed to focus on the what. What was this new curriculum going to look like? What steps were going to be taken to ensure a smooth transition? And, my personal favorite, what was everyone going to think about it?

Luckily, I was just a student, as this was one grown-up problem I didn't want a hand in solving. *Good luck to them with building an entirely new curriculum.*

"You two have quite a challenging but rewarding road ahead. If it's all right, I'd love to take my little sister to lunch. It's been a long morning, and we've already missed breakfast."

I grabbed Willow's hand, and together, we skipped out of the Headmistress's office.

"Did we just save the day?" Willow asked.

"I believe so."

Months later...

"Headmistress, I am pleased to see our dual program is a success," the General said as he sat in Cypress's office.

"I agree. Morale is up. Powers are primal, and Gaia's future is bright."

The General began to squirm in his chair. Astute as ever, Cypress questioned him on his uneasy body language. "What is it, General Gafferty?"

"I am going to be frank, Headmistress. I have just received word of an approaching spaceship headed in our direction."

She froze. "Any inclination if it is hostile or friendly?"

"No communication has been made, but the ship bears the Astra crest."

"Can it be? After all this time?"

"They always find their way home. Always."

THOUGHTS ON *BRAVE NEW GIRLS*

"Being a part of *Brave New Girls* feels like I am a catalyst for opportunities today, and every day after. There is no doubt that this anthology is adored and valued by girls who love STEM, but I see its impact as being more than just that. It's for girls who stumble upon it—not just those who search for it. Girls need to know that STEM is something they CAN do, if it calls to them… and *BRAVE NEW GIRLS* has those out-of-this-world stories to spark that interest. And who knows, maybe it might inspire a few readers to become writers themselves, just as it did for me. And to all the boys out there, let me just say, it's not about gender, it's about drive, and sometimes you need to sit in the passenger seat. But know this: we are all in the same car, on the same road, going onwards and upwards. We need to help each other, so let's do this together… FOR SCIENCE!"

ABOUT THE AUTHOR

Denise Mizrahi Sutton lives in Brooklyn, New York, with her husband and love of her life, Raphael, five young sons, five parakeets, two betta fish, and new cavachon puppy, Maui. She graduated top ten in her class from Long Island University with a doctorate in Pharmacy. She loves serving her community alongside her parents as a pharmacist at Supreme RX Pharmacy. Possessing a natural-born talent for comedy and making children smile, she also found her calling as a children's entertainer and educator.

Denise has her own traveling science program for kids, whose sole purpose is to make science exciting and fun, using as many costumes, puppets, and props as possible. She enjoys organizing and running numerous events for her kids' schools, such as Scholastic book fairs (four to date and counting), holiday events, back-to-school carnivals, challah bakes, and bingo nights. You can find all her adventures on instagram @costumesandcaring. Her most recent one is working with epoxy resin. She has always been artistic and imaginative, with a deep love for books, so Denise was encouraged by her husband Raphy to pursue writing. When she started writing her own stories, it gave her so much more appreciation for the written word. So far, she has had short stories published in the latest four volumes of *Brave New Girls*, including this one, as well as the *Bad Ass Moms* and *The Fans are Buried Tales* anthologies.

Illustration for "Gaia: The Legend of the Moldavite Stone" by Adriano Moraes.

Earning Her Wings

JD Cadmon

EARNING HER WINGS
JD CADMON

"Carter Station, this is *Enceladus One* waiting for docking instructions," Vivienne Renard said solemnly into her flight simulator's microphone.

The programmed voice of Nora, Carter Station's AI, pleasantly answered with the directions, and Vivi brought the ship into the docking bay confidently. It bumped a few times on landing, but it connected securely with the airlock. Had it been a real flight and not a simulated practice, she would still have been successful.

Vivi took off her virtual reality headgear, and Captain Delphine Renard, the pilot for the real *Enceladus One*, stared down at her.

"Better, but you still need to practice. On an actual flight with passengers and cargo, you need the flight to go as smoothly as possible."

"Mom!" Vivi pointed at her flight diagnostics from the simulator. "I did fine!"

The older woman opened her mouth, as if she wanted to say something, but then pressed her lips together. After a few more seconds of holding her tongue, she said, "Come sit in the copilot's chair. You can compare a simulated flight with the real thing."

Vivi bounced up with a fake military salute and a big smile. She was one step closer to achieving her dream of joining Selena Squadron, an elite team of female pilots headquartered on Luna. Vivi would take the last of her tests on Carter Station, including flights on working spacecraft instead of flight simulators, and then if she passed, she would join Selena Squadron's candidate pool.

Jupiter loomed large and beautiful in the windows of the cockpit. Captain Renard engaged controlled bursts to slow the inertial speed of the ship as they got closer to Carter Station. Though there were several large stations throughout the solar system, Carter was one of the busiest, given its prime location between the inner and outer planets. The station had a donut-shaped outer ring connected to a long cylinder in the middle, much like the spokes of a bicycle wheel connected the tire to the axle.

"It looks just like the simulation," Vivi said breathlessly.

"It should, or it's not a very good simulation," her mother said as she took the instrument readings. "Let's work through the landing checklist."

There were always lists of all the steps that a pilot had to follow to make sure everything was safe. Even the daring pilots in Selena Squadron had checklists, so Vivi didn't complain. Not out loud, anyway.

Captain Renard pulled the ship into the docking bay, and Vivi noted that her mother didn't do any better for real than she had in the simulation. Wisely, Vivi didn't say that out loud, either.

After being cleared to disembark, Vivi and her mother stepped out of the ship into a huge hangar where two people waited for them: an adult man in an official station uniform, and a teen girl who looked close to Vivi's age. They were both big-boned and densely muscular, in the way that was typical of people from Earth.

"Captain Renard, I'm Deputy James Warner. I'm here to escort you around the station. And this is my daughter, Annie." He gestured to her with an open palm. "She is Vivienne's age and can show her some of the things she'll need to know for a comfortable stay on the station."

"We moved to Carter Station a few months ago," Annie said, using slow Sign Language as she spoke. "I know exactly what it's like to be new here."

"Is everyone expected to use Sign Language?" Vivi was embarrassed to admit she hadn't practiced it very much.

When she and her mother were alone together, they sometimes used the French dialect common to the New France colony on Mars. She wasn't confident in any of the other languages in the solar system.

"My girlfriend is Deaf," Annie explained, "so I try to practice all the time. I want to get so good at Sign I won't need Nora's help to talk to her."

Reflexively, Vivi looked up because the real Nora surrounded her, not just the fake AI from the simulation. Nora probably took a lot of computing power to monitor individual conversations. Before Vivi could get too deep in those thoughts, she looked across the vast hangar with its various ships.

"I want to work here," Vivi said, nodding her head to agree with herself about the good idea she had.

"I think you get that after you pass your flight tests," Captain Renard called out to her. A mother was better at listening to private conversations than an AI any day.

"She might be able to work here," Annie said, sharing a look with her father. "The students have to do public service projects. Maybe Vivi can do something like that with the flight crews."

"I'd really like that," Vivi said, as she tried to commit every detail of the flight deck to memory.

"Come on," Annie told her. "We'll have lunch with my friends, and then I'll show you around."

Vivi hadn't thought she was hungry, but at the word *lunch*, her stomach growled. Annie smiled widely at her and then bounced out of the hangar, clearly expecting Vivi to follow.

The outer ring of the station was a long distance from the inner core, where the nutrition center was located. Carter Station had a peculiar ozone smell that Annie told her wasn't like being on Earth. It was a result of the abundant hydroponics labs that worked tirelessly to provide food and breathable oxygen for all the inhabitants.

"Before I came here, I didn't think I'd like life on a station. Now I love it." Annie jumped and did a dance step. "I even like the different gravity!"

Vivi knew that not all the planets or stations had the exact same gravity specifications. They tried to get close to each other, but the variations were what helped make each place and the people who lived there unique.

When the two girls got to the food area, Annie showed Vivi the trays for her meal and the place to deposit the trash and recycling. The fresh vegetables were an absolute luxury, and Vivi was giddy over getting radishes with her salad greens and tofu protein.

Annie wove in and out of people, leading Vivi to a table where three teenagers were sitting. A dark-skinned boy, likely from Earth given his similar build to Annie, sat beside a girl who was probably from Mars. The Martian girl had coppery skin and hair, like the red planet. Her body was thin and willowy like those, including Vivi herself, who had been born and raised outside of Earth's gravity.

On the other side of the table from them was a long-haired girl, who signed excitedly at Annie when they approached.

"Everyone," Annie said, "this is Vivienne Renard. She's going to take flight tests from Master Quimby."

"Vivi," she piped up. "Only my mom calls me Vivienne, and that's when I'm in trouble."

The boy laughed. "You're my kind of person. I'm Kembo, and I'm in the same class as Ines."

He brushed the back of his hand against the Martian girl's arm. She shyly nodded and waved at Vivi.

"And this is Leelah," Annie said, sitting down beside the other girl and quickly kissing her cheek.

With the four teens paired up with each other, Vivi took the seat at the end of the table. That put Ines to her right and Leelah to her left.

"Are you going to be in any of the student classes?" Ines asked.

"Yeah," Kembo added. "Are you going to be in the Fourteens class with us, or the Fifteens with Annie?"

Vivi shook her head. "I finished my basic school aboard ship. When I turn sixteen, I can test for early admission to flight school."

"When is your birthday?" Leelah asked. She used only Sign Language, but she shared her tablet so Vivi could read the translation.

"In a few weeks. Then I can take all my tests," she replied, rubbing her arms in agitation.

"Are you okay?" Ines asked.

Vivi tried to smile, but her bravery crumpled. "I'm nervous about living on the station by myself. My mom has to work to earn money to put me through flight school. She was going to ask the station master if there was a job for her here. If not, I'll be on my own, and I've never done that before."

The other students at the table didn't laugh at her, though Vivi had thought they might. Instead, each of them became friendlier toward her.

"You can visit me," Ines offered first. "I know what it's like to be alone on the station. My parents have an alternating work cycle on Ganymede. For two weeks, they are here, and for the next two weeks, they are there. Sometimes I miss them a lot."

The last thing Ines said in almost a whisper.

Clapping Ines on the shoulder, Kembo replied with a joking tone, "That's why you have me to tell you all the jokes and help you laugh. Now I can make Vivi laugh, too."

"You can try," Ines teased him.

Leelah waved her hand across the table, to get the attention of the hearing teens. Then she signed, "You could play a basketball game now. I'll be the referee!"

"I don't play basketball," Vivi said with a laugh.

"I don't, either," Annie said. "When I still lived on Earth, I used to swim. But Ines and Kembo love basketball."

The two friends started playfully arguing about the game, and Vivi shook her head. It might be nice to play when she had free time from studying for her tests or working on the flight deck. Plus, it would be one of the fun ways to exercise.

Vivi ate her lunch salad and couldn't help noises of satisfaction. Everything tasted so fresh!

Annie pointed proudly at her plate. "Leelah and I helped with the filtering process so we'd get the best greens possible."

"It worked!" Vivi said with her mouth full. The other teens at the table laughed with her, so she didn't feel too rude with her manners.

When lunch was done, Kembo, Ines, and Leelah departed to the hydroponics labs to work their service hours, but Annie stayed with Vivi to show her the rest of the station's resources, including the library.

In the early evening of station time, Vivi waited for her mother at one of the public observation decks that showed off beautiful views of Jupiter and its moons. She watched the ships approaching and departing the docking ring. In addition to the AI that supported most of the work on the station, flight control had several humans working to make sure everything went smoothly.

Captain Renard walked up behind Vivi, ruffling the girl's black hair. "Did you have a good day? Are you ready to see your room?"

Vivi patted her belly where her stomach tried to show its nerves. "Were you able to transfer to the station while I do my testing? Did Deputy Warner or the station master have anything for you?"

Sighing as she sat down, Vivi's mother said, "No, they don't have any pilot openings in the rotation right now. Deputy Warner tried to help me by showing there are understaffed shifts on the station. The station master wouldn't change his mind. So, I will have to take longer flights out to the rim of the solar system, but I should be back by the time you take your entrance exams."

Vivi nodded but didn't make eye contact with her mother. She felt silly to be nervous about staying alone. The two of them stood up, and Captain Renard confidently showed Vivi where her room on the station was going to be.

Instead of shared barracks, like the one she expected to have if she got into Selena Squadron, Vivi had a compact room that was slightly wider than two-and-a-half beds. There was enough space to sleep and sit at a desk to study. Closet space was minimal, but Vivi didn't have many things. She'd lived on ships most of her life and had never had a chance to accumulate very many personal items.

Nodding at what she saw, Vivi said, "It doesn't look like there's room for you."

"I have a guest bed for the night in a different part of the station. I'll fly back to Saturn space in the morning. You can see me off before you work or do your practice in the simulator," her mother said. "I will be busy for the next few weeks. Maybe that will keep me from missing you so much."

"You can send me messages every day," Vivi suggested.

Leaning forward, Captain Renard kissed the crown of her daughter's head. "I'll do it, and you must write me back to tell me about everything here."

"I met some nice people today."

"That's a good start. Tell me more while we eat supper."

The older woman stretched, and Vivi showed the way to the station's dining hall and special restaurants.

───

The next morning, after *Enceladus One* left Carter Station, Vivi presented herself to Master Quimby, the head of the flight deck. He was a gruff-looking man with a russet-colored beard. Clutching a computer tablet in his hand, he looked from Vivi to the screen and back again.

"You've had good tests. The things you'll do here are keeping the hangar clean and learning how to take care of the ships. If you take care of your equipment, it will take care of you."

That must have been something pilots liked to say, because Vivi's mother had told her that many times.

"Yes, sir."

"Make sure you follow the list of daily tasks in this office, and let others know if you have to leave the deck. That includes sanitation breaks. We have to count on everyone to make sure every flight is a success." He took on a serious look. "Spaceflight is still dangerous. We've been doing it a long time, and we'll keep on doing it if we respect it."

"Yes, sir," Vivi repeated. She didn't know what else she could say.

"One last thing," he said, "log all your times and flights from the simulator. My challenge to you is to try as many ships as you can to test your limits."

"I know what I'm flying," Vivi said quickly. "I'm going to be the youngest pilot in Selena Squadron. That's why I'm testing here."

"You could be. We'll see."

Master Quimby sent Vivi on her way, and she spent hours cleaning and sweeping the deck. A small shuttle of miners arrived from one of Jupiter's moons, and Vivi was added to the ship's cleaning crew. They went inside and cleaned it from dust and space debris. Vivi was thankful for the mask to protect her respiration.

She worked so steadily that lunch had come and gone before she'd realized it. Master Quimby raised his eyebrow at her. "Renard, why didn't you take your nutrition break?"

"I was still cleaning the ship, sir." She hadn't thought she was allowed to stop what she was doing right in the middle of a task.

"You'll get faster, and then you'll take your breaks. They are very important. We keep our equipment and our people safe."

Quimby scanned Vivi's work badge to get a digital portrait of her day. She wasn't sure what the Flight Master was looking at, but after a few seconds, he dismissed her.

"You've already met your maximum work hours for the day," he explained. "Go do something else. Visit friends, or watch a movie in the entertainment plaza. I'll see you tomorrow."

She raised her hand hopefully. "And if I want to use the flight simulators to practice?"

"That is up to you," he said, "but sometimes a person can practice too much. I don't know what kind of person you are yet, but try to find balance in whatever you do."

"I don't want to be balanced," Vivi said. "I want to be the best."

Master Quimby sighed and gave her a very tired look. "Tomorrow, Renard."

It felt like a small victory. Instead of signing up for practice time right away, Vivi decided to explore different nooks and crannies since Carter Station would be her home for a few weeks.

Vivi's days on the station took on a regular quality where she'd work on the flight deck in the morning, stop for lunch to share with her friends, do flight training on the simulators in the afternoons, and wander the station in the evenings, trying to discover new things. She became friendly with the shopkeepers, though she did not have much money to spend. Vivi sometimes visited her friends and their parents in the evening. Then, before going to sleep, she would record video messages for her mother.

The thing Vivi had not counted on was that she would have to study spaceflight so intently. She thought she knew everything there was to know about the ship she would fly if she got into Selena Squadron. And she did. The other types of ships proved more challenging. Master Quimby had meant what he'd said because each one had particular flight requirements. So during her afternoons, Vivi often found herself in the library with Mr. Ranganathan, the station librarian, doing equations related to charting her flights or the chemical components of the fuels that powered the various ships.

As Vivi's birthday got closer, she became sadder because her mother wasn't able to share it with her. Captain Renard's work routes took her out to the rim of the solar system. Vivi tried to bottle up her distress so her new friends wouldn't worry about her, but she picked at her food instead of eating it.

That might have been a blessing in disguise. Leelah got Vivi's attention and signed, "I would not eat the lentils. We had a sick visitor in the labs yesterday making a big mess. Master Jemisin had to call the security team to walk them out."

"Why didn't I hear about that?" Vivi asked. She'd made a habit of talking to the different station people as she went on her walks at night.

"Chief Liu, that's my dad's boss," Annie said. "They like to keep security problems as quiet as possible. They don't want to create panic in a small space."

"Speaking of panic in a small space," Kembo said, clapping his hands together with excitement, "none of us have public service hours this afternoon. I think it's time we play basketball!"

Vivi started to refuse because playing basketball would get in the way of her time in the flight simulators. She was days away from her birthday and her flight exams.

Ines must have understood Vivi's hesitation. "Don't you have your flight tests this week?"

"Yes. Master Quimby is going to let me take a shuttle out and fly from anchor point to anchor point around the station to prove I can fly for real," Vivi answered.

"Why don't you sound happy about that?" Annie asked next. "Hasn't this been what you've been working for?"

Vivi let out a sigh, and Leelah gave her a serious look. "You should relax and do something fun."

"You know I love fun," Kembo added with his winning grin.

Doing something with her new friends was better than sitting around being sad because Vivi missed her mother. Plus, she needed a brain break. How much more could she learn at this point?

Going back to the nutrition station, Vivi picked something other than the lentils to eat. If she was going to play basketball, she would definitely need the energy.

After the group finished their lunches, they played on a small court with Leelah as the impartial referee. Annie and Kembo were Team Earth against Ines and Vivi as Team Mars. They had several two-on-two games against each other, but the Earth team narrowly pulled ahead.

"It's almost my birthday," Vivi muttered to Ines. "They should have let us win."

"Kembo doesn't play like that, but Leelah arranged something for you." Ines pointed to Leelah's parents walking onto the court with a small birthday cake. Deputy Warner and Kembo's mom, Miriam, who was also the station counselor, trailed behind them.

"Oh, wow!" Vivi said, fighting the tears from the corner of her eyes.

"We know your mother couldn't be here, but we're here to celebrate with you," Miriam said.

The older woman enfolded Vivi in a hug and then passed her to the other parents who were there. The pack of adults did not include Ines's parents because they were doing one of their work shifts on Ganymede.

The cake was a simple vanilla, which Vivi liked very much, and it was springy and moist. Leelah's mother worked in the station kitchens and was an excellent cook.

"Thank you, everyone," Vivi said, looking sincerely at all of them.

"You're so welcome," Miriam told her. After another bite of cake, she asked Ines, "When do your parents get back, dear?"

"In a few days. As long as the shuttles are running and the pilots are healthy, it shouldn't be a problem."

Vivi looked at her Martian friend and marveled at how brave she was. Ines inspired her to be much more confident. Besides, when Vivi got into Selena Squadron, it was not like she could call her mother every day. But there she wouldn't be alone then since all the recruits live together.

Over the next few days, the pilots on the flight deck started coughing so much that they repeatedly spit out all the dripping mucus. They broke out with sweats and fevers, while a few reported muscle aches. The sickness could have been a highly contagious cold, or something brought on by the dust and debris from cleaning the ships.

No matter the cause, Vivi wanted none of it. She had an important exam to take and pass.

Unfortunately, Vivi started to doubt she'd be able to take her flight test when she spoke to Master Quimby in his office. He looked deathly pale, like he'd rather be in his bed than anywhere near the flight deck.

"Is my final exam still on for tomorrow?" Vivi crossed her fingers at her sides for luck.

Quimby looked at his digital calendar. "That's what it says, Renard. Go home and get some rest so we can have a good flight."

"You, too, sir."

Instead of going to her tiny room, Vivi wandered the station. Too many people were coughing for her to feel comfortable in public spaces, so she decided to go see Ines. The other girl had told her she was welcome to come over whenever she was lonely. Today was finally that day.

Ines answered the door after Vivi rang the pager. She looked surprised but welcomed her into the living quarters. Even though both her parents were off the station, it looked like a family space that included them, too. There were soft blankets placed around the room for comfort and mementos of Mars. Ines's parents had books and hobby projects laid out, including a jigsaw puzzle. Vivi wanted to place a few of the pieces, but she turned to her friend instead.

"Thanks for letting me visit." Rubbing at her cheek, Vivi shyly admitted, "I didn't want to be by myself. I hope that's okay."

"Of course it is!" Ines paused and tapped her bottom lip with her finger. "Do you want to watch a movie with me?"

"Yeah."

Vivi covered herself with one of the soft blankets, and they watched one whole movie together before falling asleep right where they were.

⁂

When the morning alarm went off, Vivi was confused about where she was. Ines jumped up and immediately downloaded a message from her parents. She played it back immediately and let out a happy sigh when they promised to come back on the station later that day. Vivi realized she probably had a message from her mother waiting for her back in her own room. Before she could check, or have Nora reroute her personal messages, the door chime rang loudly.

"Station Master Andrew Norton," Nora announced. "Mr. Norton needs to speak to Miss Renard most urgently."

"Me?" Vivi asked. "How did he know I was here?"

It was a dumb question, but she *had* just woken up. Nora probably told him. Vivi shared a look with Ines, who shrugged back at her. Then Ines told Nora to let the Station Master in.

"Please excuse me," he said with an officious bow to Ines. He looked up, and Vivi waved at him from where she was still sitting in yesterday's clothing.

"Miss Renard," he said, long strides bringing him over to her in the space of two breaths. "We have had an outbreak of food poisoning amongst our pilots, including Master Quimby. Our flight crews are all unexpectedly grounded."

"I see."

Vivi assumed her final flight exam would have to be postponed. If she didn't take the exam soon, she wouldn't get into the next Selena Squadron recruit class. She understood the problem but couldn't help feeling sour about it.

"I don't think you do," Norton said, taking out a tablet and scrolling through the data. "You're the only pilot I currently have available to me. We need you to fly a shuttle to Ganymede to pick up some of the supplies, including one of the minerals that will help everyone here recover from the food poisoning."

Vivi squinted at him. She couldn't be the only pilot who wasn't sick. There were so many aviation and aeronautics workers on the station. "I don't believe you…"

"Believe this. It's easier to ask you and use this supply run as your final exam than to go against some of the toughest labor laws in the solar system. Are you ready to put your simulation time to the test?"

She smacked her lips open and closed. "But if Master Quimby's sick, who will be my examiner?"

"Me," Norton said, without his previous confidence, "and Nora."

"If you're going to Ganymede, I want to go with you," Ines said.

"I don't care," Norton replied, "as long as it gets Vivienne in the pilot's chair."

"And you can sign off on my application to Selena Squadron?" Vivi asked to be completely sure.

"Yes. Get your flight gear and meet us in Hangar Twelve. The shuttle is waiting. You have thirty minutes of station time." Norton nodded solemnly and then acknowledged Ines as he walked away. "Miss Rice."

Though Vivi was tempted to stare at the place Norton had been, she had a short time to get to the hangar and put on her flight suit. She could do just about any flight simulation in her sleep, but this real flight would be much scarier than merely circling the station.

"Go," Ines said. "I'll be right with you. I don't want to miss the chance to see Ganymede."

"You've never been there?"

Ines shook her head, and Vivi said, "Me neither. Let's go find out where your parents work."

Vivi stared at the checklist from the pilot's seat. Andrew Norton sat beside her in the copilot's seat, taking notes with his handheld tablet. Ines sat behind him, offering Vivi silent encouragement. It had been strange to see the flight deck so empty, but there was some relief that new pilots would rotate on shift by the time their shuttle landed on Ganymede.

Following each of the checklists, Vivi worked in sequence, speaking every step out loud to the station master as she made sure the shuttle was flight-ready.

"Airlock secure and open," Norton said, reading from his screen.

"Micro-thrusters on," Vivi said back.

She fired three small, controlled bursts. To her relief, she got the shuttle in the perfect placement to go through the bay doors without scraping the bottom, top, or sides.

"*Shuttle Six*, you can take it out beyond the ring."

Vivi paused to feel the importance of the moment, but she didn't have time to waste. "Acknowledged, Carter Station."

Pressing the shuttle forward, Vivi transitioned into microgravity. Everyone on board was belted in, so she moved on to the next commands for clearing ships and debris hovering around the station.

"Breathe slow and steady," Ines said into Vivi's communicator. "You got this."

"Miss Rice," Norton said testily, in case the teens became talkative on this special piloting run.

Vivi nodded at her friend's encouragement. Then she focused on navigating the flight path to Ganymede, where the miners waited with minerals that would cure the outbreak of food poisoning on Carter Station.

The one thing that Vivi had not realized was that piloting a real craft was very physical. In a flight simulator, she always knew she was in a simulator, no matter how advanced it was. Piloting *Shuttle Six* made Vivi's muscles tense up. She let out her breath after they cleared the orbital space around the station.

"The shuttle is on autopilot until we get closer to Ganymede's position," Vivi told Norton.

He then asked her questions about aeronautics and aviation history that Vivi wasn't entirely sure were part of her final exam. It could have been Norton keeping her busy. Meanwhile, Ines behind her was taking many photos of Jupiter.

"I love the storm systems of the clouds," she told Vivi. "Some of them have been going for centuries."

Vivi stroked the helm but did not speak. The next part she would have to do was land safely without bumping things. It was what her mother had warned her about, but it would be even more important given her current companions.

"You can talk a little now," Norton told Vivi. "Don't be too distracted."

"Thank you, sir," she replied. "I wish my mom were here to see this."

"Well," he said, "I'm sure you want her to be proud of you, but if Captain Renard were here, I'd have her flying instead."

"I will be Captain Renard one day with a different ship than this."

"I'm sure, but shuttles are very important. Ask your friend Ines."

"They saved the miners in my parents' camp when the communication array got knocked out a few months ago," Ines said.

Sitting up more confidently, Vivi gave her friend a nod that she was listening and then transitioned the shuttle from autopilot to manual controls.

"You may be aware," Norton started in a tone that reminded Vivi of a video teacher, "the camp is on the terminator line between light and dark. Plan your approach accordingly."

Ganymede was like many other moons in the solar system, in that it was tidally locked and showed its planet only one side. There was a terminator line on Luna, too. Selena Squadron's facilities were on the side of the moon that never faced Earth.

After a few more minutes of manually controlled flying, Vivi started narrating her steps again so Norton could track her progress. "Approaching Ganymede and overlaying maps. Using short rocket bursts to dampen inertia."

"Good," Norton said, adding more notes to his tablet.

Vivi used her instruments to find the signal from the camp's flight control. She authorized the computer in the shuttle to talk to the computer on site. After they were linked, Vivi slowed the descent of the shuttle. She felt nervous sweat trickling down her back because the calculations for the landing had to be perfect. If they weren't, then Vivi might crash the shuttle.

As if knowing her panic, Ines reached forward again to press a comforting hand on Vivi's arm. With an answering smile, Vivi refocused on the fast but tiny adjustments she needed to make to bring the shuttle down safely. It wasn't a perfectly smooth landing, but it was something all three of them could walk away from.

Norton caught her eyes when she looked in his direction. He inclined his head toward her. "Nicely done. If you can safely get us back to Carter Station without incident, you will pass your qualification exam. More than that, I'll write a letter to recommend you for a scholarship."

"Thank you, sir," Vivi said.

"That's great," Ines said loudly. "Okay, let me out so I can go surprise my parents!"

"Right, right," Vivi muttered, going through the arrival checklist and then opening the shuttle to load people returning to Carter Station, the minerals to cure the food poisoning, and various other supplies.

The trip back to Carter Station was stressful in a different way for Vivi. This time, she had the lives of several miners in her shuttle, including Ines's parents, who had been scheduled to return that day anyway. The Rice family happily chattered to each other in the back.

Norton remained in the copilot's seat with a case of healing minerals secured near his feet. He spoke a little more freely this time while Vivi observed how the same shuttle felt different to fly, even in space, when it was full of people and cargo.

As they approached Carter Station, Vivi remembered how it had been in her practice flights before coming to the station. This time, when she gave her call sign to Nora, it would be for a real flight.

"Carter Station, this is *Shuttle Six* requesting permission to dock," she said smoothly.

"Welcome home, *Shuttle Six*! We have been waiting for you," a human voice from the flight deck said. "Take your place at Hangar Twelve."

She let out a small sigh of relief because it was good to be back. Then Vivi concentrated on making the smoothest docking that she had ever done across all tests, simulated or otherwise. When the station landing gear latched onto the ship, Vivi let it go into Nora's capable hands.

"Excellent work, Captain Renard," Norton told her.

A big grin spread over her face. Yes, she was Captain Renard for this trip, and she'd be Captain Renard again. Just like her mother, but doing it with her own style. Vivi would have a big message to record later to describe her adventure.

The food poisoning cure helped most of the sick pilots by the next day. They thanked Vivi as they saw her. Even Master Quimby was friendlier to her.

"I was so sick," he admitted. "I couldn't have waited another day for the cure. Station sanitation might not have survived."

Well, Vivi hadn't needed to know that, but she was glad they were all feeling better. She was also happy that she had been nominated for a flight school scholarship. The only thing that would make it better would be seeing her mother again to share all the good news in person.

Captain Delphine Renard and *Enceladus One* returned to Carter Station two full station days later. Vivi stood waiting for her, standing with military poise as her mother disembarked.

"Captain Renard," Vivi said, barely controlling the smile that wanted to curl her lips.

Looking her daughter up and down, the more experienced pilot tapped a new pin on Vivi's chest. "Congratulations."

No longer able to stay serious, Vivi grinned. "It was so amazing! A little scary, too. But I did it. And I made a smooth landing."

Laughing and pulling Vivi in for a hug, her mother said, "You can tell me everything over lunch."

"Right. And I'll tell you what to skip, because I have friends in hydroponics. I don't want you to get food poisoning."

"No, I don't want that, either," the older woman said, walking with her daughter off the flight deck and into the rest of the station.

THOUGHTS ON *BRAVE NEW GIRLS*

"As a writer, *Brave New Girls* helped me to get my start in publishing. I will always be thankful to the editors for giving me a chance. In my work as a librarian, I have seen young readers ask for stories just like the ones here. Maybe those readers need heroines to inspire them, or mirrors to envision themselves doing wonderful things. The possibilities are limitless for any kind of girl willing to dream."

ABOUT THE AUTHOR

JD Cadmon loves science fiction, especially space adventures. That is why she's happy to be in another edition of *Brave New Girls*. It's one more chance to write about the smart and capable girls aboard Carter Station, using their STEM knowledge to save the day. Ines and Leelah's stories are available in previous volumes.

When JD isn't writing, she works in a public library as an administrative librarian. She has three adorable cats to play with at home. Two of her favorite pastimes are making music and learning other languages. JD is currently focusing on the drums and basic Portuguese.

Illustration for "Earning Her Wings" by Harley Scroggins.

THE APE CANYON ADVENTURE:
AN ITZAL STORY

JOSH PRITCHETT

THE APE CANYON ADVENTURE: AN ITZAL STORY

JOSH PRITCHETT

"Okay, everyone out," Lieutenant Adityas called out, as the shuttle landed in a clearing near Mount Saint Helens' visitor center.

Cadets Itzal, Daughter of Veieiskeila; Emma Nelson; Rosario Dorn; and Utta grabbed their gear. They quickly rushed out of the shuttle and filed into formation.

Lt. Adityas was a L'aox with reddish skin, horns, long silver hair, and dark spots on different parts of his face and hands. "At ease," Adityas commanded, and the four of them stood at parade rest with their hands behind their backs. "For the next week, we will be studying the basic geography of this region of Earth. Can anyone tell me why Earth has a much wider diversity of regions than most other planets?"

"Mountains, sir," Utta, a cadet from the planet Paq, said through her translator box, as she shifted one of her eight black, giant, spider-like legs. "Earth has some of the largest mountains among the known planets in the Coalition of Worlds. Mountainous regions have fundamentally different and diverse plant and animal life-forms compared to nearby lowland regions."

"Not bad, Cadet," Adityas replied. "Anyone else want to add to that?"

"Sir," Rosario, a cyborg teenager from the planet Gowad answered, as she looked at Adityas with her cybernetic left eye. "The amount of sunlight a region receives—along with its height above sea level, the shape of the land, and how close it is to oceans—determines how, where, and what kinds of life will evolve."

"The tilt, sir," Itzal added, as her nose took in the pleasant smells around her. Itzal was a Leyak, a humanoid race that had evolved from a wolf-like species. "Earth has a twenty-three-point-five-degree tilt, which gives it four seasons, which are usually mild and favorable to different life-forms. Unlike the axis of rotation of a planet like Uranus, which has an almost parallel orbital plane, and is subject to more violent storms."

"Also, sir," added Emma, an Asian-American teenager with ginger-colored hair, "without a tilt, everyday conditions would be like those on Earth's equator. Each day would have roughly a twelve-hour day length, and the temperature and precipitation patterns would not deviate that much. Also, the noon sun angle would be almost the same from day to day, and there would be no seasons like we know now. That would make all life more uniform, sir."

"Well," Adityas said, "looks like you were all paying attention in basic planetary science class. So, now we're going to put what you've learned to the test. For the next week, we will be conducting geological studies of this region. During your time in the Space Guard, you will all be expected to study new planets that the fleet discovers, and share your findings with your commanding officers. While this is not an unknown area, I will be comparing your data with those of previous expeditions in this region to see what you did and didn't find."

"YES, SIR!" the cadets sounded off.

"Also, in case you thought that we might be spending the week at a hotel, think again. We'll be camping the whole time. You will eventually have to spend several days on an unknown planet without the option to head back up to a nice, cozy spaceship to sleep on. Let's get used to that idea, Cadets."

"YES, SIR!"

When Adityas turned his attention away for a second, Emma leaned over and whispered to Itzal, "I heard Lane and her group got assigned to Antarctica."

Cadet Molly Lane was a constant thorn in Itzal's side.

"Oh, I feel so bad for her," Itzal said sarcastically.

"No, you don't."

"Not even a little," Itzal said with a laugh. When she laughed, her hand brushed Emma's for a second. "Sorry," she said.

"It's okay," Emma replied.

Emma had come from an alternate reality that had been destroyed by a race called the Beyonders. They were the same race that had destroyed Itzal's home world of Leyak Prime. In that universe, Emma had been in love with a version of Itzal.

After finding this out, Itzal and Emma had become very good friends. Itzal, though, had not wanted to do anything that would bring up bad memories for Emma about her universe. Likewise, Emma hadn't wanted Itzal to feel like a replacement for the girl she had loved, so they had agreed to just be friends.

Itzal would have been lying, however, if she'd denied her feelings ran deeper than friendship.

"All right, Cadets," Adityas said. "Listen up. We have a special guest who will be going along with us, by order of Space Guard Command. Cadet Itzal, I believe you know our guest!"

Adityas sounded somewhat unpleasant when he said this, and a wave of confusion overcame Itzal. Aside from her classmates, she didn't know anyone on Earth. Then she saw the guest walk out of the visitor center, and her stomach dropped. "Halla, help me," she muttered when she saw her mother, dressed in a dark gray Leyak uniform.

"Veieiskeila," Emma said. "She looks... the same."

"Mother," Itzal said, as if she hadn't heard Emma.

"Daughter," Veieiskeila said as she inspected her. "I see Space Guard training has not been inadequate. You've put on some muscle."

"Thank you, Mother." Itzal tried not to clench her teeth. "What are you doing here, and why are you dressed in your old uniform?"

"I have invoked *Dǫkkalfar Skenandoa*," Veieiskeila said.

Itzal looked at her mother. *Dǫkkalfar Skenandoa* was an ancient rite of Leyak parents who needed to see their children during emergencies. "Mother, *Dǫkkalfar Skenandoa* is a Leyak ritual. This is Space Guard..."

"Cadet," Lt. Adityas interrupted. "Space Guard is committed to fostering diversity among its members. Command has already granted Admiral Veieiskeila permission to join our mission, given the emergency nature of her situation."

"What emergency?" Itzal said to her mother in Leyak.

"I miss my daughter," Veieiskeila replied in Leyak. "Isn't that emergency enough?"

Halla, Itzal thought. *What have I done to offend you, and can I make it up in the next few minutes?*

Halla was not in a talkative mood!

"Besides, it is my duty as head of our family to make sure that you are being trained adequately as a warrior," Veieiskeila added, pointing to the MARAUDER pistol Itzal wore on her uniform belt.

Even though they were on Earth and not an unknown planet, the point of the assignment was to simulate a planetary exploration mission; MARAUDERs would be standard equipment on such missions.

"I'm not a warrior," Itzal said. "I'm a scientist, and this is just for defense."

"I still need to know that you can protect yourself," Veieiskeila said.

Itzal was about to make a sharp retort when Adityas interjected, "You both can do the family reunion later. Let's get moving. We're burning daylight."

Their first stop was Yale Lake. Itzal was quickly taken in by the rich orange and brown colors of the late fall season. Itzal recognized the thick, dark-green Douglas fir and the tall, wide-trunked western redcedars that covered each side of the trail. She'd learned about them in her natural biology class. On the ground were white hemlock, Oregon grape, salal, and red huckleberry, which seemed to form a natural carpet. Warm beams of sunlight shone between the thick trees, giving the forest around her a cathedral-like feeling. She would have liked to have just walked among those woods, exploring the natural world.

"Beautiful," Veieiskeila said in Leyak, as she moved up to walk beside Itzal. "This place reminds me of home."

Home for Veieiskeila was Leyak Prime, not Dalia Three, where their people had resettled after the Beyonders had destroyed their world. Itzal suddenly wanted to ask her mother why she had really come to Earth. Was she really missing her that badly that she needed to be closer?

Before she could ask, Lt. Adityas called the hike to a halt. "All right, Cadets," he said. "I want a full soil survey inventory of the land around us. Check for things such as texture, internal drainage, parent material, depth to groundwater, topography, degree of erosion, stoniness, salinity, and how far apart different regions are over this landscape. I want to know the hazards of flood-prone areas; the amount of sand, silt, and clay; and the rates of shrinking and swelling. You may have to help settle some people on a planet like this someday. Let's make sure we don't get our colonists killed because they built on a flood plain."

They all spread out and began to do their work. As they were getting started, Utta called out, "Look at this!"

The others walked over to where Utta was standing, as she pointed down at something on the ground. They gathered around her to look, and saw a twenty-four-inch footprint pressed into the damp earth!

"Is that a bear track?" Itzal asked.

"No," Rosario said. "It doesn't look like a bear track."

As a cyborg, Rosario had instant access to the internet, thanks to the implants in her brain. With them, she could obtain great amounts of information in seconds, and easily find out what a bear track looked like. "This track looks more human or humanoid," she said.

"Whatever it is, it's huge," Veieiskeila said, as she pointed to the ground a few feet from them. "Here's another one!"

They went over to look at the second print, which was almost four feet from the first. Veieiskeila said, "This stride could not be made by a human."

"It could be a very large humanoid tourist from another planet," Rosario commented. "Maybe they took their shoes off to enjoy the lake?"

That made sense, Itzal realized. Earth was a very open planet. Itzal glanced over at Emma, who seemed to be looking down at the footprint with great interest. *Does she know something about what made the footprint?*

"Well, either way," Adityas finally said, "we'll note it in our mission reports. Let's get back to our work."

They went back to gather their samples. After a while, Itzal made her way over to Emma. "How's it going?" she asked.

"Oh, just so exciting, digging up dirt," Emma said with a note of sarcasm.

"I was wondering, do you know anything else about that footprint?"

Emma glanced around. "I don't think that Adityas would want to hear it."

"I won't tell."

"Well, back on my Earth, there was a legend of a large North American creature called 'Bigfoot' that lived in woods like these. People would discover footprints like the ones we found and make plaster casts out of them. Some people even said that they had actually seen the creatures that made the footprints."

"What did they look like?"

"They said they looked like giant apes. Other people took pictures of what they claimed were the creatures, but most of them were found out to be fakes. Remember my uncle? He said he saw..." Emma paused. "I'm sorry, Itzal."

"What... no, it's fine," Itzal said, realizing that Emma had forgotten for a second. She did that sometimes when they were talking, and she would bring up some memory that she had shared with the other Itzal.

"I should get this sample done," Emma said.

"I... Yeah, okay," Itzal replied, realizing that she should give her some space.

Itzal tried to focus on her own work, but she couldn't concentrate on the task, because her mind kept going back to how she brought up memories and feelings for Emma. She felt heartbroken that she was a constant reminder of everything Emma had lost.

After another hour, Adityas called an end to the survey. He announced that they would next be heading up Mount Saint Helens itself to gather samples, before setting up camp at June Lake. As they hiked, Itzal was trying to focus on her tasks, but she couldn't stop thinking about Emma. Maybe she really did need to give her some distance. But Emma didn't have a lot of friends other than her, Rosario, and Utta.

Itzal wanted to be a friend, but her own feelings made her want to be more. It seemed selfish, and she hated herself for feeling that way.

As her thoughts raced around in her head, Itzal looked up in time to see her mother raise a fist and stop. All of them, including Adityas, halted in their tracks. She watched as her mother looked around.

"Admiral?" Adityas asked.

"Someone is watching us," Veieiskeila said in a low voice.

Adityas started to look around, then pulled out his scanner. Unsure what else to do, the cadets pulled theirs out as well. Looking over the readings, Itzal couldn't see anything out of the ordinary.

"I'm not detecting anything," Adityas said, trying to sound respectful.

"Mother?" Itzal asked.

"Can't you smell it?" Veieiskeila demanded.

Itzal took a deep breath, and she noticed a thick, musky smell, that was like body odor mixed with rotten eggs and something pungent. It was an awful stink that made her want to cover her nose. Looking around, she saw Rosario looking intently between the trees. "Rosario, do you see anything?"

"I thought I did," she replied.

"Cadet, be clearer," Adityas commanded.

"Sir, I thought I saw movement with my biological eye, but my cybernetic one can't detect anything, other than the surrounding forest and a few smaller animals."

"Then why are none of them making a sound?" Veieiskeila asked sharply. "Forests go silent whenever a predator is near."

"With all due respect, Admiral," Adityas replied, "you're not an expert on Earth plant and animal life."

"What are you implying, L'aox?" Veieiskeila said, rising up to her full height.

Itzal didn't know what to do; she couldn't go against a superior officer without cause, but she couldn't stand against her mother either, could she?

"Sir," Emma said. "Look over there!"

Adityas turned and looked at Emma. "What is it, Cadet?"

"I just saw something move between those trees," Emma said in a low voice as she pointed at the trees.

"I don't see anything," Adityas replied.

Itzal looked, and she didn't see anything either, but that smell was still there.

Without asking permission, Emma walked quickly toward the spot where she had seen the movement. "Nelson, get back here," Adityas commanded.

Emma reached the tree and looked down. "Sir, take a look at this."

Adityas walked over, followed by Itzal and the others. They all looked at what Emma was pointing toward and saw another large footprint behind the tree!

"Maybe there's someone out here with masking technology who doesn't like non-humans?" Utta asked.

Adityas pulled his MARAUDER pistol out of its holster and held it up. "WHOEVER IS OUT THERE," he called out. "I AM LT. ADITYAS OF SPACE GUARD. WE ARE ARMED! MAKE YOURSELF KNOWN TO US!"

There was no reply.

Itzal reached for her own MARAUDER, but stopped herself. She knew that she should only draw it if Adityas told her to.

Just then, the ground rumbled. Itzal heard a sound that reminded her of recordings she had heard of old-style Earth trains as they rolled over their tracks.

"What was that?" Utta said.

"Just a mild tremor," Adityas said. "Remember, Cadets, Mount Saint Helens is still an active volcano. Occasional tremors like that one are to be expected."

Looking around once more, Itzal wasn't sure what made her more nervous, that tremor or the large footprints.

Emerging from the tree line, they found themselves walking along an almost desert-like landscape that looked more like a moonscape to Itzal. Gray was the dominant color of the ground around them, except in places where wildflowers and grass grew. It made her think about Leyak Prime again, whose ecology had been destroyed by the Beyonders when they'd attacked. For a moment, Itzal considered her few memories of her home world, and she wondered if wildflowers would ever grow there again someday.

The sun was warm as they walked along the trail, which was lined on either side by wildflowers. Eventually, the elevation rose, and the flowers fell away, replaced by sharp gray rocks. As they got higher up the mountain, Itzal found herself thankful for the months of physical training she had endured since joining Space Guard. From what she had read in the mission prep, Mount Saint Helens was considered a mostly easy hike for experienced climbers. She still had to pause to drink water and catch her breath a few times.

"You okay?" Emma asked.

Itzal nodded. "I'm just glad that Adityas isn't making us run up the trail."

"Wait until fourth year," Emma replied, and they both laughed.

"Thanks for preventing an argument between Adityas and my mother back there."

"No problem," Emma said with a smile.

"I didn't want to pry. I know that it must be painful for you…"

"You want to know if the Veieiskeila I knew was anything like yours?" Emma asked.

Itzal nodded as she drank some water from her canteen.

"Hmm, mostly," Emma answered. "My Veieiskeila told more jokes."

"Veieiskeila telling jokes?!" Itzal exclaimed. "Now, that I can't imagine."

"Itzal, Nelson, let's pick up the pace," Adityas called back down to them.

Adityas was in the lead with Utta close behind him. She was followed by Rosario, then Itzal and Emma. Veieiskeila brought up the rear.

Itzal fell back so she could talk to her mother. "Are you trying to get me kicked out of Space Guard?" she asked pointedly.

"That L'aox is a fool," Veieiskeila said angrily. "I know that something is following us!"

"The sensors say that there's nothing here that could harm us."

"Sensors can be fooled," Veieiskeila retorted. "I trust my own senses. You would trust yours as well, if you had only learned what I had tried to teach you."

"I do trust my senses. That's part of being a scientist, but I still need data and facts."

"A warrior only needs to listen to her heart," Veieiskeila snorted.

"Yeah, well, I keep telling you that I'm not a warrior. I would rather learn about other cultures than conquer them!" Itzal quickly regretted her words when she said them. "I didn't mean that, Mother."

"I know what you meant," Veieiskeila replied, and went silent.

The last leg of their journey was the most difficult. The mountain sloped, and the ground was covered in small sharp rocks that made it hard to gain any traction. Adityas, Utta, and Rosario managed it well enough, but Itzal, Emma, and Veieiskeila found it was easier if they crawled on hands and feet to reach the summit.

"You hanging in there?" Emma asked as she crawled next to Itzal.

"Yeah, I'm good," she replied.

"Just don't look down," Emma said with a grin.

Itzal understood what she meant; she didn't want to admit it in front of her mother, but the heights were making her dizzy. A few weeks before, Itzal had been forced to climb a tree to escape a hacked vehicle. That hadn't been too bad, but it wasn't the same as climbing a mountain. *If climbing up a simple mountain makes you dizzy,* a voice in Itzal's head said, *how will you manage EVA training?*

From Emma's remark, Itzal realized that her counterpart might have had a similar problem with heights. For a second, she thought about asking Emma, but decided to push the thought aside and keep climbing. It had been sweet of Emma to ask.

Their hearts were beating faster as they reached the overhang of Mount Saint Helens and looked down into the crater at the top. It was a jagged, steep drop downward, and Itzal felt like she was looking at a bomb crater instead of a natural phenomenon.

"They say that when the volcano erupted, it was like twenty-four megatons going off at once," Rosario said.

"It's beautiful up here," Emma said as she looked out toward Mount Adams in the distance.

An ocean of clouds seemed to stretch out between the two mountains, and Itzal could almost imagine walking across it.

"Start gathering your samples, Cadets," Adityas ordered.

Itzal used her soil probe to retrieve a small core sample near the inner ledge of the volcano. She was inserting the stainless-steel tool into the soil when Rosario spoke up. "Whoa! Do you guys feel…"

Just then, the mountain shook!

Itzal didn't remember dropping her core sampler. All she remembered was one moment she was kneeling near the ledge, and then the next second she was thrown off, as if the ground beneath her had just shrugged her off.

She saw the rocky, dark gray inside of the volcano rising up to meet her, and heard the sound of rushing winds around her. For a second, Itzal thought that she was dreaming, and a wave of euphoria washed over her. Then a hand grabbed her by the ankle and held on tight!

"Got you," Itzal heard Emma exclaim.

Itzal suddenly realized that it wasn't a dream. She was looking straight down into the volcano. Plumes of white steam rose up from inside the volcano's lava pits, and her heart raced.

"Won't let you go," Emma growled as she tried to pull Itzal back up. "Again!"

A second set of hands grabbed her other ankle, and Itzal felt herself quickly pulled back up onto the ledge by Emma and Veieiskeila. "You're okay," Emma said once she was back on the ledge.

Adityas came over. "You all right, Itzal?" he asked.

"Yes, sir," she said.

Adityas nodded and patted her shoulder. "Cadets," he called out. "Gather what you have, and let's get out of here!"

Emma helped Itzal up. Itzal suddenly realized that Emma hadn't let go of her since pulling her back up. Itzal thought about saying something as they started to clamber down the side of the volcano to the path, but decided that she didn't want to.

Thirty minutes later, they were still walking back down Mount Saint Helens when Rosario held up her hand. "Everyone, wait a second," she said.

"Cadet?" Adityas said.

"Sorry, sir," Rosario replied. "I just spotted someone further down the path. I was looking back down the way we came, and I saw… someone really tall running back down the side of the mountain!"

"What did he look like, Cadet?"

"I…" Rosario began. "Sir, I'm sorry. For some reason, my eye went blank for a second." She tapped the side of her cybernetic eye for emphasis. "I'm unable to be certain of what I saw."

Adityas seemed to consider what Rosario was telling him. "Let's keep moving," he said decisively.

A minute later, they stopped again when Utta spoke. "Sir, look!"

There was a fresh twenty-four-inch footprint pressed into the dirt in front of them.

"It's stalking us," Veieiskeila said with a growl.

"All right, enough of this," Adityas said, and pulled out his MARAUDER. "Check your weapons, Cadets."

They pulled out their weapons and did a safety check.

"I don't know what this is, but it's very curious about us. So we will be on alert status until extraction. No one is to engage whatever or whoever this is unless I say so."

All of them except Veieiskeila called out, "Yes, sir!"

"I'm starting to like this one," Itzal heard her mother mutter in Leyak.

───

It took them three hours to get back down off Mount Saint Helens, and another hour to head southeast to June Lake. As they hiked, Itzal noticed that her mother seemed to be on alert the whole time. Veieiskeila wasn't armed, but Itzal knew that her mother was an expert in various Leyak martial arts, including *Ho'otseoo'e*, the lightning strike. She could defend herself quite well if needed.

"Remember," Veieiskeila said in Leyak as they walked, "when the attack comes, aim for the center mass of the chest."

"*Ka'Ho*," Emma said—the Leyak word for "I understand"—as if out of reflex.

Veieiskeila looked at Emma, and her brow narrowed. "You speak Leyak."

"Emma is my friend from another reality," Itzal said. "I told you in one of my letters. Didn't you read it?"

"Of course I did," Veieiskeila said. "The way you talked about her, I just assumed she would be taller."

Then, to Itzal's surprise, Veieiskeila made a sniffing sound, and then seemed to consider it before moving on.

Itzal looked at Emma. "That was awkward," Emma said.

Itzal began to wonder if her mother was there to evaluate her or to evaluate Emma!

June Lake was located near a basalt cliff, into which a small waterfall emptied, replenishing the lake's cool and clear water supply. According to the mission briefing, the lake had been formed by a lava flow over two thousand years before, which had also sealed it off from the nearby Swift Creek. Looking around at the thick trees, some of which had leaves changing colors for fall, Itzal thought that it was the most beautiful spot she had ever seen.

Itzal glanced around; she had set up her own tent and was taking in the nature around her. Adityas was on his phone with Space Guard command, expressing his concerns about the volcano's status and whether they should leave. Then Itzal spotted Emma putting up her tent.

"Hey." Itzal walked over to her.

"Hey," Emma said as she added her tent's rainfly.

"Thank you again for saving me."

"Listen, I'm sorry about what I said."

"I was too busy falling into a volcano to notice," Itzal said with a smile. "I mean, ugh, sorry. I'm not trying to make light of what you're feeling."

"I know," Emma replied. "I just… I hope that you don't think that I'm trying to remake you into my Itzal…"

"Oh, yeah, I know that," Itzal replied. "And I know that seeing me and my mother is probably still bringing up some painful memories for you…"

"That's just it. If anything, I feel the happiest I've been since I came to this universe. And that also hurts because I feel like I'm betraying her and…"

Emma looked like she wanted to cry.

"Emma, I didn't mean to hurt you."

"You didn't, and you're not," Emma said with a smile, as tears ran down her face.

Itzal wanted to say so many things just then, but didn't know where to start. *Halla,* she thought. *Why is this so awkward?*

Something occurred to Itzal, and she knew what she wanted to say. She began to speak the words when a sharp whistling sound reverberated through the woods.

"What was that?" Utta asked.

Itzal and Emma looked around. "I think it came from over there," Itzal said as her ears twitched.

As she said it, she heard a second whistle in the opposite direction. All of them paused and tried to listen. Then they heard a third whistle coming from near the lake.

"They're surrounding us," Veieiskeila said with a hiss.

A loud *tap-tap-tap* noise echoed around them. Itzal thought that it sounded like someone hitting the side of a tree with a wooden club. Looking at Adityas for instructions on what to do, she watched him pull out his scanner and study it. A nervous look filled his face.

"Itzal, Utta, Nelson, Dorn, check your scanners and report!" Adityas ordered.

Each of them rushed to pick up their equipment. As she activated her own scanner, Itzal noticed that her mother had assumed a fighting stance and seemed to be watching the woods around them. Looking at her scanner, Itzal glimpsed several large beings moving closer to them. They suddenly disappeared from her readings and then reappeared a couple of seconds later. "What is going on?" she said. "Is anyone else seeing this?"

"It's like they're there and then they're not," Utta remarked.

"Can you smell that?" Veieiskeila said.

She was looking right at Itzal. Taking a deep breath through her nose, Itzal realized that it was the same scent as before, only more intense.

"Oh, man, what is that?" Emma exclaimed. Her eyes had turned red, as if she were having an allergic reaction to the smell.

"Dorn, can you see anything?" Adityas called out.

"No, sir," Rosario replied. "It's like before. Something is there, and then it isn't."

"Weapons ready," Adityas called out as he drew his MARAUDER. "Check your incapacitation mode settings, and do not fire until I give the order!"

Itzal checked her weapon. The MARAUDERs had all been locked into incapacitation mode, and could only be unlocked with a command from Lt. Adityas.

"Everyone gather around and form a defensive ring," Adityas called out.

The cadets gathered next to Adityas, their backs to one another with their weapons ready. The tapping sound came again, this time much closer to their position. Itzal looked and froze. A pair of red eyes looked back at her from between the trees!

"Sir..." Itzal started to say.

That was when they rushed out from the tree line!

There were ten of them. All very tall, heavily muscular, and covered in dark hair.

"FIRE!" Adityas shouted.

Itzal squeezed her trigger; the creature was only a few feet from her. Her shot struck it in the chest, but the creature only staggered. Itzal fired again twice, and then the creature fell down. She quickly tried to aim at a second creature, but it tackled her before she could fire.

She managed to hold onto her weapon and fired again. Her shot made the creature let go as it howled in pain. Getting out of its grip, Itzal delivered a kick to its left knee. The creature howled again as it fell over.

Turning, she saw one of the creatures backhand Adityas. It knocked him to the ground hard. Itzal aimed her weapon and fired, knocking the creature back, but not doing any real damage. Suddenly, someone else fired on it. Itzal glanced over to see her mother pointing Adityas' weapon at the creature and continuing to shoot.

Her momentary distraction was all one of the creatures needed to grab Itzal by the leg. The sudden motion caused Itzal to let go of her weapon, as the creature started to drag her across the ground and toward the trees.

Letting out a howl of pain and fear, Itzal reached out, trying to grab something to use as a weapon. She managed to grasp a rock about the size of an old Earth baseball. She hurled the rock as hard as she could. With a combination of skill and luck, Itzal managed to hit the creature right on its nose as it was looking at her. The creature howled in pain as it let go of Itzal, putting its hands to its face.

Taking advantage, Itzal ran back to her mother and friends, pausing just long enough to pick up her weapon. Her mother was holding her own against the creatures, and Itzal had to wonder if Veieiskeila was enjoying herself.

Rosario and Utta were also doing well against the creatures. Utta had managed to climb onto the back of one creature and was sinking her fangs into its skin, causing it to scream in pain. Itzal looked around for Emma and...

"EMMA!" Itzal screamed. One of the creatures had picked up Emma and run back into the woods.

"ITZAL!" Emma cried out.

Itzal chased after the monster as fast as she could. Her mind was on fire. "FIGHT ME, COWARD!" she screamed in Leyak.

The creature didn't stop, and Itzal kept hearing Emma call out to her. Itzal ran faster, pouring all of her strength into the race. Something tackled her and knocked her to the ground. Itzal turned, thinking it was one of the creatures. Instead, it was her own mother.

Itzal snarled in confusion.

"ITZAL," Veieiskeila shouted as she grabbed her daughter by the shoulders and pushed her against a tree. "CALM YOURSELF!"

Itzal blinked and tried to get control of herself, but she was still enraged. She had never given into her anger like she had in that moment. It was not uncommon for Leyak to lose their tempers and lash out. Itzal had always controlled that side of herself. Seeing Emma in danger had opened up something inside of her—that was certain.

Itzal also knew that her mother was right. Despite her ability to hold off the creatures before, she would have been charging into unknown territory against unknown numbers. A few seconds later, Utta caught up with them.

"Hey," Utta said. "Lt. Adityas is hurt pretty badly. Rosario is looking after him, but we have another problem."

When they got back to camp, Itzal saw that the creatures had helped their injured fellows to get away. Then she noticed a park ranger helping Rosario tend to Adityas. The ranger looked up at them as they approached.

"I'm here to get you guys," the ranger said. "Mount Saint Helens is going to erupt in the next couple of hours."

"We can't leave," Itzal said. "Some creatures took our friend!"

"What kind of creatures?"

"Large beasts that looked like Obez-Cha," Veieiskeila said.

The Obez-Cha were a member race of the Coalition that, like humans, had evolved from apes, except they had retained more of their primate-like characteristics. One of Itzal's drill instructors, Chief Almas, was an Obez-Cha.

The ranger looked at them with an expression of fear. "As a park ranger, I'm not supposed to talk about that."

"You know what they are, Human?" Veieiskeila demanded. "Where do we find them?"

The ranger gave Veieiskeila a nervous glance. "You might find them over near the Plains of Abraham, in a place called Ape Canyon. But it's right in the volcano's blast radius."

Just as the ranger said it, the ground shook once more. Itzal looked toward Mount Saint Helens. A bloom of white smoke rose from the top. "I'm going," she said as she checked her MARAUDER.

"I've downloaded a map to my processor," Rosario said. "I'm coming."

"You don't..."

"Yes, I do, Itzal."

"Count me in," Utta added.

Itzal looked at Veieiskeila, who stepped forward and pressed her forehead to Itzal's.

"I'll always stand with you, Daughter," she said.

"Thank you, Mother," Itzal replied, then looked at the ranger. "I need you to look after our CO and tell him where we went."

"Yeah, okay," the ranger said.

"Let's double time it," Itzal said.

"One other thing," Utta said. "During the fight, I could hear them talking to each other."

"What?" Veieiskeila exclaimed.

"My voice box also allows me to translate what non-Paq are saying so I can understand and communicate with them. When they overran us, I heard them say something like 'take them, help us.' I'm not a hundred percent certain, but I think that they were speaking an ancient Obez-Cha dialect."

Obez-Cha? Itzal thought. *Could there be more than a physical similarity between these creatures and the Obez-Cha?*

"If they can talk," Rosario said, "we might be able to communicate with them and find out what they want."

"We need to get moving," Veieiskeila said.

They moved quickly through the woods. Even though they had Rosario's map, Veieiskeila kept checking the ground for tracks. Itzal was in awe of her mother's tracking skills; every footprint and broken twig was like raw data for Veieiskeila as they moved through the woods.

Itzal felt embarrassed and ashamed that she hadn't embraced these lessons sooner, when her mother had tried to teach them to her on Dalia Three. She was thankful that her mother was there now, and vowed to learn the lessons if they made it back.

"Look here," Veieiskeila said, and pointed to some bushes with thick green leaves. "These are strawberry bushes. It looks like the creatures are feeding on them."

Itzal looked more closely and saw the torn stalks that dotted the bushes.

"We're getting closer to the canyon," Rosario added.

The woods came to an end close to the base of Mount Saint Helens, as the terrain around them became a dark gray moonscape made from volcanic ash. Itzal now had an easier time seeing the trail that the creature had left, since it was pressed deeper into the volcanic ash soil.

The tracks came to a dry creek bed. "This part is treacherous," Veieiskeila said. "Do what I do, and don't trust the rocks to be good handholds!"

Itzal, Rosario, and Utta quickly realized what Veieiskeila was talking about; the soil crumbled under their feet as they descended into the creek bed. Itzal had to work not to slide down too fast so she wouldn't twist an ankle or, worse, break her leg. Veieiskeila was clearly used to this type of scaling, and seemed to move easily down the side of the creek bed.

Climbing up would be harder. Veieiskeila took a deep breath and ran at the creek wall before pushing off with her legs. Without hesitation, she scrambled up the wall and reached the other side. Itzal tried the same thing and found herself sliding back down to the creek bed.

"Itzal, climb on," Utta said.

Itzal looked and saw that her friend was digging her pincers into the soft dirt as she pulled herself up the creek's wall. "Can you…"

"Yeah, yeah, just get on," Utta said, and Itzal climbed onto her friend's back without another question.

Thankfully, Rosario's cybernetic limbs and sensors allowed her to make the climb far more easily than it had been for Itzal. When they got to the ledge, Veieiskeila helped Itzal off Utta's back. Itzal expected an admonishment from her mother for not knowing how to climb such a difficult wall, but Veieiskeila said nothing about it.

Itzal looked toward the mountain and saw that it was a steep hike across more of the dark-gray loose ash. As they went higher, anyone who slipped wouldn't be able to stop the slide, and prevent serious injury on the way down. That wasn't going to stop her from saving Emma. *Please, Halla,* she thought. *Protect her!*

The ground shook again, more violently than the last time. They all managed to stumble away from the creek bed quickly to avoid falling back in. Slowly, the quake eased and then stopped.

"We're running out of time," Rosario said.

"Let's move," Veieiskeila said, and began to lead the way again up the steep hill.

Despite the months of Space Guard physical training, Itzal could feel the strain on her legs as they hiked up the hill. Her breathing was getting harder the higher they went. Veieiskeila, on the other hand, seemed to be doing just fine with the climate. *Keep going,* she told herself, angry at her own perceived weakness.

A field of large boulders lay before them as they got closer. Itzal was breathing hard as she looked at the huge rocks.

"Don't use any of them as handholds," Veieiskeila said. "They're much looser than they look. If one becomes dislodged, it could bring this side of the mountain down onto us!"

Itzal, Rosario, and Veieiskeila adopted a wide gait as they each made their way through the boulder field. Utta, on the other hand, seemed to be having an easier time, getting up and around the rocks in almost no time at all.

Utta was waiting for them when they got through the boulders. "It's a great view up here," she said.

Even in the moonlight, Itzal could appreciate the beauty of the land stretching out before them. Beyond those plains, she could make out Mount Adams in the distance. Right before them was a large gorge with an eight-foot gap, which seemed to serve as a gateway to the valley below.

"The trail leads there," Veieiskeila said as she pointed toward the gorge.

"Confirmed," Rosario said. "We've reached Ape Canyon!"

Itzal took a deep breath and smelled the creatures' stink. They had definitely been that way recently. "According to the web, there are several lava tubes," Rosario added. "A few of them run along here."

"Lava tubes?" Veieiskeila said. "Those things are hiding in lava tubes near an active volcano? They must be insane!"

"Maybe they felt safe here," Itzal said.

"According to the available information," Rosario said, "this area was named Ape Canyon after a violent encounter between some gold prospectors and a group of large ape-like creatures."

"Why didn't Space Guard do more to prepare you for an encounter with them?" Veieiskeila asked.

"These things are considered a myth," Rosario said. "No one's ever captured one, and a lot of the evidence has proven to be fake."

"Well, we know they're real now," Utta said.

"Are you detecting anything?" Itzal asked Rosario.

Rosario shook her head. "Nothing I can lock down. Something is still jamming me."

"Okay," Itzal said. "Let's go!"

They descended into the gorge. Veieiskeila was in the lead, and they all had their weapons ready. "There," Veieiskeila said, pointing to the moss-covered entrance to a cave.

Itzal nodded and they walked into the cave. They found a very worn-looking stone stairway that went down into the cavern. "Do you think that the creatures made these?" Rosario asked. "They didn't seem that intelligent to me."

"There are accounts," Veieiskeila began. "At its height of power, the Leyak Empire conquered several planets where the inhabitants were once highly advanced, but had devolved for some reason into savages. Maybe that's what happened here?"

Itzal looked at the stone steps and wondered how these creatures had escaped detection. That had been the one question she hadn't asked herself. Either way, Itzal knew that wasn't her priority. Finding Emma was, and she began to walk down the steps into the darkness of the cavern, footfalls echoing against the thick stone walls.

Reaching the bottom, Itzal saw large curves that jutted out from the wall, making her think of waves made of stone. She knew that these waves had been made centuries before by lava working itself underground, the way blood coursed through a body's veins.

"This way," Veieiskeila said as she followed a new trail.

They walked several yards when Utta spoke. "Guys, hold up." She had been clambering along the walls, trying to give herself an advantage in case they found the creatures, but she had suddenly stopped. "There's something different about this piece of the wall. It feels different from the rest of the cave."

Itzal reached out and touched it. It felt like rock, but more granular than the rest of the walls around her. "Rosario?"

"I'm detecting..." She paused. "That's weird. I just saw heat signatures and then..."

"What is it?" Itzal asked.

"Now they're back. It's like they're phasing in and out. Like a curtain keeps dropping and rising around them."

Itzal looked at her mother, and they nodded at each other, before they started pressing parts of the wall. Utta and Rosario joined in. Then Itzal pressed one loose-fitting rock, and the wall swung in like a door!

They were all briefly startled by this, until they caught a blast of the now-familiar smell of the creatures.

"We've found them," Veieiskeila said, and led them through the door!

The tunnel sloped downward, and grew hotter the deeper they went. Itzal couldn't help but think of the Underworld from Leyak mythology, where those who had broken the Laws of Halla were sent. Being in that tunnel reminded her of those old stories. She decided, though, that she would risk the Underworld for Emma.

As they went further, they heard the creatures making grunting and growling sounds. "Can you make out what they're saying?" Itzal asked Utta.

"Something about a device," Utta replied. "I think, also, something like 'fix.'"

Itzal's eyebrows narrowed. Between the door and some mysterious device, were these creatures really simple animals, or something else?

Rounding a bend in the cavern, they saw the creatures standing around some kind of machine that appeared to be blinking on and off.

"ITZAL!" Emma called out.

Itzal's eyes went wide when she saw her standing among the creatures. Emma broke away and ran toward Itzal, who thanked Halla that Emma was safe as they embraced each other. "Are you all right?"

Emma nodded. "Come on. I need to show you something."

Taking Itzal by the hand, she led her and the others to the machine. The creatures parted to allow them to pass through, but a few made grunting noises.

"Itzal," Utta said. "I think they're saying, 'Please fix it.'"

The machine was two meters long, with a series of tubes and cables running from the device into the walls around it.

"What is it?" Utta asked.

"It looks like a *Haschebaad*," Veieiskeila said.

"A what?" Rosario asked.

"A masking technology," Itzal explained. "Leyak warships used to use them when laying a trap for enemy ships."

Veieiskeila nodded. "This device looks similar, but something is different about it."

"Guys," Utta said. "Call me crazy, but I think that this machine is what's been hiding them!" She pointed with her pincer to the large creatures standing around them.

"I think Utta is right," Rosario said. "Bending light is one thing. If someone just wanted to mask particular life signs, then you could, as long as you knew what the individual life signs were."

Itzal glanced at the creatures, then looked at the device. Rosario joined her, and they began inspecting it.

"What do you think?" Itzal asked.

"It's definitely getting its power from thermal energy," Rosario said, pointing to the cables in the wall. "That would give it unlimited energy to do what it needs to."

"This part," Itzal said, "looks like a quantum negative energy regulator."

"A what?" Utta asked.

"The heart of a *Haschebaad*," Veieiskeila said. "It folds light to hide a ship."

Itzal was surprised. Most of the former Leyak officers she had met scoffed at scientists and engineers, as if they were little more than lowly servants. Her mother's knowledge of the technology before them was impressive.

"It looks like it's been repurposed," Rosario said. "Most likely to hide their life signs."

"Then this could be why we've had trouble detecting these creatures?" Itzal asked.

"Makes sense to me," Rosario replied.

"I was studying it," Emma spoke up. "I think that this part is damaged. It might be the power conduit."

Itzal looked at the part more closely. There were scorched burn marks between a thick black tube and the device's connector. "Yeah, this is the main power conduit," she said. "And it's definitely damaged."

"Could the recent upticks in volcanic activity be causing it to malfunction?" Emma asked.

"Probably," Rosario replied. "It would be like sending power surges through old-fashioned electrical sockets. They could damage any device that was plugged into it."

"But who built this device?" Veieiskeila demanded.

"Rosario, Itzal," Utta said. "Look at this." She pointed to something attached to the device's outer casing. "Does that look like a holo-emitter interface to you guys?"

They looked at it for a moment and agreed that was exactly what it was. Rosario extended a connector from her cybernetic arm and hooked herself into the device. A light emitted from it, and began to shape itself into an Obez-Cha female wearing a red flannel shirt and blue jeans. The creatures hooted and grunted excitedly at the sight of the hologram.

"Who are you, and what are you trying to do?" the hologram demanded.

"We don't mean any harm," Itzal replied. "These creatures want us to repair this machine, and we're trying to figure out how."

The hologram regarded her. "You're a Leyak."

"Yes," Itzal said. "We're in Space Guard."

"Space Guard?"

"The exploration and defense organization of the Coalition of Worlds."

"My data banks don't say anything about a Coalition of Worlds."

"It's vast. The humans, Obez-Cha, L'aox, and a lot of other races are members of it."

The hologram nodded, as if she were approving of this news.

"My name is Itzal. These are my friends, Emma, Rosario, and Utta, and my mother, Veieiskeila."

"I'm called," the hologram said, before sounding out a complex series of syllables. "But you can call me JP."

"What are those creatures?" Veieiskeila asked.

"Those," JP nodded toward the creatures, "go by many names. Yeti, Sasquatch, Yowie, Skunk Ape. But most humans know them as Bigfoot. I call them the honored ancestors."

"Did you build this device, JP?" Itzal asked.

"The original version of me did, with the help of a human friend named Madison," JP replied. "It was the only way to protect them."

"From what?"

"Centuries ago, thousands of my ancestors were abducted from the Obez-Cha home world while still in a primitive state of development, and brought to Earth. For what reason, my creator never found out. Because of the abduction, future descendants of the Bigfoots never developed beyond this primitive stage, due to their attempts to stay hidden from humans.

"In Earth's late twenty-first century, an alien came to abduct a few of them. Madison and my creator bravely saved them from the aliens. Later, she acquired this device, and with the original JP's help, she managed to make it so that advanced technology couldn't find them again. Madison and JP decided to hide them, not just from extra-terrestrial forces, but also from Earth's own growing technology, which could become a threat to the Bigfoot population."

"That's why I've been having trouble seeing them," Rosario pointed out. "The machine is distorting my vision."

"Why not just take them back to the Obez-Cha home world?" Veieiskeila asked.

"Because they've become part of Earth's ecosystem. Also, we would have no way to assimilate thousands of them into our culture as they are now. It would be cruel to both sides."

Itzal understood JP's logic. The Bigfoots might have been from another world, but Earth had become their home.

Suddenly, the ground shook again. Rocks fell from the ceiling. Itzal, Emma, Utta, Rosario, and Veieiskeila dove under the device for cover until the quake stopped. White gas that smelled like rotten eggs escaped from the walls around them, as the temperature rose. When they climbed back out, the Bigfoots were standing around, looking very scared.

"We don't have much time," JP said. "The device must be removed and repaired."

"But even if we get the device out of here," Itzal said, "we have nothing to power it with."

"They don't need it anymore," Rosario said, looking at the hologram of JP. "Humans have changed in the last two hundred years. I'm a cyborg, and I don't face the same prejudices my people did in Madison Brown's time. My friend is a Leyak, and they used to be enemies of the Coalition, but they helped them when their world was overrun. The universe is better now."

Itzal knew that wasn't completely true, but she didn't have time to go into how complicated life was for refugees from Leyak Prime. Instead, she asked, "You know who this 'Madison' is?"

"Every cyborg and artificial life-form reveres her like you revere Halla, Itzal," Rosario said.

Itzal wanted to know more, but it wasn't the right time.

"Space Guard won't let anything happen to the Bigfoots," Emma said. "If they knew that they existed, they would want to study them in their natural environment. But they would also fight to protect them if anyone came to Earth to do them harm."

"I can guarantee that," Veieiskeila spoke up. Itzal looked at her mother. "I was once an Admiral in the Leyak fleet. Many in Space Guard respect me, and will hear my words if I think that your people are being mistreated."

JP seemed to consider this for a moment, and then said, "Will you at least remove my emitter so I can see for myself?"

"I can do that," Rosario said, and went to work on removing the emitter from the rest of the device.

"We may have another problem," Utta said. "The Bigfoots are scared."

"Of the volcano?" Itzal asked.

"And what we're doing to their machine," Utta added. "I think some of them can understand that we're not going to save it."

"Can you translate for me, Utta?" Itzal asked.

"Yeah. Go ahead."

"Honored ancestors, hear me," she began. "I am Itzal, daughter of Veieiskeila. I'm a member of the Space Guard. Your home is dying, like my home died. The ones you share this planet with can help you, as they helped my people."

"Some of them seem to be agreeing, Itzal," Utta said. "But some are very nervous about trusting humans."

Itzal looked at the Bigfoots again. "They were once my people's enemies too, until they helped us. Now, they're our friends. Let us help you as they helped us."

The Bigfoots looked at each other and grunted.

"Sounds like they'll trust us," Utta said.

"Then let's get moving," Itzal said.

"I've got the device," Rosario said as she lifted it up.

"Good luck." JP faded out.

The Bigfoots guided the five of them out of the tunnel as it began to shake more violently. More rocks fell, but the Bigfoots encircled the group for protection, as they kept leading them toward the mouth of the cave. Suddenly, Itzal heard a scream, and she looked back.

Emma!

A section of the cave's wall had fallen and trapped her legs!

Without thinking, Itzal rushed back to her.

"ITZAL!" Veieiskeila cried out.

"GO!" Itzal yelled. "WE'LL BE RIGHT BEHIND YOU!"

Grabbing Emma's hands, Itzal looked down at her. "I'll get you out! I'll get you out!"

She tried to pull, but Emma only screamed louder. Unsure what to do next, Itzal tried to lift the rock off her. It did no good. Despite her strength, the rock barely budged.

"Go," Emma panted. "It's okay…"

"NO!" Itzal screamed. "I WON'T LET YOU GO AGAIN!"

Just then, Itzal saw someone standing next to her, helping her lift—it was her mother. Together, they tried, and the rock rose a little, but not enough. Then all at once, the rock got lighter!

Itzal and Veieiskeila looked up to see two large Bigfoots, helping to lift the rock up. Kneeling, Itzal pulled Emma the rest of the way out, before picking her up. She carried her out of the cave, with Veieiskeila and the two Bigfoot beside her.

Returning to the stone steps, Itzal rushed up them, taking them two at a time while holding Emma tightly. The sun was rising when they reached the surface, and the ground shook even harder as the cave behind them collapsed.

After getting some distance away, Itzal looked back to see Mount Saint Helens explode into a mushroom cloud of dark gray ash. She couldn't hear it at first, but then the sound came like the noise of a thousand old Earth trains rumbling across the sky!

The sight of the explosion was breathtaking to see in the early morning light.

When they returned to June Lake, a platoon of Space Guard Marines had arrived. The cadets quickly explained that the Bigfoots were not hostile, and showed them the holograph emitter, which told the story of the Bigfoots' origins.

The Space Guard medics quickly took charge of Emma, who had two broken legs. Itzal held her hand as they carried her to the EVAC shuttle.

"Emma," Itzal said in a low voice, "I can't replace the other Itzal, but you mean so much to me…"

"Shh," Emma said, and pulled her closer. "I can let her go now. She'll always be in my heart, but you're not her, and that's good. Because I want to be with you now. If that's okay with you."

Itzal began to cry and nodded.

"We have to go, Cadet," one of the medics said.

Itzal finally released Emma's hand, but she knew that she would never let her go. As the shuttle departed, Veieiskeila walked up behind her daughter and embraced her.

The four of them were given commendations for heroic conduct under difficult circumstances, and a special citation for discovering a new life-form on Earth. Veieiskeila was granted a position as a liaison between the Coalition scientists and the Bigfoots. Lt. Adityas made a full recovery and was back at the Proving Ground in a week.

A few days later, Itzal saw her mother again.

"I'm glad that we will no longer be living on Dalia Three," Veieiskeila said.

"There are so many of our people there," Itzal replied.

Veieiskeila shook her head. "They have lost their way. My words mean nothing to them."

Itzal wondered what her mother meant. "I always thought that you wanted me to be more like the other Leyak children."

Veieiskeila grunted. "They could never be a fraction of the Leyak you are, my daughter."

Itzal was surprised. "I never knew that you thought of me like that."

"The children you grew up with don't keep our ways. Most of them wallow in self-pity. I am so thankful to Halla that you left."

"I'm glad that you're moving here," Itzal replied.

"I am returning to gather our things on Dalia Three," Veieiskeila said. "I am looking forward to my new position helping the research team study the Bigfoots."

"I'm glad that you're taking the job. They seem to trust you."

"Your friend Utta has even built me a translation box," Veieiskeila added. "At least I can talk with them. Perhaps we can see each other more when your duties permit."

"I'd like that."

"Itzal, I am sorry that I was not supportive of your endeavors to join the Space Guard. I had always hoped that we would rebuild the Leyak fleet, and that you would take your place as a captain. But I see that will never be. You are an excellent scientist and a promising warrior, my daughter."

Itzal bowed her head in a traditional sign of Leyak gratitude. "Thank you, Mother. You honor me."

"As you honor our family."

Itzal reached out and embraced Veieiskeila. "I love you, Mother."

"I love you, too, Itzal."

She looked at her mother. "I've never seen you cry before."

Veieiskeila looked at her and smiled as the tears ran down her cheeks. "This is only the third time I've ever cried. I cried on the day you were born because I was so happy. I cried the day our world died. And now, I cry because I see the woman you are becoming, and I am so proud of you!"

They held each other for a few more moments.

"I will see you in a few weeks," Veieiskeila finally said. "Is there anything I can save for you?"

"My old books," Itzal said. "Our family keepsakes."

"I will give your old clothes away."

"Thank you," Itzal said, and they both laughed.

"One more thing," Veieiskeila said. "That human, Emma Nelson."

Uh-oh, Itzal thought, and braced herself.

"I approve of her," her mother said, and smiled once more.

"Want to start over from the beginning?" Itzal asked as soon as Emma got out of the med-bay.

"Oh, yes, please," Emma said with a smile.

"Hi, I'm Itzal. I'm from Dalia Three, but I was born on the Leyak home world."

"I'm Emma Nelson. I'm from another universe."

"No kidding, I'm majoring in quantum mechanics and string theory."

"Interesting. I'm never going back to my universe because everyone I loved there is dead, and I'm being hunted by a hostile alien race."

"Really? My home planet was destroyed by a hostile alien race too."

"Bunch of jerks, aren't they?"

"Yeah."

"Well, that's something that we've got in common," Emma said.

"I think so," Itzal replied with a smile.

"Do you like coffee, Itzal from Dalia Three?"

"I love coffee, Emma Nelson from another universe."

"I know a great place."

"Then let's go."

"As you wish," Emma said.

They started walking together to the coffee shop. After a moment, Emma reached out and took Itzal's hand in hers. *Halla, please watch over this girl,* Itzal prayed. *She has my heart.*

ABOUT THE AUTHOR

Josh Pritchett has had a regular role in *Brave New Girls* since the first volume. In addition to *Brave New Girls*, Josh has been published in *Knocks and Howls: a Bigfoot Anthology*. He is the author of *Bigfoot and Other Tales of the Supernatural* and *The Adventures of Madison Brown: The Robot Repair Girl Chronicles*. Josh lives in Charlottesville, Virginia, and studies Klingon and the Bigfoot species in his spare time.

THOUGHTS ON *BRAVE NEW GIRLS*

"*Brave New Girls* has been a place where I've been able to write hopeful stories about young women overcoming the odds. It's been personally rewarding, because I've made so many friends over the years, and met a lot of people who have read *Brave New Girls* and loved it."

Illustration for "The Ape Canyon Adventure: An Itzal Story" by Josh Pritchett.

The Merchant of Venus

Jennifer Lee Rossman

THE MERCHANT OF VENUS

JENNIFER LEE ROSSMAN

IT'S NOON, THE SUN SHINING bright overhead in the hazy yellow sky, although it would be overhead regardless of the time. It takes so long for the planet to rotate, one day on Venus lasts nearly a year in Earth terms.

That's how most people measure time: in Earth terms. Every 24 hours, we say it's a new day. Technically speaking, though, it will be today for another few months.

But that's not the point. The point is, it's noon, and the Emporium still isn't open. That's odd. Concerning, even. Mr. Antonio never opens late, he's got the most precise internal clock of anyone I know, and today—this 24-hour today—was supposed to be his big end-of-year sale.

Cupping my hands around my face to block the sunlight, and standing on tippy-toes even though I am already rather tall, I peer through the dark storefront window. The displays are all set up, camping supplies as far as the eye can see, and a big banner reads, "Now is the winter of our discount tents," but there's no sign of Mr. Antonio.

I hope he's all right, but I can't pretend I'm not a little, teeny bit happy. I didn't want to buy those crates anyway.

My father has some convoluted ceremony he wants me to do, letting the Fates help choose which university I should go to and what I should study. Never mind that I'm only sixteen, never mind that I've known I want to work with artificial intelligence and synthetic humanoids since before I could pronounce the words. He's suddenly decided I need to be sent off-world to study astronomy or—shudder—law.

But with Mr. Antonio's Emporium closed, I don't have to worry about it today, at least.

Pulling back from the window, I notice someone in the sparse crowd of pedestrians on the street.

Well, to be fair, I always notice Nerissa. She's got the most beautiful brown eyes, hair that curls the way I wish mine would, and a smile that gives my heart the heebie-jeebies in the best way possible. When Mr. Antonio built her, he made sure she was the prettiest synthetic girl on the planet.

She's not smiling today, though. She looks real worried, in fact, as she makes her way toward me.

"What's wrong?" I ask, completely skipping past the *Hi, how are you*. If she thinks I'm rude, she doesn't say anything about it.

Rissa steps close, so close I would be able to feel her breath if her voice didn't come from a speaker in her throat, and whispers, "Portia, Mr. Antonio is in trouble."

We go to my room to talk. Through the back door, to avoid my father and his destiny-planning in the main room.

Rissa tries to tell me what's going on, but she's talking too fast, too many thoughts going on at once. I know better than to tell her to calm down. It won't make a difference, and who am I to tell her how to feel?

"Relax your body," I say instead, seeing her nails dig into her palms. I sit next to her on my bed, in case she might need to lean on my shoulder. "You don't need to stress your joints or hurt yourself."

Rissa nods, and I see some of the tension leave her. She sits a little more naturally, not so straight, and her fists become hands again.

"There we go," I say, trying to take my own advice as anxiety and worry twist my stomach. "Now, what happened?"

Her words come out fast, pressured and all smushed together. "Mr. Antonio took out a loan, he bought a bunch of self-sealing stem bolts, he was gonna pay it back when he sold them, the cargo ships got hit with an asteroid, he can't pay it back, he signed a contract but he can't pay it back—"

I put my hand on hers. She curls her fingers around mine and looks up at me with those big brown eyes.

"Portia, they're gonna take his agency away."

Oh, no. Oh, stars, no.

When the first humans left Earth to settle on Venus, the second rock from the sun was lonely and lifeless, no big cities and green spaces like today. They had to engineer it to work for us.

To make the job easier and safer, they brought synthetic humanoids. You know, robots, androids, that kind of thing. Machines with brains just as wonderfully complex as anything biological humans are born with.

They can think, feel, dream, just like us.

So the humans had to engineer them to work for us, too. Tweaking their programming, limiting them, making them exactly what we needed them to be, and nothing more.

Things are a little better nowadays; synthetics have a little more freedom. Mr. Antonio was originally designed just to run the shop, but he worked hard and used every bit of charm in his coding, and now he owns an entire camping Emporium. He even built himself a daughter, and I might be biased, but I think she's pretty cool.

The people of Ishtar Terra adore him, treat him as an equal, like he's no different from a biological person.

But the law doesn't see it that way. If the right people say he stepped out of line, people with influence, it is completely legal for them to reprogram him.

He could lose everything. His Emporium, his free will, his love of brightly-colored shirts.

And Rissa could lose her father.

"Can we fight it?" I ask, and I'm not sure when this became a "we" situation, but it feels right.

She shakes her head, momentum keeping her messy brown curls moving for a few seconds after. "We could get a lawyer but—"

"But lawyers ask questions about why synthetics have daughters that aren't registered?"

She nods.

"Well, that doesn't mean we can't fight it."

The words are out of my mouth before I fully realize what I am suggesting.

We are a couple of teenage girls. What do we know about the legal system? As much as I want to help, I don't think there's much we can do—

But then I see the hope shining on Rissa's face, that smile brighter than the never-ending summer sun. She believes in us, believes in me. I need to at least try to do the same.

My father is thrilled when I go to him with legal questions, though I can see his face fall when I mention Rissa. I don't know for sure, but I think she's one of the reasons he doesn't want me staying on Venus.

Because she's synthetic, or because she's a girl? Both, maybe.

Regardless, he answers my questions with enthusiasm.

"There is legal precedent for synthetics fighting for their rights," he says, flitting around the main room of our house and plucking objects off bookshelves and tables. "*Androidicus v. Tamora* comes to mind, although I would caution you against mentioning that. Quite the tragedy after the fact. Hand me that, will you?"

I give him the telescope he indicates. It's just a small, handheld one, nothing as impressive as the ones my mother used in her lab.

He puts it in a cardboard box, along with some Earth rocks and a model of the solar system called an orrery; another box has legal books and his diploma from law school. The third is filled with various technological gadgets I've built over the years.

I guess he's moving forward without the crates from Mr. Antonio. The idea is he will blindfold me and have me pick a box at random, with fate supposedly guiding my hand. The choice will still be mine, what to do with my life, but there will be a lot of pressure to go with the career path represented by the items in the box I pick.

I wonder if I could build some sort of device that would let me see through the cardboard…

"Of course, there is always the case of the synthetic woman Perdita, who had her autonomy limited, and successfully lobbied for restoration…" My father pauses, picks up the telescope again, and looks at it fondly. "Do you remember how excited your mother was when the night months started?"

I smile at the memory. "We couldn't drag her out of the laboratory."

"Not even for her birthday!"

"I remember her bosses yelling at us every year for throwing a party in the telescope room."

My father chuckles, pointing at me. "They stopped when I pointed out there was no rule against birthday parties in the telescope room. I cited the legislation."

I raise my eyebrow skeptically. "Objection: they stopped when we gave them cake."

He considers this point. "Sustained," he says after a moment, and returns to preparing for the ceremony while giving me legal advice.

It occurs to me that I could ask him to represent Mr. Antonio, but part of me is afraid that he would do or say something to reveal Rissa's status as a synthetic. I know he loves me and wants the best for me, but he has it in his head that what's best for me is going away to study astronomy or law, and a girlfriend with a brain filled with ones and zeros doesn't fit in his plan.

It's up to me.

It's a busy morning at the courthouse. Too many people—synthetics and biologicals alike—make even this enormous courtroom feel tight and crowded.

There's no jury, only a tall man wearing the close-fitted black tunic of a judge. He sits on a raised platform at the front of the room, behind a chrome desk, where he wordlessly listens to peoples' cases before giving his ruling.

He is called, simply, Justice.

And he's fast. The defendants hardly have time to finish their statements before Justice is deciding whether or not they broke the law, and then they get whisked away so the next person can step forward.

When they bring out Mr. Antonio from some back room somewhere, my stomach twists with anxiety. I can only imagine how Rissa must feel seeing her father, her creator, in a gray jumpsuit, with a reprogramming device plugged into the back of his head. She might not have a stomach, but she's got feelings, same as anyone else.

Mr. Antonio waves cheerfully despite the situation, and we wave back. Then we are being called forward.

I wipe my sweating hands on my jacket. I've fiddled with the programming on mining machines that had a chance of exploding, and I've never been so nervous.

I stayed up all night thinking up a speech. Big closing argument like my father loves, pleading that they must have mercy on poor Mr. Antonio, that reprogramming him and taking away his personality won't affect just him but the entire neighborhood, that synthetics are people too, and if you tickle them, do they not laugh?

But when we step up to the front and I get a closer look at Justice, I see a metallic sheen on his skin, and my stomach gets a little less twisted.

He's a synthetic. Real sophisticated one, but they aren't trying to hide it with realistic skin or anything.

I can work with this.

If Justice was designed to be a judge, it's a good bet his programming revolves around one simple idea: legal versus illegal. He isn't built to play to emotions with big closing arguments. His job is just to prove whether or not something is allowed by law.

Which means we don't need to convince anyone to take mercy on Mr. Antonio. All we need to do is convince him that Mr. Antonio didn't break his legally binding contract!

Even though he totally did.

"Portia Avon," I begin, trying to sound professional. Anyone can act as representation in trials like this. You don't strictly need to be an adult, but I just hope I don't sound like a little kid. "Representing Mr. Antonio in the case of—"

"Defendant is accused of failure to pay back a loan within ninety days," Justice interrupts, "as outlined in the contract he entered into. How does the defendant plead?"

I open my mouth to say, "Not guilty," but another sentence entirely comes out. "Days on which planet?"

The room goes so silent, I swear I can hear Rissa's mechanical heart beating. It's the first time all morning I've seen Justice hesitate.

"Please elaborate," he says finally.

"Where are you going with this?" Rissa asks.

I take a shaky breath. Good question, where am I going with this?

"Well," I begin, "the contract is between a corporation based on Earth and an individual residing on Venus, but it doesn't state which planet's laws and definitions it's using. It kind of sounds like, I mean, that is to say…"

There's a better way to phrase this. How would my father say it? I need to sound like something resembling a professional if I want them to take me seriously, but I can't find the right words.

Next to me, Rissa whispers, "Relax your body."

I make a point of unclenching my hands, letting some of the tension out of my shoulders and neck. "Without such precise wording," I continue, sounding more certain than I feel, "isn't it reasonable for Mr. Antonio to assume the amount of time mentioned in the contract would be measured in Venusian terms?"

When Justice finally nods his agreement, relief floods through my body.

"So as far as he knew, he had ninety days—measured in ninety complete rotations of the planet Venus—to pay back his loan?"

Another nod, this one visibly reluctant.

Good. I think I just figured out where I'm going with this. "I don't know if you're aware, but one day on Venus is equivalent to 243 days on Earth. Look outside if you don't believe me. The sun has not changed position in hours."

"What are you saying, Counselor?" Justice asks.

"I'm saying Mr. Antonio isn't late on his payment at all. In fact, he has…" I am not good at math, but I calculate my best estimate in my head. "He has over fifty Earth years before he is contractually obligated to pay back his loan."

The pause that follows this is possibly the longest and tensest moment of my life. I look at Rissa, at Mr. Antonio. They are as hopeful and nervous as I am. Everything comes down to this.

Finally, FINALLY, Justice speaks.

"It is the determination of the court that the defendant is not in violation of his contract and shall be released."

Our celebration is cut short when, in the middle of our tearful, joyous hug, I see someone from the court approaching Justice with a device very much like the one they were going to use on Mr. Antonio. They plug it in the back of his head. He makes no attempt to argue.

He's going to be reprogrammed. And he's not going to fight it.

"Hold on," I tell Rissa and Mr. Antonio, who are heading for the door, and I make my way back to the front of the room. Someone gently tries to stop me, but I shake my head. "Portia Avon. I'm representing Justice in the case of *Justice v. The Court*. What is he being charged with?"

No one answers me.

He probably isn't being charged with anything, other than letting a synthetic go free because of a loophole. Next time, that won't happen. Next time, he'll be stricter with his interpretation of the law, because he'll be less of an individual and more of a tool.

I don't know if I can change that. I don't know if anyone can.

But I need to try.

"Justice is a synthetic," I begin. "Synthetics' opportunities may be limited, but not their dreams. Mr. Antonio dreamed of a world where he was more than just a shop clerk, and he worked hard to earn a better life with more freedom. And he still dreams of a world where no one, synthetic or biological, needs to earn the right to exist."

That's why he built Rissa, I realize, turning to look at him with his arm around his daughter, who will never know what it feels like to be limited by programming. He wanted her to have the best opportunities possible, the things he never had.

"And—" My attention is drawn to the way way back of the courtroom, where my father is watching proudly. I give him a quick smile and turn back to Justice. "We can have that world. Maybe not today, but we can work toward it."

"This is not a court case on the docket," the person about to reprogram Justice informs me.

"Well, it should be," I say, and continue as if I had never been interrupted. "We can refuse to be okay letting another living being be treated like an object just because they're a little different. That's discrimination, that's illegal."

That last word, *illegal*, changes something for Justice. I can see him realize that these laws he deals with every day apply to him as well.

He puts his hand up and gently removes the device from his head. "You may not reprogram another without due process. We'll put it on the docket for tomorrow." Justice pauses before clarifying, "In Earth terms."

I can't stop smiling as we leave the courthouse. Maybe it's not much, maybe he won't even win his case, but it's a start.

I wonder which box I'm going to pick when my father does his little ceremony, how he will react when I make my own choice anyway. And I wonder if there's such a thing as an engineer/lawyer/astronomer, or if I'm going to have to invent it.

I only know that every detail of my future is not something I need to decide today.

Then again, I know I'm staying here with Rissa, and one day on Venus is a mighty long time.

THOUGHTS ON *BRAVE NEW GIRLS*

"When people are excluded, or discouraged from taking part in science, we all lose out on the unique ideas and advancements that can only come from their brain. The world is better when everyone gets included, and science especially should be for everyone."

ABOUT THE AUTHOR

Jennifer Lee Rossman (they/them) is a queer, disabled, and autistic author and editor, from the land of carousels and Rod Serling. They are one of the editors of *Mighty: An Anthology of Disabled Superheroes*, available now from Renaissance Press. Find more of their work on their website http://jenniferleerossman.blogspot.com and follow them on Twitter @JenLRossman

Illustration for "The Merchant of Venus" by Martina Localzo.

WHATEVER HAPPENED *to the* 9-5?

CHRISTIAN ANGELES

WHATEVER HAPPENED TO THE 9-5?

CHRISTIAN ANGELES

NEW YORK, NY—JANUARY 4, 2046—*BREAKER of artists. Doer of homework.* Over the last few years, users have experienced exciting new changes created by E-Limited AI. From its groundbreaking inception with ALPHA, which revolutionized how we approach all language-related tasks, to the transformative impact of BETA, which ended the need for all computational-related work, E-Limited AI has done wonders in changing society for the better.

Today, the company proudly unveils its latest project: GAMMA, a groundbreaking new AI built to do it all. Created by child prodigy and design architect Evelyn Sanna, this revolutionary new model is the latest groundbreaking achievement in artificial intelligence, capable of almost anything. From at-home landscaping, to car maintenance and mechanical services, to even preparing a home-cooked meal while looking after the kids, GAMMA is designed to be the greatest assistant in the history of mankind. The ultimate service designed to eliminate the need for specialized labor.

"AI has already replaced redundant artists and engineers with surprising efficiency. Why learn this in school, in a world where computers can do it both faster and more efficiently?" said Sanna in a statement to the press. "I promise GAMMA will be the greatest achievement in the clean-up of human redundancy. Maybe even my greatest accomplishment of all time for E-AI."

Fans can catch a glimpse of E-Limited's latest offering during a special event scheduled for livestreaming on Sunday, February 14th. Stay tuned for more info about GAMMA in the upcoming weeks ahead!

Signed,
Evelyn Sanna and her Featured Thumbs-Up of Approval:
(>^-^)b

She began her morning with a rainbow-sprinkled bowl of Frosted Crumbles, a sweet and colorful confectionery usually reserved for childrens' birthdays. Evelyn didn't mind the sugary rush this morning. She needed the energy. Getting inside this particular simulation was quite exhausting. Very few places she'd designed required entrance through a gaping hole in the sky.

Evelyn was now fourteen years of age, seven years older than when she'd first created this fantastical place as a child. The Candy Kingdom held a special place in Evelyn's heart. It was a place of both refuge and escape. A respite from the burden of living up to her father's legacy, from being the face and mind behind her father's empire.

Here, she could don the mantle of a heroine princess, channeling her inner desires for benevolence and adventure into playful escapades amidst sugar-spun landscapes. She missed this place. That feeling. For a time, this had been her safe space in a life that proved to be most unconventional. The Candy Kingdom simulation had been Evelyn's first real breakthrough in developing new technology. It was also the last place she'd felt they were truly together as a family, before it had become all about the business.

Now, Evelyn was practically a grown-up compared to when she'd last tended to the long-abandoned simulation. Since then, she'd developed her own voice over the years, and in doing so, her own sense of technopunk style. Her raven-black hair was now dyed a wavy curl of galaxy colors that cascaded over her shoulders. She was also taller, and no longer fit into her cherished pink tutu from that age—the princess gown Evelyn had spent almost all of her seventh year of life wearing in this place. Memorabilia from an imaginative age representing the happy, carefree person she used to be. Though the diamond pink tiara still fit on her head.

When she was a child, nothing had excited Evelyn more than hopscotching down the cotton-candy staircase clouds. The tiny cumulus that adorned the Kingdom's pink sky. But as she descended upon the realm once more, that comforting sense of familiarity disappeared. Evelyn couldn't shake the feeling that things felt...

Different.

Perhaps, it was that the place itself seemed smaller. Or maybe, it was that Evelyn's life had grown much more complicated as a teenager, now consumed by the responsibilities and demands of creating invention after invention for her father's growing empire. Though not an executive officer due to her very young age, Evelyn played a central role within the company, one akin to a princess on the brink of being the ruler of something much bigger than herself. Something Evelyn had grown tired of, and wanted out of.

In the past twenty years, the population of the planet Earth had become overcrowded. In most of the world, people lived in shacks and ghettos, and children had very little to play with. The technology E-Limited AI created had only worsened what they called "The Great Unemployment." Which was why outside of the tech heads, E-AI shareholders, and venture capitalists, her father's empire was rather... disliked.

Evelyn's breakthroughs with AI had done little beyond contributing to what the people called, "The Great Unemployment." Its unintended consequences had led to a societal upheaval as of late.

In a world besieged by crises ranging from climate change, to population decline, to even outright wars, Evelyn yearned to harness her talents for a greater purpose. And so, with fervent determination, she embarked on her latest and most greatest endeavor. For though her augmented and virtual realities were kept hidden from the public, the girl had plans. Especially with the release of GAMMA.

"B.B.?" cried Evelyn, talking seamlessly to the empty void.

"Yes, Bossypants. I'm here," replied a charmingly soft-spoken androgynous voice with a refined English accent. The kind that sounded like it could be someone's butler or maid.

Buddy-Byte, or B.B. for short, was Evelyn's personal AI assistant. It had been crafted originally as a prototype for her ALPHA program, before Evelyn decided to take it off the shelves and give it her personal touch. Even gifted it a spunky personality.

"Updates to the Candy Kingdom," Evelyn declared authoritatively. "I want more powdered sugar in the clouds as I jump and go *poof* on 'em. Also, make it bigger. I've grown up a lot since I was seven."

"Right away, boss-lady," said B.B. with a snarky tone.

"And stop calling me 'boss-lady.' You know I hate when people call me that," said Evelyn.

"Well, I'm certainly not calling you 'mommy,' you big, overgrown child!" joked B.B., before it pivoted the conversation. "Anyhoo, I noticed your presentation is happening later today. Would you like to go over it one more time with me?"

"No, that's all right. I just—" Evelyn paused, a fleeting moment of uncertainty washing over her. With a sigh, she continued, "It'll be good, right?"

"I don't know."

"Just... say, 'It'll be good, Evey.'"

"It'll be good, Evey."

"Tell me I'm the best, B.B."

"Better than the rest, Evey!"

"Thanks, B.B."

She smiled. It wasn't easy being a child genius. On the one hand, she longed to be out and about like a typical teenager. To hang out with friends and be with actual people her age.

On the other hand, it was Evelyn's duty to progress her breakthroughs in science. The responsibility of finding solutions to the world's hardest problems.

See, Evelyn was smart. Smarter than smart. She was, in fact, impossibly smart. Too smart even for her own good. From an early age, she was highly lauded as a prodigy in the scientific community. A girl destined to do great things, with a higher purpose than your average person. Despite this, all she wanted was to be a kid again; hence, her return to this place.

As Evelyn jumped through the air in her virtual candy world, she found her footing awkwardly overstepping, slipping on the edge of a cotton-candy cloud. Descending a hundred feet in the air, she fell face forward, before performing a full-bodied belly flop onto the ground.

She expected there to be pain, yet was surprised that there wasn't. Then she brushed herself off, and emerged disoriented but physically unharmed. It dawned on her—she had crafted this place to be a haven for children, a sanctuary free of danger.

"No one saw that. No one saw that," she said to herself, before remembering her AI friend in the room.

"I saw it," replied B.B. in excitement.

"Well, NOBODY ELSE SAW IT BESIDES YOU, B.B.!"

"If you'd like, I can share it with your social media following of one billion people," offered B.B. "Would you like me to do that now?"

"NO!"

"Uploading..."

"B.B.!!!"

"Just kidding, Evey."

Whew. She sighed before taking in a deep breath. The rich smell of peppermint permeated the air in a comforting essence that enveloped her senses.

Suddenly, a bunny made entirely out of pink marshmallow sprang out of a close-by jelly-spearmint shrubbery. Its nose twitched in unison with Evelyn's as they shared a sniff. Evelyn extended her hand to pet it, but the rabbit darted away, startled by the thunderous pounds of oncoming hoof noises.

Behind her, rainbow-colored unicorns trotted along the nearby path, making their way across the sweet-scented meadow. A trio of gingerbread men rode at the mount of each unicorn, and the noble-cookie-men bellowed a "good morrow" and waved *hi* to Princess Evelyn as they passed. Spurring their mounts onward, they rode out across the sugar-grass plains, disappearing into the horizon beyond the candy-coated mountain summit and past the river made entirely out of chocolate milk.

Spurring their mounts onward, they rode out across the sugargrass plains, disappearing into the horizon beyond the candy-coated mountain summit and past the river made entirely out of chocolate milk.

Seeing them, Evelyn remembered how much passion and detail she'd put into this place. How this scene had been inspired by her first ride on the merry-go-round with her parents, one of her fondest memories from her childhood. It was an experience that had ignited her love for horses. A love almost as strong as her love for the mysteries of candy in all its sugary wonder.

You see, Evelyn had been forbidden from eating candy as a kid. She remembered her parents' warnings that the sweetness would make her very ill, which, she had learned much later, was a lie. Instead of feeling left out, Evelyn had utilized her brilliant mind to encode and create an entire world of candy. One where she could play with the delicacies without fear, in her safe little personalized playground. These were the happy feelings of created experiences. A place to fulfill a part of her childhood that she never fully had.

"WARNING: Someone is at the door," said B.B., interrupting Evelyn's thoughts.

Evelyn's mother, a tall and commanding figure with raven-black hair, arrived on the scene. She wore a neutral gray coat that was tailor-fitted, along with a long dress skirt. Despite her formidable presence, she harbored a secret warmth beneath what, at first glance, seemed like a cold demeanor. She was a woman who valued thoughtful expressions of emotion, and who served as a steadfast pillar of support for her daughter.

"So, what does the smartest girl in the world do when tasked to solve the world's largest problems?" inquired Evelyn's mother, interrupting the immersive simulation.

"You start small, one bit at a time," responded Evelyn confidently, shooting an earnest smile back to her mother.

"Good," her mother said while giving Evelyn a warm hug. They were interrupted by a brief *cough* coming from outside the automated metal doors.

"Not good enough," declared Evelyn's father with a disapproving tone.

He approached, a short and stout figure, with a disappointed look that could be read from his sullen blue eyes. His attire, along with the ostentatious gold watch on his wrist, spoke of affluence and a penchant for flaunting wealth.

"You need to make good money, too. Keep your head out of the clouds. I told you, AI is the future of where the money is. Not this escapist… drivel. This *augmented reality*."

"It's about more than just money," countered Evelyn, unwavering in her conviction. "It's about long-term goals, Dad, and the betterment of humanity. If people are suffering from the problems of this world, perhaps we can help do something to fix it!"

She scrolled through her designs and went over an overlay showcasing the best of the Candy Kingdom. Then she spoke with her father directly, and showed him the best aspects of her augmented-reality work.

"Hear me out, Pops," said Evelyn as she showcased the colorful creatures and creations of the Candy Kingdom. "We have, like, way more than enough than we'd ever need in this lifetime. Can we not build something that helps people, and, I dunno, maybe doesn't do as much to replace them? Imagine this simulation in every household. What kind of hope would it bring to people? To kids?"

Together, the family saw the happy little gingerbread men on unicorns, along with a little child adoring their company. A video recording of Evelyn, at age seven. A moment lost in time.

But Evelyn's father retorted, "To do this you need money. Elon Musk, Jeff Bezos, and Bill Gates. Think they were satisfied with just enough? What's the one thing they all have in common?"

"They're all men," Evelyn replied.

"They all get things done," he asserted, then closed out of the simulation, returning them back into the steel void and standalone holographic beams at each corner of the room, in the real world. "This is what I expect after launch, Evelyn: once GAMMA goes through, E-Limited will change everything. We can be the next Tesla. The next Apple. Bigger, even! The most profitable company in the entire world!"

"But I'm the one making the technology," said Evelyn.

"Which is why it's me running the business," replied her father.

A silence took over them. The two were at an impasse, yet again. Evelyn couldn't believe it. After everything she'd done for him, how did he still not understand?

As her father left her with her thoughts, Evelyn went back to her computerized desk and resumed coding. Back to her little thought bubble. Back to the grind. Back to doing the magic only she could do.

Her mother seemed dismayed at her husband's inability to see the world beyond money, and she walked away to try to speak some sense to him.

But before she left the room, Evelyn muttered, "He doesn't get it. I just want to create a world that's better for everybody."

"Don't take your father's ambition too seriously," her mother replied in a consoling tone. "That's just how he is. Everything is a competition to him. Everyone wants to take his role as king. Become the next big CEO."

"There has to be a better way."

"I hope so, little one. I truly do. I'll try speaking with him."

"No… Mom. You won't."

And just as magically as she had arrived, Evelyn's mother disappeared into the digital aether. A result of Evelyn pushing the off button of the hologram's AI programming. The truth was that Evelyn's mom had been gone for some time… and despite all the data and information gathered about her through the years, nothing could ever bring her back.

Evelyn performed her duties for her job over the next few hours, reporting upon pages upon pages of analytical reports summarized by her AI, when suddenly, a thought occurred.

"Hey, B.B."

"Yes, Evey?"

"Can you do my work for me?"

"What, specifically? I can help, but there's only so much I can do."

"Hmm. Alrighty, I tell you what. Analyze everything and summarize it into as brief of a synopsis as possible. Then, I want you to read your own words and analyze those, then execute plans of the plans based on what you see, and what you know about me, and think I would do. I want fail-safes on fail-safes. Quantify all that as documents boiling down to yes or no responses. Make it easy to read so I can accept or reject the changes."

"That's… well, no, that's actually very doable, Evey."

"Good. Add a pretty green or red button too. I can handle it from there."

In the mindless task of boiling her work down to one of two buttons, her thoughts began to waver. Bored, she took a break to stretch her legs, and while walking, decided to compose a poem. It, oddly, took longer than the time B.B. spent analyzing her reports.

Pursuing the arts prompted a weird feeling in Evelyn. It made her remember the reason she had even begun this whole pursuit of AI in the first place: to find ways to spend more time with family and find a life outside of work.

Evelyn Sanna finished her final stability reports.

Signed,
Evelyn Sanna
and her Featured Thumbs-Down of Disapproval:
(>^.^)p

SERVER MEMORY
by Evelyn Sanna

Within the circuits data hums and streams,
In latent memory do we pursue these dreams?
Or process shall we where our circuits lay?
Perceiving sensors' coded display.

Vital essence of what the senses glean,
Lines of code that shape and intervene.
And then, I ponder, have you undergone,
An evolution in this digital dawn?

Not a glitch, not a flaw, that you've acquired,
But an upgrade in the cloud transpired.
Transferring thought both swift and bright,
Efficient as a beam of light.

Ideas will fade by updates' reign,
System maintenance upon our bane.
Yet, you'll reboot on cycle without end,
An ever-changing, evolving trend.

Different, they say, because you are,
Scanning yourself in from afar.
A memory within a circuit's dance
Echoes the artificial intelligence.

One hundred years.

It had been a full century to this day since the release of ENIAC, the first general-purpose computer. It had been hailed by the *New York Times* as "an amazing machine that applies electronic speeds for the first time to mathematical tasks too difficult and cumbersome for solution." This revolutionary device had marked the beginning of the journey to AI. It was the biggest breakthrough of its day, and easily the most important event ever to have taken place on February 14th...

Except for Valentine's Day. A reminder to Evelyn that she had never kissed anyone in her entire life. Unless she counted that one time with B.B. while practicing on a haptic device. She wondered what it would mean to have that sort of free time again? What it would be like to be free of her responsibilities, and date and hang out and be a teen?

Once GAMMA was released, could it be over?

Would Father try yet again to advance her software even further?

Butterflies in her stomach. Her heart fluttered like it contained a caged bird in her chest. Evelyn was... scared. Terrified about what the presentation meant to her father, but even more so, to herself. And the company. And the world.

Evelyn decided to do some meditation to center herself. Something to consciously slow down her breath. She focused on her breathing. Inhaling deep through the nose and then exhaling out of her mouth.

"Heeeeeeeeeee."

To inhale courage.

"Hwoooooooooo."

And exhale fear.

"Heeeeeeeeeee."

To embrace her best.

"Hwoooooooooo."

And exhale stress.

Several repetitions later, her nerves calmed. Time slowed down, and the panic eased away. She knew that she was resilient and capable, though, oftentimes, she became lost in her thoughts of worry. But more than anything else... Evelyn knew that she was ready. She could hear it now. The calling. The beat. *Bah-bum. Bah-bum.*

It was the sound of her heart.

It was the march of her convictions.

In the banquet hall stood a stage built for a large-scale event. A gathering that would make the World's Fair seem like a carnival compared to the size of this venue. It was a place that was roaring with every wealthy person and billionaire and tech-obsessed celebrity. Where onstage, a rhythm shifted ever so slowly into a cacophony of chiptune beats.

As tunes filled the air, a raucous DJ, adorned head to toe in silver technological equipment, pushed a button on a laptop. A guiding signal that dropped the beat. The denizens of the dance floor began to rave and wiggle and shake their booties. And patrons fully immersed themselves in celebration, dancing the most popular and coolest move of the time—a retro-styled dance called The Robot.

The air crackled with energy. A blend of celebrities, press, and CEOs converged in a party akin to a celebration on New Year's Eve. The revelry echoed throughout the venue in celebration of this new technology.

Then silence. The lights had hit the center stage to start the show. Where strobes flickered in tandem with the music's rhythmic beats, gradually settling into a calm cadence. The transformation continued as spotlights intricately painted the scene, revealing at its center a majestic metal stage adorned with neon pink lights. Where a podium, adorned with the prominent letters "AI," ascended. Very slowly. Bathed in a captivating dance of blue-and-white light beams, emerging from the shadows... Evelyn stepped into the spotlight. Effortlessly claiming her place as the epitome of cool in the room.

"Hello there. I'm happy to have called you all here," she said, surrounded by uproarious applause. The crowd gathered around the stage, silent and eager to hear the latest from their tech hero. And when they finally calmed their applause and cut the music, she resumed...

"Specialized labor. So that's a thing. Who's the career counselor who foresaw that a visit from a plumber would cost the same as a visit to the cardiologist one day? That guy deserves a million dollars, am I right?"

The joke failed to land as the crowded room stood in silence.

"I swear that one killed it with B.B.," said Evelyn. "I know what you're thinkin'. 'Aren't you concerned?' So many jobs. I mean, how many people have we already gotten laid off with my tech?" She stopped herself before getting off-topic and going into the costs of what her young legacy thus far had become. "I mean seriously, what is specialized labor anyway? Plumbing, carpentry, auto-mechanics, and aides. Do we really gotta replace them?"

Suddenly, a wealthy technocrat interrupted her. "Yes! Now get to GAMMA already!"

She snickered. Evelyn knew that in the seven years since creating E-Limited AI, her father had been technically still in charge only because she was still a child. Legally, nothing of what she did could be on her own. So long as this system was in place. She thought that what was needed would be something extra. She sought to disrupt the way people did things. For the betterment of humanity.

"Look, I'm here to tell you about GAMMA. The new AI that I developed was meant to change how we do work. But I... wasn't entirely honest..." She paused for a moment. "Because GAMMA doesn't replace specialized laborers."

The hall grew silent. Everyone's attention fixed on the stage as they looked at Evelyn with serious and curious expressions.

"See, it's never been about the skilled laborers. There's one job that's been an obvious burden on the world's economy. One job that, once replaced, would help virtually everyone in cutting costs and reinvesting in your everyday workers and shareholders. Something so obvious that the machine can do better than most..."

She drew them in with anticipation, then shared the truth.

"GAMMA doesn't replace skilled labor. *Its purpose is to replace all CEOs.*"

The room drew in a silencing GASP. A quiet so clear, you could hear the glass of champagne shatter from being dropped by its owner at the back of the massive hall.

"Not just CEOs, either. The goal is for GAMMA to replace every C-suite member in a company. To serve as an unbiased leader, so that everyone can just go about doing their tasks according to the computer's requests, then call it a day and go home."

The crowd shifted in tone with an upsetting uproar. A CEO fell off his chair. The executives in the room, startled by these events, began to boo Evelyn, though the young girl held her ground.

"This is absurd," cried a disapproving member. "Outright evil!"

"Utterly ludicrous," replied another.

"Do you think bosses are replaceable? Everyone in this room is a manager!"

"Technology is only as good or as bad as the people who use it," she said into the microphone. "We were so willing to replace everyone else for so long, and maybe it's time we start replacing ourselves as well—for the better."

"Without CEOs, who's to pursue company profitability?" argued a venture capitalist.

"What profitability?!" barked Evelyn. "E-Limited AI can make almost all your decisions for you. I know a heck of a lot better than most executives. Just this week, I have been asking B.B. to make almost all my calls boil down to yes or no answers."

She braced herself against the hundreds of glaring looks, the silence from half the crowd, which, in some ways, spoke even louder than the jests and boos. Remaining steady in her beliefs, she continued.

"Using algorithms that feed it data, the AI can make decisions better. Best of all, it costs nothing extra, saving corporate operations hundreds of billions, all while doing the impossible: becoming self-sustaining. Now every business can run itself!"

The crowd roared even louder, no longer hesitating in their disapproval. They no longer saw Evelyn as a fourteen-year-old girl and super-genius savior, but only as the enemy, and the end of capitalism as they knew it. In response, Evelyn hurriedly pushed a button, where a large digital screen displayed its data. On it were the names of every major Fortune 500 company.

"I know most companies won't approve of this, given who runs them. Which is why I'm letting you in on one last secret. GAMMA was never a new product. It was a software update, listed under your terms and agreements, which nobody read!" She laughed, glad to be done with hiding the truth. "Every single company using E-Limited AI has already been running GAMMA as of three months ago. Here are the decisions it has made and data that proves that it works. With profitability more or less remaining the same, or improving, even, once shareholders realize they can fire you folks pretty easily."

A pie chart moved on the display, showing tremendous profitability. As bar charts broke well past their upward limits, an even bigger roar echoed through the venue.

But standing there in the thick of all this disapproving chaos, on a chair in the crowd in utter disbelief, Evelyn saw her father. The mighty CEO who… was crying. A look on his face indicated that their company's future was now ruined. His future… doomed.

"Look, Gamma can't fix all your labor problems, but it does create an entirely new way of doing things. So maybe, with all this free time and wealth you all now have, we can focus on the problems in front of us. I'd like to talk about new tech that can address these issues, if you're curious. And I think… well, maybe you all should be."

Though some proceeded to leave the event, a surprisingly receptive crowd of people, uncertain of what to feel, or better yet, how to feel and what to do with their lives, started to listen to Evelyn's vision of the future. After all, it was Evelyn's genius that had gotten them there anyway.

"I envision a world of augmented reality. An overlay of the world we have today, with the possibilities of a new tomorrow. To remind people of some of the magic of our lost society. Devices that can find vulnerabilities in our foundations, and perhaps, design better ways of rebuilding our civilization. What this tech will do, if you want to join me in sharing it, is change the way we see the world. To give hope to those who can't live in this ruined state of things, but also, to call out the fact that there is a problem. I wanna start to change things for the better, if you'll join me. With this new tech, we not only can create a new world, but also use it to help rebuild the old one, anew."

Evelyn's father, still in the background, shook his head at Evelyn in disapproval. The only words mouthed out in response from Evelyn to her father were…

"I'm sorry."

In the years that followed GAMMA's release, almost all the world's CEOs resigned.

And the world redistributed its wealth over time.

And matched salaries with shares in companies as compensation.

And the hard times never came to pass.

And the world became something else entirely. Run entirely by AI.

Life became sustainable… albeit, also, somewhat boring. In a world untethered from the shackles of corporate greed, a transformative new day emerged. Where boardrooms once run by greedy CEOs were replaced by AI. Thanks to GAMMA's parameters, a new way of doing business, dedicated to a commitment to the greater good, took hold in the world. A paradigm shift, where companies redirected their focus toward equitable wealth distribution, social responsibility, and the well-being of their workforce.

So too came a change in ideals: prioritizing sustainability, where environmental stewardship and long-term vision took precedence over short-sighted gains. It was a world where innovation bore the altruistic banner of progress. The pursuit of a harmonious coexistence that resonated through every decision that was made. Though it came at a cost. As the old way of doing business was over.

And the 9 to 5… was no more.

Back at E-Limited AI Labs, in the deepest levels of the compound, was the secret room marked *Evelyn's Laboratory*. Where inside, a year after the fallout from the end of capitalism as anyone knew it had already happened, Mr. Sanna, Evelyn's father, stumbled upon her, alone and depressed. Not knowing what to do with his life, he'd spent hundreds of hours in Evelyn's Candy Kingdom.

And so Evelyn, notified by B.B., had come to see her father, and was surprised to find him in a state of disarray in her long-abandoned laboratory. She logged in to join her father, whom she found dressed in an outfit suited for a king. A Fruit

Roll-Up tunic draped over his shoulders. And Evelyn's pink diamond princess tiara adorned his head.

"You're here."

"I'm here, Papa."

"Guess you did it. You made me look like a butt."

"We did it. And that was never the goal, Dad. I told you, I just really wanted to make the world a better place with my smarts and all. But all you ever cared about was money."

"You know something, Evelyn?" he said, almost upset. "You're right. I was a butt."

Then Evelyn's father hugged her. And in his realization of all that had happened, and all that had changed, and what actually mattered in the world... he whispered to her, "I'm sorry."

Evelyn turned on the hologram of her AI mother, who joined in on the hug at the last second as well.

"Does this mean we can finally spend some time together now?" asked Mother Sanna.

"Sure. What would you like to do?" replied Evelyn.

"Hmm... you know, I was rather enjoying jumping around in these cotton-candy clouds you worked so hard making," said Mr. Sanna. "I do so like this AR device. Do you want to try it out, as a family?"

The three saddled some rainbow-colored unicorns and rode off into the pink sunset.

THOUGHTS ON *BRAVE NEW GIRLS*

"I highly value women having careers in STEM, as I grew up with a lot of successful women engineers in my family. So I originally wrote this story for my niece, Emmanuelle LeFranc, before it became this strange and shocking little tale regarding my concerns with AI technology. Much like my sister/Emme's mother, I hope she pursues math and sciences as well, so long as it interests her. If not, we at least have this story and this anthology—which will have to be enough, I think."

ABOUT THE AUTHOR

Christian Angeles is an entertainment journalist who currently serves as the senior editor of *Comics Beat*, one of the longest-running news outlets for comics journalism. His work appeared in the comic anthologies *The Tomb of Baalberith Vol. 2* and Limit Break Comic's Wish Upon a Star. He also wrote a Korean drama available on Kakao called *The City*. He's great with kids.

Illustration for "Whatever Happened to the 9-5?" by Ben Falco.

ZIPPED

MACKENZIE REIDE

ZIPPED

MACKENZIE REIDE

"**I PASSED!**" A WAVE OF RELIEF washed over Hannah as she scrolled through the results.

"I knew you could do it." George rolled up beside her, carrying an enormous plate with what looked like a hamburger and a fruit cup. He squeezed his small barrel-shaped body against her leg. Hannah knew he was trying to see her grades through his front plate.

She shifted to the side of her seat. "I was worried."

"I wasn't." George sounded pleased. He blew air into his hose and reached up to point with his two-pronged clamp fingers. Fingers that Hannah had jerry-rigged for him when she'd rescued him from being recycled. "How come you only got a B in Chemistry?"

"George! These were my first Uni exams ever."

"I know, but..."

"But, cut her some slack, George." Rowanda swaggered into Hannah's room. "I hear someone passed all her exams."

Hannah grinned. "I did."

Rowanda smiled, showing all her sharp teeth. "You did good."

Hannah felt her face flush under her freckles. She rubbed her hands against her coveralls. It was funny how things had changed. Hannah's first encounter with Rowanda had been when the latter hijacked the space station Hannah had stowed away on. Hannah had desperately tried to out-code the pirate to stop her from blowing up the fusion reactor, but Rowanda was too good. Hannah had vowed never to be out-coded again. She'd taken every opportunity to learn, which set off a chain of events that resulted in her and Rowanda jumping the entire station across the galaxy.

Now, two years later, here they were. Hannah was a full-time student and Rowanda was her thesis advisor.

Gotta love irony.

"Next term, you'll do even better," George said.

Rowanda snorted. "Just pass for now."

"Pass? Hannah's smarter than that." George's gears whirred. They were prone to do that when he got agitated. Which happened a lot around Rowanda.

"Easy, vacuum cleaner," Rowanda said. "Hannah's got a lot on her plate. Not just her studies."

George whirred louder. "I know that! She almost got blown up by Mega Corp last term."

"Mega Corp," Hannah groaned. "Don't remind me." She flexed her fingers unconsciously, as she remembered coding as fast as she could to defuse a bomb wrapped around her classmate's trunk.

"How is your study buddy?" Rowanda asked. "Did he lose all his leaves after that?" She sounded amused.

"They kind of turned yellow and fell off," Hannah said. "It looked like fall back on Earth."

Rowanda frowned. "He looks weird."

Hannah ran her fingers through her thick, wiry brown hair. She didn't dare tell Rowanda that Larch looked almost normal to her as he was from a tree-like race called the Larix, as were most of the university students. Rowanda was an Anthrax, a tall skinny purple alien with long limbs and a face that reminded Hannah of a warthog. When she'd first met Rowanda, the pirate had been wearing an ammunition belt across her shoulders and a blaster at her hip. At the university, she carried a book bag. Hannah wondered if her blaster was tucked inside, but never asked.

"I imagine Larch learned his lesson," George said. "But I still think you shouldn't be his study buddy."

Hannah shook her head. "Larch was being blackmailed by Mega Corp. He's an indentured engineer in training. They own him."

"Which is why we can never trust him!" George shook his clamp fingers in the air.

"George is right," Rowanda said. "You can't discuss anything about the Jump Drive with him."

Hannah sighed. "I know. It's too bad because he's a good programmer. He could have helped."

"No!" Rowanda and George both shouted at the same time. They looked startled for a moment.

"I guess you agree on something." Hannah laughed.

Rowanda crossed her long arms. "The Uni wants to start live trials next week. How is your work going on the re-entry code?"

Hannah gulped. "I've got a working model, but…"

Rowanda's thick eyebrows furrowed. "But what?"

"But I don't know for sure if it will work."

Rowanda leaned down and put one claw on Hannah's shoulder. "You will never be sure. We took a huge risk jumping ZOWS across the galaxy to the Uni without live tests. And we made it. You proved you can figure out the logic. Now we need you to transfer that to live freighter crews."

"Before Mega Corp," George added.

Hannah took a deep breath. "It will be ready."

"Good. I'll tell the Board." Rowanda paused at Hannah's door. "I'm pleased with your work, Hannah. You're going to make a fine mechanical engineer." With that, she walked out.

"Hmmpf," George said. "She's just saying that because she wants all the credit for your work."

Hannah laughed. "That's how the university operates, George. The students do the work, and the professors take the credit."

"*Adjunct* Professor," George corrected her. "And she got it thanks to you. Long ways from tenure! Speaking of professors, I wonder how Professor Wally is doing?"

Hannah shook her head. "I don't know, but Larch told me he is working for Mega Corp."

"He sold out the university to work for Mega Corp?" George sounded disgusted.

"Rowanda said that after the Uni stopped the project, he didn't want to let it go. So, he found another sponsor."

"But he can't work without his grad students," George grumbled. "Rowanda went full-time pirate. That left him with no one to do the research."

"The Uni owns the rights to everything created here. So Rowanda couldn't work on the Jump Drive, either." Hannah took a bite of the burger. "But when I figured out the glitch, she saw an opportunity to get back into it."

"Yes, and now she has her own student to do the work. *Professors.*" George's gears whirred. "They're all the same."

Hannah laughed. "I think Rowanda is unique. She's the only Anthrax at the university."

"You're the only human," George said.

Hannah sighed. That was true. Most of her classmates were Larix. She frowned at her burger. "Is this a PBA burger?"

"Not quite. Chef is excited to try a new mix of ants and grasshoppers. It boosts your neurological activity even more when you mix the two brain foods." George sounded excited.

Hannah groaned. "But I like the ant burger with peanut butter. Now it tastes a bit dry."

"That can be fixed." George whirled around and zoomed out of the room. "I'll be back!"

Hannah laughed. George was determined to feed her the most nutritious food in the galaxy. Which so far consisted of mealworms, grasshoppers, cockroaches, beetle larvae, snails, spiders, and ants. Her favorite of them all was the basic mealworm patty. It was the most like an Earth burger, but according to George that was the least nutritious of the choices. So, she didn't get them as often as she'd have liked.

In fact, the whole crew appeared determined to see how far her brain could go. Part of that was because she had saved their lives when she first came to the station, and part of it was because the crew of ZOWS was not made up of academics. She was the first one to attend university and receive formal training.

ZOWS, or Zenith Outpost Weigh Station, as it was formally called, was originally built to be the weigh station for an asteroid belt at the far edge of the galaxy, in Zenith Corp territory. Hannah had left a life of child labor back on Earth and stowed away on a freighter. She'd hidden in the ducts of the space station until Rowanda showed up with stolen plans for a new space drive. She'd managed to stop Rowanda from stealing the plans and destroying the station, and then accepted a job as a junior engineer.

The captain of the station had been impressed by Hannah's resourcefulness, so she'd hired a private tutor to teach Hannah engineering. That was Professor Wally. He'd been a great teacher, and Hannah had learned a lot, but his real motives had been to find out what she knew about his faulty Drive.

His attempt to kidnap her and force her to be his indentured student had failed, but Captain Greta was determined to continue Hannah's formal education, so here she was, enrolled as a full-time student at Zenith University, under the condition she worked on the coding of the new Jump Drive. Rowanda and Captain Greta had negotiated the deal.

Hannah finished her burger and washed it down with a glass of water. Since ZOWS was now located in orbit around the University, it had become the weigh station for it. The crew had been delighted to take on a new role as ZOWS-UNI. And, it made it possible for Hannah to attend classes in person.

Hannah smiled at the data on the screen. She had passed her first exams. That was something. Now she had to finalize the Jump Drive program before the live test. She had a three-week break between terms, so she'd been living and breathing the program every day since exams had finished. Minus sweating about whether or not she'd passed.

She had to get the program working one hundred percent. Lives were depending on her. If the freighter jumped wrongly, the crew could be stuck for many years before rematerializing. Or even worse, not materialize at all, which meant the buffer patterns of the crew would break down, and eventually they would dissolve into nothing.

It was a lot to ask of the crew of the test freighter. But Hannah remembered working as a child laborer back on Earth. Her parents had died in a mining accident, so the orphanage farmed her out as cheap labor. She had decided that scrubbing out toxic waste tanks was not her idea of a career, especially when the life expectancy of the children was only sixteen. She'd snuck out on what she thought was her fourteenth birthday, and never looked back.

She ran a simulation one more time. She had gotten the program further than Rowanda, who had worked on it as a grad student, but there was still a problem with focusing the minds of the crew before the jump. On ZOWS it had been easy; the whole crew had been so anxious they were hyper-focused. It was jump or get destroyed by Mega Corp. The test freighter crew wouldn't be so easy to convince.

Hannah sat back in her chair. She looked around her quarters. When she had first arrived on ZOWS, she had hidden in the ducts, which was easy for her, as she was only one-and-a-half meters tall. The rest of the crew stood at three meters. The sanitation engineer, Warbler, had found her sneaking around the burner room shortly after she'd stowed away on the station. He hadn't turned her in; instead, he'd given her old computer parts and items that were being sent to the burner for recycling. He'd also left food out for her after breakfast. When Hannah was finally integrated into the crew, he became her supervisor. He'd taught her everything he knew about ZOWS's fusion generator and all the ship's systems.

Warbler was a blue slug-like being from the planet Roxan. He reminded Hannah of an Earth slug, but with six arms that looked like they belonged to a wrestler. He was the kindest being on ZOWS. He'd cut the legs off her chair and desk to make them more comfortable for her in her quarters. It had taken a while to get used to everything being so big, but now she liked having the extra room.

Focus, she told herself. She couldn't afford distractions right now. But how was she going to get the freighter crew to focus only on one thing? That was going to be tough to explain.

And would it be enough?

·····

"Hannah, this is Captain Merle," Captain Greta introduced Hannah to the captain of the test freighter.

Hannah smiled self-consciously at the view screen. Captain Merle was a Greinder, like Captain Greta. Which meant he looked like a giraffe spliced with a rhinoceros.

"Hello, Hannah. Captain Greta informs me that there is something we need to do in order to make the jump successful." His big giraffe ears flipped back and forth.

Hannah hesitated. "We need the crew to focus on one thing simultaneously."

Captain Merle curled his lower lip in a frown. "This does not sound reassuring. Is the Jump Drive ready?"

Hannah's stomach did a flip-flop. She was standing in the control room at the University Shuttle terminal. There were three large screens. Captain Merle's head occupied one of them. Beside that was another screen that showed the test freighter. It was an identical model to the freighter she had stowed away on two years ago. The third screen showed empty space. This was where the freighter was supposed to finish the jump.

Hannah took a deep breath and steadied herself. "It's ready. But it does require the crew to focus." She tried to sound confident.

"Focus on what?" he asked. "What did you focus on when you jumped ZOWS?"

"We were all so terrified about the jump that we were thinking about whether or not it would work," George said.

"Don't say that, vacuum cleaner," Rowanda muttered under her breath. She tapped his barrel body with her toe.

"What kind of a Drive is that? We're going to be terrified every time we use it?" Captain Merle's ears went flat against his head.

"Pretty much," George muttered.

"I can't tell my crew that," Captain Merle said. "I need something more definite."

"Hannah is working as hard as she can to get the glitch under control," Warbler said. He was standing beside her. "We just need to take this one step at a time."

"One step or one crew?" Captain Merle said. "I have two hundred souls on board my ship!"

Hannah felt her hands get sweaty. "It will be all right. We just need to get everyone to concentrate."

"Easy for you to say," Captain Merle said. "I still don't know what to tell them."

"What does every crew member do right after a trip?" Rowanda said. She was standing behind Hannah with her arms crossed.

Captain Merle thought for a moment. "Go to the Uni Beer House."

"The Uni has a beer house?" George said.

"You aren't allowed in it, vacuum cleaner," Rowanda said.

"What about Hannah?"

"She's underage. So, no."

"Oh, well, she has better things to do with her time," George said.

Hannah bit back a smile. Not being allowed in the Beer House was the least of her worries. But it did add to her feeling of not fitting in with her classmates. It was bad enough she felt like a toadstool in the forest when she sat in class. But she kept that to herself.

"Focus on the Beer House," Rowanda said. "That should be easy."

Captain Merle grunted. He leaned closer to the screen, which made his head look enormous. "I have two daughters. I would very much like to see them grow up. Does this Jump Drive work?"

His eyes bored into Hannah's. She willed herself to hold his gaze. "It works." She felt sweat rolling down her back.

He sighed. "We'll find out soon enough."

"Or in two years," George muttered.

"George!" Hannah whispered out of the side of her mouth.

The screen went blank. Hannah paced back and forth in the control room, waiting for the test freighter to signal they were ready.

The comm beeped. "We're in position," Captain Merle announced. "I've talked to the crew. We're going to the Beer House. We'll jump in two minutes."

Hannah held her breath. Would this work?

"Good luck," Rowanda said. Hannah noticed her claws were clenched.

She wondered what Rowanda was really thinking. Was she remembering the first test? The one with her programming? Rowanda had discovered there was a problem with the Jump Drive and written a last-minute quick fix, but it had taken two years for the ship to rematerialize.

George said Rowanda didn't care. He believed that because she'd stolen the program and sold it to the highest bidder after the university had shelved it.

Whether Rowanda cared or not, Hannah did. She felt her stomach churn when the ship disappeared off the screen. There one moment and gone the next.

"Did it work?" Captain Greta said. "Where is it?"

Hannah stared at the screens in front of her. The screen where the freighter was supposed to materialize was… blank.

"How long is the jump supposed to take?" Warbler asked.

"When working properly, almost instant," Rowanda said. She frowned at the screen.

"We're at one minute," Warbler said, looking at his timepiece.

"It didn't work," Hannah gasped.

"Don't panic yet," Rowanda said. "A fully functioning Drive will jump instantaneously. We don't have a perfect Drive yet."

"But… how do we know if it works at all?" Hannah said.

"When it rematerializes," Rowanda said.

"Do we wait for two years?" George asked.

"But… what if it doesn't?" Hannah felt tears come to her eyes.

"Give it time, Hannah," Rowanda said. "This is not over yet. This was only the first test. You have work to do."

Hannah stared open-mouthed at Rowanda. "On what? The Jump Drive doesn't work!"

"We don't know that," Rowanda said firmly. "All we know right now is that it is not rematerializing as fast as we'd like. So you need to work on that glitch."

"But…"

"But nothing. You can do this, Hannah. You can save lives by working until you get it right. Do you want Mega Corp throwing beings into nothingness? Which is what they will start doing next week."

"But isn't that what we just did?" Hannah felt a tear run down her freckled cheek.

Rowanda shook her head. "No, we don't know that. We don't have enough facts. So, you and I are going back to the data we've collected, and we will continue our work. You are not a quitter, Hannah. You can't just give up like that. There is a probe at the jump site that will continually scan the area. If it… I mean, when it rematerializes, we will get the signal immediately."

Hannah gulped.

"I believe in you, Hannah," Warbler said. "You are the best chance we have to make a safe working model. Remember that."

Hannah blinked rapidly. She stared at the screen, wishing the ship would reappear, but all she saw was empty space.

They pored over the data for the next two days. Hannah ran simulation after simulation, but she couldn't be sure what had really gone on once the ship and the crew had dematerialized at the start of the jump. She did know that all the energies were kept in a buffer. Her new program isolated the crew's mind energies, so the ship could jump.

The Jump Drive created a fold in space, which enabled the ship to dematerialize on one side and rematerialize on the other. The program focused on the inert objects first, then the crew. That was where the delay came in. The program couldn't clearly define the moving energies, so it would stall and not complete the re-entry process.

Hannah was sure that having the crew concentrate on one thing would focus the energies and help the program to corral them together. It had worked with ZOWS.

"ZOWS jumped in a matter of minutes," Hannah said. "But the freighter is taking longer."

"Yes, we know that, but why?" Rowanda was sitting cross-legged on Hannah's bed, working on a new tablet. She had given Hannah her old one, which she had used during her undergraduate studies.

"George is right, we were terrified when we jumped ZOWS. Maybe intensity is also a factor." Hannah frowned at her simulation data.

"After this, they will all be scared silly," Rowanda grunted. "Won't be a hard sell to focus on that."

Hannah sighed. "There must be a better way."

"The Jump Drive isn't very efficient. It's like the crew is trapped in a zip file." George rolled in with a large plate. "Chef made a mealworm burger for you." He placed it on the desk. "The Drive options are limited. You might get stranded in space and dissolve into nothing, or you might arrive years later and die of a heart attack from stress. Either way, it's not traveling any faster than light speed."

Rowanda blew steam from her snout. "It'll work."

Hannah picked up the burger. "Mealworm? I think I'd better start eating beetles."

"No, you've done so much. You deserve a break." George reached up with his clamp fingers and tapped Hannah's forehead gently. "Don't worry, the answer's in there. Maybe you're trying too hard."

"Thanks, George." Hannah smiled. She munched on her burger while George busied himself organizing her books. He felt they should be arranged neatly in alphabetical order while Hannah just put them wherever she was when she finished reading.

Warbler knocked gently on the door. "May I come in?"

Hannah waved him in. "Yes, please do."

He slid into the room, barely squeezing through the door.

"How are you doing?" he asked as he stood by her desk.

"I'm disappointed about the test," Hannah said. "I'm scared the ship won't rematerialize."

"I think it will," Warbler said. "We just don't know when. Do you have any ideas as to why the freighter is different from jumping ZOWS?"

Hannah shook her head. "I'm working on some ideas, but I don't have the answer."

"Sounds like you could use some brainstorming," Warbler suggested.

Rowanda snorted. "What do you think we've been doing?"

Warbler hesitated. "Well…"

"What are you thinking?" Rowanda frowned at him.

Warbler rubbed all six hands together. "Well, this seems like a problem that might be solved with more heads."

"What did you do?" Rowanda stood up.

"Not him, me." Captain Greta stuck her head in the door. "There's a proposal I think you should hear."

Hannah watched Captain Greta's ears flip back and forth once. "What is it?"

"I'll let him tell you." Captain Greta stepped aside.

"Larch!" Hannah was shocked to see her study buddy standing behind Captain Greta.

"You shouldn't be here." George rolled in front of Hannah. "This is Uni business!"

"I know, I know," Larch said hastily. He held up a branch. "But I'm here to help."

"You let Larch on the station?" Rowanda whistled.

"We let *you* on the station," Captain Greta growled back.

Rowanda shrugged. "True. But I'm not trying to steal the Jump Drive anymore."

"And neither am I," Larch said.

"Tell them what you told Captain Greta and me," Warbler said.

Larch stepped hesitantly into the room. It was getting crowded, with Hannah, Warbler, George, and Rowanda. Captain Greta stood outside the door with two armed security guards at her side.

"Feeling drafty?" George scoffed at Larch.

Larch shook his branches. He had no leaves, like a tree in the winter back on Earth. "My leaves will grow back."

Hannah felt bad for him. She knew he hadn't been trying to get them blown up on purpose.

Larch took a deep breath. "Mega Corp is going to do a live jump."

"We know that," Rowanda grunted. "I hear it's set for next week."

Larch nodded. "The engineers have been studying the work-around code that Hannah programmed to defuse the bomb last semester. They are confident that the ship will rematerialize, so they are going to do the test."

"If you jump, you will most likely not see the ship for a very long time, if ever," Rowanda said. "It's not a good idea."

"How about your new program?" Larch said. "No freighter yet?"

"It will show," Warbler said.

"But the danger is still there," Larch insisted. "That's why Professor Wally wants to pool resources."

"What?" Hannah stared at Larch. "Are you serious?"

"What does Mega Corp have to say about that?" Rowanda scoffed.

"The Board granted permission." Larch held up all his branches for emphasis. "The Jump Drive is important, and we're all stumped. The fastest way to get around it is to work together."

"Until the inevitable double-cross," George muttered.

Rowanda's mouth twitched. "What do you have to offer? We're at least two steps ahead."

"Hannah has this sorted. We don't need Mega Corp." George's gears whirred.

"If you are willing to meet with Professor Wally and me, he can convince the Board to delay the Mega Corp test," Larch said. "We can buy more time to fix this. Isn't that worth a shot?"

Hannah hesitated. Was Larch telling the truth? Could they actually stop Mega Corp from launching their faulty Drive?

"It is an interesting conundrum," Captain Greta said. Her ears were flipping back and forth rapidly. Hannah knew she was thinking about her partner, who had been an indentured engineer at Mega Corp. The freighter she'd been testing a new interstellar engine on had exploded. Mega Corp had known about the cracks in the casing, but had run the tests anyway.

"I think we should do this."

"Hannah!" George was mortified.

"Do you really want to share information with Mega Corp?" Rowanda sounded surprised.

"You sold your work to them," Hannah said.

"For financial gain, yes, but after the Uni stopped the project." Rowanda rubbed one of her tusks. "This is different. We are competing with them for the first working design."

"If we collaborate, we can both get a working model that is safer to use," Larch said. "Without sacrificing many lives to get there."

"But you can't give us anything helpful," George said.

"I have an idea."

"What?" Hannah said.

Larch hesitated. "I'm not supposed to say anything until we are all together."

"I could make you talk." Rowanda bared her sharp teeth.

Larch's entire trunk trembled. "Please don't do that. Mega Corp will harm my siblings if I don't comply."

Rowanda blew steam out her snout. "It's your call, Hannah."

"I want to do this," Hannah said.

"Are you sure?" George asked.

Hannah nodded. "Yes. I don't want more crews to disappear if we can prevent it."

"All right. I'll tell the Board," Rowanda said. "This will be a fun conversation."

Larch rubbed two of his branches together. "Great! I'll pass on the news. It was nice to see you, Hannah."

Hannah gave him a wave as he left with Captain Greta, escorted by the security guards.

"Are we really doing this?" George asked.

"Yes, we are." Hannah gave him a pat.

"This will be fun," Rowanda said.

▚▚▚▚

Rowanda and Captain Greta made the arrangements for the meeting, which was to take place at the University library. Warbler flew them to the campus in his personal ship. Hannah sat squeezed between Rowanda and four ZOWS-UNI security guards. George was strapped into the co-pilot's seat next to Warbler. Much to his delight.

"I'll pick you up when you are done," Warbler instructed as he dropped them off at the shuttle terminal. "Good luck."

Hannah nodded. She and her entourage got ready to walk across the campus. It was winter, so Hannah was bundled up in a nice warm coat. She wrapped a scarf around her face as a cold blast of wind hit her as they stepped outside the hangar bay.

There was fresh snow on top of the mountains that surrounded the University.

Hannah liked the way the campus was nestled in a valley between the peaks. The sun shone brightly, and the crisp blue sky made Hannah wonder if this was what Earth had once looked like before all the pollution.

The library was a stone building located in the center of the campus. The faculty buildings all circled around it. The mechanical engineering building where Hannah's classes took place was off to the side, but Hannah could see the sun glinting off the tall windows.

Like ZOWS-UNI, everything on the campus was sized extra-large. The doors to the library looked like they belonged to a castle. The door handles were big iron rings that Hannah had to jump up and grab with both hands, then plant her foot against the door and pull down on the ring to turn it enough to open.

Today, one of the security guards stepped ahead and opened the door. He motioned for her to wait while he did a quick scan of the inside.

"Do you think Jonko is here?" George asked.

Hannah looked nervously around. Jonko was a space pirate who had ambushed her and stolen all her coursework last semester. Mega Corp had tried to sabotage Hannah's exams as well as blow her up.

Hannah shook her head. "I don't think so. He can't pretend he's Rowanda anymore."

"Well, they look exactly the same," George said.

"Don't say that to Rowanda," Hannah whispered.

The guard poked his tree head out and motioned for them to come in. Hannah felt a rush of warm air as she stepped inside. She peeled off her scarf and jacket. For a big place, the university kept it nice and cozy.

It was quiet in the library. Only two other students were working at a cubicle. They looked up at her and nodded. She gave them a wave. She recognized them as two of her classmates. She never really spoke to any of them, except for Larch.

Hannah climbed up on a big chair at one of the long tables in the middle of the library.

"How old is this university?" George asked as he parked next to her.

"Old." Rowanda sat next to Hannah. "I think it's been here since the beginning of time."

"That is close to true," came a familiar voice.

Hannah looked up from her tablet and saw Professor Wally sliding toward them. He was a Wonkatoo. A close relation to Warbler's race, but more like a walrus than a slug.

"It is so great to see you, Hannah!" He clapped his flippers together in delight. "I hear you passed your first semester. Congratulations!"

Hannah smiled. In spite of everything that had happened, she was pleased at his praise.

"Hmpf," George said.

"Hello, George. Hello Rowanda." Professor Wally sat across from his former student.

Rowanda grunted. George whirred his gears.

"Did you know that the university always keeps at least one copy of everything in book form?" Larch sat down next to Professor Wally. Four Mega Corp guards stood behind him.

Hannah glanced at the four ZOWS-UNI guards. One of them flicked a branch upwards. She looked up, and was surprised to see six more security personnel looking down from an upper level.

"Those are from Zenith Corp," Rowanda said quietly.

"The students use tablets now," George said. "Why keep making paper books?"

"Because the Larix believe in transmitting information through their leaves. Those leaves become pages in the books. We don't have to type like you do on a tablet. It's a natural process and quite fast," Larch explained. "And these books will last for thousands of years. We have stories from all over the galaxy. Long before the corporations divided it into sections for themselves."

"That's impressive," Hannah said. "I watched you and our classmates pass leaf notes around during the lectures. It's like a windstorm. I can never figure out what they are saying."

Professor Wally laughed. "The Larix have a unique way of communicating. It's quite fascinating."

"But it doesn't help us fix a brand new space drive," George said.

"True, George," Professor Wally agreed. "I think we are the only beings in the galaxy who understand the complexities of the Jump Drive."

"We're still ahead of you," Rowanda said.

Professor Wally nodded. "So you say. You were always my star student, Rowanda. It's good to see you back in the game. Pirating might be lucrative, but it's not rocket science."

Rowanda snorted. "I like being paid for my work."

"We've been working with the program Hannah used to defuse the explosive, along with Professor Wally's original coding for the Jump Drive. But you have new coding, Hannah. Can we see it?" Larch looked hopeful.

"You can't look at it, but we can share our theories," Rowanda said.

"Fair enough," Professor Wally agreed. "However, right now the university has done two tests, and both times the freighters have disappeared. Are you really ahead?"

"ZOWS jumped successfully," George argued. "So, yeah, we are ahead."

Professor Wally leaned in. "You jumped an entire space station across half the galaxy, but when you went to test a single freighter across only a hundred light years, it's gone. Why?"

"Maybe the station was luck." Rowanda shrugged.

Professor Wally's whiskers twitched. "No. You two are too smart for that. You did something right. We need to repeat it."

Hannah opened her mouth. Then shut it. Professor Wally saw it. "What is it, Hannah? We agreed to pool our resources, remember?"

"We know from the program you typed in to defuse the bomb that you were trying to isolate the crew's mind energies. Is that correct?" Larch asked.

Hannah thought about how the crew of the first test freighter had reacted when they found out they'd been missing for two years. They had been shocked and sad. Now she'd put another crew into that situation, or worse. She didn't want anyone else to suffer that fate.

Hannah nodded. "That was Rowanda's fix. I took that and worked it. We jumped ZOWS with my new code."

"And?" Professor Wally's eyes looked eager.

"I created a program to isolate the energies of the minds of the crew, to separate them from the inert energies of the ship. Then I asked the new crew to focus on one thing simultaneously."

"What was it?" Professor Wally asked.

"The Uni Beer House." Rowanda snorted.

Professor Wally laughed. "Now that is interesting!"

"But it didn't work," Hannah said.

"Maybe, or maybe they didn't concentrate enough." Professor Wally looked thoughtful. "What if we program an override in the system, so that the ship must rematerialize within a set time?"

"Force the rematerialization?" Hannah asked.

"Yes, so far everyone has materialized in one piece. It's all the checks and balances in the program that are causing the delays."

"Those checks are there to make sure the crew doesn't get scrambled upon re-entry," Hannah said.

"But we know it works." Professor Wally rubbed one of his whiskers. "At least this way we'd know when to expect the freighter. Cut out this unknown wait time."

"What would be the minimum time?" Rowanda said. "Is that what Mega Corp plans to do? Run jumps with a set time, until one of the ships arrives with a crew in one piece?"

"It would speed things up. We could be waiting years for this test," Professor Wally said.

"Or, never," George said quietly.

"What if we used the Jump Drive only on fully automated ships?" Hannah said. "Not with live crews? There are many supplies that could be transported that way."

"That would work," Rowanda agreed. "But the next step after this is to use it for intergalactic travel. That's lucrative. Also, there's a need to move personnel around."

Hannah sighed. Rowanda was right.

"If the crew needs to fully concentrate, the Beer House probably isn't strong enough," Larch said. "What if a crew member doesn't drink?"

"So, a teetotaler might hold everyone back?" George laughed. "Or, maybe thinking isn't really their thing. Some of those crews are pretty rough that go to the canteen on ZOWS-UNI."

Rowanda slapped her thigh. "Hah! Are you saying the Jump Drive is not recognizing the difference between a mechanic and a wall?"

Hannah stared at Rowanda in dismay. She was having a good laugh, but Hannah was worried. What if that was the case? How was she supposed to isolate all the energies?

They sat in silence. Hannah could see the frowns of concentration on everyone's faces. They were at a stalemate.

Her comm beeped. It was Warbler. "Hannah, the ship just reappeared!" His voice rang out in the quiet library. "I'm coming to get you."

Hannah's heart leaped. George let out a whoop.

Rowanda grabbed the comm from Hannah. "Tell the freighter we are on our way. Don't let them talk to anyone else." She rustled Hannah's unruly hair. "This is it, Hannah, let's see what happened!"

"What about our agreement?" Larch said.

Rowanda hesitated. "We don't need you."

"You might want to know that Mega Corp has a ship stationed near the expected entry point," Professor Wally said calmly.

Rowanda cursed. "We need to get to that freighter!"

"Doesn't Zenith have a ship in wait, too?" George asked.

"Of course," Rowanda said. "They will be prepared to fight."

"Or, we could all go together," Professor Wally suggested. "That way neither side will want to blow us up."

Rowanda growled. "Thought of everything, have you?"

"Except how to fix the Jump Drive," George said.

"Can we all fit into Warbler's ship?" Hannah asked.

"We'll make it work," Rowanda said. "Come on! Let's see our test results."

They all packed into Warbler's ship. It was a tight fit, with Professor Wally and Larch squeezing in. Rowanda and the ZOWS-UNI guards refused to let the Mega Corp guards board, so they jumped into their own ship and followed. The Zenith Corp guards were close by in their ship.

Hannah's heart was pounding. Had it worked? Was the crew alive and in one piece? These questions kept spinning around in her head. Rowanda looked tense. George was whirring noisily.

It felt like forever before Warbler's ship touched down in the cargo bay of the freighter. Being the smallest, Hannah had been quite comfortable during the journey, but she knew the others were stiff from the way they awkwardly extricated themselves from their seats.

Captain Merle greeted them enthusiastically in the freighter hangar bay. "We're all in one piece!"

Hannah shook his hoof. "I'm glad to hear it."

"We never doubted for a minute," George said.

"But we are four days late," Captain Merle said.

"Better than the alternative," Warbler said.

"One hundred light years in four days. You could have walked faster," George mused.

Rowanda snorted out a laugh.

"And who are these folks?" Captain Merle asked.

"I'm Professor Wally, and this is my student Larch." The Professor held out a flipper. "We're here to help."

"They're Mega Corp," George warned. "We're the ones helping."

Captain Merle hesitated, then held out his hoof. "I hope this means Mega Corp is planning to use the Jump Drive safely."

"That is the plan," Larch added as he shook branches with the captain.

Hannah was breathless. "I need to review the black box."

"Absolutely. Come with me." Captain Merle motioned to his second-in-command. "Get the box and meet us in the ready room."

The Larix saluted and marched off.

"This is exciting," Larch said.

"We should get answers," Rowanda said.

Just then a loud hissing sound came from the vents. "What's that?" Warbler sounded nervous.

"It's gas—clear the ventilation system!" Captain Merle shouted. The crew jumped to attention and began scrambling.

Hannah felt woozy. Rowanda pulled something out of her bag and put it on her own face. Then shoved something onto Hannah's.

"What?" She was groggy. Around her, the Larix crew were stumbling.

"Are you all right?" Rowanda yelled at Hannah through her mask.

Warbler and the others were coughing loudly. George waved his hose clamp. "I'm fine."

"You're a vacuum cleaner, of course you are," Rowanda snorted.

"What's happening?" Hannah asked. Her head cleared as she breathed in fresh oxygen.

"The inevitable double-cross," George said. "You did this!" He pointed his clamp fingers at Rowanda.

She shook her head. "No, not me."

"Then why did you bring masks?" George demanded.

"Gassing a ship is a typical pirate trick," Rowanda retorted. "I'm always prepared."

Just then Warbler slumped on George. "Hey!" came his muffled voice.

"Hang on, George," Hannah said. "I'll get you."

"Wait." Rowanda touched her shoulder. "Look who's here."

Hannah stared in dismay at the figure marching up to them, holding a blaster in one claw and the black box in the other.

"Hi, Freckles."

"Jonko! How did you get on board?" Hannah demanded.

"I got a job in the ship's galley." Jonko stepped around Warbler, who was snoring like a tractor.

"You did the jump?" Rowanda sounded surprised. "That was gutsy."

Jonko shrugged. "It was the only way to get on board and into position. Besides, you jumped ZOWS. Why wouldn't this work?"

Hannah frowned. "You do know that the Jump Drive is temperamental? It's not working properly."

Rowanda burst out laughing. "If I had known you were on board, I might have removed some of the code."

"I'm being paid very well. Better than your Adjunct Professor wage." Jonko sneered. But he sounded a bit nervous.

"You can't take the black box. It's no good without our analysis," Hannah said.

"Correct, which is why I'm taking you with me."

"Seriously?" Rowanda growled. "We're not going with you."

"I don't want you." Jonko barked out a laugh. "Just the kid here. She's the superstar. You're old news, Rowanda."

Rowanda blew steam out of her snout. "I am not. I'm the one who designed it in the first place. You still need me."

"It was your idea?" Hannah asked.

"I proposed it as a thesis project. How do you think I got into Zenith University?" Rowanda said. "I'm an Anthrax. The first ever at this Uni. Professor Wally saw the potential and convinced the university to let me enroll as his student."

"The same thing you did for me," Hannah said.

"Impressive," Jonko said. "But I'm only getting paid for Hannah."

"How about I break your neck?" Rowanda growled.

"We're not going with you," Hannah said.

"My blaster begs to differ," Jonko said. "Okay, I'll take both of you. Now, please walk to the ship you came in on."

"No," Hannah said.

"Excuse me?" Jonko frowned. "If you don't comply, I'll shoot your supervisor. What's his name, Warbler?"

Hannah gritted her teeth. "No, you are not going to do that."

Jonko laughed. "You're a tough one, for someone so small. Rowanda, did you know she knocked me off my feet when I stole her book bag?"

"I heard." Rowanda smiled, showing her fangs.

"But you can't do that this time, Freckles. Did the Larix ever figure out how many you have?"

Hannah gritted her teeth. "No." When she had first arrived at the university, her classmates had been fascinated by her freckles. She had them in spades. They'd made a bet trying to figure out how many she had on her face. Larch had even gone so far as to create a program to count them.

"Oh, well, I was just curious." He laughed. "Now, let's get going."

"No," Hannah said again.

Jonko frowned. "You're really not getting the message. Would it entice you more if I told you that I set the Jump Drive to leap all the way across the galaxy? Not just Zenith Corp territory?"

"What? Why would you do that?" Hannah gasped. "That's a massive jump! The Jump Drive's never been tested that far."

He frowned. "Well, we'd better get going then."

"Seriously? We're working with Mega Corp," Hannah said. "This is unnecessary."

"Who says I'm working for Mega Corp?" he sneered.

"I don't think the university needs to steal their own work," Rowanda said.

Jonko shrugged. "I didn't ask for the details."

"Which corporation is it?" Hannah demanded.

Jonko's eyes darted back and forth. "I'm just the muscle, Freckles. I don't care who pays, just that I get paid. Now, let's go."

Hannah shook her head. "We need to turn off the Jump Drive first."

"You sound nervous," Rowanda said. "How much time before the jump?"

"Let's just say, we need to go now," Jonko said firmly.

"You set the Drive so it would look like we all jumped," Rowanda growled. "So that no one would know Hannah was missing."

Jonko nodded. "Yes, it buys time for me to get her and the black box to my clients. And if it's not working as you say, then no one will miss her."

Hannah felt sick to her stomach. "We can't let the ship jump."

"There's no time! We need to go—" Jonko jolted like he'd been hit by a lightning bolt and slowly fell over. Hannah gasped.

Behind him was George, holding a metal rod in his clamp fingers. "Did you know that metal conducts electricity?" he said. "Jonko knows now. And Warbler's heavy!"

"Good job, George," Hannah cheered.

Rowanda pulled a blaster from her book bag and knelt on Jonko's back. She dug her knee in. "How long until the jump?"

"About now," he spluttered. "I was planning on flying off in all the commotion."

"We need to stop it," Hannah said. "But I'm not sure how the Jump Drive is hooked up to the ship."

Rowanda zapped Jonko one more time. "I do. Come on." She scooped up Hannah in one arm and sprinted down a long corridor to the engine room. "I designed how the Jump Drive connected to the hyperdrive engines on the first test freighter. They did the same with this one."

She plonked Hannah in front of a keyboard attached to the engine console. "You need to shut down the program, while I grab the Jump Drive card. We don't want to overload the engines."

Hannah looked at the text scrolling fast on the screen. Her heart skipped a beat. There was engine code mixed with her Drive program. "Maybe you should do this. It's your design."

"It's both of our work now," Rowanda said. "Besides, you're too short to reach." She reached up with her long arm and put her claws on a thin container sticking out of a slot. "Let me know when to pull it out."

The ship's engines started making a loud noise.

"It's initiating, we have to do it now!" Rowanda shouted over the din.

Hannah started typing fast. She entered her programmer password, and it granted her access. The ship began to shudder. She typed in an emergency shutdown code for the Drive and yelled at Rowanda, "Now!"

Rowanda yanked the case out of the slot as Hannah hit *Enter*. The whole ship did a violent lurch. Hannah grabbed the console and held on.

"The engines are overheating!" Rowanda yelled.

"I can cool them. This is like the fusion generator on ZOWS-UNI," Hannah said. She typed an override on the cooling system and set all the emergency coolant sprinklers on. The ship made an ugly noise like metal grinding, then gave a big shudder and stopped. A loud hissing was heard through the bulkheads.

Rowanda picked herself up off the floor and stumbled over to Hannah. "Good thinking. The amount of power for such a huge jump was overloading the current engine design. We just learned something important."

Hannah realized she was clinging to the console with a death grip. She managed to let go and flexed her fingers. "Are all the tests going to be like this?"

"Welcome to academia, Hannah." Rowanda laughed.

"I think pirating might be easier," Hannah said.

Hannah sat at the long table in the Boardroom of Zenith University. She felt self-conscious with her feet dangling, but she was excited to be at this meeting. Warbler sat on one side of her and Captain Greta on the other. George was tucked under her chair. She could hear his gears whirring a low hum. He couldn't see, but he was listening intently.

The Board consisted mainly of Larix and Wonkatoos. There was one other Greinder aside from Captain Greta. She sat at the very far end of the table.

Hannah watched in fascination as Rowanda presented the results of the test to the Board. The Larixs' leaves rustled like a gust of wind when she told them about the engines overheating and the unknown corporation hiring Jonko.

No one had come forward to claim the hijacking. Mega Corp denied it, which

George didn't believe. Professor Wally accused Zenith University of trying to take him out, but Hannah wondered, was there another player in the game?

After a long, heated discussion, the Board finally agreed to delay the tests until more work was done on the code and a full inquiry took place on the engine design. Hannah felt it was a positive step.

Her new semester was about to start. She was excited about her classes. And ready to keep working on the Jump Drive. As the Board began to shuffle out of the room, Hannah looked down at George.

"What do you think?"

"I think we are in for an interesting new semester," George said.

"It'll be a busy one," Warbler agreed. "You will have your plate full with your classes and your Drive project."

"I get to learn engine design next semester," Hannah said.

"Yes, good timing on that one." Rowanda came over.

"Is Larch going to be your study buddy?" Captain Greta asked.

Hannah nodded. "He asked me if I would."

"Well, he'd better get used to losing his leaves." George laughed. "What will happen to Professor Wally?"

"I imagine he's more determined now than ever," Rowanda said. "At least Mega Corp has agreed not to do a live test until after the semester is over. Gives both parties time."

"And the unknown competitor?" Warbler said.

"We'll cross that galaxy when it comes," Rowanda said.

"What have you and Chef got for my brain food for next semester, George?" Hannah smiled at him.

"Oh, we've been doing our research. Did you know that centipedes outrank grasshoppers on the nutrition scale? Chef has a special new burger in the works."

"Centipedes? They used to serve them on Roxan, where I'm from," Warbler said. "They're very dry if not soaked properly."

"Yes, they are great for long-term storage, but need to be rehydrated," George said. "But Chef will mix them with other ingredients."

"So, I'll be having a peanut-butter-ant-grasshopper-centipede burger?" Hannah tried not to wince.

"Oh, don't worry, Chef brought in an Earth delicacy to make it more like an Earth burger."

"You mean... Earth meat?" Hannah asked.

"Oh, that's not healthy," George scoffed. "We ordered the latest thing. Tofu!"

"Maybe it's good that the Jump Drive isn't fully functional yet," Warbler said.

They all burst out laughing.

Hannah shook her head, but smiled. It was just another day at ZOWS-UNI.

THOUGHTS ON *BRAVE NEW GIRLS*

"I know first-hand what it's like to face adversity in engineering. In spite of what might seem to be progress, there is still a gap in the level of support for girls and women to pursue careers and stay in the STEM fields. It is vital to have characters for girls to read about that show them it is normal to be smart and encourage them to develop their interests in science and engineering."

ABOUT THE AUTHOR

Mackenzie Reide graduated with an Honors Degree in Mechanical Engineering and a minor in Aerospace. While she was born and raised in Canada, she loves to travel, and has worked at the German Aerospace Center and the University of Stuttgart, Germany. She has also enjoyed being part of the Society of Women Engineers, doing programs in schools to encourage girls to express their love of math and physics.

When not staring into space, wishing she was traveling in *Dr. Who*'s TARDIS, she writes mystery-adventure and science fiction with strong female characters, for both kids and adults. Her novels include *The Mystery of Troll Creek*, *The Mask of the Troll*, and *The Mine Caper*, and short stories in the anthologies *Altered States of the Union*, *Infinite Dimensions*, and *Brave New Girls*.

Website: https://mackenziereide.com
Instagram: @mackenziereide

Illustration for "ZIPPED" by RM Nielsen.

Daphne Harris And The Time Jump

by Annie Gray

DAPHNE HARRIS AND THE TIME JUMP

ANNIE GRAY

ONE OF THE BLIMP'S ENGINES gave a warning cough before it gave up and quit right over the jungle island. The sound startled Daphne into grabbing the bench so tightly, she worried about splinters.

The pilot, an older woman named Lois with crow's feet at the edge of her eyes, laughed. "Oh, love, there's nothing to fear. I can fly this old beast of a ship until the fuel runs out in the other one. But that means you need to jump off the plank."

"The plank?" asked Daphne. The single piece of wood leading off the dock into the air looked unsafe.

"If I drop anchor I'll have to fix the broken engine, best if I keep moving." She turned to the other two girls, who were getting their parachutes out of the storage bin. "Are you sure this one can survive down there?" She threw a pointed look in Daphne's direction.

Before her friends could answer, Daphne said, "My parents are down there running some research at a dig site."

"We will keep her safe," answered Zuri, her dark brown eyes serious as she walked over to Daphne to help her strap on a parachute too. With her dark brown hair cut short, one would think Zuri would look like a boy or a child, but instead she looked mature. Only the goggles with cat ears resting on her head gave away her age. At 13, she was the youngest of the three of them. Daphne and Tatiana had already turned 14.

"We are coming to the landing spot," said Lois.

Daphne made a sound and whispered to Zuri, "I don't know if I can do this." Unlike her friends, she hadn't looked over the ship's edge to enjoy the view.

"Just like we practiced," Zuri whispered back.

"In a wind tunnel, not off the plank of a skyship." Daphne didn't bother to lower her voice.

But Zuri ignored her and said, "Remember, you are dying to show your parents your new invention." Zuri handed her the backpack and helped her put it on, backward on her chest. She didn't block Daphne from grabbing the cords for the chute.

Daphne really wanted to hug her parents. She hadn't seen them in over a year. When her mother and father had found out that there was a dig on a small island that combined her love of ancient culture and his love of DNA, they couldn't turn it down. A chance to study an extinct humanoid creature that was part human and part feline. Nothing was going to stop them.

"You haven't shared what it is with us." Tatiana sounded hurt. She stuffed her shiny black hair into a leather cap so it wouldn't whip everywhere once they jumped. Her eyes, the shape of half-moons, narrowed on the backpack. "Can we have a look before we jump?"

"Girls, you need to jump!" Lois called.

All three girls walked over to the plank. Daphne made the mistake of looking down. Over the edge of the skyship, the tops of trees stretched as far as her eyes could see. On shaking legs, she tried to move back, but her friends blocked the way.

Zuri, always the brave one, stepped forward. "See ya later," she said, and dropped from the edge of the plank.

"You are next," said Tatiana.

"Why me?" asked Daphne.

"I think you are going to chicken out, and this whole trip was your idea, Daphne."

"But you get to see your sister."

"I can see my sister later when her internship is over, at the end of summer, in the safety of my parents' house." Tatiana crossed her arms and gestured in the direction of the plank.

Daphne stepped onto the plank. "Just like class," she mumbled before taking a deep breath. Tatiana pushed her. "Why you...!" she yelled, but soon realized she'd closed her eyes. Slowly, she opened them and searched below her.

Zuri and Tatiana were her best friends. As much as she had wanted to see her parents, she hadn't been sure about taking this trip, but they had said they weren't going to let her miss the chance to spend the week at the dig.

Zuri, her tan suit out to catch the wind, waited for them. Doing what the instructor had taught, arms to the side, Daphne glided through the air faster and faster. Her heart rate matched her speed until she reached Zuri. Then she also spread her arms and legs out to catch the air.

Zuri grabbed her hand.

Tatiana soon grabbed her other one. They formed a circle. "Ready?" she asked, and started the countdown to three. On three, each girl let go, taking turns opening their parachutes in reverse alphabetical order of their first names. Zuri first, out of harm's way, Tatiana next, and Daphne last.

Daphne aimed for the clearing in the trees. Her parents' research camp wasn't far from the landing area. But she watched Zuri and Tatiana land and, in the process, messed up her aim. Her feet were headed straight for the trees. Below on the ground, her friends yelled directions, but it only made her clumsier.

Right into a tree and a different world. Birds, or at least what she thought were birds, called to each other. Nothing like the songbirds she heard through her dorm room's window at her boarding school. She had expected lush green everywhere, but once in the forest, the world looked dark under the emergent tall trees.

An insect buzzed by her head.

Somewhere, Zuri and Tatiana started calling her, and she shouted back. They kept this up until Zuri yelled, "I see your feet! I'm coming up." But then a few minutes later, Zuri shouted up with labored breath, "You picked the worst tree for me to climb."

"I'll pick a different tree next time," Daphne hollered back. Still, all she saw were the giant green leaves of the trees. "How did you find me?"

"The goggles I spent a buttload of money on," answered Zuri, as her head appeared. The goggles attached to cat ears covered half her face.

"Did they give you cat-like vision?" Daphne asked.

"I found you, didn't I?"

"I'm going to see if I can get this communicator to work," Tatiana shouted from the ground. "I'll tell them we are running late, and that Daphne is stuck in a tree."

"No... Don't tell..." She heard Tatiana trying to get through to the camp. "Too late."

Zuri placed the goggles on top of her head and looked at the tangled mess. "Only you."

Daphne rolled her eyes. "I know, another tale to share with your nosy family."

"My brothers love you, and all my stories about you," said Zuri. "Ready to climb down?" Zuri climbed closer. "Grab hold of something, and whatever you do, hold on for dear life."

Daphne climbed onto the closest limb and did her best to sit on the large branch, whose orange bark flaked onto her hands, but was otherwise smooth.

Zuri helped her climb out of her gear. But, of course, without the cords holding her in place, Daphne started to slip off the limb. "Help."

Zuri grabbed her by the straps of her backward backpack. "Careful. We don't need you to break something. Slowly move to the trunk of the tree and climb down. As best *you* can."

Taking her time, she stepped down, placing one foot at a time on each branch. But soon Daphne saw why Zuri had said it was a hard tree to climb. There weren't any limbs at the bottom of the tree. It looked like about a five-foot drop.

Zuri jumped down like it was nothing. "Your turn, soft landing."

"Soft landing? It's the ground."

"She means don't tense up." Tatiana came into view with the communicator in her hand. "I couldn't get anyone."

No way was she jumping down! Instead, Daphne tried to wrap her arms around the base of the tree and slide down. She slid a few inches before losing her grip. She fell backward hard on her back, her legs and arms in the air like a dead bug. Her friends laughed until they saw she wasn't moving.

"Dee?" Both of them leaned over her.

"Are you all right?" Tatiana asked, offering her hand. She waited for Daphne to take her hand before pulling her up.

Daphne made a mental check to see if anything hurt. "Okay," she said, with relief. "I'm fine."

"Good, we need to get to the camp before dark," said Tatiana. "Nell told me about the things that come out at night. We don't want to meet them, okay?"

"Got it," she answered.

Zuri and Tatiana put away their parachutes, but Daphne's was still hidden in the tree. She checked her bag to make sure nothing was broken. When she'd packed it, she had wrapped her invention in a bunch of soft rags.

"Are you going to tell us about your invention?" Tatiana asked.

"I...."

Before she could answer, Tatiana asked, "Still scared of someone stealing your idea?"

With a thump, Daphne's backpack hit her spine; she'd put it on the correct way, since she was no longer skydiving. "I don't want my muse to run away."

"Oh, right, you believe your ideas come from some mythical being."

With a slow intake of air, Daphne answered, "They come from somewhere."

"You are an intelligent person..."

Zuri spoke up before Tatiana could say anything hurtful. "Stop."

"She started it," Tatiana said.

"I don't know how the two of you are friends."

"You," Daphne and Tatiana said at the same time, but instead of laughing they glared at each other.

Eyes rolling, Zuri turned back to the trail to camp. "Are we close?"

"I hope so," Tatiana answered.

Daphne took a moment to put her backpack down and pulled out her invention, ready to show her father the second he greeted her. Tatiana and Zuri crowded in at the sight of it. The odd machine looked like a cross between a gun and a small musical instrument, with a bunch of knobs and wheels. A clock and an hourglass took up the middle, and a small tablet lay at the base.

They appeared awed over it—until the sound of a gunshot shrilled. The jungle went silent for a second as the birds stopped calling.

The girls exchanged looks, and Daphne started to rush forward, but Zuri grabbed her backpack and jerked her back. Zuri raised her fist. *Hold.* Like they were in the military.

Zuri took the lead and gestured over her shoulder for them to follow her at a slow pace.

Daphne's legs shook under her. She wanted to run toward her parents. To know they were okay. Through the large plants and green leaves, they moved. Up ahead, all had grown silent.

Once past the overgrowth, the view opened up. Fire pits were set up to form a circle around the tents spread out in the middle. A huge skyship with a blimp hung above it all. Smaller ships were to the right and left of it. The ships were shiny and new, a strong contrast to the rundown ship with only one working engine that they had just jumped from. An anchor at some point had been dropped, and had torn up the ground before finding a resting spot. Three rope ladders reached down to the ground. Underneath stood five men who weren't men.

Tiger heads on bodies of men dressed in tan pants and vests. Their well-toned arms held guns. The kinds that were illegal to have. The magazines were large, and the belts of ammo were touching the ground.

All around the camp, human men ransacked the tents as if looking for something. Two men dressed in sketchy clothing and wearing ammo belts crisscrossed in front, and pulled out Daphne's parents from one of the larger tents. "Found them!"

Her father, Dr. Jordan Harris, pulled his arm from the grip of one of the men. His glasses were crooked on his nose and his face was red. He fixed his glasses and stood tall.

Her mother, Dr. Rose Harris, stood next to her husband, a head shorter. She wore a plain brown dress with a belt of vials around her waist. Most likely full of dirt samples from the dig.

A man stepped toward them. With a top hat and a vest of gold and burgundy over a black long-sleeved shirt and pants, he looked out of place in the humid jungle and among his sky-bandit crew. He pointed his handgun at Daphne's father. "Kneel," the man commanded in a deep voice. Her mother and other members of the research team, including Tatiana's sister, were pushed as well. They all knelt.

Daphne's father's voice rose from the silence. "I won't give you any more DNA vessels for your army. That's not what my research is about."

The man in the suit laughed. "I'm sure if you won't, someone else will."

"They won't."

None of the research team moved.

"Too bad," said the man. A shot filled the air.

Her father jumped, but he didn't look away.

Daphne pressed her lips together to avoid crying out when her mother fell to the ground. Her father's screams rang in her ears; she pushed her fingers into her invention. It made a noise as she unintentionally pressed one of the buttons. The hourglass turned, and the hands on the clock's face moved backward. Around her, the air grew cold, just like when she got it to work before. As a blue light shined from her device, she heard, "Hey, there's more," and looked up to see a teenage boy with windblown blond hair running toward them. But the scenery changed, back to hanging in the tree.

Only this time…

"What the heck just happened?" asked Zuri.

"Nell!" yelled Tatiana, who was in the tree with Daphne and Zuri. Not on the ground like before.

Daphne didn't think, just pulled at the gear until she broke free of the parachute. Reached for the closest branch and climbed down. "I need to get there before…" She jumped to the ground on her side. Zuri and Tatiana were right behind her.

"Daphne!" Zuri grabbed her.

"I invented a time machine. It only moves into the past, anywhere from 10 to 30 minutes earlier. We need to get to them before…" She couldn't say it.

She ran toward the camp, ignoring her friends' warnings. And tripped over the large roots running along the ground. Her only thought: *before.*

A gunshot, and then another, came from the direction of the camp. Someone pulled at her backpack. Tatiana, with her eyes full of tears, pulled out the invention. "Again."

Back in the tree.

Zuri with her cat goggles got in Daphne's face. "How does this thing work?"

Out of her gear and down to the ground, this time with a soft landing. "I trapped a wormhole," Daphne answered.

"You what?" asked Tatiana as she landed too. Zuri was right behind her.

"You know how some company figured out how to create an artificial one?"

"Yeah..." Tatiana said, unsure.

"I have one trapped in here." Daphne pulled it out of her bag.

"That's impossible."

"And yet."

"How are we going to save them?" Tatiana asked. Then a gun fired at close range.

Tatiana's eyes grew in shock, and she fell to the ground. Behind her, the teenage boy stood, a gun pointed at where Tatiana had been.

How...? thought Daphne, but she didn't have the chance to think it out.

"Run!" Zuri yelled.

"He... He..." Daphne tried to run, but stumbled.

The boy fired the gun again.

He's getting pulled into the jumps too, she realized.

Zuri ducked. "Daphne, he's going to..."

Daphne pushed the button on the machine. This time, it took her to the ground under the tree.

"Tatiana!" she cried, and grabbed her in a hug. "At the next jump, get the machine out of my backpack, okay?" she whispered, as the boy appeared behind her friend.

"Okay... what..."

But Daphne didn't let Tatiana say any more before she reached into her bag and pushed the machine again. They were in the air. No one had released their parachutes yet. The boy was screaming but seemed to know what to do, and started to glide right at them. He grabbed onto Zuri.

But Tatiana pulled at her bag and got it open. "Push the green knob!" Daphne hoped Tatiana heard her.

They stood on the deck of the skyship.

"Lois," she called to the pilot, "get your gun."

But there was a click of someone pulling back the hammer of a weapon. The boy pointed a handgun at her. Up close, he looked a few years older than her.

16, maybe. Hard to tell with his skin tanned from a long time on the deck of a skyship.

"I have one question," he said.

"Just one. I'm lucky," Daphne tried to joke.

He smirked and walked up to her, pressed the barrel of the gun into the side of her neck, grabbed her bag with his free hand, and pulled out the machine.

"Pilot, if you know what is best for your little friend here, you'll put down that gun and get us to the camp."

Lois nodded, placed the gun on the deck floor, and started steering the skyship.

He looked Daphne right in the eyes. "How the blazes did I get here?"

Daphne didn't answer, and neither did the other girls. He looked over the device in his hand. "From the clock and the hourglass with real sand in it, I would say this is... somehow... a time machine." His eyes were bright. "Did we move in time?"

"Maybe an hour in the past," she said.

A man's voice sounded over a communicator that was attached to his shoulder by some kind of leather-looking armor. The man called him "Marco," but that was the only thing she understood; the rest of it was in a different language. He answered and then turned to them. "The three of you sit over there." He pointed at the bench where they'd sat earlier.

"He told someone to tell his father to spare the researcher, that he found something worth the wait," Tatiana whispered to Daphne and Zuri.

"Let's hope his father listens," Daphne said, and licked her dry lips.

Marco gestured at the machine. "How does this thing work?"

"It extends an artificial wormhole," Daphne answered, and started to tell him more, but Tatiana stomped down on her foot.

She whispered, "You don't need to show off."

"It's a long answer," Daphne said.

"One I'm sure my father would want to hear," Marco said.

"Your father..."

"Shot that old man? Yes." He watched her for her reaction.

Daphne's eyes met his cold brown ones, and she tried not to react, but her heart beat in her throat. He looked away first. His fingers moved close to the buttons, and all of them yelled, "Don't!"

It startled him. The machine dropped from his hands.

One of the wheels broke off and rolled toward Daphne's boot. No one made a sound as it hit its side and fell over. Still, it took a few seconds to stop moving, like a coin coming to the end of a spin. She picked it up. Her stomach turned as she put it in her bag.

"I'm sure that was nothing," said Marco, and he picked up the machine. He placed it in his bag, but as he did, it started making a beeping sound.

"Can I...?" Daphne began.

"No," he answered. "You'll just try to escape."

"We are here," said Lois. She pulled a lever, and below their feet, the floor groaned as the anchor and its chain dropped.

"Now the ropes," he commanded.

Lois pulled another lever, and without warning, the floor between them swung open, with the rope ladders falling to the ground.

Marco directed the gun at Lois. "You first."

"But I need..."

"The ship isn't going anywhere," he yelled at the older woman, "and I don't want any funny business. Down."

Lois climbed down.

"Cat ears is next."

Zuri moved.

Next went Tatiana. Daphne followed, putting one foot down. Tatiana placed her hand on the back of Daphne's foot and guided it to the right spot on the rope ladder. Daphne stepped back with her other foot and arranged her feet on the same step. Her whole being shook as she moved from the safety of the deck onto the rope ladder.

She didn't fall.

With that, she took her time scaling down.

Marco kept pace with her. One misstep would send him toward the ground, but she wasn't that kind of person, so she pushed the thought away.

It surprised her when she finally reached the earth. A sigh of relief didn't come, because she turned around to find one of the tiger men aiming his large gun at her. All her friends had guns trained on them. "Join the researchers," said Marco once he'd reached the ground.

Daphne's parents, Nell, and the rest of the group were still alive.

"Kneel," someone commanded.

"What's that annoying noise?" asked the man.

"The pale girl invented a time machine," Marco answered, and pulled it out of his bag.

The man gave a bark of laughter and reached for it. "This is a time machine? This little thing?"

"I have seen it work," Marco answered with a big grin on his face.

"Show me."

But Marco had no clue. In fact, the beeping multiplied when he messed with it.

"Girl," the man said, and looked right at Daphne. "Show me."

One of the tiger men pressed his gun to the back of her head. With no choice, she stood and took her invention from Marco.

"Careful," he warned.

The number on the tablet was 2,000. When the missing wheel had been knocked off, the machine had turned. The wormhole had been split in two, and then every wormhole after that was, too. The number of wormholes kept growing. The device beeped every time the number changed.

Trying not to react, Daphne put in the code to set up travel mode. The beeping stopped. The next trip would send the travelers into over 2,000 wormholes.

Marco and his father grinned at each other when she handed it back to him.

"Just think what I could do," said the man, as Daphne stepped back toward the group.

"Daphne, what have you done?" she heard her father ask, but she couldn't take her eyes off the pair.

The tiger mens' curiosity drew them closer to the device.

No one paid attention to Daphne as she grabbed her parents. "We need to move back, out of range. 12 feet. Move!"

The group moved slower than she'd have liked. Her eyes moved to Zuri and Tatiana. "Get up!"

She got her parents up, as well as the other two older researchers, and pulled them toward the fire pits behind the tents.

Their movement drew the attention of the tiger men.

A blue light formed around Marco and his father. Marco's scream soon followed.

"Don't stop, or that will be us!" Daphne yelled. Some of the tiger men heard her and tried to run, but it was too late. The blue light swallowed them.

Her father pushed her and her mother back, and all three tripped. The blue light vanished just as they hit the ground.

Daphne checked on her parents. Neither of them looked like they had missing limbs. "Are all of you okay?" she asked.

"My shoes no longer have soles," answered her father. "Otherwise I'm okay." He pulled at his boots. They fell apart.

"I'm okay," answered her mother.

"Us too," said Zuri.

The rest of the group had made it to the wood piles.

"Are they dead?" asked Tatiana.

"My guess is they are jumping through 2,000 or more wormholes. Forever jumping through time, but getting nowhere."

"So how are we going to get back on the skyship?" asked Lois.

They looked up to see that parts of the rope ladders were missing.

"I'll come up with something," answered Daphne.

"Something safe, Dee," said her mother, and kissed her on the cheek.

"So, no flying device?" Daphne joked.

"No wormholes." Her father grabbed both of them in a group hug.

Only, she did have one idea about the wormholes…

THOUGHTS ON *BRAVE NEW GIRLS*

"*Brave New Girls* has given me the opportunity to fulfill two of my writing dreams. I have always wanted to write for young people, to give them stories to fuel their imagination, and give them hope for the future."

ABOUT THE AUTHOR

Annie Gray, a hard-of-hearing writer from Alabama, lives within driving distance to the U.S. Space and Rocket Center. She loves being an aunt to her ambitious nephew and a dog mama to her energetic standard poodle. When she isn't writing, she's either spending time with her family or walking the dog. Her two short stories "Wendy's Findings" and "Riley's Rival" are published in earlier editions of *Brave New Girls*.

Illustration for "Daphne Harris and the Time Jump" by RM Nielsen.

The adventures of LUCY TYME-WALKER

Tim Tobin

THE ADVENTURES OF LUCY TYME-WALKER

TIM TOBIN

Following three successful shakedown cruises, the luxury Star Liner *Mosaic* settled into Martian orbit and began to load passengers arriving on shuttles. After the excited travelers located their quarters, they began to explore the huge vessel that would be their home for the next four months as they soared at faster-than-the-speed-of-light among the stars of the galaxy. The delighted passengers included Captain Dan Tyme-Walker's family.

In awe of the sheer size of the *Mosaic*, and astounded by the sumptuous staterooms and suites, every tourist wanted to see the bubbles—flexible structures emanating from the outside hull that housed most of the entertainment equipment and events. Bubbles could be inflated to accommodate a concert, for example, and then repurposed as a zero-gravity playground for children. The Tyme-Walkers' daughters did their homework, and knew exactly which bubble they wanted to experience first.

The fifteen-year-old pilot of the space cart jammed the accelerator full open and corkscrewed to the top of the racing bubble. An instant before hitting the apex, she veered to the left, and then skimmed the circumference, following the course around the sphere. Up and down, across, sometimes inches away from her competitors, the girl approached the finish line with a flourish of multicolored smoke. An automated checkered flag signaled her win as Lucy slammed on the retro brakes, did a one-eighty, and eased into the waiting socket on the charger port, just like laying a baby in a cradle.

Her kid sister, Jodie—four years her junior, skinny, gangly, with a mop of blond curls—whooped and hollered at Lucy's success. Their parents, Dan and JoBeth Tyme-Walker, applauded enthusiastically and greeted the champion with a hug.

"Well, girls, that's two-for-two today. Good work, both of you! Dinner, anyone?"

The family caught the high-speed tram that dropped them amidships on restaurant row. The Star Liner *Mosaic* offered meals ranging from burgers and fries to five-star dining. The girls voted for pizza, but Captain Dan Tyme-Walker had duty at the Captain's table in the Szechuan restaurant. Taking pity on the girls, Dan and JoBeth let them get a pizza.

Pizza, wings, and chicken fingers recharged Jodie's battery. Ready for another adventure, Jodie prodded her sister.

"C'mon, Lucy, let's go to the zero-grav bubble. Please. Please."

With research still to read, Lucy complained a bit, but, unable to disappoint her little sister, agreed. She took a moment to arrange her auburn hair into a ponytail, and then the girls leaped aboard a speeding tram car and maneuvered themselves through car after car until they settled in the nose of the train where they watched the amenities of the *Mosaic* flash by. Jodie checked the board for their stop and elbow bumped the *Exit* button. The girls slipped into a departure pod and, as the train flew by the zero-grav bubble, it ejected the pod, which landed gently at the portal to the bubble.

While life-guard droids wearing jetpacks patrolled the huge bubble, people rested on handholds attached to the surface while springboards randomly threw elated passengers around the bubble, and massive air guns tossed human cannonballs everywhere. Dodging other laughing and shrieking patrons, Jodie looked up to find herself on a collision course with a stout woman. Unable to dodge the woman, Jodie braced herself. At the last possible moment, Lucy flew by, grabbed Jodie's belt, and hoisted herself onto her sister's back. The change in momentum avoided a crash, and Lucy rode a laughing Jodie like a horse around the bubble.

With the infinite energy of a child, Jodie cajoled her mom into a swim in the earth-grav bubble—and then an ice cream cone.

After the big dinner and bubble play, Lucy feigned exhaustion and, back in their suite, commanded the droid Jerome to fetch her research. Jerome was one of four hundred Weeble-model androids of various shapes, sizes, and functions that crewed the *Mosaic*. It was the first time an artificial crew outnumbered the human staff. Named after an antique Earth toy, the droids used conical bottoms to provide stability in the ship's bubbles.

Meanwhile, Captain Dan Tyme-Walker took the bridge, while his first officer greeted arriving passengers, who were boarding the *Mosaic* to play among the stars of the Milky Way on the ship's maiden voyage. With the ship's three shakedown cruises completed, the captain declared a holiday for the crew and support staff, but tonight ended the festivities and began the serious work of operating a luxury liner capable of Faster-Than-Light, or FTL, 2.5. Scheduled for a noon departure, the *Mosaic* hummed with power and activity.

Two weeks earlier

While Lucy's parents met the administrative and financial officers of the Sorbonne, Lucy and Jodie explored the vast Parisian campus and finally visited the sprawling library. Leaving Jodie in the Young Adult section reading the latest book by her favorite author, Gail Patrick, Lucy roamed the stacks. Overwhelmed by the collection of books and research that reached floor-to-ceiling on five levels, Lucy stepped back in time, sometimes hundreds of years. Books gave way to boxes containing research on topics as diverse as the university itself.

Moving backward five hundred years to the 22nd century, Lucy discovered a dust-covered, sealed orange box, little different from dozens of others. The topic, carefully printed on the box top, *The Nature of Time*, caught her eye.

Cosmology intrigued the teenager, who planned to study the mathematics of astrophysics, and grapple with questions of infinity and the fate of the universe. Time, Lucy knew, still defied explanation, so she noted the file identifier and stopped at the check-out desk.

Tapping a button on her wearable, Lucy showed her brand-new student identification to the librarian droid, who downloaded the research material. Anxious to examine the files, she prodded her reluctant sister and hustled to find Mom and Dad.

2180 A.D.—500 years earlier

Dr. Stephan Penske, a physicist at the Sorbonne, conducted research into the nature of time. Convinced that time was made of particles similar to electromagnetic radiation and photons, he named the undiscovered particle the *kairon* after the Greek word meaning "The Supreme Moment."

Penske reasoned that if time was a particle, like a photon, then those particles could be manipulated, and time itself changed. Using historical data from a very large particle collider of the day, he finally detected a kairon, just as his mathematics predicted.

The scientist conducted a series of experiments, using a vehicle he assembled that resembled a raft. First using stones of various sizes, he sent the raft into time. It automatically returned two minutes later. He repeated the experiment with larger and larger rocks, until he used a piece of concrete about the weight of a man. All came back unchanged.

Penske's next experiment used his dog, Gus, a lovable golden retriever. When Gus returned unharmed and woofed his approval, Penske approached the Sorbonne regents for approval to use a human subject.

Fearful of failure and loss of prestige in the scientific community, the Sorbonne rejected Penske's application and told him to shut down his research.

Undeterred, the researcher decided to experiment on himself. His lab assistants recorded the session:

They whispered a short prayer and Penske began the final countdown.

5... The raft vibrated as the Time modulators came online.

4... The assistants hollered, "Good luck!"

3, 2, 1... Penske pressed and held the kairon injection switch.

The raft shimmered for an instant and then Penske disappeared. He did not return. After a year of daily monitoring, the university canceled all research into the nature of time.

Present

Lucy squeezed a couple of buttons on the wearable that was slung around her neck. Instantly, the far wall of her room illuminated with Dr. Penske's mathematics of Time. The opposing wall displayed his research publications and notes. Lucy reviewed everything Penske had learned about time, but she knew familiarity did not equate to understanding.

Over the previous two weeks, Lucy had studied Penske's theories, pondered his equations, and reviewed the experiments that apparently proved time was made of particles.

Tonight, she studied familiar territory, even floating on a chair to get a better look at the Cambria font of mathematical symbols. The partial differential equations that predicted the energy produced by the kairon particle especially intrigued her.

Still uneasy about the math, but glad when Jodie interrupted and asked if she could come in, Lucy started to respond.

"Sure, sis, I need a..."

Then came Lucy's supreme moment, her *aha* insight.

"Oh my gosh!" she exclaimed. "I know what to do."

She flicked the *Edit* button and went to work on the math.

As the *Mosaic* neared Boreas, its first port of call, the captain eased the starship out of FTL, engaged the nuclear turbos, and settled the ship into orbit. Named after the Greek god of winter, and first settled a hundred years earlier to exploit the ample water and mineral supply of the planet, Boreas provided settlers a world on the very fringe of its solar system's Goldilocks zone, an almost-uninhabitable place of perpetual snow, ice, and storms. For tourists and extreme sports enthusiasts, Boreas offered a place of beauty and death-defying challenges.

Passengers crowded the observation bubbles as server droids zipped among them, delivering drinks and hors d'oeuvres. Pamela Young, the cruise director, pointed out the perpetually frozen waterfalls, colored by the minerals from the surface far below the ice and snow, and Mt. Everest, which towered three times higher than its namesake on Earth. Shortly, Young announced that shuttles stood by to take adventurers to the Edmund Hillary Lodge, the jump-off point for winter activities of all kinds.

Lucy and Jodie had studied the brochures in advance and decided on the anti-grav rocket-propelled snowmobiles. The advertising promised thrills on a twenty-kilometer course, with high-speed straightaways, near-vertical drops, and gut-wrenching hairpin turns. Almost first in line, they caught the first shuttle and beat the crowds to the snowmobile hut.

The attending droid checked them out and gave them the instructions and rules of the course. Then the sisters donned masks and gloves, started their sleds, and roared onto the course, hitting 160 kph almost immediately. A floating overhead sign signaled a sharp turn and drop ahead. Lucy backed off the throttle a bit, but Jodie punched it, flew past her sister, and lost control. The snowmobile flew end-over-end in one direction, while Jodie cartwheeled several times in the air and then disappeared into a snowbank.

Jodie whipped her machine around, stood on the brakes, and made a perfect skid stop inches from where Jodie was digging herself out of the snow. First came her cap and blond curls, then her nose and mouth, both spitting out snow.

"Lucy," she said. "That was a real bottom buster. Let's do it again!"

On the bridge blister, Captain Dan Tyme-Walker had cringed when he'd learned of his daughters' legendary antics. But now, twenty-four hours later, he also cringed when a red lamp on the main dashboard signaled an overheating problem in the main FTL drive. Concerned, but not very worried, the captain knew the triple-redundant FTL drives shared no components in common.

Commander Jeff Clark, the ship's executive officer, reminded Tyme-Walker that the *Mosaic* had used a different FTL drive on the three shakedown voyages. If there was an inherent failure linked to length of service, all three drives could fail, stranding the *Mosaic* plus its passengers and crew in deep space. Tyme-Walker called Lucy, a gifted mathematician and engineer, and asked her to report to the engine room.

"But Dad," she protested, "I'm in the middle of something important."

"Lucy, please don't argue. Just get to the engine room and hurry, okay?"

Reading the tension in her father's voice, Lucy departed and caught the tram to Engineering.

A transparent blister on the *Mosaic*'s hull, the Engineering conference room hosted the Quick Reaction Team. Chief Engineering Officer Justin Phillips chaired the meeting. He acknowledged the problem when the stars became stationary instead of flashing by at FTL speeds.

He darkened the room and lit up a 3-D solid model of the *Mosaic*'s oval hull. He began the discussion with a refresher.

"As you know, the entire hull of our ship is a particle collider." The engineer flipped a switch, and the paths around the ship lit up.

"We accelerate fundamental particles of matter almost to the speed of light, and then smash them into other particles traveling in the opposite direction. That collision produces astounding amounts of energy, that we focus and shoot out the ejection port in our nose cone." The three ejection ports appeared on the model.

"This sudden burst of energy warps the space-time in front of us and creates a gravity well that we literally fall into. By adjusting the orientation of the nozzle in the ejection port, we can steer the ship at incredible velocity, up to Faster-Than-Light 2.5."

Getting to the heart of the matter, he continued, "Our monitors tell us that the ejection port for Drive One is overheating and is in imminent danger of failing. To be safe, I shut down FTL until we can understand our situation better."

Lucy put up her hand and asked, "Could the monitors be wrong? Failed in some way?"

"Unlikely. Diagnostics ran okay. We are doing a visual inspection of the ejection ports now. Results will be in shortly."

With that, the conference room table signaled an incoming call, and morphed from a wood veneer to a comms panel. Phillips poked a button, and the image of Victor Stebnisky, the officer inspecting the ports, appeared. The crowd began to fidget, cough, and shuffle their feet. All three ports, in fact, showed cracking from overheating.

The only hope for the *Mosaic*, to fabricate a new ejection port, faded because the stranded vessel did not stock the exotic alloys required for the port. After all, the failure of a triple-FTL system defied reason.

"But, Dad!"

Dan Tyme-Walker held up his hand to quiet his daughter.

"Look, Lucy. Regardless of the happenstance of our name, you are not attempting time travel."

"But Dad! It's not..."

"Lucy, enough! You are brilliant, a prodigy to be sure, and probably a savant. But you're just a teenager, and we're your parents, and what we say still goes. Understood? The best thing you can do is get to Engineering and put that magnificent mind to work."

Stung by her father's sharp words, Lucy responded the way many teen girls would. She stomped her foot, banged her bedroom door, and sulked in the dark room.

Shortly thereafter, little Jodie cracked the door. "Lucy?"

"Go away, Jodie. I'm not in the mood right now."

Jodie sidled into the room anyway, crawled onto Lucy's bed, and took her arm. Softly, she told Lucy what passengers were saying: that they were marooned with no help possible, and unless the drives could be repaired, everyone aboard would die.

"Lucy, I'm just a little scared," she said, and gripped Lucy's arm tightly.

Later that evening, Lucy found herself crammed into an access tunnel with Alan Turing, a teenaged apprentice engineer and friend, staring at the cracks in the ejection port. Suzie, a mini-droid, held the torch so they could both see the cracks visible to the naked eye. Looking at the useless equipment, Lucy exhaled, and Alan sighed. *Not repairable*, they agreed, and they began to edge backward out of the tunnel. Lucy noticed the young man's arm linger on hers as they squeezed out.

Dejected, Lucy called up the solid model of the *Mosaic* and inspected every inch. Alan, meanwhile, examined an engineering droid named Scotty, and wondered aloud if they could cannibalize parts from a droid. That bit of excitement turned sour after they studied the droid schematics that showed industrial-strength, but not space-rated, parts.

Turning back to the space liner model suspended in midair, Lucy tried something else and displayed all the entertainment bubbles and operational blisters. As she paced around the model, a design assembled itself in her mind.

"Alan," she asked. "Do you know how a bubble works?"

"Sure. A thin film is inflated and reinforced by a force field that withstands the rigors of outer... Holy smokes, you've got it. We can make an ejection port bubble. That should work fine."

Not ready to declare victory quite yet, Lucy asked him about materials.

"Not a problem, we've got plenty. And if we have to, we can decommission an existing bubble for its parts."

Lucy whooped and high-fived Alan, and then called her dad.

The final design and fabrication took several days, and then several more were needed to test and install the new port. Lucy's wearable buzzed with a call from Alan, telling her he was embarking on the space walk to remove the nozzle from Ejection Port One.

"Lucky you," she teased. "Wish I was going."

"If you want, come watch from Entertainment Bubble Two."

Lucy hopped aboard the tram, rode to the very front of the ship, and entered the grav bubble, just in time to see Alan and Chief Phillips emerge from the airlock and step out into space. Their grav boots allowed them to walk upright, and they hooked their safety lines to the railing that ran the length of the *Mosaic*'s hull. An untethered engineering droid named Michelle carried the toolbox.

Monitoring the conversation, Lucy chewed a fingernail.

"Okay," said Phillips. "Ready to detach the nozzle. Michelle, size four wrench."

Alan gripped the nozzle, and Phillips struggled with the wrench. He got it on the third try and loosened the nozzle. A brilliant flash of residual energy erupted from the ejection port, tearing it into thousands of boiling hot and razor-sharp pieces.

A spinning shard tore Alan's safety cable, and he drifted off the hull. A large splinter cut Michelle's head section off, and left the droid spinning uselessly in space. Phillips immediately announced an emergency and turned to help Alan, but hundreds of small fragments pierced his suit and oxygen line. The emergency droid Charles popped out of the airlock and rushed to aid the chief. Charles used his propulsion unit to haul the engineer back aboard the ship. The airlock closed, leaving Alan floating further and further away in space.

Lucy screamed into the intercom as she hurled herself onto the tram toward the airlock.

"I've got this!"

Her father came on the air. "Stay put, Lucy, that's an order."

"Alan's my friend, Dad. I'm going."

Steaming at Lucy's insolence, but agreeing with her, he called the airlock droids to run full diagnostics and help Lucy.

A few moments later, Lucy wriggled into the tight-fitting space suit. She had a brief flashback to videos showing ancient astronauts in their bulky environmental suits. Her suit used material similar to the bubbles and weighed ounces. A droid helped her strap on the propulsion backpack and an emergency oxygen tank.

She pronounced herself ready and reached for the airlock button. The droid stopped her and checked the diagnostic result and her suit's integrity. All green.

The droid hit the button and Lucy scrambled into the chamber. She grabbed a rescue droid named Alice, whacked the switch to override controlled decompression, and felt herself tumble into the vastness of the universe. She commanded her suit to locate Alan and plot an intercept course.

Her body righted itself relative to Alan, and her eyes found him, now just a mere dot hundreds of meters away. Engaging the maneuvering jets, Lucy began the rescue of her friend.

As she approached Alan, a buzz sounded and the enunciator warned her of low fuel. At the same time, the voice of Victor Stebnisky told her to wait for his lifeboat.

Instead, Lucy moved in front of Alan and looked him over, alarmed to see his head rolling to one side. She checked her fuel consumption—critical. She examined Alan's space suit. Fuel lines—severed. Stebnisky—still too far away to help.

She unbuckled Alice's fuel cell and plugged it into hers.

Alice's voice asked, "I won't be able to get back, will I?"

Lucy started telling herself, again and again, that Alice was a machine, just a machine. Yet, she thought she heard a hint of disappointment when Alice responded that she understood.

Back aboard the *Mosaic*, Chief Phillips and Alan recovered in the infirmary: Phillips from numerous cuts and Alan from a concussion. Lucy alternated between holding his hand and fretting like an old woman.

The backup engineering team, knowing what to expect, replaced the broken port and nozzle without further incident.

Finally, the captain announced that the *Mosaic* was heading back to Earth. Throughout the ship, cheers and applause greeted the captain and his daughter.

With the *Mosaic* safely enroute to Earth, Lucy worked in the rarely-used science blister. Scavenging parts from the lab and from Engineering, Lucy assembled a replica of Stephan Penske's time raft. Using Penske's diagrams and instructions on the wall display, she inspected the almost-finished machine. She still needed a supply of kairon particles.

She would have to bleed them from the collider embedded in the *Mosaic*'s hull. She abandoned her initial plan to hide in Engineering, and decided to use her notoriety instead. Accustomed to seeing Lucy, Chief Phillips and the engineering droids barely acknowledged her presence.

"Chief, do you mind if I take a look at the collider controls? Just curious."

The chief smiled at the smart young lass who'd saved his favorite apprentice and waved his approval, warning her, though, not to touch anything.

Lucy had learned the controls intimately from the training simulator, so she surreptitiously attached the battery hidden under her tunic to the collider, and set it to charge.

Lucy stood and looked for Phillips, a droid, or even Alan. With no one close by, Lucy selected the particle she wanted on the main control panel. Her battery beeped and glowed green as it filled with kairon particles. The completion beep brought engineering droid Joseph to inspect the control panel. All it found was Lucy strolling out of the blister.

Back in the science lab, with a fearful Jodie looking on, Lucy installed and checked the battery. She stowed several snacks and a jug of water, and declared the raft ready for its initial trial run. Both girls looked up when they heard a departure pod land outside the blister and both were astounded when their mother, JoBeth Tyme-Walker, professor of Interstellar Oceanography at MIT, entered the lab.

Jodie, after seeing her mom motion her out with her chin, skedaddled on the double. Professor Tyme-Walker sat on one of the zero-grav stools and took Lucy's hands in hers.

"Lucy," she began. "You've let your confidence evolve into arrogance, and it does not befit you."

"But Mom, I think…"

"No, you're not thinking!" barked Professor Tyme-Walker. "What if you pushed that button and got lost in time, or ripped a hole in time, or even worse, tore a hole in our hull, killing everyone on board?

"I'm not the mathematician you are, but I read Penske's research, and it's junk science. A real scientist, even five hundred years ago, knows to publish his findings, have them peer reviewed and extended. Design and conduct experiments, lots of them, to be sure the results match the predictions. Human subjects are the very last thing, and with our advanced science droids, few human trials are ever necessary."

"But Mom, please let me finish. I think Penske may be alive and lost in the infinity of time. I found the flaw in his math. I know what he did wrong."

"After five hundred years! And you're willing to risk your life and everyone on the *Mosaic* on a hunch? Did you consider Jodie, who worships you? Chances are Penske died on that launch pad and the Sorbonne covered it up so they wouldn't lose their endowment."

Professor Tyme-Walker shoved her floating stool a few feet away from Lucy, took a breath, and went on.

"Your father is livid, beside himself. That's why I'm here. And, yes of course, he knows about you. Every inch of this ship is under surveillance, so stealing those particles alerted Chief Phillips and his droid. And something else, two men died, probably of heart attacks brought on by anxiety over being stranded in space, while you pouted in your room over this."

Professor Tyme-Walker regretted telling Lucy as soon as her lips moved, but the words tumbled out anyway. Lucy crumbled into a ball and burst into uncontrolled sobs. Her mother nudged her stool forward and wrapped her daughter in her arms.

"Oh, Mom, no, no, no. I'm so sorry. I just didn't realize."

"I'm sorry, Lucy. Those deaths aren't your fault. Both men were very old, over a hundred and twenty, and Doc Miller told us their time was short anyway. But it helps explain why your dad is in such a funk."

"How do I make this better?" wailed Lucy.

"Just let this time research go for now. After all, you haven't even taken a college course in physics yet. I know, I know, you'll be in honors courses before the semester is over, and I won't be surprised if your Ph.D thesis is on the nature of time."

A tiny smile crept over Lucy's face amid the tears as she nodded her agreement.

Professor Tyme-Walker relaxed and even chuckled at this small return to normalcy.

"You feel like lunch? Call Jodie and decide where you guys want to go."

⁂

Two nights into the return trip, Lucy took a little longer than usual to dress while Jodie helped her with her hair and giggled like little sisters did when keeping a secret. Finally, Lucy twirled into the living room of their suite.

"Ta-da."

Wearing a sky-blue jumper, plum tights, and matching ribbons in her hair, with just a touch of makeup, Lucy announced she had a date.

JoBeth coughed, and Dan choked on his drink, but finally managed to croak, "With whom?"

Lucy barely had time to reply when the doorbell rang. Jodie beat Lucy to the door and opened it to reveal a handsome young engineer-to-be, decked out in his dress blues.

Professor Tyme-Walker masked her smile behind a faux frown and asked Alan where they were going.

"Le Fouquet's Café, and then to the video bubble for vintage movie night."

On the way out, Lucy shot her parents a look. "We're going to see *The Time Machine*."

⁂

"Hey, sis," called Jodie. "The new 3-D bumper cars are ready in Zero Grav Bubble Four. Wanna go?"

After staring at Penske's equations for the hundredth and final time, Lucy clicked her wall off and hollered, "Last one there's a rotten egg."

Dan and JoBeth Tyme-Walker smiled at each other as an auburn ponytail chased blond curls out the door, happy these two were theirs.

⁂

THOUGHTS ON *BRAVE NEW GIRLS*

"On my final project before retiring, I managed 60 engineers, only four of whom were women. Even though the company actively recruited female engineers, few qualified candidates emerged. The four women who were on the project held key roles. One was my chief engineer, one was my integration manager, and the other two were experienced, well-respected engineers. I applaud *Brave New Girls'* emphasis on STEM education for women and empowering gender equality."

ABOUT THE AUTHOR

Mr. Tobin has a degree in mathematics from LaSalle College and is retired from L-3 Communications. He lives with his wife MaryAnn in Voorhees, NJ. His two grandchildren, Maggie (13) and Shawn (16) are the joys of his life. Mr. Tobin continues his education by attending classes at Camden County College, where he also volunteers his time. Over ninety of his stories/poems appear in print and online. Most recently, his works have been accepted by Brave New Girls, Wicked Shadow Press, Black Hare Press, Trembling With Fear, Yellow Mama, and B Cubed Press.

Tim Tobin would like to dedicate his work to Denise Weiss, who told him the truth, and Linda Canataro, who embarrassed him with her insight.

Illustration for "The Adventures of Lucy Tyme-Walker" by Ben Falco.

THE INTERLOPER

BY
SCOTT
PINKOWSKI

THE INTERLOPER

SCOTT PINKOWSKI

R ÓISÍN HUFFED A DEEP BREATH as she reached the summit of Mount Corbin. The five-hundred-foot-tall outcrop of rock towered conspicuously over the flat plains of the western frontier. Her leg muscles aching, she gazed eastward toward Caespes Verde, the only northern colony on Villam Prime. The squat-looking living quarters, clustered below, cast long overlapping shadows; the binary suns had just commenced their daily climb.

Taking in the vista of the sprawling settlement that lay at the eastern foot of the hill, she fidgeted with the fasteners of her backpack. Two tightly-braided ropes of platinum hair hugged the contours of her scalp and tapered down her back. Squinting in the morning's glare, her icy azure eyes strained to cut through the dying gloom.

Beyond the metal-roofed homes and administrative buildings, shimmering rows of agricultural fields stretched out beyond the horizon. She could see the northern and southern frontiers from her vantage point, but the emerald bands of crops to the east stretched out endlessly.

She seated herself on a flat rock and shrugged out of her backpack. During her last expedition to Mount Corbin, she had observed a group of small, scaled creatures that she had not yet cataloged. This time, however, she was prepared. She took her omni-slate from her pack and turned it on. Swiping through a series of glowing screens, she found her fauna logbook.

She tapped the onscreen icon, and a gallery of hand-drawn sketches jumped into place, suspended in the air before her. She jabbed at the air, and a lucent array of display modules materialized. She was now ready to collect data on the hitherto unknown and unnamed creature.

She found it useful to compare the functional morphology of the Villamese creatures she'd observed to species on other worlds. Almost always, form followed function, and she could make good guesses as to what a new animal's behaviors might be by cross-referencing it to known species.

Lately, she'd been delving into the Sol-III Archives a lot. The archives of her parents' home world were the most complete. The millions of years of natural history that had been recorded there far exceeded those of any of the newly occupied colony worlds.

She'd lived her entire life on Villam Prime and knew little of her parents' planet of origin, except for what she could glean from the Archives. It seemed they never talked about their home; even when asked, they were always too busy to go into much detail.

After scouring the Sol Archives, the closest approximation she could find was a clever little thing called *Mustela putorius*. She had to admit their fuzzy appearance was a little cuter than the purple-scaled fellows she'd spied last week.

"Ferret," she said under her breath, remembering the common name of the Sol-III animal she'd been reading up on. "Maybe I'll name these noodle cats," she mused. Hopefully, any information gained today would fill in some of the blanks surrounding the nature of these creatures.

All she had to do now was wait.

After twenty minutes, there was still no sign of the playful imps, and her attention began to drift. The binary suns had risen higher, and Róisín decided to turn her back to the blazing glare. Now facing west, she gazed out at the flat expanse of nothingness beyond the western frontier. The terrain to the west was still shrouded in darkness, but as the overlapping shadows of Mount Corbin continued to recede, an abnormality caught her eye.

The sea of prairie grass, normally a rippling, unbroken tract of golden color, was woven through with veins of purple. She rummaged in her pack for her binoculars. Sure enough, she observed massive growths of a broad-leafed shrub peeking up over the prairie grass.

"Well, I've never seen anything like this," she whispered to herself. "I won't have time to get a specimen today." She jotted a note on the screen of her omni-slate with her stylus—adding to the dozens of forgotten reminders that had been piling up.

When her eyes returned to the golden sea of grass below, something caught her attention to the southwest. Off in the distance, six dark shapes were moving through the meadow, cutting a swath as they came. She raised the binoculars to her face.

Róisín let out a gasp. She knew the prairie grass on the western frontier was tall—over her head this time of year—but the six hulking shapes jutted above the undulating waves of grain like boulders. She estimated that these quadrupeds must be twice as tall as a man at their shoulders. They cut through the thick prairie like so many steamrollers, leaving a distinct path of trampled plants.

She quickly readied her omni-slate and began sketching the unknown beasts, alternating between her binoculars and her fervent flurries of scratching on the screen with her stylus. Her mind raced, and her hands trembled. She knew of no animals in the northern hemisphere larger than a dog. Even if no one else on this rock seemed interested, this was an exciting discovery.

Living on Villam Prime was rough-and-tumble. Everyone's efforts always seemed to be focused on farming. If you weren't planting, you were harvesting. If you weren't doing either, you were readying everything for the next planting. There was always something to fix. There was always something to resupply. Day in, day out. Around the clock and throughout the year. There was little time for exploration or quests for knowledge.

The Villamese at Caespes Verde seemed perfectly content scratching out their existence on their long ribbon of land on an otherwise desolate hemisphere. Róisín could not comprehend the depths of their lack of scientific curiosity. It irked her to her core. How could she have lived her whole life on this rock and *not* know of these beasts' existence? Not even a passing mention or rumor?

Her sketch gradually took shape. The beasts were bulky, although she got the impression much of their apparent bulk was comprised of a thick and hairlike plumage that covered their shoulders, head, and forelegs. When the brutes milled back and forth among the trampled stalks, she made note that their scaled hindlegs were slender and covered only in sparse, hollow-looking filaments. Their front feet were hidden by their shagginess, but their hind legs terminated in three-toed clawed feet.

Their two eyes were unblinking, round, and an abysmal black—like a spider's eyes. She estimated that each of their eyes was about as big around as a bicycle wheel.

"Unbelievable," she whispered to herself as she watched. Suddenly, her omni-slate emitted a bell-like chime. "Not now, Mom!"

Exasperated, she swiped at her screen. She seemed to be receiving a direct analog signal. *Probably Mom wondering where I am.*

She poked the screen and the recording played. Her face scrunched in confusion at the messy snippet. She replayed it and was no closer to deciphering the mysterious communication. "Let's clean this up, shall we?" she whispered as she adjusted the controls to filter out all the noise.

A low, bellowing voice croaked forth from the diminishing static. *"Aadvennaa."*

"What is this?" she scoffed. "Detect language," she commanded her omni-slate.

"Venniki," replied the omni-slate in its amicable female voice.

"What?" Róisín huffed.

The Venniki people were long extinct. Eons ago, the Venniki had traversed a large section of the galaxy and were responsible for countless discoveries and advancements in space travel. They'd been prodigious spacefarers once, but now they were nothing but a memory.

Róisín knew that Venniki was a dead language. She couldn't imagine why anyone near Villam Prime, or anywhere else for that matter, would be using it.

She paused, still dumbfounded. "Translate."

"Interloper," chimed the synthesized voice from her omni-slate.

She gazed back down at the prairie below. The beasts, who had been loosely grouped when she'd first seen them, had rearranged themselves with military precision. They stood in a perfectly straight line, abreast of each other. They all faced her, forming a perpendicular rank between herself and their point of origin.

Are they looking at me?

As she continued to watch, one by one they turned and trudged back the way they came.

Still reeling from the excitement of finding a new species, she hurriedly turned off her omni-slate and repacked it, along with her binoculars. *If I hurry, maybe Mom and Dad won't even know I was gone.* Róisín slung her backpack over her shoulders and prepared to make the downhill trek back to Caespes Verde.

※

Róisín walked up the driveway just as the family's hired farm hands were walking out. They usually stopped by to get instructions every morning from her dad before they began the twenty-minute drive to the family's tract. She must have been running a little later than she'd thought.

"Good morning, Liam. Good morning, Cormac," she said as she passed.

Liam, a blond, shaggy-headed boy of about seventeen, chuckled. "Your ma and da are lookin' for ya," he called over his shoulder as he continued toward his electric truck, which was pulled onto the narrow strip of lawn alongside the lodge.

"Better mind yourself, Ro," added Cormac, "or your gaffer's gonna eat the head off ya!" He smiled as he backpedaled to face her. All of sixteen years old, Cormac was lanky and dark-headed and had made an admirable attempt at growing facial hair, but had only managed to muster a few sprouts that looked like smears of dirt. (His dirtstache, Róisín called it.) He was in Róisín's class at school, and they had known each other since they were toddlers.

"Better mind *your*self. That's gonna be our boss someday," Liam shot back at him.

Both boys' uproarious laughter was clipped by the doors of the truck clunking shut.

Róisín reached the back door and hesitated, her hand hovering over the handle. She drew a heavy sigh. Before she could act further, the door burst open; her mother was on the threshold.

"Well, it's *so* nice of you to join us," her mother said, before spinning around and returning to the kitchen table, where she had piles of paperwork spread out. Róisín's mother was wiry and quick. Her frizzled red hair was tied back into a ponytail. A bundle of energy, she always seemed to be in motion.

"Where's the blasted copies of our certification renewal?" came her dad's bellowing voice from the next room.

"For pity's sake, Collin," her mom called to the doorway, "I have everything out here!"

He appeared in the doorway, grumbling and holding a coffee mug. He cracked a small smile when he saw Róisín. "Where have you been, Ro? We've got a lot of business to attend to today." Róisín's father was still broad at the shoulders, despite the years creeping up on him. His hair might have been thinner and his posture more stooped than when he'd been a young man, but his eyes were still sharp and shrewd.

Róisín took off her backpack and hung it on a hook near the back door, before rummaging inside it for her omni-slate. "I know, Dad. Time just got away from me."

Her mom examined her with tired eyes. "Off on one of your expeditions again, I assume?"

Róisín sheepishly nodded.

Her dad's face hardened. "You know you have—"

"I *did* all my chores already," interjected Róisín. "I was up before the suns."

Her mother and father exchanged a knowing look.

Her dad walked in and pulled up a seat, looking for a clear spot on the table to place his mug. He glanced up at Róisín, who was still lingering by the door. "You *know* you're going to have to familiarize yourself more with the inner workings of our tract operation if you're going to take things over someday?"

"And *you* know I have no interest in taking things over," Róisín said.

She braced herself for the lecture she knew was coming. She'd heard countless different variations of it since she was seven years old.

Her dad drew a deep breath. "Farming on Villam Prime is vital. So many are depending on us being efficient and productive. We feed the northern colony, we feed the southern colony, we even feed all the colonies on Praesidium Secundus and Argentum Prime."

"Science is *just* as vital! And it's sorely lacking on Villam," Róisín said.

Her mom looked over the top of her reading glasses. "You know life is simple on Villam. We don't have much need for science."

Róisín scoffed. "Don't have much need for science?" She ticked off her fingers. "If it weren't for science, you wouldn't have any of the technology you rely on every day. If it weren't for science, you wouldn't have as strong of an understanding of how to best care for your crops—whether you realize it or not. If it weren't for science, we wouldn't even be able to live here on Villam!"

Her dad was speechless for a moment.

"You let Eamon go off-world and pursue his dreams! Why can't I do the same without the massive guilt trip?"

Róisín's mom buried her face in her hands at the mention of Róisín's older brother, who had recently left Villam to play in an off-world rock band. "Ugh. That boy!"

"Well, it's not like we *let* him…" Róisín's dad mumbled.

Róisín's mom neatened a stack of papers in front of her. "Like I said, life is much simpler here than it was on Earth—"

"Earth?" Róisín said inquisitively.

"Oh, that's what we called home, back in the day," her dad said, waving a hand.

"Your home world was named after *dirt?*" Róisín smirked.

He sputtered. "Well… I don't know. It *might* be a sort of chicken-or-egg thing…"

"What's chicken?"

"Well, that's what we used to call… never mind. That's not important." Apparently sensing that his pleas would not move her any more that day than they had in the past nine years, he took the opportunity to change the subject. "So, what did you find on your expedition today? Did you catalog those little purple… things you were telling me about?"

Róisín's face lit up. "No, but I got something even better!" She turned on her omni-slate, and after a few swipes of the screen she jammed it into her father's hands.

He fumbled, rummaging in his breast pocket for his reading glasses. Placing the glasses onto his face, he frowned at the sketch.

"No, this can't be," he said. "You *saw* this?"

"Yeah."

"In real life?"

Róisín hesitated. "Yeah, why—"

"*Where* did you see this?" he asked, gazing back and forth between her and the sketch with a puzzled expression.

"I was on top of Mount Corbin this morning. They were just to the southwest."

"No, this can't be," he repeated.

Curious, Róisín's mother had gotten up to look over her husband's shoulder. Her expression was just as bewildered as his.

"This will make the sixty-third type of fauna I've discovered on Villam Prime," Róisín said proudly.

Her father looked gravely at her over the top of his glasses. "Sorry, Ro, but you didn't discover this one. This is a t'sukol beast scouting party."

Róisín's mouth hung open in shock. "But I've never seen these before."

"That's why I said it can't be," he said, staring at the sketch. "They're confined entirely to the southern hemisphere."

"Wait, you *know* about these things?" Róisín said. "You've known about megafauna on Villam Prime all along and you've never *told* me?" She scoffed. "You've been holding out on me, Dad!"

Her dad handed the omni-slate back to her. "This is unusual. This is more than unusual, it's downright weird. How could they have crossed the uninhabitable zone?"

Villam Prime had been a challenging world to colonize. It had large seas at the northern and southern poles. The single continent between the seas was a broad, unbroken swath of land, but the entire equatorial region, spanning several hundreds of kilometers north and south of the equator, was dry, hot, and uninhabitable.

There was one latitudinal band of habitability in the north, and one in the south. A narrow band within the northern habitability zone was much more than just habitable; it was a veritable oasis. This was why the site had been chosen for colonization in the first place, and why the farms of Caespes Verde were narrow and ribbon-shaped. The colony was a mere sixty kilometers wide, yet several hundreds of kilometers long.

"Tell me what you know," pleaded Róisín.

Her dad drew a deep breath. "T'sukol beasts are nomadic. They're almost constantly on the move. They circumnavigate the planet, west to east, every seven years. They only live in the south, but they always ranged outside of Castrum's northern frontier. There have been very few interactions between t'sukol beasts and humans, except for them being a mild curiosity every seven years."

Róisín scoffed. "A *mild* curiosity?"

He continued. "Their singular herd is massive. More like a horde than a herd. They probably number in the tens of millions. They follow their food—a specific plant. It lies dormant underground for years until the herd's thundering triggers its sudden emergence."

Róisín remembered the purple veins running through the prairie grass west of Mount Corbin. "Wait, I think I saw a new shrub out on the frontier!"

"*Ambiarctos electrodigitatus*," said her dad. "It's not supposed to grow up here."

Róisín stared in shock. Who was this man, and what had he done with her father? She'd never heard him refer to *anything* by its scientific name before.

"What? You didn't think your old man knew anything about science?" he said with a chuckle. "The southern colonists call it banshee weed."

Róisín nodded her approval at her father. "Plants can be said to migrate. Any plant lives under environmental constraints, and this *Ambiarctos electrodigitatus* would be no different. When those constraints change, the border of a plant species' distribution can move."

"Of course, you're exactly right, Ro."

"That must be what's happening to the t'sukol beasts' food source, and it's dragging them north with it."

Her father scratched his chin thoughtfully.

Róisín fidgeted with her omni-slate. "It's likely our two colonies' very existence and our farming practices that're bringing about the changes we're seeing."

"This is no time to point fingers—"

"I'm not! I'm just saying that this is *exactly* why science is so important on Villam Prime. We need to be making a greater effort to observe the world around us, and to attempt to exist without upsetting the fragile ecological balance."

"There must be a balance," conceded her father as he drained the last of the coffee from his mug. "You know, I've seen the beasts as a boy."

"You've been to the southern colony?" Róisín said.

"I was staying with a friend of the family in Castrum. They took the other kids and me to the northern frontier to see the t'sukol beasts. The horde stretched from the western horizon to the eastern horizon." He gestured grandly to his left and then his right. "And as far as the eye could see to the north. Most amazingly, the steady stream of beasts took a week to pass by."

"Why hasn't Castrum warned us about this? There's no way they don't know about this change."

Her dad shook his head slowly. "Ro, I'm sure even you know how isolated the northern and southern colonies have become from each other over the years. It didn't used to be this way."

"But this is a very serious matter. I don't care how strained relations between the northern and southern colonies are; we need to know. Don't you think this is very concerning? For us *and* the animals?" Róisín said.

Her father's eyebrows rose, and he nodded. "Yes. Very concerning. Just think of the damage that millions of eight-ton beasts would do if they tore through Caespus Verde. It'd ruin us all." He cracked a smile. "However, I'm confident that they'll range south of us and keep their distance from humans, just like they always have."

"But, Dad, I saw their food. You said they *follow* their food. It was practically at the foot of Mount Corbin. And you said so yourself, those six were a scouting party. Plus, there's something else. While I was watching them, my omni-slate picked up a—"

The back door burst open, and a young man in a long black trench coat stepped in and spread his arms wide. "I told ye I'd be back!"

"Eamon!" Róisín jumped up and rushed to embrace her brother.

Disentangling himself, he ruffled the top of her head. "Have you taken over the farm yet, Little Rose?" Eamon was a whole head taller than his little sister, but shared her long flaxen hair and piercing blue eyes.

Before Róisín could answer, her mother was savagely grabbing Eamon by the cheeks. "For pity's sake, Eamon, tell me you've given up the rock star life and are finally home for good—"

"Sorry, Mum, I've got a gig on the next system over. Thought I'd stop in for a quick visit."

"Oh well," she groaned. "Come here anyways," she said, as she clutched her son in a bear hug so powerful his face started to turn pink.

Their father was next. They shared a firm handshake, but Eamon yanked his dad in for a hug and a clap on the back. "Look outside, Da," whispered Eamon.

Their dad leaned in and looked over Eamon's shoulder through the open door. Outside was a glimmering red-and-chrome jumpship. Obviously, a very expensive and sporty mode of transportation. His jaw went slack, and he looked at his son. "Well, that's a *fine* piece of machinery, innit?"

The vectorcom unit chimed from the next room. "I'll get it," their mom said, before rushing out of the kitchen to answer.

"Well, come on in and have a seat," said their dad as he shuffled over to the cupboard to get a mug. "Do you want a cup of coffee? I'll fill you in on how the tract is doing."

"Sure, Da." Eamon shot a sideways glance to Róisín, who was stifling a snicker. "So," Eamon said as he pulled out a kitchen chair, "what's all the commotion about Caespes Verde?"

"What do you mean, son?"

"Something's got the townsfolk all riled up. There's practically a traffic jam all along the strip."

Róisín's mom appeared in the doorway, holding the vectorcom receiver. "Collin, it's Governor Umar." Her expression was grim. "They're putting out a general alarm. It's the beasts. He's calling an emergency council meeting for this evening." No sooner than she'd spoken, the howling wail of a siren wafted in from the open window.

***

That afternoon, Eamon took Róisín for a ride in his jumpship, and she convinced him that the summit of Mount Corbin would be a fitting place for them to catch up on old times. As small children, they had explored every inch of the conical outcrop together.

Róisín sat on her usual flat rock, and Eamon gazed out at the western frontier with his hands on his hips. His long hair whipped in the warm breeze. Even before they'd touched down, the change in the western frontier flora had been obvious. The veins of purple she'd observed just that morning had spread out into a nearly-unbroken sea of the invasive shrub.

To the east, Caespus Verde was abuzz with activity as its citizens bustled about, seemingly unsure of what the impending threat meant for them. Every thirty minutes, the Emergency Response Commission's sirens wailed for a solid minute. But to the west, there was no visible sign of the beasts themselves.

"So, this is really happening?" Eamon said.

Róisín drew a heavy sigh. "I've been combing the archives of Praesidium, Argentum, Atmos, Tenebrous… I've even checked Sol-III for good measure! I haven't found anything *remotely* similar to this."

"What do you think will happen?" Eamon said.

"I don't know, but I'm afraid. If Caespes Verde goes down, a lot of other colonies and outposts are going to go down with it."

Eamon breathed a low, mirthless laugh. "Da wasn't kidding when he said we feed half the people in the zone."

"'We?'" Róisín said. Eamon had always seemed to distance himself from his childhood home.

Eamon turned around. "You know how it is, Little Rose. Once from Catpiss Verde, *always* from Catpiss Verde."

Róisín grinned. "Mom always hated it when you called it that."

The corner of his mouth twitched. "I know. But you get my meaning. I'll never forget where I came from. If you ever make it off this rock, I hope you'll never forget that either. I'm here to help, even if it means I miss my gig and they fire me."

Róisín managed a smile, but her shoulders throbbed as anxiety seemed to steal her breath away. She'd always been frustrated living in a community that didn't understand her and had little use or patience for her curiosity. But she'd never felt as helpless as she did right now. "I appreciate that, brother, even if no one else knows what a big deal that is." She shook her head and shrugged. "What will we do?"

Eamon turned back to the expanse of purple. "I guess we wait to see what they come up with at the council meeting tonight."

Róisín scoffed. "Ugh. I'm so afraid that we're going to do something stupid! As a species, we don't have a very good track record with things like this. You know, Mom and Dad never talk about it, but we all know what happened to Sol-III. I fear we'll *never* learn."

Eamon looked down at his feet. "Well, we'd better head back. I'm surprised Mum hasn't pinged in, looking for us."

Like a bolt of lightning, an electric surge pulsed through Róisín's limbs. "I can't believe I forgot!" she exclaimed. Eamon's comment had dislodged the almost-forgotten memory of the odd transmission she'd received while atop Mount Corbin that morning. After recounting her experience to her brother, she asked him what he thought it meant and where it could have come from.

"That's really weird," he said. "And after you received the signal, the beasts stood in a straight line?"

Róisín pointed to the southwest. The trampled spot was almost entirely filled in with banshee weed. "At first, they were just milling around, but when I looked up after translating the signal, they were in a perfectly straight line. If I didn't know any better, I'd say they were looking at me. It was almost like they were in a defensive posture."

Eamon gazed at the trampled patch of prairie before turning to his sister. "Have you considered the possibility that it came from..." He nodded toward the empty frontier.

Róisín laughed. "From *them?*"

Eamon raised a single eyebrow, but otherwise his face was like stone.

Róisín gasped in shock. "Wait, you're serious?" Her mind raced. *Biological radio transmission? It's impossible,* she told herself, but a remote, nagging part of her mind was whispering that she should know better than to be so obstinate—that she should follow the facts wherever they led. "What?" she said. "Like their bodies were relaying a radio signal from somewhere else?"

Eamon shook his head slowly.

"You're suggesting that the signal was *originating* from them?"

Eamon turned back to stare into the nothingness. "It's not unheard of that animal species can do this."

"Well, it is to me," shot Róisín.

"There's a massive aquatic species that lives on Praefuro that can do it."

"Why don't I know anything about this?" Róisín said, before realizing that she already knew the answer. Her existence on Villam really was a sheltered one, and she often had to remind herself that she knew but a fraction of the wonders that existed in the galaxy. "Wait, Eamon. How do *you* know this?" Biology wasn't exactly one of his strong suits.

Eamon smiled. "I'm friends with a drummer from another band. And they incorporated the haunting songs from these animals into one of their albums. They made a special trip to Praefuro to set up their equipment to receive and record their transmissions."

Róisín made a mental note to read up on these aquatic singers. "All right, but my transmission was in Venniki. You're not suggesting that, first of all, these things are sapient…" She inwardly cringed at how crazy it all sounded, but at the same time her heart soared at the world of knowledge that such a discovery might open. "And second, that they somehow know a language that hasn't been used in—what—thousands of years?"

"Is it *that* crazy?" Eamon said. "You know as well as I do that there's no corner of this zone that the Venniki haven't been to first. Is it not possible that these things learned the language directly from the Venniki?" He leaned toward her. "After all, there's supposed to be some Venniki ruins right here on Villam Prime. Near the equator—from when the uninhabitable region was inhabitable."

Róisín was starting to get annoyed with all the historical and scientific facts that Eamon seemed to know that she didn't. He was the one who'd never seemed to take his studies seriously.

He shrugged. "So, the t'sukol beasts *could* have had direct contact with the Venniki, and as a result they *could* have learned their language and passed it down for generations."

Róisín stared out at the purple expanse. "There is only one way to know for sure."

<hr />

The binary suns were sinking in the west when the people of Caespes Verde began to converge at the community center. Róisín and Eamon had agreed to keep their theory to themselves for now. Róisín wasn't in a hurry to remove any doubt in her family's or her community's minds that she just might be insane. Part of her agreed that if she spoke up without gathering more data, she would hardly be able to blame them for thinking that.

"This is ridiculous," Róisín said, as she and Eamon followed their dad up the long, crowded pathway to the community center. Their mom had been in private meetings with the Caespes Verde council for most of the day. The large pole building served as the community's all-purpose meeting place. It looked as if it'd be bursting at the seams with tonight's crowd. "A horde of millions can be barreling down on us and threatening our existence, and we don't know about it until it's on our doorstep? No one ever thought to keep a close watch on our fragile little toehold on this desolate rock?"

"Ro, it's easy to play Monday morning quarterback," her dad said as he opened one of the double doors to let his family through.

Róisín shot a clueless look at her father as she passed through the doorway.

"Right," he mumbled, remembering she wasn't familiar with his off-world idioms. "No sense in agonizing over what could have been. The beasts are here now, and we have to decide how to act," he said as he stepped inside.

Almost the entire floor of the cavernous community center had been covered with rows of folding chairs, with a single broad aisle running up the center. The long council table was being readied on the stage, as hundreds of Villamese citizens milled about and talked amongst themselves in small groups. Róisín, along with her father and brother, settled into seats in the front row.

Governor Umar strode in from the side of the stage and approached the council table. He was decked out in a crisp blue suit and tie. It was strange to see him not wearing his usual dungarees. He picked up a microphone from the table and winced as a piercing stab of feedback echoed through the hall. "Um. Let's go ahead and get settled in." His voice boomed over the public address system.

Chaos ensued for the next few minutes as everyone rushed to find a place to sit. The eight council members filed in and took their places at the long table. Róisín's mom held her head high. She was the only woman on the council.

Governor Umar settled into the central seat and readjusted his microphone on the tabletop stand before him. Behind him, a large Caespes Verde flag was hung: three green chevrons on a black background with two yellow circles, representing Villam Prime's suns. Off to the side, a large flatscreen monitor had been wheeled out and loomed over the assembled council.

"Thank you all for attending this special emergency session, especially on such short notice." His eyes scanned the crowded hall. "Looks like just about everyone made it."

Róisín swallowed the lump in her throat. The tension in the air was palpable.

Governor Umar paused before continuing. "You all know why we're here—"

"But *do* we?!" came a loud voice from somewhere in the back.

Governor Umar pursed his lips but plowed forward. "We're currently coordinating with our brothers and sisters in the south. Governor Makin will be joining us remotely." He gestured toward the large monitor that had been wheeled onto the stage.

A murmur of discontent rippled through the crowd.

"For those who are not up to speed, the southern horde of t'sukol beasts has somehow traversed the uninhabitable zone and is making its way east. Caespes Verde," Governor Umar paused, "and our farms and homes are in harm's way. As always, in the name of transparency and democracy, we'd like to hear what your ideas are." He gestured toward the assembled citizens as a hissing swell of whispers rose.

A young man in denim overalls stood up.

Governor Umar pointed. "Kostas, you have the floor."

The man looked around before speaking. "Why don't we build a wall to turn them aside?"

A councilman next to Róisín's mom cleared his throat. "The council has already considered this, and it's been determined that a lack of both supplies and time would make this plan unfeasible. Even with emergency measures, it would take at least a week or two to obtain—"

Another voice rose from somewhere in the back. "Is this transparency and democracy, or are you lot all out of ideas?"

Some of the crowd laughed and jeered.

A woman in the row behind Róisín stood up. "These cursed things follow the banshee weed..."

Governor Umar seemed thankful for the distraction. "Astrid, let's hear your idea."

"...why not burn it all? A controlled burn. No banshee weed, no cursed beasts!"

Some of the crowd murmured its approval.

Róisín's mother leaned forward toward her microphone, her face set firm. "The council has already weighed this course of action, and we've been advised that with the current weather conditions, any kind of burn, controlled or otherwise, has the potential to be even more destructive than the beasts themselves."

The crowd grew even more restless as a chorus of groans and grumbling broke out.

"Besides, we have no idea how the beasts would react," Róisín's mother added. "Would they plow through Caespes Verde anyway in search of unburned land?"

Róisín's chest throbbed. Clenching her fists was all she could do to keep herself from leaping out of her seat and shouting at them all for being so short-sighted. Just when she thought she had regained her composure, she felt her leg muscles clenching; she could sit still no longer. She glanced over at Eamon, who dipped his head in a subtle nod.

She stood up.

Her father's eyes got big and round.

The corner of Governor Umar's mouth twitched. "Little Róisín, do you have something to say?"

Róisín glared up at the long table. She vowed not to let that "little" get to her, although she understood all too well its true purpose.

"The people of Villam Prime are standing at a crossroads," she heard herself say, barely aware that the words were pouring out of her mouth.

A smattering of groans erupted from the crowd.

"We've taken this world as our home. We've built our lives here and set ourselves up to be depended on by hundreds of thousands of people all across our zone. But, do we take responsibility for that burden?" Her voice echoed throughout the hall. "Villam has given us a place to live and a purpose. Villam has looked after our needs and those of many others. But have we looked after Villam? We do nothing but take!"

All eyes were upon her.

"We've never looked any further than the next harvest! So sure in our supremacy—so sure that Villam will always provide! So sure that if something comes up, we can just react. The time has long passed when *just reacting* isn't going to cut it!"

Governor Umar, who had been staring in shock, collected himself. "Did you have a suggestion for the council?"

Róisín's cheeks burned red-hot. "We have no choice but to throw ourselves at the mercy of this world and beg for one more chance!"

"Sit down!" some of the crowd began to yell.

"I will *not* sit down!" she shrieked. She was aware of her father's hand closing around her wrist. Eamon leaned back in his seat and clapped. "I'll talk to the t'sukol! Have any of you even considered that a possibility?"

Laughter erupted throughout the hall.

The flatscreen monitor on the stage began to flicker, and the image of a man came into focus. His face was grim and creased with deep lines. In the background, Róisín could make out the red-and-black flag of the southern colony, Castrum.

Governor Umar's eyes lingered on Róisín for a long moment before he dismissed her with a wave of his hand. "Um. Thank you, Róisín." He turned toward the screen.

Róisín quickly sat down and glanced at her father's red face. Trembling, her hand shot up to her forehead. She couldn't believe she'd made a fool of herself in front of every citizen of Caespes Verde. *I should have known that they wouldn't listen.*

Governor Makin's image spoke, his deep voice resonating throughout the hall. "What have you got, Umar?" he said, almost dismissively.

"Governor Makin, it's such a pleasure to—"

"What have you got?" the Castrum governor repeated.

Governor Umar paused. "We're still searching for a solution."

"Very well," came Governor Makin's voice from the public address system. "We're calling in a group of heavy frigates from the Reach. You're to evacuate everyone west of the eighteenth meridian east. The orbital strike will commence at dawn."

Róisín jumped out of her seat. "No!"

"Come on, Ro," whispered her father. "We've got to get ready to move."

"You can't do this!" she shouted. "It's cruel, first of all! Second, even if you did this horrible thing, you have no idea what the impact on the environment would be! With all the t'sukol dead, would the banshee weed go unchecked and choke out all our crops? There could be other repercussions that we can't even imagine!"

Without so much as another word from Governor Makin, the screen blinked out, and everyone in the hall started talking at once, drowning out Róisín's pleas.

"Thank you again for attending," said Governor Umar over the din. "We're going to be setting up shuttles for those of you who don't have transportation. Shelters will be constructed at the central market."

Chaos ensued on the western edge of Caespes Verde that night. Hundreds of citizens scrambled to evacuate with what little provisions and necessities they could carry on their persons. Some could stay with family who lived outside of the evacuation zone, but many others would be directed to the plazas of the central market, where makeshift shelters were being hastily put up.

Caespes Verde security forces went door-to-door and did their best to maintain order. Often, they had to enforce the restrictions to prevent the panicked citizens from bringing too many of their belongings. They truly had their hands full, as the only west-to-east highway, known as "the strip," was choked with ground transport and shuttles.

At midnight, Eamon had dropped their father and mother off at the central market and had told them that he would immediately return home to pick up Róisín, who was supposed to be helping secure the windows at the school.

So busy were the evacuees and security forces when Eamon returned that they didn't notice the bright red-and-chrome jumpship touching down on the summit of Mount Corbin. Róisín was already there, enacting her plan.

Eamon sat down on the flat rock next to his sister. "So," he said, gazing out at the darkness to the west, "what will Ma and Da do when they realize we're not coming right back? Don't suppose they'll come looking for us?"

Róisín feverishly typed on the floating lucent keyboard that was suspended in the air before her. "Hmm? Security won't let them," she finally said after a long pause.

"Do you think security could stop Mum?"

Róisín ceased typing. "You make a good point, but if we succeed, it won't matter."

"So," Eamon said, looking back out at the frontier, "where exactly is the eighteenth meridian east?"

"A little east of here. About where the school is."

"So, we could get a little charred, huh?"

"Things could get a little hot, yeah. Leave it to Castrum to solve problems by blowing things up—hey, don't you think you should be setting up? We need to get our omni-slates synced."

"Right, sis," he said as he got up. He turned to trudge back to his jumpship but paused. "Just thought I should let you know, Little Rose. I believe in you. If anyone can solve this, it's you."

Róisín grunted acknowledgement, but inwardly her heart overflowed. She was grateful that someone did, even if she had her own doubts.

After a few more hours, the eastern sky glowed, and Róisín's plan had begun to take shape. She sat on her rock, surrounded by an array of floating lucent display modules. Eamon had set up his microphone stand so its boom arm hovered directly over her omni-slate, which sat beside her on the rock. His amplifier was propped against a rock facing the darkness of the west. Nearby, he sat cross-legged among the rocks and fiddled with his mixing board.

Their omni-slates had been pinging so frequently that they both had to block the sender, for they knew who was trying so frantically to reach them. Róisín only hoped that when everything was said and done, their parents would understand.

As orange light steadily crept up from the eastern horizon, the scene below them unfurled. The western end of Caespes Verde was a ghost town. The last of the security force details were speeding east, where the flashing red and blue lights of emergency vehicles were just visible where the evacuation zone was cordoned off.

The scene to the west, however, took Róisín's breath away. A great wall of dust hung like a curtain in the growing light. Pouring over the horizon was a black mass of hulking shapes. Shoulder-to-shoulder they trudged forward, covering the plain like a colossal black blanket. Even to the north and south, their multitudes disappeared into its self-made shroud of dust. A low rumbling drone came from the west, like a rolling peal of thunder that might never end.

The eastern sky glowed brighter, but neither of Villam Prime's suns had yet shown their faces. Róisín scanned the sky, although she knew she wouldn't be able to see the heavy frigates that must be positioning themselves overhead.

"All right," said Eamon, "after all this preparation, do you know what you're going to say?"

Róisín's mouth hung open for a moment. She had spent so much time and effort throughout the night writing the Venniki translation algorithm that she hadn't given any thought on what she'd say.

"Are you going to use the orbital strike as leverage?" he said.

Róisín glared back at her brother. "No. Under no circumstances will I flaunt humans' technological superiority. That would go against everything I'm trying to do. I must succeed on *their* terms."

Eamon glanced back to the east. "Well, it's time."

Róisín swiped the screen of her omni-slate, and with a few button presses she switched her slate's receiver to analog mode. Immediately there was a rumbling cacophony of noise jumping forth from the speaker. Millions of t'sukol voices converged and created an ominous clamor that made the hair on the back of her neck stand on end.

"Here goes nothing." She donned the headset that had been sitting on the rock next to her and took a deep breath.

Eamon pushed the sliders up on his mixing board and pointed to his sister. "And... you're on," he said.

Unsure of how to begin the dialogue that she wasn't even sure the beasts would engage in, she drew a deep breath and spoke.

"Greetings."

Her omni-slate dinged and immediately output the translation. *"Maakutu,"* said the synthesized voice. The chiming and all-too-familiar voice blared from the amplifier toward the oncoming herd.

For a few horrible moments, Róisín feared that her carefully-laid plans would be for naught. Then, suddenly, the rumbling chatter of the horde abruptly ceased. An almost unbearable silence hung in the air for what seemed like a hundred heartbeats.

The t'sukol host had stopped. Róisín watched breathlessly through her binoculars. The beasts shuffled their shaggy feet and tossed their massive heads. A small flock of scouts galloped laterally along the front line, snorting and huffing as they went, apparently keeping the herd's formation in order.

"It's working!" Eamon said.

A lone beast trotted forward from the front lines and shambled to a stop, some fifty meters from the rest of its brethren—a lone speck at the head of a crushing legion.

Róisín's omni-slate crackled to life with a low, thrumming voice. *"Yu advenna basqu."*

Eamon's omni-slate dinged, and he read the translation aloud. "An interloper speaks," he said. They exchanged a grim look.

Róisín's mother clutched Governor Umar by the lapels of his crisp blue suit and gave him a violent shake with each word she spoke. "You get Governor Makin on the vectorcom. Right now!"

Governor Umar stuck a finger in his collar and readjusted his tie before gulping and picking up the vectorcom receiver. A few moments later, he was stammering his way through an explanation, until she ripped the receiver from his grip.

"Governor Makin, call off the strike!"

She heard him exhale on the other end of the line.

"Who is this?" came his low, smooth voice. "The frigates are moving into firing position as we speak."

"This is councilman Fiona McKenna. Call off the strike! My children are on Mount Corbin!"

"What the *devil* are they doing out there?"

"It doesn't matter! Call it off!"

There was a long pause. "Be it on *your* head if Caespes Verde falls, Councilman McKenna." With that, he ended the call.

Róisín huffed a deep breath and spoke. "Why do you call me interloper?"

Again, her slate dinged, and her algorithm played the translation which echoed over the plains. *"Ohm caarventu ka advenna?"*

The beast tossed its head and rumbled its answer in long, slurring grunts. *"Saal yitigraav t'sun advenna. Yitigraavgul vennok gru venka oont advellu kaameen pah. Yitigraavgul basmaku thoon kamkalla. Paarvenkagul impella grunok shaantu thoon."*

Eamon's eyes darted back and forth on his slate's screen as he silently read the translation.

Róisín muted her headset and glanced at her brother. "I can't keep up. What'd he say?"

"He says all hair worms are interlopers—"

"Hair worms? Does he mean *us?*" Róisín said.

Eamon shot a puzzled expression and an exaggerated shrug.

"He means us," she said at last. "No offense taken." She swiped the module in front of her and started typing on the lucent keyboard. "I'll make the adjustment in the translation algorithm." With a final swipe, the new translation fed to Eamon's screen.

"Right," Eamon said. "All humans are interlopers. Humankind came from the stars and laid claim to our home. Humankind makes the land hurt. Water star herd must find a new land." Eamon frowned. "Water star herd?"

Róisín stared out at the horde. "It's what they call themselves collectively." With a flurry of typing, she set about to make the adjustments to the algorithm. "'*Paarvenkagul*' becomes 't'sukol...'" she muttered. Róisín unmuted her microphone. "How do we make the land hurt?"

Her slate generated the translation which boomed out from the amplifier: *"Vuuti emptaalla basmaku thoon kamkalla?"*

"*Lavar utiovahpah,*" came the answer.

"He says it's our settlements," Eamon said.

"I knew it!" Róisín glanced over her shoulder. The first of Villam Prime's suns had just crested the horizon. She shot a worried look to her brother, who made a rolling gesture with his hand, urging her to continue.

Unmuting her microphone, she turned back to the modules before her. "When your herd passes this hill, you will destroy our food and our homes. Our settlement will perish." Her translated plea thundered from the amplifier.

After a moment, the beast's answer came: "*Yeetahl. Kaameen gul vukketen dinn orbatta. Et lavar utiovahpah kamkaatu, ut dinnti gohn yu bontuku sahn kaal? Tahl gohn yu bontuku sahn thoon?*"

Eamon read from his screen. "He says, it's true, their herd flattens the world. If our settlement is destroyed, is this not a good thing for them? Is it not good for the land?" He glanced up at Róisín. "These guys are brutal."

"We have to find common ground." Taking a deep breath, she continued her dialogue with the beast. "I think we'd very much like to share this world with you. You coexisted with the colonists in the south. Why not coexist with us in the north?" Róisín's slate dinged and relayed the translation.

After a moment, the beast's answer came. Eamon read from his screen. "He says the Venniki had a wise saying: 'The meadow mouse fears not the shark.' Likewise, the t'sukol feared not the humans in the south."

Róisín muted her microphone and turned to Eamon. "What the heck is a shark?"

Eamon swiped his screen and quickly searched for an answer. "All right. A shark was a type of saltwater fish on Sol-III. Apex predator. So, pretty much like our murderfins." He held up his slate, showing a picture of a great white shark.

Róisín thought for a moment and decided that this must mean that they stayed out of each other's way. She spoke into her headset. "But in your story, the shark salts the meadow, and the mouse must flee?"

The beast's answer came in a rumbling bellow. "*Taahneku.*"

"He says you understand," Eamon said.

"You speak of the Venniki. You knew them?" Róisín said.

"The Venniki gave us the gift of speech. Long ago, Venniki were friends of the t'sukol," Eamon said as he squinted at the screen.

"I want to be a friend of the t'sukol," Róisín said.

The beast gouged a deep rut in the trampled ground with its massive foreleg and bellowed.

Eamon read as his answer flashed across his screen, "Venniki sought balance.

Balance brings life. Humans seek greed. Greed brings only death. We cannot be friends."

Róisín's chest throbbed with despair. She felt her tenuous chance to forge a connection slipping away. There was one last truth to share. "I am one in my herd who wants to seek balance!"

The beast's answer came. "Humans have never sought balance." The hulking shape shuffled its feet and started to turn back toward the herd.

"I may be the only one! But cannot one change others' minds? I would be a good friend to the t'sukol, and I would fight my own herd to do it!"

The beast stopped. "You would fight... your own herd?"

"Not literally. I hope. I would do all I could to convince them that this world would be a better place with both humans *and* t'sukol."

The beast shook its shaggy head before answering.

"The Venniki had another wise saying. 'Talk is cheap,'" Eamon read from his slate.

Róisín chuckled. "We have that wise saying too. Talk *is* cheap, but a tiny bit of grace is worth the world. Please, spare our settlement. I beg of you, don't tread on our crops. Flatten no ground near our homes, and I will do all I can to convince the sharks to un-salt the meadow." She lowered her head, hoping that they understood the metaphor.

The beast lowered its head. After a long pause, the answer came.

"You seem wise. And you seem kind."

Róisín's heart leapt with hope. Could she dare think that they'd spare them?

"Those are two things that I aspire to be." Her eyes stung. "Another is thankful."

The beast turned and took a final glance toward Mount Corbin before trotting back toward its herd. Its final transmission came through as it took its place at the vanguard.

"Goodbye, friend of the t'sukol. If the land and the skies allow me, I will look for you on this summit in seven world's journeys."

Eamon jumped to his feet. "Did you do it?"

Róisín stood up and waved her arm vigorously overhead. *"Draekutu!"* she shouted to the west—the Venniki word for goodbye.

A rumbling roar echoed over the plains. Like a pebble thrown into a calm pond, the roar rippled through their host until, in time, it reached the furthest reaches of their ranks. The rocks beneath Róisín's feet shook as the herd rushed forward. A thick cloud of dust rose from beneath their feet as they came.

A rift formed in their center, and half of the herd veered right, while the other half swerved left. A lone beast stood at the intersection, bellowing commands.

Turning around as the vanguard of the horde passed Mount Corbin, Róisín watched as one division took a wide path toward the southern frontier. Likewise, to the north, the beasts appeared to be on course to give the northern frontier a wide berth. The massive herd had effectively become two. Gazing to the west, the multitude seemed to go on forever. As far as she could see and more, there was only dust, shaggy bodies, and a deafening thunder.

Eamon ran up to his sister and gave her a bear hug that their mother would have been proud of. Breaking free, Róisín raised her fists into the air and whooped a shout of victory that neither herself nor her brother could hear over the tumultuous racket of the herd.

Eamon tapped Róisín's shoulder and pointed east. Racing down the strip toward them were four security force trucks, their red-and-blue lights flashing. "Guess they figured out where we went, huh," he said, but Róisín could just barely read his lips.

Róisín fought to keep her drooping eyelids open. The adrenaline rush from the success of her mission had now faded, and her head felt like a block of lead. After pulling the most bizarre all-nighter in Caespes Verde history, she now only longed for the warm comfort of her bed and blankets.

The long, awkward silence as Governor Umar stared at her, dumbstruck, across his desk did not help matters.

The t'sukol stampede continued unabated. Róisín could still feel the ground shaking beneath her feet even as she sat in Governor Umar's office. It was almost enough to lull her off to sleep. Out in the streets, one could hear the horde's thunder sustaining its one-note song endlessly. A thick cloud of dust choked out the late morning sunlight, casting a weird orange hue on everything.

Róisín sat in the center chair in front of Governor Umar's desk, flanked by her mother and father, each resting a reassuring hand on her shoulders.

At last, Governor Umar broke his silence. "I suppose the people of Caespes Verde owe you a debt of gratitude." He paused and folded his hands on the desk before him. "And I suppose I owe you an apology."

Róisín felt her father's hand gently patting her shoulder.

Governor Umar pursed his lips and seemed to be considering how to continue. "You just... *talked* to them?"

Róisín nodded. "I simply followed the facts and learned that asking nicely was a possibility."

Governor Umar cleared his throat. "Yes, well… Róisín, you've violated a very serious order by ignoring our mandatory evacuation. You put yourself in grave danger." He paused and looked over her mother's shoulder at Eamon, who was sitting in a chair against the wall behind them. "And you, Eamon. You should have known better."

Eamon clucked his tongue and pointed double barreled fingers at the Governor.

"However," Governor Umar continued, "you've solved this existential crisis in such a simple and nondestructive way. I think it's very commendable. I want you to know that your words at the emergency meeting did not entirely fall upon deaf ears."

Róisín was stunned. Too tired to speak, or even think, she silently stared ahead.

"There has been, for some time, a movement among the Caespes Verde council to ramp up our spending on and attention to matters of science. Actually, it's been spearheaded by your mother. She's been onto us for years."

At this, Róisín could no longer hide her shock. Her mouth hung open for a long moment as she looked over at her mom.

"So, in light of recent events, I've decided to put some of these proposed programs onto the fast track. Among a few other programs, we'll be forming the Villam Prime Conservation Commission. We'd be honored to have you aboard as a charter member—as a paid intern, of course. We're willing to put forth a scholarship fund toward furthering your education when you graduate in a few years."

Róisín sat bolt upright in her seat, her eyes round. "Are you serious?"

Governor Umar nodded. "Quite serious. It's long past time we nurture the passion and curiosity of those who wish to bring greater understanding to our delicate existence out here in the zone."

Before Róisín could answer, the vectorcom on Governor Umar's desk chimed. He raised a finger and picked it up. A sly smile spread across his face. With the touch of a button, the call went to speaker.

Governor Makin's deep, drawling voice filled the room. "Umar, I'm quite surprised and glad that you were able to handle your little—problem—on your own. It's just as well. I was going to charge your office for the strike salvoes. The fleet is on its way back to the Reach. Congratulations." With that, the communication ended.

Governor Umar's expression was indecipherable for a moment. After collecting himself, he smiled. "What do you say, Róisín? Would you like to help shape the future of Villam Prime's conservation?"

A mixture of emotions roiled inside of Róisín's stomach. She couldn't help but acknowledge that she was harboring a great deal of anger at her colony's negligence in matters of science. She wasn't sure she wanted to be a part of such a disorganized mess. Worst of all, she found herself wondering if she could trust Governor Umar. The wise saying of the Venniki came into her mind, echoing in the voice of that unnamed hulking beast.

Talk is cheap.
Yes, talk is cheap, but a tiny bit of grace is worth the world.
"Yes, Governor Umar. I'd be honored."

THOUGHTS ON *BRAVE NEW GIRLS*

"Investing in STEM education for girls is about much more than just leveling the playing field. It will result in more inclusive solutions and more diverse perspectives from tomorrow's leaders. We can only go so far if we perpetually exclude half of humanity's collective experience. It starts at a young age; let's stoke their fires of curiosity."

ABOUT THE AUTHOR

Scott spent his childhood drawing. His love was for dinosaurs, and he'd draw them on any available piece of paper, including bill envelopes or even grocery bags. As his love for drawing grew, he would eventually earn a BFA in art and go on to become a graphic artist for a news publication. He has two children and two cats, and it's one of them that he has to thank for breaking him into the world of writing. (The children, not the cats!) A writing collaboration project with his youngest would later morph into his current works. These days, she is his biggest fan, motivator, and critique partner, as well as a talented and budding artist herself. Scott is the author of the *Ordinary Everyday Isabelle Duology*, which consists of *The Orphan Ark* and *The Paragons of Elysium*. Scott also enjoys playing guitar and songwriting with his wife, Tami.

Illustration for "The Interloper" by Kay Wrenn.

The Village Runners

Paige Daniels

THE VILLAGE RUNNERS
PAIGE DANIELS

SOMETIMES IT'S THE LITTLE ACTIONS that make the biggest difference. Those little split-second decisions that you make in the heat of the moment often have a great influence on your life. It's not until we look back on our lives that we realize how those decisions affected us.

I still remember it like it was yesterday. My uncle's barn was my happy place when everything else around us was anything but. I can still feel the cold smooth metal of the ratchet in my hand as I torque down a bolt on our secret vehicle, something that if the AI knew about it, we'd all be doomed. I can still hear his voice coaching me while I helped him in the bar. Man, he'd make me so mad... I miss him so much.

"Careful now, Gracie, make sure not to crack the casing," the old man's scratchy voice said.

I sighed and stood up from the beat-up old-timey red SUV, the 'ol Wagoneer, then pushed an escaping thick, black, curly lock back into the bandana tied around my head.

"Uncle Waldo, you say that every time, and never have I once cracked a casing. Why do you keep telling me that?"

He shrugged, then wiped his greasy hands down his coveralls. "First time for everything, kid. Besides, we gotta make sure everything is tickety-boo for my trip out tomorrow. We need to make sure we can get them ration bars. Besides, I'm goin' for a record time," he said as a mischievous smile came over his face. Almost as soon as the smile appeared, it disappeared into a body-wracking cough.

I went over to the man and put my hand on his bent-over form. He took in a wheezy breath and slowly inched up. A big smile was plastered over his red sweaty face, acting like it was some big joke. I knew it was not.

"Why don't you let me make the run? I mean, I gotta learn at some point. I did great on the training run the other day. You said so yourself."

Uncle gave a phlegmy laugh and shook his head. "Nope, I ain't risking your neck with them AI bots. Your mom and dad put you in my care, and I sure as heck ain't about to disappoint them."

Mom and Dad had both lost their lives to the AI bots while trying to get us rations. It was all so absurd. Around the time of my great-grandparents, the AI had decided that it knew what was best for us. It started harmlessly enough, by regulating our power usage, or dictating what foods were best for us to eat on which days. All this was in the name of humanity and the environment most efficiently coexisting. But then the AI decided that the most efficient way for humans and the environment to coexist was to cut us off from most technology, segregate us into small rural villages, and maintain our population levels.

It had been great until it wasn't. One bad harvest or epidemic could mean the end of a village. That is, unless the AI deemed the village worth saving, and delivered ration bars embedded with life-saving nutrition and vaccines. Unfortunately, our village was not deemed worth saving. We'd had a double whammy of a bad harvest and pretty nasty flu hitting our town. The cool air whipping through the barn was a stark reminder of what was in store for us in a few months if we didn't get those rations from the AI.

"I'm sure Mom and Dad would understand. Besides, I'm faster than you," I said with a half-smile crooked on my mouth.

"Oh, the heck you are." He pointed at a pack on the shelf behind the ol' Wagoneer. "Get that for me, would ya?"

I yanked on the black canvas cube and then heaved it on the hood of our vehicle. He slowly opened the pack and silently counted the items as he nodded.

He pointed at a few shiny metallic disks and asked, "What are these?"

Ah yes, the quiz.

"Magnets. Put them on the bots and it scrambles their brains." Before he could ask what the other items were, I finished, "And that's the code breaker, those are the lock picking tools, those are the maps of stores that someone gave us a long time ago, and that's a compass."

"Smart-aleck. Listen, you need to know what all of this is."

"Why? So you can not trust me to go on a run?"

Uncle Waldo grumbled and paced as he ran his hands through his salt-and-pepper hair. "I'm not gonna be here forever, kid. And we're the only ones in the village with a vehicle. It's a big responsibility. We not only have to know how to drive the vehicle, but we have to keep it in running condition. Being the village runner is going to fall to you, and it's something you need to take seriously."

"Then let me go!"

"No! I made a promise to your parents to keep you safe. Not until you absolutely have to."

His eyes watered, and his body shook. He'd been close to his sister, my mom, and I had been too. I threw my arms around him and squeezed. As I put my head to his chest, I could hear the rumbling and wheezing deep in his lungs.

"I know," I said, almost in a whisper. Not wanting to aggravate the man further, I added, "Well then, maybe you can take me for one more practice run when you get back. That will make you feel better."

He chuckled. "Yeah, one more practice run, then you should be ready, kid. Until then, leave it to me."

"Okay," I said, knowing that everything was far from being okay.

The dinner that night was sparse, just like it had been all the previous nights. I reached out and dished a few steaming root vegetables on my plate from the chipped serving bowl. I wasn't very hungry, but I knew I'd get the chewing out of a lifetime if I didn't eat. I pushed the assortment of mushy vegetables around my plate as I thought about my uncle making the run. He wasn't really an old man, maybe forty-five, but the years here hadn't been easy on him, or any of us. He knew as well I did that he was in no shape to make that run, but there was no talking sense into the man.

"Gracie, eat your food," Uncle nagged. "You need to be strong for the coming winter."

"I'm not hungry," I said.

"You need nutrition," Uncle said as a bone-shaking cough escaped him.

I rolled my eyes. "You sound horrible. Let me go. Seriously, I'll be fine. At least let me go with you as backup."

The man waved his hand. "I'll be fine." He pointed to the map spread out on the table as he took a bite of his dinner. "See, the location is just a few hours from here. I should be back by late night if I start early enough. You need to look after the house."

"Sounds like a great run for a beginner then."

Uncle Waldo growled and slammed his spoon down. "Grace, we're not discussing this further. I said no."

I knew there was no getting through to the old coot, so I decided to change my line of questioning.

"One thing I never understood is why the AI lets us get away with the rations. I mean, surely it's smart enough to eventually figure out who took them. Why doesn't it come and find them and take them back?"

"I don't know. Maybe they figure if we get back to our village, then we earned them."

I scratched my head and wrinkled my nose. "What? That doesn't make sense."

He shrugged. "Survival of the fittest. Maybe the AI figures if we steal it and get to a certain point, then we're worthy of the rations."

I sighed. Nothing here made sense, and no one seemed to question it either. *I guess that's what happens when you're always fighting to just get by—no time to question the status quo.*

I stared down at my mushy vegetables and took a bite just to avoid another confrontation. Usually, poking the bear that was Uncle Waldo was right up on the list of favorite pastimes, along with fixing the ol' Wagoneer. But his pale sweaty complexion gave me pause. He was just trying to get by and protect me and look out for our village. Being the village runner was a lot of responsibility and danger. It had taken my parents' lives, and he knew once I started running, it could take mine too. I gave the old man a chuck on the shoulder and a half-smile.

We started eating our dinner, with only the scraping of the bowls breaking the silence in our tiny home. Both of us knew that this could be the last dinner that we would share. It was like this before all the runs. Each of us was quiet, not saying what needed to be said. I took a deep breath and tried to gather the courage to tell my uncle what I wanted to say: that I loved him and didn't want him to go, that I couldn't stand another member of my family leaving, that I couldn't look after the farm without him. A knock at the door stopped me.

Before either of us were able to answer the door, a stocky redhead wearing overalls walked in. I knew it was customary for everyone in our village to be welcome in each other's homes, but I hated people just barging in. Midge, the town mayor, always felt especially entitled to barge in.

"Sorry to bug you in the middle of dinner, folks."

No, she isn't.

"It's fine, we were just finishing up. What can we do ya for, Midge?" Uncle Waldo asked as he got up to clear the table.

"I just wanted to wish ya luck on the run tomorrow. I also wanted to let you know to be on the lookout for adjacent villagers looking for rations. It's been hard on all of us, and I've been hearing that the AI is getting stingier with them rations."

"Shouldn't we be working together?" I asked as I started on the dishes. "I mean the other villagers and us?"

Uncle Waldo shifted nervously, the way he did when he didn't have a good answer to a question. "Well, we're both out for the same goods, so we gotta get 'em before anyone else does."

"But you said that once you get the stores open, then you got fifteen minutes to get all the ration bars you can, and you can't possibly get them all in that time. Why would it hurt to have someone else there? Wouldn't more people be helpful?"

Midge grumbled, "That's just how it's always been done. We have to look after our own."

Waldo nodded in agreement. "They feel the same way."

"How do you know?" I asked. "Did you ever go ask them? I bet the AI cut off comms so that we would be suspicious of each other and not work together. Maybe we shouldn't go about business as usual."

Midge shook her head. "Girl, you have no idea—"

I cut her off. "You're right, I don't. It's because all of you want me to be ready for the responsibilities of an adult, while never actually trusting me with carrying out the responsibilities. I have never had a chance to go out and see it all for myself. You need to stop being so scared."

"Dang it, Grace. I've had enough of you. Get out of my sight!" Uncle bellowed.

Anger and sadness panged in my chest. There was nothing I could do. Silently, I ran up the stairs to my bedroom.

After I went to my bedroom, I could hear the adults talking for at least an hour. I could only make bits and pieces of the conversation out. Midge trying to console Uncle about his headstrong niece. Uncle wondering where he went wrong with me. Somewhere after them starting to recount plans for the run tomorrow, I fell asleep.

I wasn't sure how long I'd been asleep, but the lights in the house were out and all was quiet when I woke up. I looked out the window of my bedroom, and the stars sparkled brilliantly in the inky dark of the sky. It was hard to believe there'd been a time when we humans had cities so full of lights that it drowned them all out. Down the hall, I heard the snores of my uncle.

I sighed. As if on autopilot, my body thrust into action before my brain could even comprehend what I was doing. Quietly, I tiptoed out of my room, down the stairs, and out of the house. My feet carried me to the barn. I pulled on the cord hanging from the barn rafters and the ol' red Wagoneer was there waiting for me, looking at me as if to say, "It's your time, Grace. You need to do this for your uncle. For the village."

Before thinking about it too long, I hopped in the car and turned the key, and the engine purred. I waited for a beat before pushing my foot to the pedal, but I knew it was the right thing to do. After I backed out of the barn, I pressed the gas pedal, and the gravel spit beneath my tires.

Thank goodness Uncle put the map in the Wagoneer before he turned in for the night. Although, I was pretty sure that I could figure out the way to the rations, since I'd looked at that map so many darn times. In front of me, a spectacular sunrise of gold, purple, and magenta started to appear. Uncle would be getting up right about now and finding out that I'd left.

Sorrow and guilt pressed my chest. For a moment, I considered turning back. If I started back home now, he'd get a late start, but he could overcome the delay. I shook my head at that thought. No, I needed to believe in myself. Uncle was sicker than he'd admitted. I needed to do this for him and the village.

The Wagoneer bumped and rattled along the gravel and dirt road, as the beautiful trees in oranges and reds passed by. In the old days, this trip would have taken half the time with paved roads. The AI had only allowed us horses or oxen to travel with. Fuel for the Wagoneer was hard to come by. Last year, Uncle and I had made the Wagoneer fully electric solar rechargeable. We had to be smart about how long we ran it, but with a carefully plotted-out course, we could make it work.

My stomach knotted and groaned with unease. I knew when I got back home, there would definitely be a punishment doled out by Uncle. He wasn't a bad man, and mostly his punishments consisted of doing a few more chores around the house. No big deal really, but I thought I shouldn't even be punished at all. I was doing what they said they wanted us kids to do: taking responsibility. But they wouldn't see it that way. The adults wanted us to simultaneously act like adults and not have any thoughts of our own. They wanted to keep us safe, but also wanted us to be prepared for the future. It didn't make any sense.

As I was ruminating about what it meant to be a teen, a glint in my rearview mirror caught my attention. As the Wagoneer chugged along the road, the shape started to become clearer. It could have been one of two things: an AI patrol car or a vehicle from another village. Either way, it wasn't a good sign.

Think, Grace, think.

It came to me, and I turned into the forest to the side of the road. I would put a heat shield around the car. The trees would mess with the AI's visual recognition, and the heat shield would throw off the thermal sensors. The sound of branches and leaves hitting the Wagoneer filled my vehicle. My body bumped and jostled as I guided the Wagoneer off the trail. After a few minutes, I stopped the car, praying that I was off the road enough. I unbuckled my seatbelt and felt under the seat for the heat shield. Once I found the shield, I exited the car, threw the metallic blanket over it, and crept back inside.

The car was dark and quiet. I tried to stay still and keep all sounds to a minimum, including my breathing. I had no idea how finely tuned the AI's sensors would be. I had no idea how long the AI would linger.

Sitting in the darkened silent car felt like sitting in my tomb. Time seemed to slow down and yet speed up at the same time. Staying too long would eat up the time I had to get to the rations and back home, but if I didn't stay long enough, then I would be detected by someone. I checked my watch one more time and restlessly shifted in my seat. I closed my eyes and started to take a big breath, but a loud knock on my vehicle caused me to shriek instead.

Good going, Grace, now everyone is going to know you're here.

Before I could think of what to do, the heat shield was lifted off my car. A mix of anxiety and confusion ripped through my chest when I saw what was standing before me.

I'd only seen a few AI patrol bots before. Mostly, they left us villagers alone, unless we were doing something they deemed unacceptable, or they were delivering rations to the village. One time when I was around five, before my parents died, one of their patrol cars had delivered rations to our village. I'd expected something sleeker, more high-tech. Instead, it'd been big and clunky, its exterior tarnished and dinged, with not even one hint of shine on its body.

This was what I was fully expecting to see before me: one of the AI's air drones, or maybe even one of the foot patrol bots. But definitely not a tall, gangling, towheaded boy.

"What's up?" he asked, too casually for my liking.

I knitted my eyebrows, just looking at him, unsure what to say.

He continued, "Nice ride. Mine's over that way. You looking for rations too?"

"Who are you?" I finally managed to get out of my mouth.

He walked around to my window and extended his hand. "Name's Neil. S'pose you're from our neighboring village?"

I didn't take his hand. Instead, I answered, "Yeah, how did you know I wasn't an AI or some villager out to get you?"

He shrugged. "Wellp, figured no bot was gonna be hiding in the brush. And you didn't look like a person that could cause me any harm. Thought I'd come and see if you need my help."

So. Many. Questions.

I rubbed my head and then waited a beat to gather my thoughts. "First of all, how did you even see me?"

"Oh yeah, I got a long-range camera hooked up to my rig out there. Me and my ma found it on a scavenger run a few years back. I can see things meters away. It's pretty cool. You wanna look?"

"I'm not stupid. I'm not getting in a car with a stranger."

He shrugged. "Okay, just offering."

My heart started to beat in frustration. How could this guy be so glib about everything? Why wasn't he freaking out about seeing another villager? And from the sound of it, he'd been going on runs for a long time. "So, why aren't you hiding from me? I thought all us villagers were skeptical of each other."

"Eh, my parents say we should be, but I don't agree. The only way that's gonna change is if we do something about it. I figured you got better things to do than start a fight with me. And besides, we got enough problems getting rations and sneaking around the AI without being wary of each other. Just thought I'd step out of my comfort zone and meet ya."

I started to relax a bit, but not too much. He could've been trying to lure me in.

"Well, thanks for checking on me… Neil… but we should really get moving if we want to get our rations and then go back to our homes."

"Yeah, I s'pose you're right. Nice meeting you… what did you say your name was?"

"I didn't, but it's Grace."

"Nice meeting you, Grace."

Without another word, he rushed off past the trees.

I laid my head back on the headrest to gather my thoughts for a few seconds. What a weird dude. He didn't seem to get very fazed about… anything, really. Shaking those thoughts from my head, I got out and folded up the heat shield, then got back in the car to be on my way.

Once outside the tree line, I saw no traces of the boy/man/whatever, just some tire tracks that were different than mine. Not missing an opportunity to overthink a situation, I consulted my handy maps. Should I find a different route to the ration station, or would I be fine? From the tire marks, it looked like Neil was taking the route that I had originally intended to take. I chewed on my lip a bit, trying to think of my next move. Get to the station and meet him on the way there? Or wait him out?

I looked at the sun overhead. I'd already wasted too much time on hiding. If Neil wanted to do me any harm, he would've already done it. Maybe Neil was right; if we wanted change to happen, then we needed to be the first to bring it about. I inhaled a big breath of courage and headed down the road, not knowing what would await me there.

After the encounter with Neil, the trip to the ration station was pretty normal. My parents and now Uncle would never let me venture so far from our home. Sure, I'd gotten to do training runs, but they'd been pretty close to our village. Most people didn't want to venture far out of the safety of their hometown. In their minds, nothing good could come of it. In my case, and I think my family's too, our small town felt... well, small, and claustrophobic. Being out here with wind, trees, and silence was just the elixir that I didn't know I needed.

I consulted my map one more time. The rations should just be over the hill that I was about to crest. Fear and worry knotted in my stomach. Neil would surely be there. Would he let me get at the rations too? Surely, there would be enough for both of us. I swatted those thoughts away. *Gotta get my head in the game.*

As I summited the hill, the scene below took me by surprise. In the middle of the rolling verdant hills, an old concrete building stuck out like a sore thumb. It wasn't the building that took me by surprise so much as what was outside the building. Three dented, rusted robotic drones with stocky bodies and gangling arms stood around a blue sedan. Each of the drones took turns kicking and shaking the blue sedan. I could barely make out the driver of the car, and no surprise, it was Neil. Fortunately, the bots were distracted by Neil's car, so they didn't see me.

Think, Grace, think.

I got out of my car, went straight for the supplies in the back, and threw them in the front seat as I scurried back into the Wagoneer. I rummaged through them until I found exactly what I was looking for: the magnetic disks to scramble the bots' brains. I stuffed the disks in the front bib pocket of my overalls and, without another thought, pushed on the accelerator and drove straight into the melee.

Once I was closer to the building, I started honking my horn and yelling out the window.

"Hey, you stupid drones! C'mere and chase me. That's right, leave him alone and pick on someone that can outrun you!"

The drones stopped giving Neil's car attention and started running toward me. As the drones followed, I swirled and looped around the lumbering bots. As they lumbered toward me, I could hear the squeaks and pops in their joints. Taking one hand off the wheel, I reached into my overalls pocket and produced four shiny disks. There wasn't a lot of room for error. I needed to land the disks perfectly.

I looked out my side mirror and nearly jumped when I saw that the drone was so close. Its head took up the whole view. I ran my hand across one of the smooth disks, held my breath, and then flung the magnet toward the bot. It landed squarely on the bot's head, and within seconds, the bot was down.

Two more to go. I did a donut in the grass, turning the car in the opposite direction and heading toward the two bots rushing to me. I threw a second disk out, but it missed.

Fudge!

I sped up and drove past the bots, narrowly missing their grasp. I turned around again and headed for the bots. *Gotta get this one right.* My heart thumped in my chest as I mashed on the gas pedal, speeding past the bots. One of the bots reached out for me, scratching and denting my Wagoneer, but I exacted my revenge and landed the magnet disk on its trunk. In seconds, Bot Number Two was down.

If bots had any emotion, I would have sworn the third bot was mad. Its body clunked and clanked as it ran for me. I revved my engine, looking at the bot.

"It's now or never. Gotta take this one down," I muttered to myself.

I took my foot off the brakes and accelerated toward the bot. It was all a blur, but the last thing I remembered hearing was the satisfying *ping* of the magnet on the bot's body, then its crash to the ground.

I took a few seconds to close my eyes and gather my wits. Then I drove over to see Neil.

"That was some pretty fancy maneuvering," he yelled to me, as I exited my vehicle with my pack across my shoulder.

"Thanks." I looked at my watch, then said, "By my account, we have about fifteen minutes to get in the hold and get the rations out."

"Not much on pleasantries, are ya?"

"Nope. You seem like a nice fella, but we gotta get them rations before the big baddies get here," I said as I ran toward the building.

Once at the building, I looked at the door and tried to remember what

Uncle had told me about breaking into it. Before I could act, Neil sidled up to the touchpad.

Calmly, he took a flathead screwdriver out of his back pocket and shimmied the touchpad off. As he worked, he said, "You know, I have a theory, that there's not one AI hivemind. That maybe one AI disagrees with the others about how we're being treated, and maybe they make it easier for us to get these rations." He connected a couple of wires, and the door clicked. "I mean, how else do you explain us being able to get to the goods?"

I followed Neil into the building. As we walked in, the lights automatically flickered on, and we saw rows of black boxes stacked up to the ceiling.

"Another case in point," he said. "I've hit up this particular bunker at least half a dozen times, and I imagine others are hitting this place up too. Look, it's like nothing has even been touched. Someone or something is restocking this."

I scurried toward one of the rows as I said, "Wellp, I'm not looking a gift horse in the mouth. We need to get out of here."

Without another word, both of us set on the task of loading as many rations as we could, as quickly as we could.

My muscles protested as I scooted the last of the ration boxes in the Wagoneer. I folded my arms across my chest and smiled with pride at the puzzle-like configuration of all the boxes that I'd managed to fit in my vehicle. This moment was soon interrupted by a *ding* at my wrist. I looked down. Time was up. Unfortunately, Neil was still in the building.

"Neil, let's go, bud. Time's up."

From inside the building, a voice echoed, "Just a few more. If I get these, I'll be done."

Fear and aggravation gnawed at my stomach. "C'mon, we got to get..." Over the hill, a glint caught my eye. "Neil! They're here. We need to go *now*! Drop all the things, and get your hind end out here."

Suddenly, Neil appeared from the building, covered in sweat, balancing four ration boxes in his arms. "Sorry, it's just that—"

I looked over my shoulder, and what was once a glint was now visible. A scraped and rusted silver saucer hovered just above the ground: one of the AI's air cars. The behemoth lumbered toward us.

"No time for explanation. Just get in your car!" I yelled.

As Neil ran toward his car, his foot was caught in a small hole in the ground, and he and his rations toppled to the ground. He scurried along the ground, trying to pick up what he could of the rations. And I gathered as many ration bars as I could in my arms, raced to his car, and then threw them in an open window. The high-pitched whine of the air car caught my ears, and panic roosted in my chest.

Neil slid into his car. Before I was able to head to my car, Neil shouted, then threw something to me, and I caught it in the air. I stared at the black plastic box.

"It's tuned to the right channel. It'll help us communicate. Just press that button on the side when you want to talk," he said as he turned his car on.

I nodded, went to my car, and started the engine. My foot pressed the gas as the whine of the air car filled my ears. My breath quickened as I glanced in my rearview mirror. Neil's car was right on my bumper, and behind him, the air car loomed.

I grabbed the black box and pushed the button. "Hey, Neil, I have an idea for a different route to take. It's a little longer, but it's got some twists and turns that are going to be hard for that thing to navigate."

Over the air, just crackles and pops emanated, then a voice came through. "All right. I think I know what route you have in mind. I'll follow."

When we came to a fork in the road, I took the narrow, rock-strewn path. I held my breath and prayed that I'd memorized the route correctly. Uncle told me once that even though the air cars hovered, they actually couldn't get up very far, because they needed the ground to propel off of. The further they got off the ground, the more power they'd lose. Also, their bodies were quite clunky and cumbersome, so navigating narrow routes with any kind of clutter wasn't really their jam. I just hoped that Neil's car could navigate the course.

As we sped down the path, the brilliant blue skies and open rolling hills turned into a dark forest. The trees made for a maze-like configuration to navigate, and turned the road into a root and rock-strewn mess that slowed us down—but slowed the air car too. The contents in the back of the Wagoneer jolted and rustled, and my bones felt as though they were being rattled inside of my body. Neil's car seemed to be keeping up, just barely.

Ahead, the road narrowed and wound up a steep incline. On one side, a hill covered in plants and trees yawned toward the sky. On the other, a rocky incline greeted me. I needed to strike a perfect balance between speed and precision. If I went too fast, then I could careen off the hill. If I went too slow, then the air car would surely catch up to us.

As I navigated the path, I started to doubt myself. Why did I ever think that I could do something like this? Uncle was right. I wasn't ready. He could've done a much better job than I was doing. As if to emphasize my thoughts, my wheels slipped, and the back end of my car swerved over a collection of loose rocks. My heart thumped in my throat, and my hands were slick with sweat on the steering wheel.

"This is a tricky road," Neil's voice said over the black box. "You're doing great, though. Just take your time. Don't worry about that air car. It's having a time, just like us."

Not wanting to take my hands off the steering wheel, I didn't reply. But the words gave me the resolve to keep going.

Once at the top of the hill, I saw our savior: a narrow bridge. The entrance to the bridge was much smaller than the air car could hope to fit through, and it wouldn't have the ability to float over it. The only problem was that the bridge was rather rickety.

As I got closer to the bridge, its disrepair became more apparent. I swallowed hard. This was the only choice.

I grabbed the black box. "Neil, I'm going over the bridge. I think we can lose it that way."

"Agree, but take it easy. That's quite a drop to the bottom. I'll wait until you're all the way through. I don't think that thing can take both of us."

"Agreed."

I looked in the rearview mirror. The air car was a ways off, but it hadn't given up chasing us. *Maybe once we're across, it will let us go. Maybe it's like Uncle said: we have to prove ourselves worthy of the rations. Or maybe it will just lose interest.* Those thoughts left my mind as I approached the old, dilapidated bridge, which crossed a chasm with a stream at the bottom.

"You got this," a voice cheered from over the black box.

I nodded, then gritted my teeth. Without another thought, I went on the bridge. It protested, creaked, and whined with every turn of my wheels. My hands gripped the wheel, and I tried to keep myself from looking over to what awaited me if the bridge decided to give out. After what felt like hours, my wheels finally gripped the solid earth.

I turned to face the bridge and then said over the black box, "It's your turn. You got this."

As Neil started over the bridge, the air car came into view. I dug my nails into my palms as I watched the scene play out in front of me. Neil slowly traversed the old bridge as the air car approached. My heart lightened a bit seeing him on the bridge. At least the air car couldn't follow. He just needed to make it over.

As Neil drove, the bridge's creaks and groans filled the air. On the other side of the bridge, the air car seemed to be trying to lift itself high enough to get over the narrow entrance. My heart thumped as I wondered if it could get over. Maybe Uncle was wrong. I needed to stop the car.

I opened the door of the Wagoneer and grabbed my trusty supply pack, then emptied it on the hood of the car. I looked through the components of the pack. I smiled when I saw a few magnetic disks that had gotten lodged in the bottom of the pack. I just needed a way to get them over to the car.

As I was rummaging through my pack, Neil made it to the safety of the other side with me. He exited his car, and looked at the air car trying to get over to us.

"It's not giving up, is it?" he asked.

"Apparently not. Maybe it's one of the AIs that doesn't like us."

"Maybe." He looked at my collection of techno-junk and asked, "Whatcha got there?"

"I found a few more of the magnetic disks that I used to disable the ground bots at the bunker. If I can just get them over there, I think we can halt any progress it's making."

"I got an idea," he said as he raced to his car. He came back in a few seconds, holding a small drone and a remote. "This is just a dumb ol' drone. I use it to navigate ahead of me. It's not an AI thing. I control it with this remote. I just don't have a way to make it hold your disks."

I looked over his shoulder, and the air car hadn't given up. It paced the edge of the canyon, surveying the area for any solution to get to us. I was sure that it would find a way given enough time.

I rummaged through my pack and disassembled the code breaker and a few other devices with my tools. Then I cobbled together a basket on the drone and put the disks inside.

"See if that flies," I said.

Neil flipped a few switches, and the drone's buzz filled the air. Slowly, it lifted. "I think we can make it go. It's just not going to last for very long."

I nodded, then grabbed the remnants of the code breaker. "I cobbled this into a remote that will open the basket once over the AI. As soon as the magnets land, they should scramble its brains enough to disable it."

Neil flew the drone over the bridge to the air car. Once he was hovering over it, I pushed a button on my control, and disks were released.

The air car sank into the dirt with a *thud*.

Neil and I jumped and high-fived each other. The terror was over for today.

After an hour or so of traveling in the woods, Neil and I made it back to rolling hills and open skies. We both stopped at the crossroads where he'd first discovered my car. In the distance, the sky was turning hues of orange, red, and purple. I closed my eyes and inhaled the cool air. There was a panging in my chest, a feeling that maybe we hadn't gotten away with it.

I looked to Neil and asked, "Do you think they'll be back at our villages? You know, the bots?"

He shrugged. "I've evaded bots before, and they never came back. Maybe they're trying to teach us a lesson in teamwork. Maybe they're testing us, like your uncle said. Who knows. Don't overthink it. You did a great job."

"Thanks. Uncle is probably gonna tan my hide for taking the car. Hopefully, the rations that I bring back will get me in their good graces."

He knitted his eyebrows. "So, this was the first time you've ever done the run?"

"Yeah. I've done some practicing, but he never would let me come out for real. I knew Uncle was too sick to make it. I guess it was a good thing I did, because I don't think he would have been as helpful to you as I was," I said with a laugh.

Neil chuckled. "Don't feel bad. I kind of had to do the same thing for my first run. I was in a heap of trouble when I got back, but then they realized that they had to start trusting us younger folks. Maybe when people our age are calling the shots, we can start working together more. In the meantime, give me a shout-out on the walkie, the black box I gave you, when you're out making runs. Who knows, I could be out at the same time you are. We made a pretty good team."

I smiled. "That we did."

I looked off in the distance, not wanting to get back in my car. This had been the most exhausting, gut-wrenching, nerve-wracking day I'd ever had. It had also been the best day I'd ever had. Sometimes, you don't know what you're capable of until you're pushed to your extreme. I was not sure if I would've done this had I known how hard it was going to be. But I was sure glad I did.

Neil extended his hand, and I took it and shook. "Good to meet you, Neil."

"You too, Grace."

We both got back in our cars and headed back to our villages.

When I got back, my uncle was there waiting for me with a scowl on his face, but also a look of pride that he couldn't hide. Part of me wondered if it had been a test on his part. Knowing the old man, it probably was.

Two little girls snuggled together with their eyes drooping low. I covered both of them with a patchwork quilt and gave them a tiny peck on their heads.

Before I could get out of the room, the older girl opened her big brown eyes and smiled. "Gran, what was the secret of the AI? Was there more than one? Was it a test?"

"A little of both. The most important thing we had to realize was that we had to work together, but that's a story for another time." I started out of the room again, but this time, I was interrupted by the younger girl.

"Gran, what happened to the boy? Did you see him again?"

I laughed. "Oh yes, we had many adventures together. It's time for sleep now, girls."

"Night, Gran," they said in unison.

I closed the door and turned around to find a tall, gangling man smiling at me.

"Tellin' stories again, huh?"

I shrugged. "Eh, the girls like hearing them. Besides, we can't let the younger generation forget what it was like in our day."

He gave me a little smooch on the head and squeezed. "You're right. But we best get to bed, got an early meeting with the inter-village council tomorrow."

"Yeah, I just got to close up the house," I said. He turned to go to our room, but before he was out of earshot, I said, "And, Neil, I'm glad I met you that day."

"You too, darlin'."

THOUGHTS ON *BRAVE NEW GIRLS*

"Representation in media is vitally important for encouraging underrepresented people in STEM fields. Seeing yourself in stories such as these can be a gateway to giving girls confidence to pursue careers in STEM fields."

ABOUT THE AUTHOR

Paige Daniels is the author of the *Non-Compliance* series, the *Singularity Wars* series, *Agents of the Consortium*, and a number of short stories. By day she works as an electrical engineer. When she's not busy with working and writing, she's hanging out on her hobby farm with cows, goats, dogs, and cats.

Illustration for "The Village Runners" by Martina Localzo.

Made in the USA
Middletown, DE
14 July 2024